DELIVERY AFTER DARK

GANSETT ISLAND SERIES, BOOK 28

MARIE FORCE

Delivery After Dark
Gansett Island Series, Book 28
By: Marie Force

Published by HTJB, Inc.
Copyright 2025. HTJB, Inc.
Cover Design by Diane Luger
Print Layout: E-book Formatting Fairies
ISBN: 978-1966871156

HTJB, Inc.
PO Box 370
Portsmouth, RI 02871 USA
author@marieforce.com

View the list of Who's Who on Gansett Island here
marieforce.com/whoswhogansett/

View a map of Gansett Island
marieforce.com/mapofgansett/

WHO'S WHO ON GANSETT ISLAND
BEFORE DELIVERY AFTER DARK

The McCarthy Family

- **Malcom John "Big Mac" McCarthy Sr.,** brother to Frank and Kevin, co-owner of McCarthy's Gansett Island Marina and McCarthy's Gansett Island Inn, married to:
  - **Linda McCarthy**, co-owner of McCarthy's Gansett Island Marina and McCarthy's Gansett Island Inn

Big Mac and Linda are parents to:

- **Mallory Vaughn James**, daughter of Big Mac McCarthy and Diana Vaughn (deceased), nursing director at Marion Martinez Home for the Aged married to:
  - **Dr. Quinn James**, trauma surgeon, medical director at Marion Martinez Home for the Aged, brother of Jared, Cooper and Kendall
- **Malcolm John "Mac" McCarthy Jr.,** son of Big Mac and Linda McCarthy, co-owner of McCarthy's Gansett Island Marina and owner of McCarthy Construction, father to Thomas, Hailey, Malcolm John "Mac" McCarthy III, Connor (Deceased), Emma Linda, and Evelyn Francine, married to:
  - **Maddie Chester McCarthy**, former housekeeper at McCarthy's Gansett Island Inn, daughter of Francine and Bobby Chester, sister of Tiffany Taylor, mother to Thomas, Hailey, Malcolm John "Mac" McCarthy III, Connor (Deceased), Emma Linda, and Evelyn Francine
    - **Thomas McCarthy,** son Maddie Chester McCarthy and Tom Wilkinson, adopted by Mac McCarthy
    - **Hailey McCarthy,** daughter of Mac and Maddie
    - **Connor McCarthy (deceased),** son of Mac and Maddie
    - **Malcolm John "Mac" McCarthy III,** son of Mac and Maddie

- **Emma Linda McCarthy** (twin), daughter of Mac and Maddie
    - **Evelyn Francine McCarthy** (twin), daughter of Mac and Maddie
- **Grant McCarthy,** Academy Award winning screenwriter, married to:
    - **Stephanie Logan McCarthy,** daughter of Charlie Grandchamp, owner of Stephanie's Bistro
- **Adam McCarthy,** computer programmer, father to Liam Callahan McCarthy, married to:
    - **Abby Callahan McCarthy**, daughter of Tom and Carol Callahan, owner of Abby's Attic, mother to Liam Callahan McCarthy
        - **Liam Callahan McCarthy,** son of Adam and Abby
- **Evan McCarthy,** singer, performer, owner of Island Breeze Records, married to:
    - **Grace Ryan McCarthy,** owner of Ryan's Pharmacy
- **Janey McCarthy Cantrell,** vet tech at Gansett Island Veterinary Clinic and later a veterinary medicine student at Ohio State University, mother of Peter Joseph "P.J." and Vivienne Cantrell, married to:
    - **Joe Cantrell,** son of Carolina Cantrell O'Grady and the late Pete Cantrell, co-owner of the Gansett Island Ferry Company
        - **Peter Joseph "P.J." Cantrell,** son of Joe and Janey
        - **Vivienne Cantrell,** daughter of Joe and Janey

Big Mac and Linda's Grandchildren:

- **Thomas McCarthy,** son of Maddie Chester McCarthy and Tom Wilkinson, adopted by Mac McCarthy
- **Hailey McCarthy,** daughter of Mac and Maddie
- **Connor McCarthy** (deceased)
- **Malcolm John McCarthy III,** son of Mac and Maddie
- **Emma Linda McCarthy,** daughter of Mac and Maddie
- **Evelyn Francine McCarthy,** daughter of Mac and Maddie
- **Peter Joseph "PJ" Cantrell,** son of Janey and Joe

- **Vivienne Cantrell,** daughter of Janey and Joe
- **Liam Callahan McCarthy,** son of Adam and Abby

RI Superior Court Judge Frank McCarthy (retired), eldest brother of Big Mac and Kevin, widower of the late Joanne McCarthy, engaged to

- **Betsy Jacobson,** mother of Steve (deceased)

Frank McCarthy is the father of:

- **Laura McCarthy Lawry,** daughter of Frank and Joanne McCarthy, sister of Shane McCarthy, mother of Holden Newsome, Joanna Sarah Lawry and Jonathan Russell Lawry, married to:
    - **Owen Lawry,** son of Mark and Sarah Lawry, brother to, Julia, Katie, Cindy, John, Josh and Jeff Lawry
        - **Holden Newsome,** son of Laura McCarthy Lawry and Justin Newsome, stepson of Owen Lawry
        - **Jonathan Russell Lawry,** (twin) son of Laura McCarthy Lawry and Owen Lawry
        - **Joanna Sarah Lawry,** (twin) daughter of Laura McCarthy Lawry and Owen Lawry
- **Shane McCarthy,** ex-husband to Courtney (deceased) married to:
    - **Katie Lawry McCarthy,** nurse practitioner, daughter of Mark and Sarah Lawry, sister to Owen, Julia (twin), Cindy, John, Josh and Jeff Lawry

Frank McCarthy's Grandchildren:

- **Holden Newsome,** son of Laura McCarthy Lawry and Justin Newsome, stepson of Owen McCarthy
- **Jonathan Russell Lawry,** son of Laura and Owen
- **Joanna Sarah Lawry,** daughter of Laura and Owen

- **Dr. Kevin McCarthy,** youngest brother to Big Mac and Frank

McCarthy, psychiatrist, divorced from Deb McCarthy, married to:
  - **Chelsea Rose McCarthy,** former bartender at the Beachcomber, mother to Summer Rose McCarthy

Kevin is the father of:

- **Riley McCarthy,** son of Kevin and Deb McCarthy, employed by McCarthy Construction, married to:
  - **Nikki Stokes McCarthy,** manager of McCarthy's Wayfarer, identical twin sister of **Jordan Stokes,**
- **Finn McCarthy,** son of Kevin and Deb McCarthy, employed by McCarthy Construction, married to:
  - **Chloe Dennis McCarthy,** owner of Curl Up and Dye Salon
- **Summer Rose McCarthy,** daughter of Kevin and Chelsea McCarthy

The Lawry Family

- **General Mark Lawry,** imprisoned former husband of Sarah Lawry Grandchamp, father of Owen, Julia, Katie, Cindy, Josh, John and Jeff Lawry
- **Sarah Lawry Grandchamp,** daughter of Russ and Adele, ex-wife of General Mark Lawry, mother to Owen, Julia, Katie, Cindy, Josh, John and Jeff Lawry, married to:
  - **Charlie Grandchamp,** father of Stephanie Logan McCarthy

Sarah is the mother of:

- **Owen Lawry,** co-owner of the Sand & Surf Hotel, brother to Julia, Katie, Cindy, John, Josh and Jeff, stepfather to Holden Newsome, father to Jonathan Russell Lawry and Joanna Sarah Lawry, married to:
  - **Laura McCarthy Lawry,** co-owner of the Sand & Surf Hotel, sister of Shane, mother of Holden Newsome, Jonathan Russell Lawry and Joanna Sarah Lawry

- **Holden Newsome,** son of Laura McCarthy Lawry and Justin Newsome, stepson of Owen Lawry
  - **Jonathan Russell Lawry,** (twin) son of Laura McCarthy Lawry and Owen Lawry
  - **Joanna Sarah Lawry,** (twin) daughter of Laura McCarthy Lawry and Owen Lawry
- **Julia Lawry Taylor,** officer manager, McCarthy Construction and performer at Stephanie's Bistro, sister of Owen, Katie (twin), Cindy, John, Josh and Jeff, married to:
  - **Deacon Taylor,** Gansett Island Harbor Master and police officer, brother of Police Chief Blaine Taylor
- **Katie Lawry McCarthy**, nurse practitioner, sister to Owen, Julia (twin), Cindy, John, Josh and Jeff, married to:
  - **Shane McCarthy,** employed by McCarthy Construction, brother of Laura
- **Cindy Lawry**, hair stylist at Curl Up and Dye, sister to Owen, Julia, Katie, John, Josh and Jeff, engaged to:
  - **Jace Carson,** biological father of Kyle and Jackson Chandler, ex-husband of Lisa Chandler (deceased), bartender at Beachcomber and plumber at McCarthy Construction
- **John Lawry**, former police officer, director of security at the McCarthy's Wayfarer, brother of Owen, Julia, Katie, Cindy, Josh and Jeff, involved with:
  - **Niall Fitzgerald,** from Ireland, musician at Island Breeze Records, and performer at the Beachcomber
- **Josh Lawry**, engineer, brother of Owen, Julia, Katie, Cindy, John and Jeff, not present on Gansett Island
- **Jeff Lawry**, computer science degree, employed by McCarthy's Construction, brother of Owen, Julia, Katie, Cindy, John and Josh, engaged to:
  - **Kelsey Gordon,** nanny for Mac and Maddie McCarthy

The Martinez Family

- **George** (deceased) **and Marion Martinez,** co-founders of Martinez Lawn & Garden, parents of Alex and Paul Martinez

- **Alex Martinez**, son of George and Marion Martinez, brother of Paul, father of George Alexander Martinez II, co-owner of Martinez Lawn & Garden, married to:
  - **Jenny Wilks Martinez**, former lighthouse keeper, fiancé to the late Toby Barton, mother of George Alexander Martinez II
    - **George Alexander Martinez, II**, son of Alex and Jenny Martinez
- **Paul Martinez**, son of George and Marion Martinez, brother of Alex, stepfather to Ethan Russell, father of Scarlett Marion Martinez, co-owner of Martinez Lawn & Garden, member of Gansett Island Town Council, married to:
  - **Hope Russell Martinez**, nurse, mother of Ethan Russell and Scarlett Marion Martinez
    - **Ethan Russell Martinez**, son of Hope Russell Martinez, adopted by Paul Martinez
    - **Scarlett Marion Martinez**, daughter of Paul and Hope Martinez

The James Family

- **Jared James**, billionaire, co-owner of The Chesterfield and Marion Martinez Home for the Aged, adoptive father of Violet James, married to:
  - **Elisabeth "Lizzie" James**, co-owner of The Chesterfield and Marion Martinez Home for the Aged, adoptive mother of Violet James
    - **Violet James**, daughter of Jessie Morgan, adoptive daughter of Jared and Lizzie James
- **Jessie Morgan**, seasonal worker at the Beachcomber, abandoned infant daughter now in the care of Lizzie and Jared James
- **Dr. Quinn James**, trauma surgeon, medical director at Marion Martinez Home for the Aged, brother of Jared, Cooper and Kendall James, married to:
  - **Mallory Vaughn James**, daughter of Big Mac McCarthy and Diana Vaughn, sister to Mac, Grant, Adam, Evan and Janey

McCarthy, nursing director at Marion Martinez Home for the Aged, EMT for Town of Gansett Island
- **Kathleen "Kendall" James,** attorney, divorced from Phil Tobin, mother of:
    - **Elias Tobin,** 12, son of Kendall James and Phil Tobin
    - **Henry Tobin,** 10, son of Kendall James and Phil Tobin
- **Cooper James,** owner of party boat, youngest brother of Jared James and Quinn James, living with:
    - **Gabrielle "Gigi" Gibson,** lawyer, reality TV star, friend to Jordan Stokes and Nikki Stokes McCarthy

Other Gansett Island Residents...

- **Luke Harris,** co-owner of McCarthys Gansett Island Marina, father of Lillian Alice "Lily" Harris, married to:
    - **Sydney Donovan Harris,** interior designer, mother of Lily, widow of Seth, mother of the late Max and Malena
        - **Lillian Alice "Lily" Harris,** daughter of Luke and Sydney
- **Ned Saunders,** best friend to Big Mac McCarthy, Gansett Island cab driver and real estate owner, stepfather to Maddie McCarthy and Tiffany Taylor, married to:
    - **Francine Chester Saunders,** ex-wife of Bobby Chester, mother of Maddie McCarthy and Tiffany Taylor
- **Tiffany Taylor,** daughter of Francine Chester Saunders and Bobby Chester, sister of Maddie McCarthy, mother to Ashleigh Sturgil and Adeline "Addie" Taylor, owner of Naughty & Nice, married to:
    - **Police Chief Blaine Taylor,** brother of Deacon Taylor, stepfather to Ashleigh Sturgil, father to Adeline "Addie" Taylor
        - **Ashleigh Sturgil,** daughter of Tiffany Taylor and Jim Sturgil, stepdaughter of Blaine Taylor
        - **Adeline "Addie" Taylor,** daughter of Tiffany and Blaine Taylor
- **Jim Sturgil,** ex-husband of Tiffany Taylor, father to Ashleigh Sturgil, deceased in *Hurricane After Dark*

- **Jack Downing,** RI State trooper assigned to Gansett Island, widower of Ruby, dating:
  - **Piper Bennett,** employee at the Sand & Surf Hotel
- **Seamus O'Grady,** from Ireland, manager of the Gansett Island Ferry Company, guardian to Kyle and Jackson Chandler, married to:
  - **Carolina Cantrell O'Grady,** widow of Pete Cantrell, mother of Joe Cantrell, grandmother to P.J. and Vivienne Cantrell, guardian to Kyle and Jackson Chandler
- **Lisa Chandler,** (deceased) ex-wife of Jace Carson, neighbor to Seamus and Carolina O'Grady, mother to:
  - **Kyle Chandler,** son of Lisa Chandler and Jace Carson, guardian child of Seamus and Carolina O'Grady
  - **Jackson Chandler,** son of Lisa Chandler and Jace Carson, guardian child of Seamus and Carolina O'Grady
- **Dan Torrington,** celebrity defense attorney and friend to Grant McCarthy, married to:
  - **Kara Ballard Torrington,** daughter of Chuck and Judith Ballard, owner/operator Ballard's Launch Service
- **Dr. David Lawrence,** Gansett Island doctor, former fiancé of Janey McCarthy Cantrell, married to:
  - **Daisy Babson Lawrence,** friend of Maddie McCarthy's, housekeeping manager at McCarthy's Gansett Island Inn
- **Truck Henry,** Daisy Babson Lawrence's abusive ex-boyfriend
- **Tobias "Slim" Fitzgerald Jackson Jr.,** Gansett Island pilot, married to:
  - **Erin Barton Jackson,** twin to the late Toby Barton, who was engaged to Jenny Wilks Martinez
- **Linc Mercier,** US Coast Guard Commander, stationed at Gansett Island
- **Mason Johns,** Gansett Island Fire Department Chief, engaged to:
  - **Jordan Stokes,** Activities Director at Marion Martinez Home for the Aged and reality TV star, identical twin to Nikki Stokes McCarthy

- **Victoria Stevens O'Grady,** Gansett Island midwife, married to:
  - **Shannon O'Grady,** from Ireland, deck hand on the Gansett Island ferries
- **Rosemary Enders,** (deceased) grandmother of McKenzie Martin, close friend/neighbor of Duke Sullivan
- **Duke Sullivan,** owner of tattoo studio, engaged to:
  - **McKenzie Martin,** bookkeeper, mother of Jax
    - **Jax Martin,** infant son of McKenzie Martin and Eric
- **Eric,** ex-boyfriend of McKenzie, father of Jax
- **Sierra Mancini,** owner of Refresh and Renew Massage Studio
- **Ace,** works with Duke at the tattoo studio
- **Billy Weyland,** owner of the gym, deceased in *Hurricane After Dark*
- **Morgan Weyland,** brother of Billy
- **Rebecca,** owner of the South Harbor Diner
- **Doc Potter,** island veterinarian
- **Rev. Joshua Banks,** pastor of nondenominational church
- **Fiona,** took over Ryan's Pharmacy when Grace was on tour with Evan
- **Evelyn Hopper,** owner of Eastward Look, grandmother to Jordan Stokes and Nikki Stokes McCarthy
- **Oliver and Dara Watkins,** lighthouse keepers, parents of Lewis (deceased)
- **Monique,** sister of Dara Watkins
- **Candice,** works at Abby's Attic
- **Dr. Cal Maitland,** former island doctor and ex-fiancé of Abby Callahan
- **Bobby Chester,** estranged father of Maddie McCarthy and Tiffany Taylor, ex-husband of Francine Saunders
- **Matilda,** Gigi and Jordan's show producer
- **Libby,** Owner of the Beachcomber, part-time EMT

The Children of Gansett Island

- **Thomas McCarthy,** 7, son of Maddie Chester McCarthy and Tom Wilkinson, adopted by Mac McCarthy

- **Hailey McCarthy,** 5, daughter of Maddie and Mac McCarthy
- **Connor McCarthy,** deceased son of Maddie and Mac McCarthy
- **Malcolm John "Mac" McCarthy III,** 2, son of Maddie and Mac McCarthy
- **Emma Linda McCarthy,** 9 months, daughter of Maddie and Mac McCarthy, twin sister of Evelyn Francine McCarthy
- **Evelyn Francine McCarthy,** 9 months, daughter of Maddie and Mac McCarthy, twin sister of Emma Linda McCarthy
- **Ashleigh Sturgil,** 7, daughter of Tiffany Taylor and Jim Sturgil, stepdaughter to Blaine Taylor
- **Adeline "Addie" Francine Taylor,** 1, daughter of Blaine and Tiffany Taylor
- **Holden Newsome,** 3, son of Laura McCarthy Lawry and ex-husband, Justin Newsome, stepson to Owen Lawry
- **Joanna Sarah Lawry,** 2, daughter of Owen and Laura Lawry, twin to Jonathan
- **Jonathan Russell Lowry,** 2, son of Owen and Laura Lawry, twin to Joanna
- **Peter Joseph "P.J." Cantrell,** 5, son of Joe and Janey Cantrell
- **Vivienne Cantrell,** 2, daughter of Joe and Janey Cantrell
- **George Alexander Martinez II,** 2, son of Alex and Jenny Martinez
- **Scarlett Marion Martinez,** 1, daughter of Paul and Hope Martinez
- **Ethan Russell,** 9, Son of Hope Russell, stepson of Paul Martinez
- **Lillian Alice "Lily" Harris,** 3, daughter of Luke and Sydney Harris
- **Liam Callahan McCarthy,** 2, son of Adam and Abby McCarthy
- **Summer Rose McCarthy,** 2, daughter of Kevin and Chelsea McCarthy
- **Violet Catherine James,** 5 months, biological daughter of Jessie Morgan, guardian child of Jared and Lizzie James
- **Kyle Chandler,** 8, son of Lisa Chandler (deceased) and Jace Carson, guardian child of Seamus and Carolina O'Grady

- **Jackson Chandler**, 7, son of Lisa Chandler (deceased) and Jace Carson; guardian child of Seamus and Carolina O'Grady
- **Jax Martin**, 1
- **Elias Tobin**, 12, son of Kendall James and Phil Tobin
- **Henry Tobin**, 10

CHAPTER 1

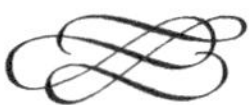

She'd come to despise the words *bed rest*. Abby McCarthy was slowly going mad from being stuck in a Providence hospital bed for eight weeks. It was unbearably boring and oddly exhausting despite how it might sound to those who craved more time in bed. A person could lie around only so much, and then they had to get up and get on with it. Except she couldn't get up or get on with anything until she safely delivered the four baby boys competing for space in her belly.

The lack of activity had made her feel weak and useless. She couldn't even help her husband, Adam, take care of their son, Liam. Thankfully, Adam and Liam were staying nearby at Adam's uncle Frank's house and came to visit every day, which was the highlight of Abby's endless days confined to bed. Their visits were never long enough for her, though, because Adam could entertain Liam in a hospital room for only so long before their almost two-year-old got antsy.

One day this week, or maybe it was last week — who could keep track when every day was the same as the last one? — Liam had fallen asleep in her arms and taken a two-hour nap. Poor Adam never got a break, though. He couldn't leave Liam with her in case he woke up.

As of tomorrow, she'd reach the thirty-week mark, which was a significant milestone for a quad pregnancy. The longer the babies "cooked," the doctors had said, the better their chances for avoiding numerous scary complications. They were giving her two more weeks to percolate, and if the babies didn't come on their own, they'd be delivered by C-section.

While she didn't relish the idea of major surgery, she also wasn't thrilled with the idea of giving birth to four babies naturally. Neither option was particularly appealing, especially since she'd have five little ones to care for afterward.

She couldn't imagine fourteen more days of this tedium, so she was hoping her baby sons took mercy on their mother and decided to get the heck out of their increasingly cramped accommodations sooner rather than later.

The days had begun to run together weeks ago. She couldn't recall what'd happened when, such as what day Liam had napped with her. Hopefully, the pregnancy brain would let up by the time she had four new babies to care for.

Four. New. Babies.

Even with thirty weeks to prepare, the thought of welcoming *four* infants at the same time was incredibly overwhelming. She'd been told a while ago that it was likely she might never conceive. Well, she'd shown "them." She'd conceived, all right, and then some.

Her body was so swollen as to be obscene. She was careful to keep her belly covered when Adam was there so he wouldn't run away in horror. If he knew she was thinking that way, he'd be angry. He told her every day how proud he was of her, how amazing she was and how lucky they were to soon have five sons to grow up together and be the best of friends.

Five sons.

Five more McCarthy boys.

Just what the world needed.

Her mother-in-law, Linda, had teased her about what she was in for. "I had *only* four, and they nearly killed me," Linda had said when she and Big Mac had come to visit last week.

They'd shared a big laugh because Abby was well acquainted with the original four McCarthy boys, as she'd dated Grant for more than a decade before marrying his brother a couple of years ago. Adam and his brothers were capable of a ridiculous amount of mischief, separately and together, which she often found entertaining. Would the nonsense be as entertaining if her own children were perpetrating it? Probably not.

Her goal in life was to raise five respectful, well-behaved boys. The fact that mischievous McCarthy DNA ran through them would make that goal more difficult to achieve, but she was up to the challenge.

Or so she hoped…

Her favorite McCarthy boys came strolling into the room, cheeks flushed from the December chill. In addition to all her other complaints, she'd missed autumn, her favorite time of year on Gansett Island. They'd go home to winter in full swing and the holidays looming, on top of everything else. She'd done some online shopping for their nieces and nephews, as well as for Liam. Thank goodness for her laptop, a Wi-Fi connection and Netflix, which had helped to keep her entertained.

"Mama, we go to the park and play on the slide!" Liam's brown eyes were big with excitement.

Adam lifted him onto the bed so Abby could hug her baby. She missed taking care of him more than just about anything. She also missed snuggling with her handsome husband, which was all but impossible due to her massive belly.

Liam allowed her to hug him for close to a minute before he squirmed free, ready to move on to the next thing. They had some toys for him in the room, and he ran over to play with his trucks while Adam bent to kiss her.

"I'd ask you what's new," he said, smiling, "but your updates have gotten really boring lately."

Abby laughed. "I'm the most boring wife ever."

"I'm just teasing, and you know it. You're growing four little men in there. Nothing boring about that."

"How are you guys doing?"

"We're okay." He gave her a guilty look before adding, "He slept with me again last night."

"Adam! We talked about that."

"I know, but I can't be mean when he's crying."

"It's not being mean. It's being *firm*. There's a difference."

"I suck at that."

"At this rate, he'll sleep between us until he goes to college."

"No way. Trust me, he'll want his privacy by the time he's twelve."

"That's ten years from now. Do you want him between us every night for that long? And besides, what'll it be like when there are *five* of them between us? These boys will do whatever Liam does."

"I'll try harder tonight."

"Yes, you will."

"He's just so damned cute and snuggly, and I'm lonely without you."

"Adam…"

"I hear you, honey. I'll work on it."

"Do that before we have a baseball team in bed with us."

He laughed. "I love when you're stern with me. It's hot."

"Oh please. Nothing about me is hot except a body temperature set to roast because these boys of yours are overheating me."

With Liam occupied with his toys, Adam sat on the edge of her bed, took her hand and brought it to his lips. "You have no idea how beautiful you are. In fact, you've never been more beautiful than you are now, full of maternal power as you prepare to give birth to a rare double set of identical twins."

Though she felt like an ugly whale, she appreciated his efforts to raise her self-esteem. "If you say so."

"I say so, and I'm the husband, so whatever I say goes."

Her scowl made him laugh again. "I can't wait to be home with you and our boys. I miss our life on the island.

"Same. I miss sleeping with you." He waggled his brows. "Among other things."

"Speaking of that, you should use the remaining time on the mainland to get yourself a vasectomy, because now that I know you're packing super sperm, you're not coming near me again while that thing is still active."

He made a sad face. "I'm deeply offended on behalf of my thing and my super sperm."

"Whatever. Get the snip. Have your parents or mine come over to watch Liam. They're always happy to help."

Adam released her hand and put his over his package, as if protecting it. "I take back every nice thing I said about you."

Abby laughed hard and then burped, which made her laugh even harder. The heartburn, burping and flatulence had been ridiculous as her pregnancy progressed.

Adam laughed with her and then kissed her. "Even if you're planning violence against my manhood, I still love you."

"You'd better still love me. This is all your fault." She curled her hand around his. "Won't be much longer. I have a feeling we're getting close to the finish line. There's nowhere left for them to go in there."

"I hope so for your sake. I'm afraid you'll go loco before they arrive."

"I'm hanging in there, thanks to you and our families and the visits from our friends. Everyone has been amazing. My girls on the island call or text every day. They're planning a shower for when we get home, since we left somewhat abruptly." In a Life Flight helicopter, no less, after she went into early labor.

"That's very sweet of them."

"The theme is Four of Everything."

"Ha, good idea."

"I sure hope we're home in time for Christmas." The only way they wouldn't be home by then was if there were complications with the babies, which neither of them wanted to think about.

"I hope so, too, but if we're not, I'll make sure we celebrate right here."

"I know… I just miss everything."

"Home stretch, love."

Abby rested her hands on her massive belly. "Literally."

Laughing, he kissed her and rested his forehead against hers. "I'm so ridiculously proud of you."

"I'm ridiculously proud of you, too."

"What? Why?"

"It's not easy taking care of a two-year-old completely on your own for weeks on end, while also working."

"That's nothing compared to what you've been doing."

"It's not nothing. Knowing he's with you makes it possible for me to get through this."

"How about we be proud of us?"

"Yes, that works. We're going to have to stick together to get through the next eighteen years."

"I'm here for it. I'm here for all of it."

And he would be. She knew that without a shadow of a doubt. A long and difficult journey had led her to this moment with this man, and even as she went nuts from the boredom, she couldn't wait for their babies to arrive and to watch their five sons grow up with Adam by her side every step of the way.

. . .

Sierra Mancini hated funerals, but of course, everyone did. No one got up in the morning, gave a good stretch and thought, *Today would be a great day for a funeral.* Since she'd lost her mother and two much-loved grandparents in the span of eight months a few years back, she'd avoided them and the memories of deep grief whenever possible.

Today, however, she'd pulled herself together to support Billy Weyland's older brother, Morgan, who'd lost the last of his immediate family when Billy died during Hurricane Ethel. Sierra had been friends with Billy and had been part of the island-wide effort to support Morgan in the months since the tragic loss of his brother.

For a time, it'd been assumed that Morgan wasn't going to have a funeral for Billy, but then he'd decided there needed to be something, hence today's gathering at the island's nondenominational church, presided over by Pastor Joshua Banks, who'd also been a source of comfort to Morgan since Billy's body was found in the Salt Pond.

The whole thing was so dreadfully sad that it would've been much easier to sit it out, to schedule appointments at Refresh and Renew, her massage studio, to do anything other than sit in the pew next to her friend Duke Sullivan and his fiancée, McKenzie Martin. The two of them were stupid in love, holding hands even in church. For a time, she'd had "feelings" about the way they'd fallen madly in love over a couple of weeks in the fall.

Duke had been Sierra's backup plan. She'd thought that if neither of them ended up with anyone by the time they were forty, maybe they'd try to make a go of it. Except Duke had harbored no such thoughts, and when she'd shared her vision of the future with him… Suffice to say the entire exchange with one of her closest friends had been mortifying. Especially since McKenzie had been waiting for Duke in his bed while she talked to him outside.

Ugh. She couldn't even think about that night without wanting to cringe. Thankfully, neither Duke nor McKenzie had held Sierra's drunken confession against her, and they'd gone on as friends as if nothing had ever happened.

But for Sierra, that night had served as a wake-up call. For one thing, she'd all but stopped drinking after that, limiting herself to an occasional glass of wine to be sociable, but no more whiskey or vodka, which was what had gotten her into trouble that night. She'd also decided to get real about her love life and stop looking for reasons to avoid men and relationships and everything that went with them.

Over the years, she'd been on a lot of first dates, a few second and third dates and even dated one guy for a month before he got tired of being "stuck on an island" and set out for more exciting parts. That disappointment had been followed by a go-nowhere relationship with Kyle, one of the deckhands on the ferries. Was it any wonder she'd become bitter about all things dating and men and was sick of looking for something she was probably never going to find?

In addition to cutting back on alcohol, she'd been listening to self-help books while she worked, hoping to find the secret to a happy single life in one of them. So far, the answers remained elusive, but she wasn't giving up. If she was going to be by herself for the rest of her life, she was going to find a way to be content in that life, even as everyone around her was blissfully in love, pregnant and raising kids—or planning to be soon.

Not that she was dying to be married or anything like that. However, it would be nice to have someone to hang out with after work, someone who was hers and hers alone. That wouldn't suck, as long as it was the right guy and not another in a string of noncommittal idiots who were looking for a mother, not a partner.

Was it too much to ask to find a grown-up man who knew who he was and what he was about and wasn't looking to her to take care of him or fix all his problems for him? She'd found that, yes, it was too much to ask.

There'd been an outbreak of love in her group of friends, and she'd gotten to see Duke so happy with McKenzie, as well as her friend Jace Carson with his love, Cindy Lawry, and even Dr. Kevin McCarthy and his wife, Chelsea, who were expecting their second child together... Each of them had taken enormous risks with their hearts and well-being and had hit the jackpot with amazing partners.

She wanted what they had and had hoped to find that special connection for herself but wasn't willing to leave Gansett to make it happen. That was the last thing she wanted to do. She loved her island home and had a nice business running the only massage studio, but the lure of true love had her considering her options as another long, lonely winter loomed before her. Sierra was fine during the madness that invaded the island in the spring and went on until well into October. But it was this time of year, when everything slowed down, that the loneliness set in, and she expected that to be worse this year without Duke to hang out with the way they used to when he was single, too.

Sierra knew a lot of people who'd found their person on Gansett, so that gave her hope that she might find someone right there. But if not, she wasn't willing to shake up her whole life, even if it meant finding her soul mate. No, if he was out there, he needed to come to her, because she wasn't going anywhere.

Before she'd had a front-row seat to Duke falling so hard for McKenzie, she would've scoffed at the notion of soul mates. Whatever that was. But now she'd seen it and felt the palpable energy between the two of them, and damn it, she wanted some of that for herself, even as she acknowledged the unlikelihood of finding it on a tiny remote island miles off the coast of the smallest state. What were the odds?

Not great...

She was stirred out of her thoughts when the service began with a rousing rendition of "How Great Thou Art," sung by Julia Lawry, bringing back childhood memories for Sierra of going to church with Nana Ann, who'd had a beautiful singing voice. Tears filled her eyes as she remembered holding hands with her nana and singing along to songs with familiar tunes, including "Amazing Grace," which had been a particular favorite of her nana's. Julia's voice was so beautiful, it took Sierra's breath away.

Pastor Banks led the congregation through a series of opening prayers. Some of Billy's friends from the gym did Bible readings. It was almost comical to see the muscular dudes, decked out in poorly fitted suits as they attempted to show decorum and respect for their late friend.

Billy's friend Niall Fitzgerald performed "Danny Boy," one of Billy's favorites of the songs the Irishman regularly performed at the Beachcomber.

Sierra had heard that Billy was cremated and that his ashes were contained in the urn on the altar, giving the whole concept of "dust to dust" new meaning. She was glad no one could hear her thoughts as she tried to pay attention to the lessons to be found in the readings and in Pastor Banks's comforting words. As always, her ADD kicked in, and her mind wandered in a thousand different directions.

"Are you okay?" Duke whispered.

Sierra nodded. "I'm fine." That was a lie, as it was impossible to sit through a funeral without thinking of the funerals for her mother and grandparents. The emotions were like muscle memory, built into her wiring now, even if the loss of Billy wasn't as difficult for her as those had been. He'd still been a friend and far too young to die, which was the hardest part of this for her. He'd been only a few years older than her, and his death had served as yet another reminder that life wasn't a dress rehearsal.

When Morgan stood and walked to the lectern, his wavy dark hair combed into submission and a black suit showcasing his broad shoulders, Sierra sat up a little straighter, eager to hear what he had to say.

CHAPTER 2

$\mathcal{H}$e'd debated whether to have the funeral in the first place and had engaged in a full-on argument with himself about doing a eulogy. Now that he stood before the packed gathering, Morgan Weyland wished he'd asked someone else to speak about Billy.

He'd decided to have the service because that's what his late mother would've wanted. So he'd done it for her—and for Billy and the many people who'd loved him.

"I want to start by thanking you all for coming today and for the way you've stepped up for me over these last few surreal months. As many of you know, Billy and I were raised on here on Gansett, along with our late sister, Amanda. Unlike my sister and me, Billy loved this island with his whole heart and soul, and while Amanda and I were plotting our escape, he was figuring out a way to stay forever. He founded the gym right out of high school in the hope that it would allow him to live here forever.

"Billy, congratulations on achieving that goal. You did it, pal. You spent your entire life on this island you loved with all your heart. After spending these last few months here with all of you, I can see why Billy loved it so much and had no desire to leave. It's been a reminder to me that even if I wanted out of here as a kid, it's always been a special place made up of incredible people who show up in good times and in bad.

"Thank you for the meals, the cards, the endless support, the kind words about Billy and for everything you've done to prop me up during the awful days when we were looking for him and every day since we found him.

"If my brother were here, I'd punch him in the face for putting me through this."

The congregation laughed, as he'd hoped they would.

"We were always wrestling, trying to outdo each other, tripping each other and generally acting like fools when we were together. We drove our poor parents crazy with the bickering, trying to one-up each other, constantly competing to see who could do what stupid thing better, faster or with less blood.

"We spent a lot of time in the island's clinic when we were growing up. Billy held the record for the most stitches, while I was the broken-bone champion. We wore those titles with honor and considered them proof of a well-spent childhood."

Morgan paused to contend with the lump that suddenly appeared in his throat. *Please, Ma, help me get through this and not bawl my head off in front of all these people. I'm doing this for you...*

"Our sister, Amanda, died from meningitis when she was in college. Over the next five years, we lost both of our parents to accidents. For a time there, it felt like the universe was out to get us, but Billy and I... We hung on to each other and got through it. Somehow. I'm not sure how I'm supposed to get through this without him to hang on to. He was my best friend, my favorite person to annoy and the only one in the world I talked to every day. That's how I knew for sure he was gone. He stopped answering the phone and texting me back. He'd never do that to me unless he had no choice."

A few people sniffed, and he saw tissues being passed around.

"Billy worked his butt off establishing the island's only gym and made a huge success of it. I was so proud of him, and I'm thankful now that I told him so every chance I got. Like many of you, who, like me, grew up here and escaped to the mainland as soon as we could, the island looks different to me as an adult. I loved coming out here to spend a weekend with Billy. I'll cherish those memories forever. A lot of you have asked what I plan to do with the gym, and for now, the only plan I have is to keep it open because that's what he'd want me to do. I'm taking it day by day, week by week, so I guess I'll just say we'll see what happens for now.

"I'll never know what possessed Billy and Jim to try to ride out a hurricane on a boat, but if I know Billy, he was worried about losing the boat he loved and didn't want to be out there alone. They probably figured they could muscle through it together. I can't bear to think of what they went through… I'm not a very religious person, but if there's an afterlife, I hope Billy is with the ones we've loved and lost.

"Thank you again for being here for Billy—and for me—and for reminding me why my brother loved it here. I'll never forget how you all took care of me during one of the worst times in my life."

He wiped away tears as he left the lectern and made his way back to his front-row seat. As he went, his gaze connected with Billy's friend Sierra, who was openly sobbing as Duke Sullivan comforted her.

He'd gotten to know her a little as she'd brought meals to the gym, each time asking if there was anything she could do to help him. While he'd appreciated her kindness, he also found himself looking forward to her visits, as she was not only sweet and kind but also one of the sexiest women he'd ever met.

Not that he had time for such thoughts while figuring out how to run a gym and dealing with his brother's estate, among many other current challenges, including his own job, which had been put on hold when his brother went missing in the storm. He'd have to make a decision about that situation before too much longer, but that didn't need to happen today.

The last time Sierra had come by the gym, she'd left a gift certificate for a massage at the time of his choosing. She'd put a note in it to let her know when he was ready, and she'd find the time. He wasn't sure he'd be able to handle having her hands all over him, which was a thought he absolutely should not be having as Reverend Banks led them through prayers for Billy's eternal soul.

Morgan was still trying to decide whether he wanted to keep Billy's ashes with him or inter him with their parents and sister on the mainland. If he had to guess, he'd bet Billy would want to be on the island some-where, so maybe he'd sprinkle the ashes in some of his brother's favorite places.

All at once, he was awash in tears at the thought of dealing with what was left of his brother. He wanted Billy here with him, not in an urn on the mantel or lost to a stiff breeze. How could he have risked his life when he knew Morgan had no one else? How could he have left him to face the rest of his life alone? What was he supposed to do now? Billy had poured everything he had into the gym, and the thought of closing it was almost as heartbreaking as losing Billy.

He couldn't let that happen.

But at some point, he had to get back to his own life. His boss had been supportive, telling Morgan to take whatever time he needed and that the job would be there when he was ready to return, but his patience would run out eventually.

After the service, Morgan stood by the door and greeted everyone who'd come to pay respects to Billy. He'd had so many friends, most of them through the gym, but there were fishing friends, poker friends, softball friends and others who'd helped to search for him.

"Let us know if we can do anything for you, Morgan," his high school classmate—and onetime baseball teammate—Mac McCarthy said when he and his wife, Maddie, stopped to say hello. After she'd brought a meal to the gym, one of the guys had told him she and Mac had five young kids at home.

"Appreciate all your help so far, and thank you for the food. This community doesn't mess around when it comes to helping others."

"That's one of the things we love best about Gansett," Maddie said. "We're all in it together out here."

"That's what Billy said, too. Being here again has brought back a lot of memories."

"He'll be missed," Mac said. "And you have been, too. I hate the reason for it, but it's nice to have you back in town. Let's get together and have a beer when you catch your breath."

"I'd like that. Thank you so much for coming."

Mac's parents, Big Mac and Linda, were right behind them with hugs and offers of help. Big Mac had been his and Billy's Boy Scout leader once upon a time. They were followed by Ned Saunders and his wife, Francine.

The people kept coming. Some he knew, others he met for the first time, all of them with something kind to say about Billy and generous offers to help him with anything he needed.

"Everyone is so nice," he said to Jace Carson, who'd been one of Billy's good friends at the gym.

"That's Gansett for you." Jace put his arm around his fiancée, Cindy

Lawry. They'd checked on him daily since Billy went missing and had been steadfast in their support as he planned the memorial service. "Everyone is heading over to the Beachcomber for drinks in Billy's honor, if you feel up to joining us."

He'd closed the gym for the day since most of the patrons were planning to attend the service. "That sounds better than cleaning out Billy's stuff and figuring out what he did with all the important paperwork. His filing system makes no sense whatsoever."

"That'll keep until tomorrow," Cindy said. "Come with us. Be with people who care."

He glanced back at the church, which was now empty except for Reverend Banks, who was straightening up the altar. Where had Sierra gone? She hadn't stopped to see him on the way out. Would she be at the Beachcomber with the others? And why did that matter? It didn't. He had enough to deal with as it was. The last thing he needed was additional complications—and that woman had *complicated* written all over her gorgeous self.

But he didn't want to be alone after the emotional service, so he nodded to Jace and Cindy. "Sure," he said. "Let's go."

You should've said something to him before you left the church, Sierra thought as she sipped from a glass of wine that she planned to nurse for as long as she could make it last at the Beachcomber. She'd closed the massage studio for the day in deference to the funeral and was indulging in a rare opportunity to day drink. Usually, that led to an early bedtime, but she was taking it slowly so she wouldn't be lights out by five o'clock. After this day, she'd much rather be here with friends than home alone with her thoughts.

Morgan had been surrounded by people after the service, and Sierra hadn't wanted to add to the crush when she could check on him at the gym tomorrow. On one of her visits there, she'd left him a gift certificate for a free massage whenever he was ready for some relaxation. She hoped he would take her up on it. Some guys were funny about massages. They thought they were about sex when that was the last thing on her mind when she was caring for a client.

"Hey," Duke said when he pulled up to the stool next to hers. He had longish dark blond hair, twinkling blue eyes, a full beard and sleeve tattoos.

"Hey, yourself." Weeks after she'd made a fool of herself with him, she still found it difficult to look at the man who'd been her best friend for years.

"Nice service for Billy."

"Yes, it was."

"My heart goes out to Morgan. He's lost his whole family."

Sierra thought that was a sweet thing for Duke to say, considering he'd never had a family to call his own until he met McKenzie and her son, Jax. "He's been through a lot for someone so young." She'd guess that Morgan was in his late thirties. "You think he'll stick around after he settles Billy's estate?"

"Word on the street was that Billy didn't have a will, so it'll go to probate. That'll take a while. In the meantime, he can keep the gym open or pay taxes and insurance on an empty building. If I had to guess, he'll keep the gym running until it's all sorted."

"What about his own life and job?"

"I'm not sure what he's doing about that. He must be on a leave of absence or something."

"Do you have a will?" she asked Duke.

"I do now that I have McKenzie and Jax to think about. If something happens to me, everything goes to them—the property, the studio, my truck, savings, all of it."

"You've already done that?"

"Yep. Kendall James helped me with it while Dan Torrington was in Maine. She walked me through every step of it, and I signed it a couple of weeks ago. I feel better knowing it's done."

"I'm trying to imagine what it would be like to care so much about someone else that you'd leave everything you own to her—and her son—a few months after meeting her."

Duke shrugged as he smiled. "When you know, you know. The only thing I want in this whole world is to make a family with the two of them and anyone else who might come along."

"So you guys might have more kids?"

"We've talked about it. I'm all for it. I love being a dad to Jax and watching him grow."

"Sometimes I can't believe you're the same guy who avoided domestic stuff like the plague for your whole life."

Duke chuckled as Jace put a draft beer in front of him. "Thanks, Jace." To Sierra, Duke said, "Sometimes I can't believe it either. Mostly, I can't believe how lucky I am to wake up with her every morning and to hear the little guy chirping in his crib or see how thrilled he is to see me when I go to get him."

"I'm happy for you, friend, despite my bad behavior."

"You didn't do anything wrong, Sierra."

"I feel like a total ass every time I think of that night."

Cringe.

"I don't want you having another thought about that. I'd hate for something silly like that to mess with one of my best friendships." He nudged her shoulder. "So you can stop acting weird around me, like something has changed when nothing has, as far as I'm concerned."

"Everything has changed for you."

"Maybe so, but some things should never change, and you and me— that's one of them. I miss you popping in to help yourself to my candy and doing lunch together and hanging out after work."

"I figured McKenzie wouldn't want you doing that stuff with me."

He gave her a look full of amazement. "She knows how much my friends mean to me, that you guys are the family I never had. She'd never want to come between us. That's not who she is."

"Oh." Now she felt doubly stupid about keeping her distance from him since that night. "Okay."

"Are we good?"

"Yes, of course."

"I want my friend back, Sierra. I miss you."

"I'm right here."

"Will you start bugging me in the studio between clients again and stealing all my candy?"

"If you insist."

"I do."

"Where's McKenzie, anyway?" The two of them and McKenzie's little boy were usually joined at the hip.

"She had two client meetings and is coming here with Jax when she's done." He took a sip of his beer. "Oh, hey, there's Morgan. I'm glad he came."

"Me, too." Sierra was unreasonably happy to see him surrounded by people who wanted to help. Although why she cared so much about someone she barely knew was a mystery to her. Perhaps it was the tragedy of Morgan losing the last member of his immediate family under such awful circumstances.

She felt for him what anyone with a heart would, or so she told herself as a tingle down her spine indicated it might be something more than that. *You can lie to others, but you can't lie to yourself.* She could almost hear her grandmother's voice as one of her favorite phrases echoed through Sierra's mind.

"Are you okay?" Duke asked.

She glanced at her friend to find him watching her with an intrigued expression. "What? I'm fine. Why wouldn't I be?"

He shrugged. "Funerals can have weird effects on people. This one reminded me of when Rosemary died. The church-smells and the music bring it all back."

Duke had been close to his next-door neighbor, who'd been more like a mother to him than anyone else had ever been. McKenzie was her granddaughter, and he liked to think Rosemary had fixed them up from the great beyond.

"I hope it brought back the good memories, too."

"It did, but it was a reminder of the loss," Duke said.

"It reminded me of losing my mom and grandparents, but I wanted to be there for Morgan. I really feel for him losing the last of his original family. That's got to be brutal."

"For sure, but at least he had them to begin with. He'll carry them with him for the rest of his life."

"True, but he'd rather walk beside them."

"Yeah, for sure."

While Duke chatted with Jace, Sierra kept her eye on Morgan as he worked his way through a room full of people offering condolences. Even from a distance, she could see that he was graciously accepting the outpouring, but his tension was equally apparent.

Sierra hoped he took her up on the free-massage coupon soon. If anyone had ever needed what she had to offer, it was him.

CHAPTER 3

They were killing him with kindness, Morgan thought as he shook hands and received hugs from a few people he remembered from back in the day and others he recognized but didn't really know. They'd known Billy, though, and had nothing but nice—and funny—things to say about him.

His brother had been making people laugh all their lives with his quick wit and sardonic take on just about everything.

"I always looked forward to his greeting at the gym," Oliver Watson said as he stood with his wife, Dara, her sister, Monique, and Linc Mercer, the Coast Guard officer who'd led the search for Billy and Jim. "You never knew what he'd have to say, but it was always entertaining."

"That was Billy. He was very proud of being the class clown in high school."

"I can picture that," Oliver said, smiling.

"Our parents weren't as thrilled by it as he was."

Dara laughed. "I love that."

"Billy told them it would always be his proudest accomplishment, and they said they feared for his future."

"He did just fine despite that," Oliver said. "I loved the atmosphere at his gym. Everyone did. And it came directly from him."

"That's nice to hear. He had a special way with people. He always found some way to connect with them."

"He was great at that," Oliver said. "We won't keep you, but please know we're here if there's anything we can do for you, man."

"Thank you. Everyone is so very kind."

"That's Gansett for you," Dara said. "We've found the community of our dreams here. We were supposed to come for a year and then move on, but we're not going anywhere."

"I'm glad to hear you've found a home here."

"Do you think you'll hang out here for a while longer?" Linc asked.

"I'm not sure yet. I've got to figure out what to do about the gym and clean out Billy's house and stuff. I'm not making any big decisions yet, but I do have a job and a life of my own to get back to at some point. My company has been supportive of me taking an extended leave."

"That's nice to hear," Monique said. "You should take all the time you need before you make any decisions."

"That's the plan. One day at a time."

Morgan's high school classmate Luke Harris and his wife, Sydney, came over to speak to Morgan, so Oliver and his family stepped aside.

He'd barely made it inside the room, and he'd been there for thirty minutes.

Duke Sullivan brought him a draft beer. "Figured you might be getting thirsty."

"You figured right. Thanks."

"We won't keep you," Luke said. "But if there's anything we can do, please feel free to reach out."

"Appreciate that," Morgan said.

"If I may," Sydney said somewhat tentatively, "I've been where you are after losing my husband and children in a drunk driving accident. If you need to talk to someone who gets it, please call me." She handed him a business card. "Any time."

"That's very kind of you. I'm sorry for your losses."

Sydney hugged him. "And I'm sorry for yours."

After they walked away, Morgan glanced toward the bar and caught Sierra looking at him—again. He raised a brow in inquiry.

Her face flushed with color as she looked away.

What's that about? he wondered, intrigued by her, which was ridiculous in light of how tumultuous his life was at the moment.

Even as he had that thought, however, he was still intrigued.

"I FEEL SO BAD FOR MORGAN," Monique said as she sat with Linc across the table from her sister and brother-in-law. "What do you suppose he'll do now?"

"Hard to say," Oliver replied. "He'll probably want to find a way to keep the gym open as it's a pretty successful business."

"Is it?" Dara asked. "I wouldn't think gyms make that much."

"Billy told me it's all about the people who sign up and then forget about it. He said half his members rarely came in, but they kept the membership for someday when they decide to get in shape."

"So it's like a psychological thing, then," Monique said. "That's interesting."

"I've been guilty of that very thing," Linc said. "Having the gym membership that I rarely use because I'd prefer to run or be outside to work out. Billy has made a lot of money off me since I moved to the island."

Monique wasn't sure what possessed her to reach over to squeeze his well-developed biceps. "Where'd these come from, then?"

He grinned at her. "Free weights at home."

"Ah, I see." That smile of his made her insides flutter any time he directed it her way. After weeks of texts and FaceTime chats, she was happy to be back with him again, even if it was for a sad occasion. He'd told her he dreaded Billy's funeral after leading the effort to find his body in the Salt Pond, so she'd come to offer her support.

She hadn't told him she was coming and had truly enjoyed his stunned expression when she slid into the pew next to him in church.

And then he'd made it worth the trip by reaching for her hand and holding on throughout the service.

Under the table, he rested his hand on her leg, which was all it took to set off the low hum of desire that'd been building between them since the first time they hung out months ago. He'd invited her back to his place that night, but she'd declined because she was leaving early the next day.

Fresh off an ugly divorce, she hadn't been sure she could handle a one-night stand with him. Now, though, she was fairly confident neither of them was interested in one and done. He'd repeatedly asked her to come back to the island for another visit and had offered to come see her on his days off.

They hadn't made any plans yet, so that was why it'd been fun to surprise him, even if it was for a funeral.

Oliver spotted Jared James across the bar. "Let's go say hello," he said to Dara.

"Be right back," she said as she followed Oliver over to see their friend. Oliver had been working with Jared to learn the investing business and was now doing that full time from the island and having great success with it.

"Alone at last," Linc said as he put his arm around her.

Monique rested against him, warning herself to slow her roll, to be careful, to not risk more than she could afford to lose. She ought to pull back, to keep her distance, but that was the last thing she wanted to do after missing him so much.

"It means a lot that you came today."

"I was hoping it would be a good surprise."

"It was the best. I was feeling really low about it, and you made me feel better."

"I'm glad."

"How long can you stay?"

She gave a little shrug. "My stay is open-ended."

"I love open ends."

She laughed at the dirty way he said that.

"What about work?"

"I'm off for a bit." She'd taken a leave of absence from her job as the branch manager of a bank in a Boston suburb. The job bored her, and since she'd received a decent settlement from her ex-husband, she'd decided to take a few months off to figure out her life.

"Is that right? So you're kind of footloose and fancy-free at the moment?"

"I suppose I am."

"That works out really well."

"How so?"

"I'm off for a couple of weeks myself after working around the clock during the storm and extra hours for months since then. My commanding officer told me to get lost for at least two weeks and to not check in or else he'd write me up for being a workaholic."

"What do you intend to do with this unplanned vacation?"

"I had no idea until about five minutes ago when you mentioned the footloose situation."

"I believe you're the one who called it that."

"Are your feet loose, or are they not?"

"They are," she said with a chuckle.

"As are mine. What do you say we be footloose together?"

"I'd consider that."

He pulled her in closer to him. "I'm really glad you came today. The minute I saw you, I felt better."

"In that case, I'm very glad I came, too."

Oliver nudged Dara. "Look."

"Where?"

"Your sister and Linc."

Across the crowded room, they had their heads together, whispering and smiling, mindless of everything happening around them.

"I told you there was something brewing there," Oliver said.

"I told *you* that."

"When did you tell me that?"

"One of those times when you were nodding but not really listening."

"I never do that. I hang on every word you say, my love."

She rolled her eyes. "Sure you do."

"Is she ready for something new?" Oliver asked hesitantly.

"I suppose that's up to her to decide, but I like him. He seems like a solid kind of guy, unlike the one she married."

Oliver would never get over the brother-in-law he'd once been close to cheating on Monique with a twenty-three-year-old recent college graduate. The shock of that news had stayed with him for months after it first happened, as did the blow-by-blow from one of the ugliest divorces in history. She was just getting her sparkle back after that ordeal, and he would hate to see her hurt again.

When Dara let out a little gasp, he forgot all about his concerns for Monique and focused on his wife. "What's wrong?"

Dara rested a hand over her pregnant belly. "I… I felt her move." She reached for his hand and placed it on her belly.

Oliver held perfectly still until he felt the unmistakable flutter rippling under his hand. His eyes flooded with tears as the memory of doing the same thing when she was expecting their late son, Lewis, appeared out of nowhere, leaving him staggered by the rush of emotion.

"Do you feel her?"

"Yes, there she is."

A week ago, they'd found out the baby was a girl. He'd been relieved to get that news, as the thought of another boy had left him unsettled by the notion of "replacing" the son they'd lost so tragically. A daughter would be a completely different experience for them. When he'd shared that thought with Dara, she'd agreed with him.

"Everything okay, guys?" Monique's question roused them out of their private bubble to remind him they were in a room full of people who'd be wondering what was going on.

"I felt the baby," Dara told her sister.

Oliver moved his hand so Monique could feel her niece.

"Oh wow," Monique said tearfully. "That's amazing."

The loss of Lewis had nearly ruined all of them, but this little girl… She was giving them something they badly needed: hope.

"Will we tell her someday that we were in a bar the first time we felt her move?" Dara asked, smiling.

Oliver brushed the tears off her cheek. "Maybe we can keep that part to ourselves."

She and Monique laughed and then hugged each other tightly. Monique had been an incredible source of love and support to them during the darkness. She was as thrilled about the new baby as they were.

They reached for Oliver to include him in their group hug.

When they finally pulled back from one another, laughing and wiping away tears, he noticed a few people watching them with curiosity.

"You guys all right?" his friend Jared asked quietly.

"Just felt the baby move. We might've overreacted a bit."

"No such thing. Congrats, man."

"Thank you."

"Do you know what you're having?"

"A girl."

"I hope she'll be a friend to our Violet."

"We'd love that. How long until the adoption is final?"

"Three more weeks. We're in the home stretch."

"I hope it goes by quickly for you."

"There're my girls now," Jared said, brightening at the sight of his wife, Lizzie, carrying their daughter into the Beachcomber.

Jared waved to Lizzie, who came over to join them.

"Hey." She raised her cheek for a kiss from Jared. "How was the service?"

"Terribly sad, but also lovely. Morgan gave a beautiful eulogy."

Lizzie sought out Morgan in the crowd. "How's he doing?"

"Seems to be hanging in there."

"Has he said what his plans are?"

"Not yet."

"I hope he sticks around," Oliver said. "I can attest that this is a good place to pass the time while you heal from a tough loss."

"We couldn't agree more," Lizzie said. "We love this island and everyone who lives here."

"We do, too," Oliver said.

"Did you find a house?" Jared asked.

"We've made an offer on a place on the west side. We're waiting on pins and needles to hear."

"Oh, exciting," Lizzie said. "I'm so glad you're staying."

"We are, too," Dara said. "After spending this year here, we couldn't imagine raising our daughter anywhere else."

"Violet can't wait to meet her." The baby had light brown hair, big hazel eyes and chubby cheeks.

Morgan came over to say hello, shaking hands with Jared. "Thanks for coming today."

"Of course," Jared said. "Billy was a friend. He'll be missed around here."

"If I had a dollar for every time I've heard that," Morgan said, smiling. "The outpouring has been incredible."

"That's Gansett for you," Lizzie said. "People show up."

Police Chief Blaine Taylor and his pregnant wife, Tiffany, came into the bar and walked over to see Morgan. Tiffany's ex-husband, Jim Sturgil, had died along with Billy during the storm. Their young daughter, Ashleigh, had taken her father's death hard.

Tiffany had dark circles under her eyes. Her husband stayed close to her as they exchanged hugs with Morgan.

"How's your daughter?" Morgan asked.

"She's doing okay," Tiffany said. "Good days. Bad days. You know how it is."

"I do, and I'm sorry she's hurting."

"Thank you for caring."

"Of course. I heard she used to come to the gym with her dad. Tell her she's got a lifetime membership for whenever she wants to use it."

"That's so sweet of you."

"Tell her I'm thinking of her, and I get what she's going through."

"I'll do that, and thank you again."

"Everyone here has been so very good to me. It's the least I can do."

"You should come for dinner some night," Blaine said. "You can tell Ashleigh yourself about her gym membership. She'll think it's cool."

"I'd love to."

Blaine shook Morgan's hand. "We'll be in touch."

"I'll look forward to it."

CHAPTER 4

$\mathcal{A}$fter the chief and his wife had moved on to visit with others, Oliver turned to Morgan. "That was really nice of you to think of Ashleigh."

Morgan shrugged. "I feel for a kid struggling to understand things most adults can't handle."

"Dara and I lost our three-year-old son in an accident. I was a fully grown man and almost didn't survive that loss. I can't begin to imagine how a child would cope with such a thing."

"I'm sorry about your son."

"Thanks. We're doing better, but it stays with you, as you certainly know."

"It reshapes you into a whole different version of yourself."

Oliver glanced at him, moved by the profound observation. "Yes, it does. That was well said."

"If you ever want to grab a beer with someone who gets it, I'm your guy."

"Thanks, Morgan. I'll definitely take you up on that."

"Please do. I need it as much as you do."

Everyone wanted a moment with Morgan, so Oliver went to find Dara and Monique, who were seated again at their table with Linc.

"How's he doing?" Dara asked.

"He seems to be okay, all things considered. Are you guys ready to head home?"

"I am, but Monique is going to hang out with Linc in town."

"And what are your intentions, young man?"

The other three stared at him, mouths agape.

Oliver snorted with laughter. "I wish you could see your faces."

"I can't believe you said that!" Monique said, sputtering.

"You can't?" Oliver raised a brow in her direction. "Really?"

"Well, I believe it, but I don't have to like it."

"Anyway, Linc, what exactly are your intentions toward my much-loved sister-in-law?"

"I, uh… Well…"

Oliver rolled his eyes. "Articulate."

"Leave him alone, Ollie," Dara said.

"It's a fair question," Linc said. "Let me just say that I like Monique a lot. I thought about her all the time after she left, and we've talked a lot on the phone and by FaceTime." He glanced at Monique, who seemed to be holding her breath. "I'm very happy she came back and that I get to spend some time with her while she's here. You can rest easy that she'll be very safe and well cared for with me." He looked back at Oliver. "Okay?"

"I can live with that."

Monique rolled her eyes at him. "Go away."

"Your sister is rude," he said to Dara as he helped her up.

"And you're a pain in my ass," Monique said.

Oliver grinned at her. "You love me."

"It's a good thing I do, or I might be tempted to punch your lights out."

"Easy, killer. Don't show Linc how crazy you are right out of the gate."

Linc rocked with laughter.

"I apologize for my husband and sister," Dara said to him. "If they aren't bickering, they aren't happy."

"I see that," Linc said.

"Midnight curfew," Oliver said as they walked away. "Don't be late."

Monique gave him the finger.

His work there was finished.

. . .

AFTER HE'D SPOKEN with what seemed like a hundred different people, Morgan took a seat at the bar next to Sierra.

Jace put a fresh draft beer on the bar and pushed it toward him. "On the house, my friend."

"Thanks, Jace. Appreciate you guys opening the bar early for the reception."

"No problem at all. We were glad to do it."

When Jace moved on to see to other customers, Morgan turned to Sierra, taking in her spiky dark hair, multiple ear piercings and colorful sleeve tattoos that were on full display due to the tank-style top she wore that showed off some of her considerable curves. "Thanks for being there today. Meant a lot to me."

"Oh. Sure. How're you doing?"

"Today's been a bit of a roller coaster. I hate the reason for this gathering, but the people on this island have restored my faith in humanity since Billy died."

"I'm glad you're feeling the love. It's a special place."

"Billy used to tell me how great it was and how much he loved living here, but until I experienced it for myself as an adult, I didn't really get just how incredible it is. I never would've gotten through these last few months without all the support that came my way from people I've known all my life and others I'd never met."

"They knew Billy. That's enough for them."

From behind them, Niall Fitzgerald rested a hand on Morgan's shoulder. "Just wanted to say hello and tell you I thought your eulogy was beautiful."

"Thanks, man." Morgan turned to shake Niall's hand. "Nice of you to be there and to sing for Billy. I appreciate it, and Billy would have, too."

"He was a friend. Looked forward to seeing him every day at the gym."

"So many people have said that."

"He was a bright light around here. He'll be missed."

"Thanks again. Appreciate it."

After Niall went to set up for his set, Morgan turned back to Sierra. "That Irish accent must have the ladies lining up behind him."

"He's not interested in them."

"Oh, I see."

"He and John Lawry had been seeing each other, but something went down between them recently. Not sure what, but I don't think they're together anymore."

"Is John related to Owen who owns the Sand and Surf?"

"Owen's younger brother. There're a bunch of Lawrys here."

"I know Owen, Cindy and Julia, who did such a beautiful job today."

"I was in tears listening to her. She sang some of my late grandmother's favorite hymns."

"They were our grandmother's favorites, too. That's why I picked them. The only religion we got was when we went to church with her."

"Same here. It didn't stick for me, but those hymns took me right back to being with her."

"You were close to her?"

"She was my favorite person growing up. She died when I was thirteen. That was a rough loss."

"Mine died when I was fifteen. It sucked."

Sierra held up her wineglass in a toast. "Cheers to your Nana and mine."

He touched his glass to hers. "Cheers to Nana."

NIALL HAD BEEN GOING through the motions for weeks now. Get up, go to work at the Island Breeze Recording Studio, perform four gigs a week at the Beachcomber, go home, go to bed, rinse and repeat. He'd begun to think about relocating back to the mainland to get away from the island and the memories of the man he'd fallen in love with.

John had said he needed some time to think after the intense night they'd spent together during the hurricane. He'd hoped that night would be the start of something great. Instead, the opposite had happened. John's youngest brother, Jeff, had been badly injured during the storm. John had spent a few weeks in Providence supporting Jeff and his girlfriend, Kelsey, as they recovered from their injuries.

He'd come back to the island a different person, or so it seemed to Niall. No more flirty texts or late nights spent talking and getting to know each other or any of the other things they'd enjoyed together.

It was devastating to have come so close to the real thing, only to have it yanked away like their connection had meant nothing to John.

If only he knew why. Yes, he'd been John's first significant relationship after another one had ended disastrously, but he'd tried to show him how great it could be if only he were willing to take a chance and open his heart to the possibilities.

Apparently, he wasn't able to, and Niall was working on trying to accept that, which wasn't going well at all. He had to force himself through the most basic tasks each day—showering, getting dressed, eating a little something… Even playing for the crowd at the Beachcomber wasn't the usual thrill, as it was all he could do to sing love songs with the conviction needed to be entertaining.

Life was a major drag, with no chance of anything changing to make it better. John's silence was an answer, even if it wasn't the one Niall had hoped for. Being on this tiny island, in the off-season, made it more likely they'd run into each other somewhere like the grocery store or the pharmacy or somewhere else everyone had to go eventually.

That hadn't happened yet, and he'd stopped hoping it would. What good would it do to come face-to-face with the one he wanted but couldn't have? That would only make a bad situation worse.

He sang "Brown Eyed Girl" because familiar favorites usually got the crowd singing, too, which took some of the pressure off him. Every face in the place was familiar to him since the tourists had left, which was usually comforting. Now, though, the only face he wanted to see was the only one that wasn't there.

Many of the island's year-round residents had turned out to support Billy's brother, Morgan, and a lot of them had ended up at the Beachcomber. He'd looked for John at the funeral, since he was a regular at the gym and had been friendly with Billy. If he was at the service, though, Niall hadn't seen him. Perhaps that was strategic on John's part.

Ugh, he hated thinking about this nonstop. That was the primary reason he'd stayed single after ending a long relationship back home in Ireland. He'd had enough heartbreak then and had vowed to steer clear of the whole mess when he came to Gansett. That plan had worked well until John made him forget all about his plan to stay single. And look at where that had gotten him.

Niall caught Jace looking at him with an odd expression on his face. *You okay?* He mouthed the question so no one else would hear him ask it.

Why was Jace asking him that?

After realizing he'd zoned out between songs, Niall nodded and forced his attention to the music that'd been his salvation before and would be again. If that didn't work for him, he had no idea what would.

TIFFANY HAD WANTED to come to support Morgan, but the longer they were there, the worse she felt about being away from Ashleigh. Her mom was with Ash, which was the next best thing to Tiffany herself, but she couldn't shake the feeling that she needed to be with her little girl around the clock to keep a watch on her, even if that wasn't feasible.

Ash had gone back to school a couple of weeks after Jim's body was found, and she'd done pretty well getting back into her routine. Tiffany was in regular contact with her teacher and had picked her up early a few times when she'd been having a rough day.

Nothing could've prepared her or Blaine or their extended family for the challenge of helping a seven-year-old through the sudden loss of her father. Add that to the complicated feelings Tiffany had toward Jim, and it'd been a rough couple of months.

In the last hour, there'd also been a nagging pain in her midsection that was becoming harder to ignore. She shouldn't have eaten that piece of pizza from the food table. Everything gave her heartburn in the third trimester, especially tomato sauce. She knew better, and now she was paying the price.

Except the pain wasn't the usual sting of heartburn. This was more like a hard cramp in her side that intensified every few minutes.

"What's wrong?" Blaine asked.

"Nothing."

"You keep flinching."

"Do I?"

He nodded. "Twice in the last ten minutes."

"I have a weird pain in my side."

"What kind of pain?"

"The kind that hurts." She gasped when it showed up again, harder than ever this time. "It can't be the baby. It's too soon."

"Let's get you to the clinic right now."

Tiffany bit back a moan. She didn't want to go to the clinic. She wanted to get home to her girls.

Blaine didn't give her a chance to object as he helped her up and held her while she got her bearings.

A gush of liquid between her legs caught her by surprise as she looked down to see a watery mess on the floor.

"Oh my God." Blaine picked her up and rushed her out of there so fast, her head spun as the people they passed went by in a blur of concern and curiosity. He had her to his police department SUV in a matter of seconds, buckled her in and ran for the driver's seat. They launched out of the Beachcomber parking lot with the siren blaring.

"Is that necessary?" she asked of the siren between sharp pains.

"Yeah, it is."

He drove faster than he ever had before with her in the car and pulled up to the clinic less than a minute later.

Tiffany released her seat belt and was about to get out of the car when he was there to pick her up and carry her inside.

"I can walk."

"You don't need to. I'm here."

Before she could reply, another sharp pain stole the breath from her lungs.

"She's having pain, and her water broke," Blaine said to Katie Lawry McCarthy, the nurse at the front desk. "The baby isn't due for six more weeks."

"Right this way," Katie said.

As they followed her to an exam room, they encountered their friend Dan Torrington in the hallway. "What's up, guys?"

"Tiffany may be in labor six weeks early. What about you?"

"Kara's in labor right on time. I hope everything is okay with your little one."

"Same to you," Blaine said as he deposited Tiffany on the bed in one of the exam rooms.

She was seized by another sharp pain, followed by intense pressure to push.

"Let's get you undressed," Katie said, moving quickly to help Tiffany out of her clothes and into a gown.

Nurse Practitioner/Midwife Victoria Stevens came into the room, pulling on gloves. That she didn't say hello or crack the usual joke or do anything other than get right down to business only added to Tiffany's considerable anxiety—and Blaine's, judging by the tense way he held himself.

"It's too early," Tiffany said.

"Babies have minds of their own." Vic smiled as she examined her. "And your baby is coming right now. Let's get ready to deliver."

"Is it safe to have him this early?" Blaine asked.

"We'll do everything we can to make sure mom and baby are just fine," Victoria said. "I'll be right back." To Katie, she added, "Call David. Tell him I need him."

Terrified, Tiffany reached for Blaine, and he was there to wrap his arms around her and comfort her with his presence. As long as he was right by her side, she could convince herself that nothing could go wrong.

"You're shaking, baby," Blaine said.

"I'm so scared."

"I have total faith in Victoria, David and Katie. They know what they're doing."

"What if the baby is too little?" They'd chosen not to find out the baby's sex, but Tiffany was convinced it was a boy. Everything about this pregnancy had been different from the ones with her girls.

"I'm sure he or she will be strong like Ash and Addie are."

Tears filled her eyes as her chin wobbled. "I don't want to lose this baby."

"You won't. I have a good feeling about this little person. They're showing us who's the boss from the start. Imagine what the teen years will be like."

She appreciated his efforts to help her think about anything other than the growing need to push and the fear that something could go terribly wrong.

CHAPTER 5

"Tiffany is in labor, too," Dan told Kara when he brought her another cup of ice chips and fed them to her after a particularly brutal contraction.

He wasn't sure he would survive childbirth, but he wisely kept his mouth shut since he wasn't the one doing the heavy lifting. He'd never been prouder of his incredible wife than he'd been during the interminable day that had passed since she woke him up to tell him she was in labor early that morning.

"It's too soon for Tiffany. She's not due until after Christmas."

"I guess the baby has other plans."

"Damn," she said. "I hope they're okay."

Katie came in to check on them. "How's it going in here?"

"The contractions are four minutes apart," Dan told her.

She put on gloves. "Let's see where we are."

Kara grimaced her way through the internal exam and then moaned as another contraction descended upon her.

Dan held her hand and tried to help her breathe through the pain, but the breathing exercises hadn't done much to help her, and they made him feel like he was hyperventilating. She'd wanted to have the baby on the island, while he'd advocated for the mainland in what had turned out to be one of the more intense disagreements they'd ever had. He was hoping he wouldn't regret ceding to her wishes.

If anything happened to her or the baby…

He couldn't bear to think about any outcome other than a healthy mom and baby at the end of this ordeal. And people said childbirth was the most natural thing in the world. Like hell it was.

"Why are you spinning?" Kara asked when the contraction had passed, and Katie declared them getting closer to ten centimeters dilated, at which time things would get real. Katie said she'd be back to check on them again shortly.

"I'm not."

"Don't lie to the person who knows you best."

"I'm having trouble with anticipating worst-case scenarios, which is usually my job."

"Don't do that. We're fine. This is normal, even if it seems anything but."

"You promise?"

"Yes, I promise. It's all good and will be over soon enough."

"Not soon enough for me."

She gave him a withering look. "Because it's all about you."

"It's so nice of you to realize that."

Kara laughed. "Only you could make me laugh when I'm in labor."

"That's what I'm here for. Comic relief."

As she curled her hand around his, he was thankful she still wanted him around when he'd gotten her into this situation in the first place.

"Did you text your family?" she asked.

"Not yet. I'd rather tell them when our peanut has arrived than have them stressed for hours."

"But you talked to Bertha, right?" Kara asked. "You told her Slim is on standby to bring her over?"

"I did, and she was packing her bags as we spoke."

"I can't believe she's going to take a day off from lobstering for me."

"Really? You can't believe that? She adores you, and she can't wait to meet her new great-grandbaby. I bet she stays a week."

"No way. She'll be twitching after twenty-four hours."

"Want to make a bet? I say seven full days."

"I say twenty-four hours."

"What's the wager?"

"Winner's choice."

He waggled his brows. "I'm already thinking about my prize."

She groaned. "Stand down, stud."

"Are we shaking on this wager?"

She raised her hand.

He shook it and then kissed the back of it. "My queen. The mother of my child. The love of my life. I'm so proud of you."

"Thanks. That means a lot." She looked up at him with big eyes. "It's a lot more painful than I thought it would be."

"You want the epidural?" The thought of a shot in the back had freaked her out more than the fear of pain, but that was before reality set in.

"I think I might."

He kissed her forehead. "I'll tell Katie."

DAVID LAWRENCE SAT on the edge of the bed and kissed Daisy's cheek.

His wife's eyes fluttered open, and she smiled when she saw him there.

"Sorry to disturb you." Now in her third trimester with their first child, she was tired all the time and had taken an early-afternoon nap that'd stretched into dinnertime. "I got called in to work for multiple deliveries."

"Oh, who is it?"

"I can't tell you that, but you'll know soon enough. Nothing stays secret around here for long."

"I hope whichever of my friends is giving birth has the best possible experience."

"We'll make sure of it." He kissed her. "Will you be okay on your own tonight?"

"Somehow, I'll get by, but I won't be happy about it."

David smiled. "I'll call you when I can."

"I'll look forward to that."

As he drove quickly toward the clinic, he called Victoria for an update.

"Tiffany is crowning six weeks early."

"Put Life Flight on notice that we may need them."

"Already done. Kara Torrington is stalled at seven centimeters for four hours now. We're going to move her along."

"Good plan. I'll be there in ten minutes."

"See you then."

Soon enough, it would be Daisy's turn to give birth, a thought that filled him with unreasonable anxiety. He'd spent years watching expectant fathers pace the floor while their wives or partners were in labor and had found it funny that they were so stressed out about one of life's most natural things.

Now he got it. When the most important person in your world was going through something as difficult and sometimes traumatic as childbirth, he could now see from the perspective of a devoted husband and father that it was normal to freak out.

The thought of Daisy suffering through labor set off a burst of panic inside him every time he pictured what it would be like to see his wife in a hospital bed, struggling to give birth to their baby.

Fortunately, they had a couple more months before that would be their reality. Soon, they'd have a little girl to love and adore. At first, they'd planned not to find out what they were having, but David had taken one look at the ultrasound and knew it was a girl. He'd asked Daisy if she wanted to know since it wasn't fair that he knew and she didn't. She'd said, *Hell yes, I want to know.*

They would soon have a daughter named Helen, the name Daisy loved.

He couldn't wait for that part, and neither could Daisy. She'd begun buying cute outfits and onesies and little socks that were so small, they could've been made for a doll.

Helen Lawrence.

That sounded like an old-time movie star's name. It had grown on him since Daisy had first mentioned the name Helen when they were riding out Hurricane Ethel together at the clinic. He'd tried to cancel it out by suggesting Myron for a boy, which had taken them back to square one. Over time, he'd come to see that Daisy was truly sold on Helen, and since he was truly sold on her, he'd agreed.

But he would get to name the next one.

As long as it wasn't Myron, his wife had said.

David was smiling when he walked into the clinic to the sound of a mother in active labor.

He washed up, gowned up and gloved up and was walking into the room as Tiffany pushed her premature son into the world at just thirty-four weeks.

"You have a son," Victoria announced as she quickly cut the cord and handed the baby off to David.

"A son," Blaine said through tears. "We have a son."

Tiffany wept as her husband held her close.

"What's his name?" Victoria asked as she worked on Tiffany while David tended to their son. He'd emerged with a bluish tint to his skin that'd initially concerned David, but the little guy had stabilized quickly. David suspected he might be closer to thirty-six weeks rather than thirty-four.

"Adrian Robert Taylor," Tiffany said.

"I love that. It's a beautiful name for a handsome boy."

"Why is he so quiet?" Blaine asked.

"He's awake and alert," David said. "Which is what we want to see. Five pounds six ounces and nineteen inches long."

"Does this mean we finally had a quiet child?" Tiffany asked.

"Might be."

"If there's anything this family needed, it's a quiet boy," Blaine said.

Tiffany laughed through her tears. "Are you sure he's okay, David?"

"He seems to be just fine, even though he came early." He wrapped the baby in a receiving blanket and brought him to his parents. "Adrian, meet your wonderful mommy and daddy. You're a very lucky boy."

"Hi, buddy," Tiffany whispered as tears continued to spill down her cheeks. "You're so handsome, just like your daddy."

As the baby looked at his parents with big, solemn, dark eyes, David decided he was an old soul, come back around for another trip through life.

Blaine ran a finger over the infant's cheek, seeming in awe of the miracle he and his wife had created. "Thank God you're here to save me, Adrian. Your mother and sisters are a lot, but I'm sure you'll love them as much as I do."

Tiffany laughed as she cried. "I can't believe he's here so early!"

"He knew his daddy needed him to hurry up," Blaine said. "Welcome to the world, Adrian Taylor."

"Tiffany had her baby!" Abby told Adam when he and Liam returned to the hospital to have dinner with her after a trip to the park.

"What? I thought she was due in January."

"She was. He came six weeks early."

"Ah, they had a boy, then."

"Yes, Adrian Robert Taylor."

"I like that. They stuck with the A names."

"But he's six weeks early, and here I am with no sign of these babies, who should've come by now."

"Remember what the doctor said: The longer they cook, the stronger they are."

"This slow cooker is fed up and ready to be done with this."

Adam laughed. "You're the prettiest slow cooker I've ever met."

She scowled at him. "Your potent charm is no match for my current mood, Mr. McCarthy."

"Oh, yikes, good to know." He lifted Liam onto the bed. "Mommy needs some sweetening up, and you're the only man for the job."

"Sweet, Mommy," Liam said, melting Abby's heart.

Abby held out her arms to him, and he worked his way around the monstrosity that was her pregnant belly to snuggle up to her. He smelled like fresh air with a hint of wood smoke, which was one of her favorite scents this time of year. She was sad once again to be stuck inside during her favorite season.

"How was the park?"

"Good. Daddy pushed the swing."

"He's a good daddy."

"Uh-huh. When can you go to the park?"

"Your brothers will be here soon, love, and then we can all go together."

"I don't want brothers."

"I know." Abby smiled at Adam. They hoped he'd change his mind once the babies arrived. "They'll be your best friends."

"You're my best friend. And Daddy."

"Aw, we still will be. You'll just have more best friends."

"Don't want more."

Abby hugged him tighter. "Just you wait. Those boys are going to be so much fun."

He shook his little head, but for once, he wasn't struggling to get free, so she let him have the last word on the matter.

She and Adam were worried about his lack of excitement about his new siblings, but Linda had told them it was probably because he couldn't conceptualize having four new baby brothers arrive all at once. What was a lot for them was even harder for a two-year-old to process.

Linda had assured them that Liam would be an awesome big brother.

They hoped she was right about that.

"I'm stir-crazy," Abby said as she stroked Liam's silky, dark hair.

"At most, you have two weeks to go."

"That feels endless."

"Home stretch, baby."

"Emphasis on *stretch*. It can't happen soon enough for me."

"Don't forget that after it's over, we're going to have five kids aged two and under. So we should probably enjoy this peaceful interlude while it lasts."

"This interlude isn't peaceful for me."

"I bet you'll look back at it and yearn for some time to yourself to lounge around in bed."

"I don't think I'll ever want to lounge around in bed again."

"Yes, you will. We're going to be so tired that bed will be our favorite place for totally different reasons than it used to be."

"You must wonder if you'll ever have s-e-x again."

"We will."

She made a scissor gesture with her fingers. "Not until you're snipped."

Adam winced. "Yes, dear."

"I'm not gambling with your super swimmers again. I've learned my lesson times four."

"I should've done it while we were here, but I'm not sure Liam would be down for having both of us laid up at the same time."

"Probably not, but please make the appointment to do it as soon as you can so we can get that over with."

"Yes, dear. Is he asleep?"

"I think he might be."

"Make room for Daddy." Adam crawled onto the bed and put his arm around her. "I've missed the snuggling."

"Me, too. So much."

"Soon enough, we'll be back to normal."

Abby laughed. "Nothing is ever going to be normal again."

"New normal. It's going to be awesome. You'll see."

"Me and my six McCarthy boys. Awesome. And smelly. Pee on the toilets. Sneakers everywhere. Fourteen tons of laundry per day, not to mention the food."

"We could have one more and try for a girl."

"Shut your mouth, Adam."

Grinning, he said, "Yes, dear."

"And stop gloating about how you knocked me up with four babies and outdid all your brothers."

"Did I or did I not outdo all my brothers?"

"You're shutting up now, remember?"

"I'm just asking, and I should get to enjoy this a little bit."

"Not while I'm stuck in a bed. Talk to me about gloating after we're home with our four miracles."

"I'll put a reminder on my calendar to bring this up with you then."

"You do that."

He caressed her face. "I miss this."

"What?"

"Lying in bed, bickering with you. It's my favorite thing to do."

"You're very good at it."

"Pushing your buttons—all of them—is the most fun I've ever had."

"No one has ever pushed my buttons—all of them—as well as you do. And I felt your chest expanding as I said that."

"You think you know me so well."

"I know you better than anyone, and don't tell me your chest isn't expanding."

"Maybe just a little. After all, I did knock you up with four babies all at once. No McCarthy boy in history has ever done that."

"Congratulations on your remarkable accomplishment."

"Now that's the attitude I'm looking for."

Abby sighed. "I want out of here so badly."

"I know, hon. You've been a trouper. I'm so proud of you."

"Thanks but so have you. Taking care of Liam on your own, while working and visiting me, hasn't been easy either."

"My part has been much easier than yours, and we're not going to fight about that. It's true."

"I keep telling myself two more weeks. Two more weeks."

"Or less."

"That'd nice. We need to finalize names for these boys. I'm under tremendous pressure from my mother, who wants to embroider things."

"Where's the list?"

"On the tray table."

Adam sat up and reached for the piece of paper they'd referred to as the brainstorming document. "Did we agree we're not doing all L names?"

"Yeah, I don't think we can do that and meet the goal of having Irish names that're recognizable and not hard to pronounce."

"Okay, so are the top contenders still Beckett, Ryan, Rory, Eamon, Murphy, Cormac and Patrick?"

"I haven't added any new ones to the list, so yes, those are the top ones. Murphy is my favorite, because that was my grandmother's maiden name."

"I'm still not sure how I feel about Murphy McCarthy."

"Murphy Callahan McCarthy." They'd agreed to use her family name as the babies' middle name, like they'd done with Liam.

"But no one will call him by the full name. They'll call him Murph McCarthy."

"I like that."

"Okay, we'll put that one first in the final column."

"One down, three to go," Abby said. "What's your top pick?"

"Rory. I like that a lot."

"Me, too. Put it in the number two spot."

"Two down."

"Your turn to pick," Adam said.

"Cormac," she said.

"I dig it, but..."

"What?"

"Will people call him Mac?"

Abby groaned. "Probably, and we cannot have that."

"No, we can't. So what's your second choice?"

"My other grandmother's maiden name was Crosby. What do you think of that?"

"Crosby. What would people call him?"

"Um, Crosby?"

"But there's no nickname."

"Cros?"

He made a face that indicated what he thought of that. "I don't love the nickname, but I do love the connection to your grandmother. Any other family names we could draw from?"

"My mother's mother was a Kane."

"With a C or a K?"

"K."

"I like that. Kane Callahan McCarthy."

"Do we have a winner?" she asked hopefully.

"I think we do."

"Yes!"

"Your turn to pick the last one. What's it going to be?"

Adam studied the list thoughtfully. "I'm going with… Beckett."

"Beckett Callahan McCarthy. Will we call him Beck?"

"Maybe, but that's okay with me. You?"

"Yeah, it's got a nice ring to it. Beck McCarthy."

"So our holiday card will say with love from Adam, Abby, Liam, Murphy, Rory, Kane and Beckett McCarthy. How does that sound?"

"Unless…"

"What?" Abby asked with exasperation.

"Do we want each set of identical twins to have the same initial name?"

"Adam! We had it decided, and you're throwing that into the mix now?"

"I'm just asking."

"No, I'm putting my foot down as best I can while on bed rest. Those are the names we're going with. Murphy, Rory, Kane and Beckett. They don't need matching names. They're already going to have matching faces."

"That's true. Good thing you're here to talk some sense into me."

"How many times in our lifetime together will you have reason to say that?"

"Probably hundreds."

"Thousands."

"Easy, babe. It's not like I'm Mac or something."

"That's true." His eldest brother was famous for regularly getting himself into trouble with his wife, Maddie. "And thank goodness for that."

"He texted me earlier to ask how we're doing. The kids are excited to meet their baby cousins."

"Aren't we all? Nice of him to check on us. How are they doing?"

"All the kids have had colds that have made everyone miserable, especially their parents."

"Five kids with colds. I can't imagine that."

"I hate to point out that we're about to have five kids."

"Trust me, I know."

"So it *could* happen."

"Be quiet, Adam."

"Yes, dear."

Abby shifted in the bed to find a more comfortable position, which was becoming harder all the time. Every position was uncomfortable lately, and the grinding pain in her back that'd started yesterday was beginning to become unbearable.

"What's the matter?"

"My back is killing me."

"Let me take Liam."

"I don't want to let him go. I miss him so much."

"I know, hon, but you don't want to get your back acting up worse than it already is."

"True." Abby kissed the top of her son's head and surrendered the sleeping child to his dad, who settled him at the foot of Abby's bed.

"Want me to rub your back?"

"Oh, would you?"

"Of course. Whatever my baby mama needs, I'm here for it."

He helped her to turn onto her side, which was easier said than done, and got behind her to rub her lower back.

"That feels so good." Her entire midsection felt tight with a rolling tension that seemed to be worsening by the minute, along with a pervasive pressure that could no longer be ignored. "Adam…"

"Yeah, hon?"

"Um, I think I might be in labor."

CHAPTER 6

As things began to wind down at the Beachcomber and the crowd thinned to the usual suspects, Sierra was thinking about heading home but didn't feel right about leaving Morgan there by himself. Duke and McKenzie had left to get Jax home to bed, and Jace was visiting with customers at the other end of the bar.

Morgan had been nursing a third beer for more than an hour and had eaten the chowder and burger Jace had brought him.

"On the house," Jace had said again.

Sierra had noticed tears in Morgan's eyes after Jace said that and at several times during the outpouring of support from everyone who'd come by to see him.

Her heart ached for him, which was weird since she barely knew the man. But she understood the pain of losing someone irreplaceable and how the hard part had only just begun.

"So, um, what're you doing tomorrow?"

"Opening the gym and going through the stuff in Billy's office. I swear he lived there more than he did in his place upstairs."

"You've been staying there? At his place?"

"Yeah. I figured, why pay for something when that's available?"

"Is it hard to be there?"

"It's not terrible. I'd only been there a couple of times, so it's not full of memories."

"Oh, well, that's good, I guess."

"I feel him more at the gym than I do there. The gym was his real home."

"Definitely. He was in his element."

"I enjoyed watching him do his thing there. He was like the mayor of Gansett, greeting everyone with an inside joke or a comment that made them laugh."

"He used to call me Touchy because I'm a massage therapist. At first, I thought he meant that I was prickly, which I can be at times, but he just laughed and made a massaging motion with his hands to let me know that's where the name came from."

"That sounds like him. Our grandfather had nicknames for everyone. Billy got that from him."

"What did he call you guys?"

"Billy Bluster and Morgan the Menace."

"Menace, huh?"

"I was always getting into stuff when I was really little, so he gave me that name, and it stuck. Billy called me Menace, and I called him Bluster. It's weird to think how those names kind of end with me. No one else in the world knows about them now."

"I know about them. I'll keep them safe for you."

He glanced over at her. "That's very kind of you. Thank you."

"Of course."

"Would you want to…"

She held her breath, waiting to hear what he might say.

A long moment passed in which he didn't finish the thought.

"Would I want to what?"

"I was going to ask if you wanted to get dinner sometime, but then I thought maybe that wouldn't be fair since I have no idea which end is up right now or whether I'm coming or going."

"I'd love to have dinner with you sometime, and it's okay if you're not sure of anything. Neither am I, and I didn't just suffer a devastating loss."

"So you're saying it's not just me who's a total mess?"

She laughed. "Not at all."

"That makes me feel a little better."

"Whatever I can do to help."

When he smiled, it changed his entire countenance, giving her a hint of what he might be like when he wasn't caught in the depths of grief.

The man was a handsome devil all the time, but that smile…

"I should get going," she said. She put two twenties on the bar to pay for her drinks and the cup of chowder she'd had for dinner, as well as a tip for Jace. "I've got an early morning at the studio."

"I'll walk you home since I'm heading that way."

"How do you know where I live?"

"I asked Duke. He said you live over the store."

"Oh. Okay." She wanted to ask why he'd felt the need to ask Duke where she lived, but she couldn't seem to say the words.

"I was curious about you," he said, saving her the trouble.

"Oh. You were?"

"Uh-huh."

About what? Was he going to finish that thought, or was that all he was going to say? He'd spun her into knots with a couple of tiny little sentences that packed a big wallop.

"Let me just say thanks to Jace before we go." He walked over to where Jace was and leaned across the bar to shake the bartender's hand.

Sierra followed him since he was headed toward the exit.

"Thanks for everything," Morgan said. "Appreciate it."

"Wish there was more we could do for you."

"This was what I needed today. I won't forget it."

"We're here if there's anything we can do. Cindy would want me to include her, too."

"I didn't get to tell her that the meatballs she made were the best I've ever had."

Jace smiled. "I'll let her know. She'll love hearing that."

"See you at the gym."

"I'll be there after work tomorrow."

Morgan gave him a thumbs-up and then gestured for Sierra to move toward the door ahead of him.

She caught the curious look Jace directed her way but didn't get the chance to shrug or do anything other than be swept up by Morgan.

And would that be such a bad thing? To be swept up by a guy like him?

Though she barely knew him, she liked everything she'd seen so far, especially his grace during one of the worst times of his life. He'd thanked everyone who'd come to see him, remembered what they'd brought to the gym for him, had shaken a hundred hands and received pats on the back from people he didn't even know but who'd known Billy.

He'd impressed her repeatedly during that long day.

When she got home, she'd be texting Duke to find out why he hadn't told her that Morgan had asked about her. Hello, best-friend code violation.

As they walked through town, Sierra took note of the festive white lights in every storefront window and the garlands wrapped around the streetlights. In the ferry area, they would pass the Christmas tree made of lobster traps that was an annual tradition on the island.

"You've gone quiet on me," Morgan said as they walked through the nearly deserted downtown area toward the ferry landing, where the gym and massage studio were located close to each other across the parking lot from the ferry.

"Have I?"

"Yep. What're you thinking about?"

"I guess I'm wondering why you were asking about me."

He glanced at her with a raised eyebrow. "For the same reason I asked you to have dinner with me."

"Which is?"

"I like you. I appreciate you coming by the gym to check on me, bringing me food and asking what you can do to help."

"Lots of people have done that."

"Maybe so, but you stand out in a crowd."

Not once in her entire life had a man ever said anything to her remotely close to that, and she was floored by how it made her feel to hear such a thing. "Oh, well, thank you."

"You're welcome. Surely you must get compliments all the time."

"Ah, no, not that often," she said with a laugh that sounded nervous to her. Did it to him as well? She hoped not.

"What's wrong with the guys around here?"

"Um, well…" None of them was interested in her, but she couldn't tell him that. It would make him wonder what was wrong with her, which she asked herself all the time as one friend after another fell madly in love with their soul mate while she was left to watch from the sidelines.

"You don't have to answer that, but perhaps their inaction will turn into my good fortune."

Now, what in the hell was she supposed to say to that? Was he seriously interested, or was it her imagination? "I, um, I guess I'm confused because I thought you weren't sure if you were sticking around, and I'm, well, I'm pretty much a lifer around here."

"I've been thinking more about hanging for a while. The island needs the gym, and the people here have been so amazing since everything happened. Whereas I've gotten a few texts and cards from my friends back home. Here, it's been a whole other level, and a lot of the newer people hardly know me."

"That's how it is on Gansett. This community is unlike any other I've ever been a part of, and that's why I'm a lifer. I can't imagine living anywhere else."

"Can I let you in on a secret?"

"Sure."

"I used to hate the winter here so bad that I'm afraid I'll go nuts having to do another one."

Sierra laughed. "That's my favorite time of year, even though business is a lot slower. It's my rest-and-recharge season. I light the fire, make soup in the Crock-Pot and spend entire days in my pajamas. It's delightful."

"That sounds very relaxing."

"It is."

"Do you ever get bored?"

"Nah, there's always someone inviting everyone to do something. People do dinner parties with friends they don't have time to see in the summer. There're birthday parties, nights at the Beachcomber, Christmas parties. I rarely spend more than a day completely alone before someone pops up to ask me to hang out. I absolutely love autumn, winter and spring here—much more than summer, when we're straight-out seven days a week. That gets old real quick."

"I'll bet it does."

"We're very thankful for the people who come here to vacation and spend their money. They keep us in business. But some of them are a bit extra. We've all seen enough of them by Labor Day. Don't quote me on that, though."

"Your secret is safe with me."

As they approached her place, she wished the walk had been longer.

"Can I make a confession?" he asked as he eyed the studio.

"Of course."

"I've never had a massage."

"What? Never?"

"Nope."

"Oh my God. You don't know what you're missing. You have to come in. I want to be your first."

He laughed. "I might just take you up on that."

"You should. It's the most relaxing thing you can imagine."

"I'm not so sure that having your hands all over me would be relaxing."

Sierra nearly swallowed her tongue. What the hell did she say to that?

His low chuckle had her looking up at him to find him watching her with dark eyes filled with amusement and something else not as easily identified. "Sorry. I don't mean to embarrass you."

"I think you quite enjoy embarrassing me."

"When are you going to have dinner with me?"

"When do you want me to have dinner with you?"

"How about tomorrow night? I'll make a reservation at Stephanie's. I hear that's good, and I haven't been there yet."

She pulled the coat she'd never bothered to zip closed against the stiff breeze coming off the water. "It's very good, but you don't need a reservation anywhere this time of year."

"I'd hate to leave anything to chance for such an important engagement."

"You're kinda making my head spin with all your pretty words."

"Am I?"

She nodded, feeling as breathless as she'd ever been around a man.

He stepped closer to her, tipped her chin up and laid a soft, sweet kiss on her lips that surprised the hell out of her.

"Pick you up at seven tomorrow?"

"Seven thirty is better. I have a client until seven."

"Seven thirty it is. See you then."

"Okay."

"Sleep tight."

"You, too."

As she used her key in the door that led to her apartment upstairs,

Sierra wondered if she'd sleep at all as she picked over the last twenty minutes and reviewed each of the amazing things he'd said to her. She was still dazzled when she crawled into bed and snuggled under the down comforter she needed this time of year.

She'd felt a spark of… something… in past encounters with him, brief as they'd been with her stopping by the gym to bring him something or to ask how he was doing before jumping on the elliptical for an hour. If she'd started to look forward to seeing him, well, that was her problem, or so she'd told herself.

Sierra had also wondered if he was just being nice to her the way he was to everyone who'd come by to support him through a tragic time.

But as of an hour ago, she could now say he wasn't just being nice. He was interested in her and realizing that changed everything. She hadn't dated anyone in more than two years. Or was it three? Jeez, it was more than three years since she and Kyle, the ferry boat mate, had broken up after dating for six months.

Sierra still saw him around once in a while, but that'd been going nowhere fast from the start. She'd stayed with him thinking it was better to be with him than to be alone, but she'd learned that being lonely in the wrong relationship hurt worse than the loneliness that came from being single.

After they'd finally called it quits, she'd been relieved and had never once missed having him around. Duke had told her then that everything was a learning experience, but she was tired of worthless experiences that hadn't taught her anything other than she was better off alone than with someone who wasn't good enough for her.

Morgan was different. He was an actual grown-up who'd been through a lot in his life but still seemed to have his shit together. And he'd said things to her that no man had ever dreamed of saying, which made him the first one with the power to truly hurt her if she wasn't careful not to get too caught up in whatever game he might be playing.

She'd start being careful tomorrow. For now, she wanted to fall asleep thinking about how he'd looked at her when he said she stood out in the crowd and perhaps the inaction of other men would turn into his good fortune.

· · ·

DAN TORRINGTON WAS LEARNING that labor wasn't for the faint of heart as Kara's stretched into the eighteenth hour, and the medical team seemed to become less animated with every half hour that went by.

Kara was exhausted and as pale as Dan had ever seen her, which had his nerves stretched to their absolute limit.

He'd given in and called his mother an hour ago, and she'd assured him that a long labor was perfectly normal, especially with a first child. He'd been relieved to hear that his sister Barbara had been in labor for thirty hours with her first baby, not that he'd wish that on anyone. But it had been good to hear from his mom, on top of the assurances from Victoria and David that everything was progressing according to plan.

He rubbed the back of his neck, which had gone tight with tension hours ago, trying to get some relief.

Kara awakened out of a doze when another contraction started.

Dan held her hand and talked her through it, encouraging her to breathe and all the other useless things he could think of to say.

"I think I want the epidural," she said when it was finally over.

When they'd come in earlier to do the procedure, she'd panicked and decided to keep trying to go without it.

"Are you sure, hon?"

"Yeah, I can't do this anymore. The pain is too much."

"I'll tell Victoria." He kissed her forehead. "I'll be right back."

"We'll be here."

Dan left the room to find Victoria and David in a break room at the end of the hallway, standing as they had something to eat. "Sorry to bother you guys, but Kara is interested in the epidural. This time, she means it."

"I'll be in right away to assess whether she's still in the zone to have one."

"There's a zone?"

Victoria nodded. "We don't like to administer an epidural if she's crowning or about to deliver because it can slow things down. I'll take a look and see where we are. Be right there."

"Thank you."

"Of course. How're you doing?"

"I'm fine. Just worried about her."

"Have you eaten anything?"

"Not since this morning." The thought of eating had made him nauseated because he was so worried about Kara.

"You should have something so you don't pass out and give us another patient to tend to." Victoria gestured to the pizza on the table. "Have some. We have plenty."

Dan's stomach growled.

Victoria and David laughed.

"Don't mind if I do."

"Help yourself, friend," David said.

"How much longer will this go on?" Dan asked between bites of the delicious pepperoni pizza.

"We're giving her four more hours, and then we'll consider our options," David said, "but please don't worry about anything. She's doing great, and this is a very typical first labor, as hard as it is on both of you. And also, the baby is tolerating labor well, with a strong heartrate."

"That's a relief, but I'm worried about Kara. I hate to see her suffering."

"She's a warrior," Vic said. "She's got this."

"Thanks for the reassurances. I'm going back to check on her. Thanks for the pizza."

"Sure thing," David said. "Hang in there, Dad. You're doing great, too."

"If you say so."

"I say so, and I'm the boss around here."

"Puleeze," Victoria said. "We all know who the boss is, and it ain't you."

"You see what I put up with?" David asked.

Dan laughed, relieved to see them goofing around. If they were doing that, they weren't overly concerned about Kara. "I see, and I wish you well, my friend."

"I need all the good wishes I can get with all the women in my life bossing me around," David said.

"Let's go check on Kara," Vic said as she thoroughly washed her hands.

In the hallway, Dan took a second to reply to Kara's grandmother Bertha's text checking on her progress.

Slow going, but she's hanging in there.

Keep me posted.

Will do.

Love you both.

Love you, too.

When he entered the room, Vic was examining Kara as his wife gritted her teeth from the added pressure.

"You're there," Vic said. "We're ready to push."

"So no epidural?" Dan asked.

"Nope, but don't worry. She's got this. I'll be right back."

Dan went to Kara's bedside and took the hand that didn't have the IV attached, kissing the back of it. "I'm so proud of you, sweetheart. I already knew you were incredible, but now I know you're a superhero."

"I don't feel like one. I'm scared of this next part." Her eyes were full of tears. "I should've gotten the epidural when I could."

"I'm sure you'll rock this the same way you rocked the first part."

"If you say so."

"I say so, and you know how I love to hear myself talk."

She laughed and then gasped at the start of another contraction.

Dan talked her through it while feeling ridiculous because nothing he said would help. "I can't wait to meet our Dylan."

"Me, too," she said, panting through the aftermath of the contraction.

"Last chance to change your bet."

She'd bet on a girl, while he'd bet on a boy.

"She's a girl. I'm sure of it."

He couldn't wait to be a girl dad—or a boy dad. Either was fine with him, and he was thrilled to be naming the baby after his late brother. "You're going to be a mommy."

She turned her head so she could see him. "You're going to be a daddy."

"I'm so excited."

"Me, too."

"I just wish I had a magic wand to move things along for you."

"That would be nice to have right now."

Victoria returned with David and Katie, who were wearing gowns, masks and gloves and moved like a well-oiled pit crew who'd done this very thing many times before. Their obvious competence infused him with confidence that he badly needed as he prepared to support his wife through the birth.

They instructed him to get behind her on the bed while they positioned her legs and took their places, with Victoria leading the charge,

Katie standing next to Kara and David waiting to care for the baby after the birth.

"On the next contraction, I want a big push," Victoria said.

"Are you ready, honey?" Dan asked, surprised to be blinking back tears as the magnitude of the moment took hold.

"I think so."

"I've got you. Lean on me when it becomes too much."

Her hand gripped his arm as the contraction began and she pushed with all her might.

Time seemed to stop as they repeated the cycle at least ten times before Victoria instructed Kara to push as hard as she possibly could.

"Here comes your baby! Keep pushing."

Over Kara's shoulder, Dan watched as the baby entered the world into Victoria's waiting hands.

"Congratulations! You have a daughter!"

Dan could barely see her through the haze of tears as he held Kara.

"You did it," he whispered. "I love you so much. We have a daughter!"

"I told you."

"Yes, you did. I'll never bet against your mother's intuition again."

"You still owe me a hundred bucks."

"Do you take credit cards?"

"You guys are too cute," Victoria said, smiling up at them.

David brought their baby to them, wrapped in a receiving blanket with an oatmeal-colored cap on her tiny head. "She's scored a perfect ten on all her tests."

"She's already an overachiever," Dan said through his tears.

David transferred the baby to her mother. "Baby girl, meet your incredible mom and dad."

Kara held her as tears streamed down both their faces. "Hello, Dylan Adele Torrington." Adele was Bertha's mother's name, which she'd insisted they go with instead of Bertha for her middle name. *No baby needs that old name,* she'd said adamantly.

Kara kissed the baby's cheek. "I'm your mom, and that guy behind me is your dad. I'm sorry about him, but we'll handle him together."

Dan laughed as he wiped tears from his face. "Hey!" He reached out to caress the softest skin he'd ever touched. "And this is your mom. She has a smart mouth, but overall, she's pretty cool, and I love her more than anything, except you, of course."

"We need to tell all the people. They're on pins and needles by now."

"Let me see your phone," Katie said. "I'll take a picture."

Dan sent the first photo of their family of three to his family and Kara's as well as all their friends on Gansett Island with the message, *Welcome to the world, Dylan Adele Torrington, born at 7:38 pm on December 10th, weighing in at eight pounds, four ounces and measuring nineteen inches. Mom was a stud, and Dad held up pretty well, all things considered. We're overjoyed to have a daughter!*

He hoped his late brother somehow knew that he had a new niece named for him. Dan would never cease to be amazed by how the best day could somehow also reflect the worst day, proving that life went on after an unimaginable loss.

"She's so pretty," Kara said, bringing him back to the present with his wife and daughter.

They had a daughter!

"Like her mommy."

"I hate to say it," Kara said dryly, "but she looks just like you."

"Lucky kid," Dan said, because that's what she expected from him.

"We're the lucky ones."

"We sure are."

CHAPTER 7

Stephanie let out a whoop from the sofa in Mac and Maddie's spacious family room, where the McCarthy family had gathered for dinner. "Dan and Kara had a girl! Dylan Adele Torrington." Stephanie read off the vital stats that Dan had sent.

"Two babies in the same day," Maddie said, who'd become an aunt again with the birth of her sister Tiffany's son.

"What if they grow up to get married?" Mac said. "Wouldn't that be something?"

"Easy, skippy," Maddie said. "Give them a day to get acclimated before you start arranging their marriage."

"I'm just saying… That would be something with them being born on the same day."

"Like Quinn and me," Mallory said with a smile for her husband.

"Any word from Providence?" Big Mac McCarthy asked.

"Nothing since Adam texted that Abby is in labor," Mac told his dad. "I'm sure we'll hear something soon."

"Mom and I are heading to the mainland on the first boat," Big Mac told them.

"I wish we could all go," Grant said.

"We don't want to overwhelm them any more than they already are," Stephanie said. "Four infants. I can't imagine." She rested her hand on the curve of her own pregnant belly as the countdown to her delivery inched closer to February.

Mac loved nothing more than nights like this, surrounded by most of the people he loved. Adam and Abby were missing, as were his sister, Janey, and her family, who were in Ohio as Janey took the last exams before she graduated from veterinary school. Big Mac and Linda were flying to Columbus for the graduation, which was another thing Mac hated to miss.

But with five young children, including twin baby girls, there was no way he was going anywhere any time soon. That was fine, as he was where he needed to be with Maddie and their kids, but he wished he could also be there for his siblings as they achieved these significant milestones. "Question. Do we have to call the Brat doctor when she comes home?"

"I thought we'd decided to go with Dr. Brat," his brother Evan said.

Evan's pregnant wife, Grace, smacked her husband upside the head. "You're not calling her that."

"Why not? She'll be disappointed if we don't."

"I highly doubt that," their mother, Linda, said as she rocked baby Emma.

"I'm not calling her doctor," Mac said. "Unless it's Dr. Brat, and that's all I've got to say about it." Tormenting his younger sister was second nature to him, and that wasn't about to change now that she was officially about to become a veterinarian. He was crazy proud of her, and he'd tell her so as soon as he could, but he'd still poke at her because it was so damned fun.

His brothers agreed.

"I'm with you, Mac," Grant said. "Dr. Brat it is. We should get an engraved nameplate for her office so she doesn't get too big for her britches."

"Yes," Evan said, pumping his fist. "Let's do it."

"You boys never learn," their father's best friend, Ned Saunders, said, chuckling. "How many times does Mac gotta lead ya'll off a cliff before ya wise up?"

Mac puffed out his chest. "They'll never give up on me."

"Easy, big brother," Evan said. "We've learned to be more selective in how much of your bullshit we're willing to consume. In this case, the Brat will always be the Brat, doctor or not."

"We're going to have to add a wing onto the elementary school to accommodate all these kiddos," Grace said, who was also due in February with their first child.

"The town council is already talking about that." As president of the council, Big Mac was always in the know. "And they're blaming us and our soon-to-be fourteen grandchildren—and counting—for creating the need. Not to mention the kids Laura, Shane, Riley and Finn have or will have in the future."

The McCarthy cousins were contributing to the baby boom with three from Laura and her husband, Owen, one on the way for Shane and his wife, Katie, and more probably coming from Riley and Finn, the "babies" of the family, who were now married to Nikki and Chloe.

"That's funny," Mac said. "We are a prodigious bunch."

"You are indeed," Big Mac said. "We'll need a whole new wing of the school for the ones being born this year alone to our family and friends."

"Can you imagine all of them as teenagers together?" Maddie shuddered. "If they're anything like their fathers, we'll have to add to the police department, too."

"One thing at a time," Big Mac said, smiling. "We'll beef up the police when they hit the teen years. And let me just say, I sure as hell hope I live to see that."

"I'll make the popcorn," Ned said to his best friend.

"Those are gonna be some years," Linda said. "I fear this crew will put the last group of McCarthys to shame."

"I got here just in time for the show," their eldest sister, Mallory, said. She'd learned a few years ago that Big Mac had fathered her in a brief relationship before he met Linda. Mallory's arrival had been a shock at first, but she'd fit right in with the family, and now it was like she'd always been there.

"What about you?" Mac asked his sister. "You're not adding to the baby boom?"

"We're forty-one," she said of herself and Quinn. "We're too old and set in our ways to detonate that kind of bomb in our lives. We'd prefer to watch the hijinks from the sidelines and then go home to our nice, quiet house."

"That's very wise, Mallory," Linda said.

"We're inundated with nieces and nephews who'll keep us young," Quinn added.

Ned's wife, Francine, who was also Maddie's mother, was rocking baby Evelyn. "I can't believe these babies sleep through all this chaos."

"They're used to it," Mac said. "They've been listening to it since before they were born."

"We're so thankful they sleep through everything," Maddie said, yawning. "I'm not sure what we'd do if they didn't."

Mac's younger son, Mac the Third, toddled up to him and lifted his arms.

Mac scooped him up. "Is my buddy ready for bed?"

Baby Mac nodded. He was so unlike Thomas and Hailey, who held out to the last possible second before going to sleep. When Baby Mac was done, he was done.

"We'll get out of here so you can put them to bed," Evan said for everyone as the family gathered coats and the dishes they'd brought to contribute to dinner.

"Congratulations to Aunt Maddie and Uncle Mac on your new nephew," Big Mac said when he hugged them and the kids. "More nephews coming in hot."

"We can't wait," Mac said. He was so glad that Adam and Abby were in Providence at a top-rate neonatal center for the birth of the quadruplets. That sure as hell beat his twins being born in a freaking helicopter. "Give us an update when you get to Providence."

"Will do," Linda said as she handed baby Emma to her mother.

"Thanks for giving my arms a break," Maddie said to her mother-in-law and mother.

Francine settled sleeping Evelyn into Mac's right arm as he held little Mac with the left one.

"Our pleasure, honey," Linda said, kissing Maddie's cheek.

"That's what grannies are for," Francine added.

"Thank goodness for the grannies—and grandpops," Mac said. "We'd be lost without you, so don't forget about us when Adam brings four new babies home."

His parents laughed as they headed for the door.

"As if you'd ever let us forget about you," Linda shot over her shoulder, making Big Mac, Maddie, Ned and Francine laugh.

Mac helped Maddie herd Thomas and Hailey up the stairs, while he carried Mac and Evelyn and Maddie brought Emma. Five kids was a *lot*.

Thankfully, Thomas could take his own shower while Mac and Maddie bathed Hailey and Mac in the tub in their room. The twins were sleeping in their bassinets.

They got the three "big" kids down without much of a fuss, since they were tired after long days of school and preschool as well as playtime with friends and cousins that afternoon.

Mac fell into bed next to Maddie, who was reading something on her phone. "Any news?"

"Apparently, things are progressing quickly for Abby, and it looks like she'll avoid the C-section. I'm not sure if that's good news or bad for her. Pushing out four babies…" She shook her head. "Two was bad enough."

"Good old Adam had to show us all up with his super sperm. We're never going to hear the end of that nonsense."

"What would you be saying if we were having quads? And before you get any ideas, that is *never* going to happen."

"I'd probably be saying the same stupid shit he is."

"You definitely would. We'd all want to stab you by now."

"Aw, you love me." He turned on his side to face her and slid an arm around her. "Guess what?"

"What?"

"David texted me earlier today to give me the green light we've been waiting for."

"You mean the green light *you've* been waiting for."

"*We.*"

"*You.*"

"Do we have so many kids now that you don't love me anymore?"

"Oh, hush, Mac."

"I love our family. You know I do. But I also miss when it was just us."

"It was never just us. Thomas and I were a package deal."

"Yes, you were, but he was a baby, and we still had lots of time to be together without any distractions." He ran his finger lightly over her arm and loved the goose bumps that erupted from his touch. "I wouldn't trade our five kids for anything, but sometimes I really miss us."

"I know," she said with a sigh. "I do, too. But it won't always be this intense."

"You promise?"

"I do." She put her phone on the charger and turned to cuddle up to him. "I'm sorry if you're feeling neglected."

"Please don't apologize to me for anything. I stand in awe of what you accomplish every day with five little kids underfoot."

"I have an exceptional partner and lots of help from grandparents, aunts, uncles and friends."

He tucked a strand of hair behind her ear and ran his finger over her cheek. "You're the one who makes it all happen, and if I want to be in awe of my amazing wife, I get to be. Also, I don't feel neglected at all. I'm feeling nostalgic for your little apartment over Tiffany's dance studio and that pullout sofa bed that gave me a crick in my back that I still have."

She smiled. "Those were the days, my friend."

"Yes, they were."

"I couldn't wait to get out of that apartment. Remember the first time you brought me here and told me you'd bought this house for us? I thought I was dreaming."

"That was a great day, but I never go to Tiff's that I don't glance at that place and remember where it all began for us."

"I do, too. I had some hard times in that place, but the time with you was magical."

"Even though you wanted nothing to do with me and kept trying to get rid of me?"

"That didn't last long."

"My feelings are still hurt."

"Sure they are."

"Good thing I didn't let you run me off, huh?"

She ran a finger down the center of his chest, lighting a fire of desire with that simple move. "Very good thing, but your own stubbornness is how you ended up with five children."

"That and my endlessly sexy wife who can turn me on with a fingertip after all this time together."

"You're a bit primed." She ran that deadly fingertip over the length of his erection. "It's been a while."

"Eighty-two days, five hours and thirteen minutes."

Maddie lost it laughing. "Are you for real right now?"

"Hundred percent for real."

"You're too much."

"You always say that."

"Well, it's always true."

He wanted her badly, but she was so tired by the end of every day with the kids that he'd never want to be one more thing she had to deal with. But if she kept running her finger up and down his shaft, he might not be responsible for what happened next.

"I love you, Madeline, love of my life, secret to all my happiness."

"I love you, too, even when you're counting the days without sex."

"It's only because I miss being close to you."

"I sleep in your arms every night."

"That's almost close enough, but not quite."

She could barely keep her eyes open, so he reached for the hand that was driving him crazy and curled his fingers around hers.

"Go to sleep, love. We'll have thousands of days to make up for lost time."

"I feel bad leaving you like that."

"Don't feel bad. Don't ever feel bad for making all my dreams come true—even the ones I'd never dared to have before you crashed into me."

"Ha. *You* crashed into *me*."

"Best day of my life."

"Mine, too, except for the blood and scabs."

He held her close to him as he throbbed with the desire that was always present when she was around.

"We need a date night soon," she said. "A whole night alone together."

"We'll make that happen."

"Yes, please."

Mac fell asleep thinking about how he could get a night alone with his beautiful wife before too much longer. With Adam's babies coming home soon, the grandparents would be in hot demand, so he'd need to act fast to squeeze it in before his new nephews made their island debut.

CHAPTER 8

"What do you feel like doing?" Linc asked Monique as they left the Beachcomber, zipping their coats against the cold December breeze off the water. His only goal was to spend as much time with her as he could.

"What's there to do?"

"Um, well, not much of anything."

"Okay, then."

"We could go for a ride, listen to some music…"

"Sure, that sounds good."

"What kind of music do you like?"

"Anything I can dance to."

He handed her his phone, which was paired with the Bluetooth in his Coast Guard SUV. "Lady's choice."

Monique scrolled through the music app until she found what she wanted and put on a song he'd never heard before, but the beat had him tapping his fingers on the wheel as he drove toward the bluffs.

"What is this?"

"'I Don't Wanna Wait' by OneRepublic and David Guetta. One of my favorites."

"I like it."

"I love to dance. It's my favorite thing."

"How do you feel about dancing with someone who's been told he has two left feet?"

She laughed. "I can work with that. I used to teach dance when I was younger. That was my favorite job ever."

"Why'd you stop teaching?"

"I needed to pay my bills and get health insurance and other adult things."

"I hate when that happens."

"Me, too!"

"It's never too late to go back to doing what you love, you know."

"Oh, I don't know. In my case, it might be. Owning a dance studio won't set me up for a plush retirement."

"And you need your retirement to be plush?"

"I don't want to be working when I'm seventy-five."

"You should think about it anyway. There used to be a dance studio here when I first arrived. Tiffany Taylor ran it. She closed it down when she opened her Naughty & Nice store, but I think the space is still set up like a studio."

"And just that quickly, I'm intrigued."

"Have you met Tiffany?"

"I don't think so."

"I could introduce you, if you'd like. You could take a look and see what you think."

"You're the devil."

"Haha. But if you wanted to meet her, I could make that happen. She had her third child today, so it might be a week or two before she's up for it, but the studio is right at her house."

"So tempting, but I'm afraid if I even look, I'll be hooked, and then what do I do?"

"Move to Gansett Island and start a business doing what you love?"

"What about my plush retirement?"

"Eh, you'll figure it out."

"Said the guy with the built-in government pension."

"Life is too short to be working in a job that doesn't make you happy."

"That's very true."

Her entire disposition had gone sober, which had him wondering what had caused that. "Are you okay?"

"Yeah, of course. Do you know what brought Ollie and Dara to the island?"

"Yes, I heard about what happened to their son. It's so tragic."

"When I tell you it was the worst thing I've ever been through… That doesn't do it justice. That little guy was the light of all our lives. For a time, I didn't think they'd survive it, and I wasn't sure I would either. At the same time, my marriage was beginning to fall apart."

"That's rough. I'm sorry you went through such a hard time."

"Losing Lewis was horrible. By the time I split with my husband, it was a huge relief, although I was surprised by feelings of failure and other fun things I never saw coming until I found out he was cheating on me with a twenty-three-year-old he worked with. Anyway… That was a long time ago now, but I agree that life is short, and we need to be happy for the time we have here."

"Dancing makes you happy, Monique."

"Yes, I'm aware of that, Linc."

"I'm just saying."

"Devil."

He laughed, which was something he did a lot when she was around. Out at the bluffs, he pulled into a parking space and cut the engine, leaving the music playing in the background.

"Is this where the teenagers go to fool around?" she asked.

"I wouldn't know. I was never a teenager out here."

"Where'd you grow up again? I know you told me once."

"In Connecticut. Westport area. Went to the Coast Guard Academy in New London, and here we are, fifteen years later."

"So that makes you…"

"Thirty-seven."

She winced. "Ouch."

"What?"

"I'm almost thirty-eight."

"That's not exactly cougar territory."

"Maybe not, but getting closer all the time."

"Far be it from me to correct you, but I would've guessed you were thirty or thirty-one at the most."

"You're too kind."

"It's true."

"Thirty-eight kinda snuck up on me. I'll be freaking *forty* in *two years*. Like, WTF is that about?"

Chuckling, he said, "You're rocking thirty-eight."

"Time's getting away from me, though."

"What do you want to do that you haven't done yet?"

"I expected to be a mother a long time ago, but that didn't happen."

"It still could."

She gave him a comically withering look. "I'm getting old for that."

"Nah. You're a spring chicken. Anything is still possible if you have the will and the desire to make it happen."

"My sister is having another baby. That might have to suffice for me."

"It doesn't have to."

"Are you offering stud services?"

He sputtered as he laughed, which cracked her up, too. Then he took her hand and pressed a kiss to the back of it. "I'd be happy to be your stud if I could help to make your dreams come true."

She tugged her hand free, seeming annoyed all of a sudden.

"What?"

"Don't say things like that. It's too painful to even think about it."

"I mean it. I've always wanted kids, too, and I'm not getting any younger either. Maybe you and I can make a go of it and have a couple of kids together."

She stared at him as if he were certifiable.

Maybe he was.

"We just agreed to spend some time together while we're both off, and you've got us making a go of it and having a couple of kids together?"

He shrugged. "Why not? What've we got to lose?"

"Um, well, our sanity, for one thing. You can't just go having kids with someone you barely know."

"I know you. We've been talking for months."

"How do you know there isn't stuff about me you don't know and wouldn't like?"

"I don't know that, but I look forward to finding out everything there is to know."

"You're being serious about this?"

Linc released his seat belt and turned to face her. "Listen, I've dated a lot of women. Been on more first dates than any guy I know. I've had one real girlfriend, back at the academy, but we got stationed in different places, and that fell apart. Otherwise, nothing has ever stuck, and believe it or not, I thought I'd be married with a few kids by now, too. But that hasn't happened. You know what *has* happened?"

"What?" she asked, seeming a little wide-eyed and breathless.

"I've finally found someone who interests me so much, I can never get enough of her company. I can't wait to talk to her again, to see her again, to be with her. I think about her all the time. That's never happened."

"Whoever she is, you ought to do something about that."

"I'm trying to, and she's being obtuse."

Monique smiled then, taking his breath away. She did that a lot. "I think about you a lot, too."

"Is that so?"

"Uh-huh."

"Like, how much is 'a lot'?"

She rolled her eyes. "All the time, especially when I should be doing other things, such as working."

"Same. I ran over a lobster trap in the work boat the other day because I was thinking about how gorgeous you looked when we were on Face-Time the other night."

"You did? Really?"

"Yep, and do you know how embarrassing it is for the commander to have to call back to the station and ask someone to send a diver to get a lobster trap off my propeller?"

"How embarrassing is it?"

"Extremely, and that's all your fault."

"Hey! Don't blame me."

"I am blaming you." He moved closer, hoping she'd meet him halfway. "That was one hundred percent your fault."

She seemed to move toward him without realizing she was doing it, hopefully as drawn to him as he was to her. The last time they'd been together, he'd wanted to kiss her—and everything else with her—but it hadn't happened.

"You know what I thought about every day since I saw you last?"

"What's that?"

"How incredibly stupid I was not to kiss you that night."

"It was kinda stupid."

"I'd like to rectify that if you're on board."

"I'm on board."

He raised his hand to her face, caressed her cheek and gazed into her eyes in the second before he moved in to close the distance remaining between them.

When her lips met his, the expression "pour gas on a fire" passed through his mind before the kiss went from easy to hot in one second flat. Holy. *Shit.* He'd had a feeling it might be like that with her. Before he knew what had hit him, they were straining to get closer, hands pressed to faces, hers tugging at his hair.

"I knew it was a mistake not to do that last time." With his forehead pressed against hers, he tried to catch his breath while she did the same.

"Big mistake. Huge."

"*Pretty Woman,* right?"

"All this and you know my favorite movie, too? A girl could get carried away in this situation."

"That'd be fine with me." He twirled a length of her curly hair around his finger. "You want to go to my place?"

"Not if we're going to make a baby."

"We can save that for tomorrow."

She laughed, as he'd hoped she would. "You're out of your mind."

"So it seems, and that, too, is your fault."

"I see how this is gonna go."

"Do you? Tell me all about it."

"I'd rather show than tell."

"Mmm, yes, please." Somehow, he managed to disentangle from her and get his head together enough to drive them the short distance to the station, where he had the commander's apartment. Bringing a woman there wasn't ideal, but he had a separate entrance from the rest of the station, and no one was around at this hour anyway. The night shift had settled in to watch TV after dinner, and unless they were called out overnight, they wouldn't emerge until the morning.

He was on vacation and free to do what he wanted, and what he wanted most was to spend as much time with the gorgeous, sparkling, sexy, funny, smart and thoughtful Monique as he possibly could. That was certainly a first for him. Often, he found himself looking for ways to disengage as yet another woman failed to stir anything in him but apathy.

Not this time.

Everything about her was different, and for the first time, he was thankful to all those unremarkable first dates for helping him to realize when someone special came along. He'd thrown her for a loop with the baby talk, but he was about seventy-five percent serious. If they both wanted kids and they both wanted each other, why not go for it? What did they have to lose?

It was madness. He knew it and didn't care.

When they got to his place, he walked her in with an arm around her shoulders. His phone connected with his Bluetooth speaker and launched into "Shut Up and Dance."

Monique turned to him as she tossed her coat onto a chair and started to groove to the song.

The lyrics about this woman being his destiny caught Linc's attention and put a huge lump in his throat as he watched her move. He liked everything about her, including her sharp intelligence, biting wit and easygoing personality. Now he could add the sexy way she moved to the list. The woman could *dance*.

She reached out her hands to include him, and he went to her, fearing he'd turn her off by being a total clod.

But when he followed her lead, he found his own groove, which was a first.

He looped an arm around her waist without missing a beat and earned an impressed look from her.

"Two left feet, my ass," she said, grinning.

"I guess it was all about finding the right partner."

She curled her arms around his neck and ended up pressed against him. "That does tend to make all the difference."

"I wouldn't know. I've never had the right partner."

"Me either."

"This is feeling pretty right at the moment."

"Sure is. How about you show me some of your other moves?"

"Oh, um, well, this is about the extent of it."

"Somehow I doubt that."

He wasn't sure what came over him that had him leaning into a dip that he pulled off rather smoothly, if he said so himself.

"Not bad, Commander. Not bad at all."

"We'll see if I can still walk tomorrow."

When she tossed her head back and laughed, he was completely captivated and couldn't resist leaning in to kiss her neck.

"Mmm." She moved against him, firing him up like he'd never been before as he walked her backward toward his bedroom while continuing to kiss the sexy column of her neck and breathe in the bewitching scent of her skin.

"Where're we going?" she asked, sounding a bit breathless.

"Somewhere more comfortable." He lowered her onto his bed and came down on top of her, propping himself up on his arms. "Are you comfortable?"

She shook her head and smiled.

"What can I do about that?"

"I've got some aches you could see to."

"Is that right? Well, I'd need to do a full exam to make sure I tend to them all."

Linc loved her laughter and the abandon with which she threw her arms over her head, giving him access to every sexy inch of her. He took his time, uncovering her slowly and learning what made her gasp and what had her lifting her hips to drive him wild.

In a final moment of sanity, he said, "Tell me to stop."

"Not doing that."

"You're sure?"

"Yes. Are you?"

"Hell yes."

She whipped the shirt over his head so fast, he never saw it coming. Then she went for his belt while he dealt with her top. Clothes went flying until they were skin to skin, which was the best thing he'd ever felt.

"Hi there."

She smiled up at him. "How's it going?"

"Better than it has in longer than I can remember."

"Same."

"Nice how that worked out, huh?"

"Very nice."

He kissed her lips and then her face and then everywhere else until she was writhing beneath him, begging for more. Before he lost control completely, he grabbed a condom and rolled it on.

She welcomed him back into her arms, running her fingers through his hair and driving him wild with her nails down his back as he joined their bodies for the first time.

He wanted to remember everything about this, so he took his time, savoring the moment in which he confirmed what he'd known for a while now—that after years of looking and hoping and more disappointment than he cared to recall, he'd found the one for him.

This… This was the thing that people wrote songs and poems about… This feeling…

It was everything he'd ever wanted, and so much more than he'd dared to hope for. He wanted it to last forever.

CHAPTER 9

*W*hen a quadruplet mom went into labor, things happened so fast, the parents' heads spun as they went from the tedium of waiting to the chaos of delivery. They were moved to an operating room in case a C-section became necessary and were immediately surrounded by people—nurses they knew well by now and doctors they'd never seen before. A doctor explained that there would be two people assigned to each baby when they arrived, which accounted for eight of the people in the room, along with others on standby in case they were needed.

One of the nursing students had taken the sleeping Liam from his dad and promised to stay with him until his grandparents arrived in the morning. "We'll be right down the hall," the young woman named Dana said. "You can check on him any time."

"Thank you so much," Adam had said as she left with Liam.

"Where's Izzy?" Abby asked of Dr. Isabella Connors, who'd been monitoring her since they arrived in Providence.

"On her way," one of the others replied.

"I'm scared," Abby said to Adam.

"You're in the best possible place, surrounded by all the right people." Adam brushed the dark hair back from her face. "This is the moment you've been training for all your life, my love. You've got this."

She frowned. "How does one train to deliver four babies at the same time?"

"I'm not sure, exactly, but if anyone has been preparing for this, you have. It's your dream come true."

"I dreamed for *a* baby, not *four*."

Adam chuckled at the emphatic way she said that. "Your dream is coming true times four. What can I say? When I aim to make you happy, I go all out."

She grimaced with discomfort as another contraction started. "You can quit that now."

They'd been given birthing lessons bedside a few weeks ago, so Adam tried to remember what he was supposed to do when she was in pain. Focus on breathing. Right. That's it. When he encouraged her to breathe, she glared at him, so he shut up and let her do her thing.

Izzy came rushing in ten minutes later, gowned and ready for battle. "I'm here! Let's have some babies!"

Murphy Callahan McCarthy arrived twenty minutes later, followed shortly after by his brothers Rory, Kane and Beckett, each weighing between four and five pounds, which had been the goal.

Murphy and Rory were identical twins, as were Kane and Beckett.

The nurses applied the colored armbands Abby had read about on a multiples Instagram account to help them keep the babies straight.

"Are they okay?" Abby asked over the cacophony of four babies crying at the same time.

"They're great," the neonatal specialist said. "They scored eight or above on all their Apgar tests, and they're breathing well on their own. Well done, Mom."

Adam released a sigh of relief at the same time Abby did. Their eyes met, and they smiled as he kissed her. "Well done, indeed, my love."

"I can't believe they're finally here."

"The noise is a pretty good indication that they've arrived."

"I suppose we need to get used to that."

"Probably so. How're you feeling?"

"Like I got run over by a tractor-trailer, but so, so relieved that they're here, they're healthy, and I can finally get out of this freaking bed."

"Should we announce their arrival?"

"We need a picture."

They waited until the doctors had brought them all four babies and posed one set of twins with Adam and the other with Abby so a nurse could take the picture for them. Thankfully, the babies had stopped crying for the moment. Then the nurse held two of the babies so Adam could send the text to their family and friends:

Help us welcome two sets of identical twins, all of them with Callahan as their middle name: Murphy and Rory (with Abby), Kane and Beckett McCarthy. They're each at least four and a half pounds and measuring between sixteen and eighteen inches. They're breathing on their own and scored well on the Apgar, which is a huge relief to Mom and Dad. Mom was a trouper through delivery and is looking forward to being OUT OF BED for the first time in almost nine weeks! She's a superstar, and I'm so proud of her. Much love to all of you!

After he sent the text, he took the babies back from the nurse as the medical personnel filed out of the room to give them time to get to know their new sons.

"What now?" Abby asked when they were alone with the babies.

"Um, well, I think we're expected to raise them into men we can be proud of."

"By ourselves?"

He knew that laughing wouldn't be recommended. "Much of the time, yes, but with lots and lots of help from grandparents, family and friends."

"There's another one, you know," she said, sounding slightly frantic.

"I heard something about that. I think his name is Liam?"

"Adam, be serious. We have *five* baby sons. *Five!*"

"Remember when we thought we wouldn't have any? We showed them, didn't we?"

"You're not being serious."

"You have to admit it's kinda funny."

"It's not funny."

"Yes, dear."

"I mean it!"

"Look at what we did, sweetheart. Look at this family we get to raise and love. Look at how beautiful our boys are." Two of them were blond, and the other two had darker hair. "Remember how rare it is to have two sets of identical twins. They've been remarkable from the start, and they're only going to be more so as they grow up. How lucky are we that we get to watch that happen?"

"Very lucky," she said as she gazed down at the babies.

"We've got this, Abs. We've already proven there's nothing we can't do if we do it together."

"That may be true, but there's one thing we *won't* be doing together until that thing is shooting blanks. You got me?"

Laughing, he said, "Yes, dear."

"THEY'RE HERE!" Linda McCarthy said to her husband as she brought him coffee in bed at six in the morning. They were booked on the eight o'clock ferry to the mainland. "Murphy, Rory, Kane and Beckett Callahan McCarthy!"

Big Mac sat up to take the phone from her so he could see the photo of their new grandsons. "Will ya look at that?"

"Thank goodness it's done and they're all doing well."

"So that means they can come home fairly soon, then, right?"

"I think so. They'll want to keep them for a week or two to make sure they're good to go, especially since they're coming to an island."

"We can pick up the car seats on the way out of town so we're ready when they're released."

"Yes, Adam texted to remind me about that."

Between Big Mac's truck and Adam's SUV, they could bring them all home. The kids would be in the market for a bigger vehicle that could accommodate five car seats before too much longer.

"Good Lord," Linda said. "*Adam has five sons!*"

Big Mac laughed. "He's always been an overachiever."

"That's for sure. I can't imagine how overwhelmed they must feel to suddenly have four infants to care for."

"Grammy and Pop are coming. Let's get moving! We've got things to do today."

They showered, got dressed and took coffee to go as they headed for Adam and Abby's house to pick up the infant car seats and some other things Abby had asked them to bring. By seven thirty, they were in line for the eight o'clock boat off the island.

"Thank goodness the weather is with us today," Big Mac said as he took in the gray skies and flat seas. December could be wildly unpredictable, which had worried him as they waited for the babies to arrive.

Their friend Seamus had held a spot on the first boat of the day for the last two weeks in case the babies arrived, and the Irishman came to greet them when he saw them in the car line.

"I guess this means congratulations are in order," he said with a smile.

"It is indeed." Big Mac showed him the photo. "Say hello to Murphy, Rory, Kane and Beckett McCarthy."

"Aw, look at them. Beautiful boys."

"Two sets of identical twins."

"Amazing. Congratulations to you all. Must be a relief to have it done and four healthy boys to shower with love."

"Sure is a relief," Linda said.

"Your family is single-handedly populating this island with the next generation," Seamus said in a teasing tone.

Big Mac laughed. "We're doing what we can to keep the island running."

"How's Carolina?" Linda asked. "I haven't talked to her in a couple of days."

"She's working hard at PT and determined to make the trip to Ohio for Janey's graduation."

One of the great joys of their lives had been when their daughter Janey married Carolina's son Joe, officially making them family to each other after years of being family by choice. Joe had hired Seamus to run the ferry company Carolina's parents had left to Joe and Caro, and she'd fallen in love with the charming Irishman who was sixteen years her junior. What'd been a big surprise to everyone at the time was now just another thing to love about life on Gansett. Seamus had been a great addition to their family.

"Are the boys coming to Ohio, too?" Big Mac asked of Jackson and Kyle, the boys Seamus and Carolina had taken in after their mother died of lung cancer.

"Nah, they're going to stay home with Jace and Cindy so they don't miss school."

Jace was the boys' biological father who'd come to the island to live close to his sons after being released from prison. He'd succeeded in turning his life around, and the friendship between Jace, Seamus and Carolina had become a blessing for all of them as they surrounded the boys with a supportive, loving family.

"That's probably for the best."

"For sure. They barely know Janey and Joe, but that'll change when they get back to the island and get to spend more time with us. We can't wait for that."

"We can't either," Linda said. "It's a dream come true to see our girl become a doctor of veterinary medicine."

"I saw Doc Potter the other day. He's counting the days until Janey gets here to take over his practice. He and the missus bought a retirement home in Arizona to spend the winters there and the summers here. He can't wait."

"It was so good of him to stick it out until Janey was done with school," Big Mac said.

"She's the only one he would've turned over the practice to," Seamus said. "He's as proud of her as you guys are."

"He's been on Team Janey since she was a teenager," Linda said. "This is a dream come true for all of us."

"We can't wait to celebrate her in Ohio," Seamus said.

"First, we've got to bring four new babies home," Big Mac said.

"Give Adam and Abby our congratulations. We're looking forward to meeting the little guys."

"We are, too," Linda said.

"Four babies all at once," Seamus said, seeming amazed.

"You never know what your kids have in store for you," Big Mac said. "All you can do is hang on and enjoy the wild ride."

"Do you have all this fatherly wisdom written down somewhere so new guys like me can refer to it as needed?"

Big Mac laughed. "It's free to you any time you need it, my friend."

"I have a feeling I'll be needing it a lot." Seamus waved to one of the dockhands, who signaled for him to start loading cars and trucks onto the ferry. "Have the best time with your kids."

"We will," Big Mac said. "Thanks for holding a spot for us for this mission."

"Family takes care of family."

Seamus walked away to direct the flow of vehicles onto the boat.

"I'm always so thankful you're the one who does the backing on," Linda said. "I stink at that."

"I gotcha, love. We wouldn't want you backing into the water, now would we?"

"Haha, like that's even possible."

He kept an eye in the mirror as he smoothly backed the truck onto the ferry. "You'd find a way." Seamus had arranged it so they'd be the last ones on and the first ones off.

Island life had few disadvantages as far as Big Mac McCarthy was concerned. But at a time like this, when his son and daughter-in-law had welcomed quadruplets on the mainland, he was chafing at the drawn-out process of getting from point A to point B. If he'd had his way, they would've been with the kids the night before, but that hadn't been possible.

Abby's parents were also heading over today, on a later boat, and similarly eager to get there.

He and Linda left the truck on the lower level and took the stairs to get more coffee and a breakfast sandwich at the snack bar. They had their pick of the tables this time of year, when it would often be standing room only in the summer. As they cleared the breakwater to leave South Harbor, the boat bobbed in the late autumn seas.

Linda cast a wary look out the window at the rolling waves and pushed the rest of her sandwich across the table to him. "I hope I don't regret eating that."

"You'll be fine. You're an old hand at this by now."

"Who you calling old?"

He smiled. "Not my gorgeous wife. She's timeless."

"Right, but that was a good recovery."

"Besides, nothing can ever be worse than your first ride to the island."

"That is very true. You're lucky I came back a second time."

"As you certainly know, you coming back and deciding to live on my island with me was the best thing to ever happen to me."

"As if it was ever a decision. I wanted to be where you were. Still do, for some strange reason."

The seas got rougher when they cleared the island's northern shore.

Big Mac reached a hand across to his wife, who held on tightly. "Remember, four babies at the other end of this ride."

"That's all I'm thinking about. I can't wait to kiss those little faces."

. . .

Adam and Abby had quickly discovered that caring for four newborns along with a cranky two-year-old in the mix was a nonstop process. They'd get one baby changed and fed, only to repeat the process three more times while trying to keep Liam entertained and safe—all without so much as fifteen minutes of sleep for any of them—except Liam—all night long. Upon the advice of the lactation specialist, Abby was attempting to combine breastfeeding with formula, since she wouldn't be able to keep up with four breastfeeding babies.

"Holy shit," Adam said to Abby in a brief lull around eight o'clock in the morning when Liam was settled in a recliner chair with cereal and Bluey on TV and all four babies were pacified—for the moment, anyway.

"Literally."

They quietly cracked up laughing as Adam stretched out on the bed next to her.

"I had no idea that brand-new babies could produce that much poo," she said. "They haven't even eaten much of anything yet."

"I think they came preloaded."

That led to more quiet laughter, because God forbid they should disturb any of their *five* children during this moment of peace and quiet.

Liam had been unimpressed with his brothers since all they did was lie there and cry—and he said they were stinky. He'd complained about the noise they made when he was trying to watch his show. His parents were counting the minutes until the grandparents arrived to provide some much-needed relief for Liam and them.

They'd told him Grammy and Pop were coming in the morning and Nana and Papa in the afternoon. He couldn't wait to get out of baby central.

"How many of the nurses do we get to take home with us?" Adam asked.

"Um, I think zero."

"How're we supposed to function without them? We have no clue what we're doing."

"I believe we're expected to figure it out for ourselves. Thank goodness we'll have a ton of help at home—and P.S., I can't *wait* to go home."

"How're you feeling?"

"Sore from head to toe, but so happy and so relieved it's over. Well, the birth part, that is. The rest is just beginning."

"In case I forgot to tell you yesterday, I'm so proud of you for everything you went through to bring our boys safely into the world. You're the undisputed star of this show, and I love you."

"I love you, too, even if you knocked me up with quads."

"I'd say I was sorry about that, but they're awfully cute, and having four at once will give me bragging rights with my underachieving brothers for the rest of our lives."

"Because that's what really matters."

"You know it, baby."

Abby yawned as she attempted to find a comfortable position to rest while the babies did. She was under no illusions that the peaceful interlude would last for much longer.

The next thing she knew, Big Mac and Linda were there, gazing down at the babies, while Adam walked a crying baby around the room. "How long was I asleep?"

"About two hours," Adam said.

"No way. I slept through that? What kind of mother does that make me?"

"The best kind," Linda said as she leaned over to kiss Abby's forehead. "The babies are gorgeous. Congratulations, Mama times five."

"Thank you, I think."

Linda laughed at the face Abby made.

"I thought five was a lot when they came one at a time. This is next-level."

"Just what I always aimed to be. Next-level."

Abby took Rory from Adam. At least she thought it was Rory. He had the blue bracelet, right?

"Rory," Adam said, smiling.

"You read my mind."

Big Mac held Liam, giving him his full attention while everyone else fawned over the new arrivals.

"Thank you, Papa," Abby said. "You're exactly what Liam needed today."

"My pleasure, honey. How about Mr. Liam and I go out for a walk and a bite to eat?"

"He'd love that, wouldn't you, buddy?" Abby asked her son, who had a confused look to him since awaking to four younger brothers who were occupying every second of his parents' attention.

Liam nodded and rested his head on Big Mac's shoulder.

"Then that's what we'll do."

CHAPTER 10

Kendall James had gotten her boys off to school and was heading to the law office she shared with Dan Torrington when the man himself called.

"Hey there. How's your little one doing?"

"Dylan had a great first night, and we're hoping to take her home later today."

"Congratulations again to you and Kara. Hope she's feeling okay."

"She's aching and tired but elated to finally hold our bundle of joy."

"Give her my best. I didn't think I'd hear from you today."

"I didn't either, but I got a voice mail from a lawyer on the mainland who says he represents the father of Jared and Lizzie's baby, who just found out the baby exists."

Kendall's heart stopped for a hot second as she pulled off the road. "What? Oh my God."

"I wanted to make you aware of it right away."

As she took down the name and number that Dan recited, she felt sick to her stomach at the thought of having to tell her brother and sister-in-law this devastating news. They were counting down the final weeks to Violet's adoption being final.

"Did the lawyer give any indication of what he's asking for?"

"No, he just asked me to call him."

"I'll take care of it."

"I'm sorry about this."

"Me, too. Let's hope he's after money and not the baby."

"That was my first thought—that he recognized Jared's name and is looking for a payout."

"As disgusting as that would be, it's better than him wanting the baby."

"Yeah, for sure. Let me know if you need help with this. I'm a phone call away."

"Will do. Enjoy your family. I'll take care of mine."

"Keep me posted."

"You got it."

Kendall ended the call and stared out the window at the ferry landing for a long time, summoning the fortitude to make a call that could upend Jared and Lizzie's family. "Please don't let that happen," she whispered to the universe.

Before she could figure out her next move, her phone rang with a call from her ex-husband.

"This day just keeps getting better." After a deep breath to calm herself, she said, "Hey." She tried to remember when she'd loved Phil Tobin more than any human on the planet. That felt like a long time ago after the ordeal he'd put her and their sons through.

"Hi. Thanks for taking my call."

She hadn't talked to him in a few weeks, but the sound of his voice had the same effect on her as always—unreasonable yearning for what used to be. "What's up?"

"I wanted to check on how you and the boys are doing."

"We're doing well. Settling into a new life here on Gansett. It's been a good move for all of us."

"I'm glad to hear that."

Fucking tears. She deeply resented them as she brushed them away. "Was there anything else?"

"I was wondering if I could maybe see the boys."

She closed her eyes, as if that would contain the flood. "The, uh, therapist thinks we should keep things as they are now for a while. The boys have made such a smooth transition here... I wouldn't want to do anything to interfere with that."

"By letting them see their father?"

"It's much more complicated than that, as you certainly know."

"I miss them, Kath. I miss you all."

"I go by Kendall now, and I'm not sure what you want me to say, Phil. I didn't create this situation. I'm just trying to survive it."

"I'm sorry," he said, sobbing. "I'm so sorry for everything."

"I know you are, but that doesn't change my reality or the boys'. I have to do what's right for them."

"I've been sober for ninety-six days. I haven't missed a single meeting."

"I'm happy for you. Congratulations." He'd made it to one hundred and ninety-four days the last time he got sober before relapsing for a third time.

"This latest rehab was outstanding. I feel different this time. I know you have no reason to believe me, but it's true."

"I hope with all my heart it sticks, for your sake and the boys'."

"But not yours?"

"We're divorced, Phil. It's over between us. I'm not sure what else you want me to say, and having this same conversation every few weeks doesn't help with the healing I'm working so hard to do. It just reopens the wound, which isn't healthy."

"What am I supposed to do? Not care about you and our sons anymore?"

"I never said that. But you need to leave us alone to recover from the ordeal you put us through. That's what we're doing here, and it's going well so far. I'll text you updates and photos of the boys, but please don't call me again. I just can't put myself through this anymore."

"My mother wants to see the kids."

"She knows she can text me any time she wants to come out."

"She doesn't want to go to the island."

"Well, I'm sorry, but that's where we live now."

"So that's permanent?"

"Maybe. We're happy here. It's peaceful. We're surrounded by family. The boys are making some great friends, and they love their school." After a pause, she added, "I have to go now. I have work to do."

"Where are you working?"

"At a lawyer's office."

"So you're practicing on the island?"

"Yes."

"When you said you were going there, I didn't think it would be forever."

"You forced us to make a whole new life for ourselves. What did you expect?"

"I don't know, but not this. Not never seeing my kids."

"There's so much I could say to that, but it's all been said a million times before. Please don't call me again."

Kendall ended the call before he could say anything else that would drive the knife deeper into her broken heart. She dropped her head into her hands as the tears flowed freely. Nothing had ever devastated her more than the demise of her marriage and the loss of the man she'd expected to spend the rest of her life with. She'd fought for him for years before she'd pulled the plug, realizing she couldn't put her life and those of her sons on hold indefinitely while she hoped for something that wasn't going to happen.

Doing what needed to be done didn't mean her heart wasn't shattered by the loss of the man she'd loved so much. There'd been times, at the beginning, when she'd feared she might not survive losing him. But her boys had been there every morning, needing her to show up for them, and one day followed another, and she'd gotten through it somehow.

Since they'd been living on Gansett Island, she'd felt as if they'd turned a corner toward a future bright with promise. That was until Phil called to send her spiraling back to day one as if all the other days had never happened.

Enough was enough. That was the last call she'd ever take from him. She'd keep her promise to text him updates and photos of the boys, but otherwise, she would have no contact with him. She had full custody of their sons and felt it was the right thing to keep them away from Phil for now. Hopefully, when the boys were older, they'd be willing to entertain having their father back in their lives. That would be for them to decide when the time was right.

Her phone buzzed with a text.

I'm sorry. I love you. I always will.

If only she could block him and permanently remove him from her life, but for as long as their sons were minors, she'd be forced to remain in contact with him. The therapist had told her it was in the boys' best interest to eventually repair their relationship with him. In the meantime, she was stuck in this emotional battlefield, never knowing when the next bomb would blow apart the fragile accord she'd found with her peace of mind.

She shook off her own problems to focus on the grenade that threatened to explode in Jared and Lizzie's world, determined to do whatever she could to make sure her baby niece stayed exactly where she belonged.

LIZZIE WAS ON THE FLOOR, playing with Violet like she did every morning before her nap, when Jared came into the room, fresh out of the shower.

Sunshine had broken through the gray clouds and cast a warm, cozy glow on Violet's playroom, which had become their favorite room in the house.

"There's Daddy."

Violet clapped her chubby hands and let out a squeal of excitement when she saw Jared coming toward them.

Lizzie could relate to that feeling as her heart did a happy jolt at the sight of her handsome husband.

"How're my ladies doing?" he asked when he joined them on the floor.

Violet reached for him, and Jared scooped her up, making her squeal with laughter when he kissed the ticklish part of her neck.

Her daughter's laughter was the most joyful sound Lizzie had ever heard. She could listen to it all day long.

Jared loved it, too, and went to great lengths to coax belly laughs from her.

They played for half an hour before Jared's phone rang.

"It's Auntie Kendall," he told Violet. "Should we see what she's up to?"

"Yayayayayayaya."

"I'll take that as a yes."

"Hey, KJ, what's up?" He listened for a second before nodding. "Of course. We're here. Come on over. Sounds good. See you then." After ending the call, he told Violet, "Yay, Auntie is coming to see us."

"What's she up to?" Lizzie missed having Kendall and the boys staying with them since they'd moved into a small house Ned Saunders had rented to them a few weeks ago. It was closer to the boys' school and to the office Kendall shared with Dan Torrington, so the move made sense. But it was quiet in the house without them.

"She didn't say. She just asked if she could stop by to see us."

"She doesn't have to ask."

"I'll remind her of that when she gets here."

Violet entertained them with her toys and baby chatter until they heard Kendall come in through the kitchen door.

"Back here," Jared called to his sister.

Right away, Lizzie could tell that her sister-in-law had been crying. "What's wrong?"

"Several things." Sighing, she sat on the footstool and held out her arms to take Violet from Jared. She kissed the baby's cheek and gave her a hug as Kendall's eyes filled.

Lizzie was immediately on edge. "What is it, Kendall?"

"Dan called me this morning to tell me he'd heard from an attorney on the mainland representing Violet's father."

This must be what it felt like to get punched in the face. The noise that came out of her sounded like a wounded animal and had her daughter turning to her in distress.

"Wh-what does that mean?" Jared asked.

"I spoke to his attorney. The man's name is Brooks Ward, and he only recently learned of the baby's existence from a friend of Jessie's."

"What does he want?" Jared asked with a hard edge to his voice. As someone who'd made his first billion in his twenties, he was accustomed to people being after his money.

"He wants to see her."

"No!" Lizzie cried. "Absolutely not!"

When Violet began to cry, Lizzie picked her up and held her close. "He's not getting near our child."

"Lizzie," Kendall said gently, "she's not officially your child yet, and until she is, she's technically his."

"How do we know that for sure?" Jared asked.

"His lawyer said Jessie was the one who gave him your number when he reached out to her after finding out about Violet. He's also willing to take a paternity test."

Lizzie couldn't bear to hear another word about this man who threatened everything she held dear. She took Violet and left the room.

. . .

"KENDALL…" Jared felt like he was coming out of his skin.

"I'm so sorry about this, Jared. I wish I didn't have to bring this news to you."

"What do we do? If we lose our baby… Lizzie won't survive it."

He wouldn't either, but he was far more concerned about his wife than he was about himself.

"I think you have to play this out, as hard as it is. Let him come see her, and maybe that'll be enough for him."

"Until his parents find out there's a grandkid, and suddenly, they're filing for custody, and of course, the courts will side with them because he's the biological father whose child was kept from him for all this time."

"Jared. Stop. I know it's very hard not to go to worst-case scenario, but it's very possible that he just wants to meet her, not disrupt the family she's found with you and Lizzie."

"I want to know his intentions before we let him see her."

"That's fair, but you should know that the court can order you to let him see her, if it comes to that. You don't want that to happen."

"I don't want any of this to happen. We're weeks away from the adoption being finalized. What'll we do if he fights us for her?"

"We'll fight back."

"This will wreck Lizzie."

"And you."

"Yeah."

"I know it's impossible not to think the worst, but let's take this one step at a time and hope for the best."

Jared would focus on the worst-case much more than the best-case outcome of this nightmare. That was his nature.

"Thanks for coming over to talk to us in person."

"I couldn't call you with this."

"Is this why you've been crying?"

She shook her head. "That's because Phil called to tell me how much he loves and misses the boys and me."

"Aw, jeez, K. I'm sorry. I wish he'd leave you alone."

"I promised him updates about the boys, but I asked him not to call me again. I can't take it. Every time I talk to him…" Tears spilled down her cheeks that she angrily brushed away. "I just can't."

Jared hugged her, and she held on tightly to him, both giving as much as receiving comfort.

"We'll get through this," Kendall said. "I promise. Dan and I will do everything we can to make sure your adoption goes through."

"Thank you."

"Anything for you, little brother."

"Back at you, sis."

After Kendall left to figure out the next steps to keep Violet where she belonged, Jared went to find Lizzie, who was lying on their bed crying as Violet slept next to her.

Jared crawled onto the bed and took her hand.

"I was thinking earlier, when we were playing before you came in, that I've never been happier in my life than I am right now. If I lose her, I don't know what I'll do."

"We won't lose her."

"How can you say that? If he's her father…"

"I'm her father, and that's not going to change. If I have to offer him every dime I have, that's what I'll do."

"We can't buy her, Jared."

"Who says? If he's found out who we are, that might be all he's after. If it is, I'll give him whatever he wants to make sure we never hear from him again."

"That wouldn't be right."

"That might be all he wants."

Lizzie sighed. "I can't even think about this without wanting to scream."

"We've got two great lawyers on our team, and they'll do everything they can for us. So let's try not to lose our minds over this."

"Too late. I lost my mind the minute Kendall said Violet's father's lawyer had called Dan." Tears slid down Lizzie's sweet face. "Look at her. Our perfect girl. Our dream come true. If we lose her…"

"We won't lose her, Lizzie. I won't let that happen."

"Some things, even you can't control."

"Have some faith in me. I'll fight for you and our baby girl with everything I have. I won't let them take her from us."

He silently vowed to keep that promise to her, no matter what it took.

CHAPTER 11

Sierra had three clients that day, which was a lot for December, not that she was complaining. Business dropped off after the holiday weekend in October, which was why she was so careful with money during the busy season. The summer months funded the rest of the year for her and her two employees. Any business was considered "gravy" at this time of year, and she appreciated her regular clients who propped her up in the off-season.

Jenny Martinez was one of her favorites. Over the years, she'd become a friend, and Sierra looked forward to catching up with her during the monthly massages that she claimed saved her body and her sanity.

Quite some time ago, Jenny had told Sierra about how she'd lost her fiancé, Toby, in the 9/11 attacks on New York City and had struggled for years before landing on Gansett as the new lighthouse keeper and meeting her husband, Alex Martinez. She and Alex were the parents of a son named George and were expecting another son in the spring. Jenny, who was now in her early forties, was concerned about the high-risk pregnancy that had so far been uneventful.

As she prepared a room for Jenny's arrival, Sierra tried to keep her mind on work and not on the handsome man who'd asked her out on the first real date she'd been on in longer than she could remember. How sad was that? Thirty-two years old, and she couldn't recall her last real date.

Pathetic.

Would she remember how to act?

That thought had her laughing as she smoothed a hand over the sheet on the massage bed and folded the top blanket back to make an inviting presentation for Jenny. With everything in place, she returned to the reception area to wait for Jenny.

She took advantage of the brief lull to respond to an email from her bookkeeper, McKenzie, who was in hot demand by everyone who ran a business on the island.

Sierra was happy for her new friend's success and how she'd made lemonade from lemons after the house her grandmother left her was destroyed by Hurricane Ethel. She was rebuilding the house with plans to eventually sell it since she and Jax were happily settled at Duke's place.

Everything had fallen into place for them and several of Sierra's other friends, including Jace, who'd come to the island hoping to have a relationship with his young sons and had fallen in love with Cindy Lawry, who was an awesome person. Even her new friend Piper was head over heels in love with Jack, the state policeman.

Love was in the air all around her, or so it seemed.

Her friends joked there was something in the water on Gansett that led to people finding forever love on a tiny island with only seven hundred year-round residents. The odds of falling in love in a small town like theirs should've been astronomically high. Alas, it happened all the time to other people.

Sierra had never been in love. She'd never even come close, so she wondered if she'd know it if it happened to her. That worried her. What if true love was standing right in front of her, and she failed to realize it? Or what if she found it and managed to screw it up somehow? The thought of living with that kind of regret made her shudder.

She was saved from delving too deeply into that dark thought when Jenny came in, bringing a burst of chilly air. Her smile lit up her pretty face as she fixed blonde hair that'd been messed up by the wind.

"It's brisk out there today," Jenny said. "I swear I saw a few flurries."

"No! Not yet."

"I know, it's too soon, but I saw them."

Sierra went around the reception desk to give her friend a quick hug. "Come in. I'm all set up for you. How're you feeling?"

"A little better now that the nausea has finally let up. It was brutal this time around. My Georgie spoiled me with a much easier pregnancy than I'm having with this little one. Of course, I was three years younger then."

"You're doing great."

"For a senior citizen, you mean."

"Oh stop." Sierra laughed as she led Jenny to the dimly lit room. "You know the drill. We'll start on your side to focus on your aching back."

"Bless you. I miss being facedown."

"You'll be able to do that again soon enough, my friend."

Sierra left her to get undressed and settled and went to the tiny kitchen in the back of the space to refill her water.

When she was ready, she knocked on the door to Jenny's room before entering.

"All set," Jenny said.

Sierra walked in, put her water on a table and got to work making sure Jenny got the best possible massage. Some clients, like Jenny, enjoyed chatting during their treatment. Others preferred silent meditation.

"How've you been since I saw you last?" Jenny asked.

"Not too bad. Relieved to be winding down after another frantic season."

"Same, girl. We've got Christmas tree sales and then we're done for a couple of months." She helped to run Martinez Lawn & Garden with Alex and his brother, Paul.

"How's your mother-in-law doing?" Marion Martinez, who suffered from dementia, resided in a care facility that'd been named for her, founded by Jared and Lizzie James for the island's senior population.

"A little better after having pneumonia in September. We were afraid we'd lose her then, but she surprised everyone by recovering. But she's still not back to where she was before."

"I'm sorry to hear that."

"We're thankful she's still with us, but it's been a roller-coaster ride these last few months. She takes such pleasure in George as well as Paul and Hope's kids, Ethan and Scarlett. She lights right up when she sees them but barely recognizes Alex and Paul."

"It's such a cruel disease."

"It is for sure."

"Did you go to Billy's service yesterday?" Jenny asked.

"I did."

"We did, too. It was so lovely."

"Yes, it was. I'm sorry I missed seeing you. It was so crowded."

"I was glad to see such a big turnout for him," Jenny said. "Everyone liked him."

"I feel so badly for his brother."

"He's been through so much. What do you suppose he'll do now?"

"He said he's planning to stick around and keep the gym open for now."

"Alex will be glad to hear that. He's a regular at the gym. He was worried about it closing, but he was more concerned about Morgan and what he'd do after such a terrible loss."

"He seems to be coping with it as best he can under the circumstances."

"Have you gotten to know him?"

"I guess you could say that. I'm having dinner with him tonight."

Jenny nearly levitated off the table. "Way to bury the lead, girlfriend! Tell me everything!"

Smiling at Jenny's reaction, Sierra said, "There's not much to tell… yet. We've gotten to know each other over the last few months, and he asked me to have dinner with him last night."

"This is so exciting!"

"Don't get out over your skis," Sierra said with a laugh. "It's very new, and who knows if it'll go anywhere? It usually doesn't for me."

"It hasn't *yet*. Doesn't mean it never will. I didn't expect to meet Alex when I did, and if you'd asked me ahead of time if I was going to fall madly in love that summer, I would've said no way."

"How did you know you were in love with him?" Sierra asked as she worked on the tight muscles in Jenny's lower back.

"That feels heavenly," Jenny said with a sigh of pleasure. "It took me a while to realize I was in love because I thought that wasn't going to happen for me again. At first, I was in lust. We had a combustible spark from the beginning."

"Lucky bitch."

Jenny snorted. "You know it. That was one hot summer, thanks to Alex Martinez and a heatwave that roasted us for days."

"I've never really had that spark with anyone. Of course, I've seen it happen to others and heard about it from my friends, but I've yet to experience it."

"Your time is coming. I can feel it in my bones."

"If you say so."

"Ask Alex, I'm good at predicting stuff like this."

"I'll take your word for it."

"Back to your question about how I knew I was in love… I was obsessed with him, which was another thing I wouldn't have thought possible before he came along. I'd been kind of just fumbling through life for years after losing Toby, and then one day, Alex was there, and everything was new again. It wasn't easy, though. We were both dealing with a lot that summer. His mother's condition had worsened, and it was putting a terrible strain on him and Paul. Meanwhile, I was an emotional disaster area desperately seeking a reset. In hindsight, it's amazing it worked out between us."

"You two were meant to be."

"I believe that. At the time, I would've said Toby was my meant-to-be, but I've since learned there can be more than one."

"I'm happy for you that it worked out so well with Alex."

"It's going to work out for you, too. I'm sure of it."

"I guess we'll see."

Jenny's assurances stayed with her as she welcomed Dr. Kevin McCarthy for his first-ever massage, which had been a birthday gift from his wife, Chelsea. She couldn't believe he'd never had one.

"Chelsea says I have to be in the buff for this. Is that true?"

Sierra laughed at the face he made as he said that. "That's totally up to you. Some people go out and proud. Others prefer to keep their underwear on."

"Chelsea told me I'm a prude if I keep the britches on."

"I'd never tell if you did."

"She'll know."

Sierra laughed and gestured for him to go into the room she'd prepared for him.

"This is so nice," he said, taking in the taupe-colored walls she'd painted herself. "And it smells amazing."

"Aromatherapy."

"I dig it."

"I'll leave you to take off as much as you're comfortable with. Then you can slide under the blanket. We'll start backside up, with your face here." She showed him the special pillow with the hole in the center. "Any questions?"

"Nope. I got this."

"I'll be back in a minute." While she was out of the room, Sierra allowed herself a brief giggle over how funny Kevin was asking about whether he had to be nude. She knew him and Chelsea quite well from the Beachcomber and would make sure he was comfortable and relaxed, but he'd cracked her up with the question. He was always such a grown-up compared to the rest of them. To see him a bit unsettled had been amusing.

She ate a protein bar and chased it with water. Then she washed her hands and knocked on the door to the room. "All set?"

"As ready as I'll ever be."

Sierra bit her lip to keep from laughing. He was too funny. "Remember, this is supposed to be relaxing."

"Gotcha."

She rubbed scented oil between her hands and held them under the face pillow. "Close your eyes, clear your mind and take a deep breath in through your nose. Exhale through your mouth. Again."

Sierra quickly discovered that he held all his stress in his shoulders and neck, so she focused on those areas while thinking about what she might wear to dinner later. The temperature had been dropping all week and was expected to hit the thirties for the first time later that night. So she'd probably wear jeans, a sweater and boots, which was boring. She much preferred dressing for warmer weather when she could show off her sleeve tattoos, although she could wear a tank under a sweater and remove the sweater during dinner.

She liked that idea. The tattoos were exceptional, in her opinion—and in Duke's. He said they represented some of his finest work. *Colorful, elaborate, detailed* and *magical* were words that had been used to describe the renderings of some of her favorite images from the fantasy novels she'd devoured in her youth. *The Lord of the Rings* had been her favorite, and Duke had helped her bring the stories to life in living color.

"How's the pressure?" she asked Kevin.

"Mmm, perfect. I can see why people love this so much."

"That's great to hear."

She shifted the blankets to find that he'd taken Chelsea's advice to go completely nude, which was no big deal to her, but…

Did it feel odd to massage the bare hips and legs of a man she knew from her favorite bar? A little, but she was used to giving massages to people she knew and maintaining her professionalism. But some, like this one, were more awkward than others. Kevin was a great guy, but as a psychiatrist, he was also someone she looked up to as a source of fatherly advice.

She'd never given her own father a massage, but if she did, she imagined it would be a little awkward like this was with Kevin. Thankfully, she got through the full treatment and sent him away relaxed and satisfied with his loose muscles.

"Will you confirm for Chelsea that I went all in?" he asked as he prepared to leave. "She won't believe me."

Sierra smiled. "What happens in the room stays in the room."

"Ah, okay. Well, she'll be glad I finally lost my massage virginity."

"Hope you'll come back again sometime."

"I'll definitely be back."

While she waited for her last client of the day to arrive, Sierra sent confirmations to three clients booked for tomorrow and replied to an email from McKenzie with several receipts she'd requested.

Her phone rang with a call from Linda McCarthy, who was due to arrive in fifteen minutes.

"Hi, Linda."

"Oh, Sierra, thank goodness I caught you. I'm so sorry I forgot to call you sooner. Abby had the quadruplets last night, and we're on the mainland. You have my card, so please go ahead and charge me for the service. I'll reschedule when I get back."

"Congratulations! Four new babies takes priority over everything else."

"I felt so badly when I realized I forgot to call you."

"No problem at all. Call me when you're back to reschedule, and no charge for today. Pass along my congratulations to Adam and Abby."

"I will, honey. Thank you for understanding."

"Talk to you soon."

Linda had been a client for years and had never once not shown up for an appointment. Having four new grandsons was a pretty good excuse for missing a session.

Sierra cleaned the room she'd used for Kevin's service and prepared for the next day before she shut down her computer and punched out for the day—two hours earlier than expected.

She had a hot date to prepare for, and as she went upstairs to her apartment, she was thankful for the extra time.

CHAPTER 12

Organ had spent a frustrating day in Billy's office at the gym, sifting through the endless piles of paperwork his brother had stacked on the desk, probably with plans to deal with it in the future. Billy had always been a master procrastinator, so the mess didn't surprise Morgan. But it was one more thing he had to deal with on top of sorting through the personal belongings in Billy's apartment. He'd been chipping away at sorting through both locations over the last couple of months, but had barely made a dent, or so it seemed to him.

Having his brother's things all around him brought comfort and distress in equal parts. While he loved the pictures of Billy and his friends as well as the mementos from a life well lived, they were each a reminder of what'd been lost for everyone who loved him.

The whole thing was so freaking senseless.

That was the part Morgan struggled with the most. Billy shouldn't have been on his boat in the storm, and they'd never know what he and Jim had been thinking when they got the big idea to ride out the storm on a boat.

Their parents had never cared for Jim Sturgil and had discouraged Billy's friendship with him in high school.

"That kid is trouble," their dad had said more than once.

But Billy had been undeterred. Even when the rest of the town turned on Sturgil after his messy breakup with his ex-wife, Tiffany, Billy hadn't frozen out his old friend. "I feel sorry for him," Billy had said when Morgan asked why he was still hanging out with the guy.

"You feel sorry for him. Why the hell is that?"

"I don't know. He's always been trying to figure himself out and never seeming to succeed."

"He had a beautiful wife and daughter that he treated like shit, from what I've heard."

"It's true. He did, and I told him that was totally lame. But I can't turn my back on more than twenty years of friendship because I don't approve of how he handled his breakup. That's none of my business."

"Dad was right about him," Morgan had said. "He's trouble, and you should keep your distance."

"I only hang out with him once in a while. Don't worry about it."

Morgan wished he'd pushed the point harder that Jim was bad news and Billy ought to keep his distance from the guy and all the trouble that seemed to follow him since he'd blown up his life in spectacular fashion.

Maybe if he had, Billy wouldn't be dead. He assumed Jim had been the one to suggest they ride it out on the boat, because Morgan couldn't see Billy coming up with that idea on his own. He'd bet his own life there'd been alcohol involved in their decision-making.

After they'd lost their dad, sister and mother in the span of five years, Billy, the fitness guy, had started to drink more than he ever had before. Morgan wouldn't have said he had a problem with it, but in recent years, he'd been uncomfortable the few times he'd seen Billy drunk.

Who knew what went on when Morgan wasn't around? Maybe it had become a problem. If so, Billy had done a good job of hiding it from him.

He'd probably never know what went down that night since Billy's phone—and presumably Jim's—had been lost in the storm.

On the desk, he found a note in Billy's distinctive handwriting. CALL CLARE ABOUT GOING OUT ON SATURDAY NIGHT, along with a phone number. Morgan studied the number for a second, debating whether he should call it to find out who she was and what she might know about his brother's final days.

He made the call and listened to it ring until her voice mail picked up. "This is Clare Reynolds. I can't take your call right now, but leave me a message, and I'll get back to you as soon as I can. If you're looking for an update on your child's progress in class, you can also send an email to my school address."

So Billy had been dating a teacher? Interesting.

"Hi, Clare, this is Billy Weyland's brother, Morgan. I found your name and number on his desk at the gym and figured I'd call you to say, well… I don't know. If you were seeing him, you might know what he was doing on a boat in the Salt Pond that night. Anyway, if you can, give me a call back." He recited his phone number, even though she'd have it in her recent calls. "Thank you."

He went back to sorting the mess on the desk, tossing anything that wasn't a bill that needed to be paid or something that looked important. After two hours of sorting and tossing, he had uncovered the desk and was working his way through an equally chaotic filing cabinet.

When his phone rang with a local number, he took the call. "This is Morgan."

"Hi there, this is Clare. I got your message."

"Thanks for calling me back."

"I've been meaning to get in touch with you. I… I'm so very sorry for your loss. Billy… He talked about you a lot. He loved you very much."

"That's nice of you to say. Did you know him well?"

"We were getting there. We'd been out five or six times and… I was devastated by his death."

"I'm so sorry."

"Thank you. I am, too. He was a special person. I'm very sad to have lost him."

"Do you know why he was on the boat during the storm?"

"He didn't say anything to me about going to the boat. I couldn't believe it when I heard he was out there in the storm."

"Likewise."

"I'm sorry I don't have more information for you."

"No worries. I appreciate you getting back to me. Take care of yourself."

"You do the same."

After he ended the call, he sat staring at the wall for a long time, thinking about the many people impacted by Billy's death.

"How's it going in here?" asked Terry, one of the guys who worked at the gym.

Terry's question roused Morgan from his contemplative state. "It's going. Our boy Billy was a disaster at organization."

"Yeah, he was, but he was amazing with the clientele. They loved him."

"They sure did. That's all I've heard for months. I suppose that was what mattered in the grand scheme of things."

"It's what made the place so successful. We all looked forward to seeing him every time we walked in the door."

That was the magic Morgan wasn't sure he could replicate. He was personable enough, but Billy had always been the gregarious, outgoing one. "That's nice to hear."

"Can I help?"

"You're already helping by covering the front desk while I clean up in here. Appreciate that."

"Sure thing. Give a holler if you need anything."

"I will. Thanks."

The guys who worked for Billy had been a source of tremendous friendship and support since tragedy struck. He was convinced he could leave them in charge of the place, and it would continue on largely as it had in the past, albeit without their buddy there to make it special.

Morgan had been amazed by how much money the gym brought in each month, with a tidy profit left over after payroll and other expenses. If he were to stick around, he could live comfortably off the proceeds and had a ready-made home at Billy's place. But did he want to assume his late brother's life on the remote island he'd worked his ass off to escape once upon a time? That was the burning question that kept him awake at night lately.

Duke Sullivan poked his head in. "Heard you're digging out the office today."

"You heard right. It's a job and a half."

"Billy told me a few weeks before the storm that his New Year's resolution for next year was going to be getting organized here and at home."

"I wish that had been his resolution for *this* year."

Duke chuckled. "That would've helped. Speak of help, my fiancée, McKenzie Martin, had begun doing some bookkeeping for Billy a month or so before he passed."

"Is that right?"

"Yep. Since the payroll and most of the bills were handled automatically, she didn't want to bother you with that while you had so many other things to deal with, but she asked me to give you her card. Give her a call when you're ready."

"I'll do that. Tell her thanks for me."

"I will. If there's anything else we can do, you can find me at the tattoo studio."

"That's good to know. Appreciate it."

"You got it."

This island… It looked different to him as an adult. He'd spent the first eighteen years of his life working as hard as he could to escape the place he'd considered a prison. His parents and brother had loved it. Morgan and his sister had *hated* it. With hindsight, he wished he could get back those years he'd spent miserable while still living with the family he'd lost one by one.

He'd wasted time he hadn't known would be so precious to him later.

In the months he'd been on the island since the hurricane, he hadn't yet been able to bring himself to drive by the house where they'd lived growing up. Back then, his dad had worked as a captain on the ferries and his mom as a nurse at the island clinic. They'd had a really nice life on the island, surrounded by good friends who were like family.

Morgan hadn't appreciated what he'd had then. He'd hurt his parents with his disdain for the island home they'd loved. He'd felt guilty about that for a long time, even more so after they died. That he was even thinking about moving back to take over the business his brother had worked so hard to establish probably had them rolling in their graves.

He thought of Mac McCarthy, who'd shared his contempt for island living back in the day, but was now married to a local woman and raising a family with her while helping to run the family's marina and a construction business, too. For someone who'd hated it there as much as Morgan had, Mac was now firmly entrenched. Maybe he could shed some light on what it was like to live here as an adult versus a kid.

Morgan looked for the contact info Mac had given him weeks ago, when Billy first went missing. He'd said to reach out if there was anything at all he could do to help. Morgan sent him a text.

Hey, it's Morgan. Was wondering if you have an opening in your crazy schedule for a quick beer one of these days. Thinking about our shared dislike of island life as kids and how you've made it work since you came back. Trying to figure out what I'm going to do about the gym and other things that would require me to relocate to a place I once couldn't wait to escape...

Mac responded a few minutes later. *Of course! I'd be glad to chat about that any time. I could probably meet you for a quick one tomorrow. I'll hit you up after lunch to see how your day is going.*

Thanks, Mac. Look forward to it.

Same!

The guy was frantically busy but had offered to make time to help him. People were like that here, even the ones he hadn't grown up with. A guy could get comfortable in a place like this, which was something he never would've thought about Gansett until he lived through the tragic loss of his brother and saw how the community had rallied around him in his time of need.

That experience had forever changed his impression of the place where he'd been raised. However, he'd been through enough loss to know that a tragedy often brought out the best in people, and while he'd been deeply moved by the response of the Gansett community, could he be happy on the island long term? Should he give up his own career as a master electrician to keep Billy's business running? He'd worked long and hard to get his master electrician license, but he was still working for someone else's company. At one time, he'd planned to start his own but hadn't yet gotten around to it.

If he ran the gym, he'd be self-employed and make as much as he had in his own job. Did he want to give up on all that time and effort he'd put into his specialty to become a gym owner? During one sleepless night, he'd made a mental list of the pros and cons, and the gym had come out on top financially. If only he felt the same passion for running a gym that he did for being an electrician.

He glanced at the clock to find it inching closer to five. Time to wrap it up for the day and go get ready for his night out with Sierra. He'd made a reservation at Stephanie's Bistro, which was known for great food, as well as entertainment by Julia Lawry.

It'd been such a gift to have her sing at the service. She'd been recommended to him by numerous people and hadn't hesitated to accept his invitation to sing for Billy, who'd been a friend to her and her partner, Deacon Taylor.

He hoped Sierra would enjoy the evening he'd planned for them.

Back at the apartment, he showered and changed into black jeans and a black button-down shirt, rolling up the sleeves to reveal his tattooed forearms. His sister, Amanda, had teased him about his all-black uniform, a memory that made him chuckle as he checked his appearance in the mirror behind the bedroom door.

He'd teased Billy about having a full-length mirror behind his door like a teenage girl would have. Billy had put him in a headlock and said he liked to be able to see how he looked before he left the house and to shut the fuck up about it.

Tears stung his eyes at the memories of his late siblings that came out of nowhere to remind him how very alone in the world he was now that Billy was gone, too. Losing Amanda had been hard enough. But also losing Billy was just cruel.

Morgan pulled himself together, put the sadness to the side and tried to get into the right frame of mind to enjoy a nice evening with Sierra. God knew he needed the reprieve from the difficulties he'd faced every day since his brother went missing. He ran some gel through his dark hair that had more silver strands than it'd had before Billy died and arranged it to his liking.

Satisfied that he looked as good as he ever did, he sniffed a couple of Billy's bottles of cologne, chose the least offensive scent and slapped on Billy's prized TAG Heuer watch, feeling a bit guilty to be wearing something that'd been so important to his brother. But life was for the living, and the watch was of no use to Billy anymore. Morgan figured he might as well wear it in his honor.

If he decided to stay on the island, he'd need to get his own place as well as his own vehicle, he thought as he drove Billy's truck the short distance to pick up Sierra. It was one thing to take over Billy's successful business. It was another thing altogether to fully inhabit his late brother's life.

CHAPTER 13

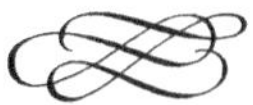

*I*n the summer, they could've walked across town to the restaurant. But with a frigid breeze blowing in from the ocean, it was too cold to walk. Morgan pulled into a parking spot outside Sierra's building as a light went on outside the door upstairs.

Sierra was down the stairs and in the truck before he could get out to hold the door for her, although she probably wouldn't want him to bother. How he knew that, he couldn't say. Call it a hunch.

"Brrr, it's freezing."

"Hey." *Great opening, Morgan. Absolutely brilliant.*

"Hey yourself. How was your day?"

"Not terrible, which is an improvement over the past few months."

"Glad to hear it was an okay day."

"How about you?"

"Two clients and one cancellation due to the birth of quadruplet grandsons, which meant I could cut out early. So all in all, a good day."

"Quadruplets, huh?"

"Yeah, Adam and Abby McCarthy."

"Mac's younger brother, right?"

"Yes, one of them. He has three brothers."

"I remember that. He was in my class, and his brother Grant was a year behind us. I didn't know the younger two. Everything all right with the babies and their mom?"

"I think so. Linda, their grandmother, didn't say otherwise when I talked to her. She sounded excited."

"That's crazy, though. Four babies. All at once."

"Right? No, thanks."

Morgan laughed.

"They also have an almost-two-year-old son."

"Five boys."

"Under the age of two."

"No, thanks," they said together, laughing.

"I think I'd prefer them one at a time myself," he said, "with a few years between them."

"I don't know if I want them at all. I go back and forth. Although, since I've gotten to know my friend's baby, I'm wavering a little."

"A cutie, huh?"

"He's adorable and so sweet. If I could get one just like him, I might be tempted. With my luck, I'd get a wild child."

"Like you were?"

"Haha, how'd you guess?"

"Had a feeling." As he pulled into the parking lot at the Sand & Surf, he realized he'd had more fun in the four minutes she'd been in the truck than he'd had in longer than he could remember. Even before Billy went missing, his life had become a bit of a boring rut. Nothing about being with Sierra was boring. "Wait for me."

"For what?"

"To get your door."

"You don't have to do that."

"I know. I want to."

"If you must."

Grinning, he got out of the truck and went around to open her door with a bow and a flourish that had her rolling her eyes.

"Don't injure yourself."

He extended an arm to her. "I'll try not to."

She gave him the side-eye, but she put her hand through the crook of his elbow and held on for the quick walk into the hotel. "It's freaking freezing all of a sudden."

"I noticed that."

He dropped his arm to hold the door for her and ushered her in ahead of him.

"Nice manners," she said as she brushed by him.

"My mom is watching. That's one of the many downsides of her being dead."

"Don't make me laugh at things that aren't funny."

"Sorry."

"You're not, though."

Inside the hotel, she went to the registration desk to hug the young woman who came around the desk when she saw Sierra come in.

Sierra turned to Morgan. "This is my friend Piper. She works here. Piper, meet Morgan Weyland."

Piper shook his hand. "It's so nice to meet you, and I'm very sorry about your brother."

"Thank you. Nice to meet you, too."

Piper tucked reddish-brown hair behind her ear and propped her elbow on the desk. "So you guys are…"

"Having dinner at Steph's."

"Together. Interesting."

"Mind your business, girlfriend."

"The way you all minded mine when I started seeing Jack?"

"No, not like that at all."

Piper laughed. "Jack's coming by after he gets off work. Meet us at the bar after dinner so I can get to know your friend."

"We'll see," Sierra said, giving Morgan a gentle push toward the restaurant.

"Very nice to meet you, Morgan," Piper called after them.

"You, too."

"Come to the bar!"

"Sheesh," Sierra said. "This place."

"You can't get away with anything."

"I know! But to be fair, we've been pretty relentless with her since she started seeing Jack Downing, one of the state police officers who works out here."

"Ah, I see. So payback is a bitch."

"Yes, and so is she!"

Laughing, Morgan gave his name at the hostess desk, and they were shown to a table by the window, near a roaring fire in the stone hearth that made up the center of the room.

Morgan held her chair and waited for her to get settled.

"Your server will be right with you," the hostess said.

"Thank you." Morgan took his seat and looked around to find the restaurant was doing a brisk business for a weeknight in December. "Is this okay?"

"It's perfect. I love the fire."

"Me, too. That's my number one prerequisite for my future permanent home. Must have fireplace."

"You're not permanent in your place on the mainland?"

"Nah, it's an apartment."

"Whereabouts?"

"South Shore of Boston."

"What do you do there?"

"I'm an electrician."

"You are?" Her eyes went wide. "Really?"

Laughing at her reaction, he said, "Really. Why? What's so great about that?"

"Ever since we had the big blackout last year, I've had one glitch after another at the studio. Maybe you could take a look for me sometime?"

"I'd be happy to."

"That'd be amazing. Our electrical grid is antiquated out here. The blackout revealed a lot of weaknesses. I think most of them are in my place."

"We'll get you straightened out. No worries."

"When word gets out that there's an actual electrician here, you'll be in hot demand."

"Is that right?"

"Oh yeah. It was like when we found out Duke's fiancée, McKenzie, knows QuickBooks. We all snapped her up, and now she's self-employed doing the books for most of the island's businesses."

"That's a good skill to have."

"She's finding that out. We literally fight over her."

"That's funny."

"Don't tell anyone else that you have this skill until you fix my shit, you got me?"

Grinning, he said, "Yes, ma'am."

"I mean it."

That made him laugh as their waitress approached the table to recite the list of specials.

"What can I get you from the bar?"

"I'll do a glass of the house pinot grigio," Sierra said.

"Sam Adams draft for me, please."

"Coming right up."

"That seafood special sounds good," Morgan said as he perused the menu. "I might have that."

"I'm thinking steak."

"Do you like seafood?"

"Love it."

"We could get one of each and do some sharing."

"Works for me."

A pretty woman with short red hair and a round pregnant belly approached their table. "Hi, Sierra. I thought that was you."

"How's it going, Steph?"

Stephanie patted her belly. "Getting closer to D Day."

"You're feeling good?"

"I feel great. Ready to meet my little one."

"Do you know what you're having?"

"We do, but we're keeping it a secret."

"That's cool. Do you know Morgan Weyland? Billy's brother. This is Stephanie McCarthy."

She shook Morgan's hand. "Nice to meet you, and I'm so sorry for your loss."

"Thanks. You're married to Grant, right?"

"That's right."

"I went to school with him. He was between me and my brother."

"He told me that. He's hoping to catch up with you while you're here."

"I'm meeting Mac for a beer tomorrow. He's welcome to join us."

"He'd love to."

"I'll ask Mac to send him the place and time."

"Perfect. Dessert is on me tonight. Enjoy your dinner."

"Thanks, Steph."

"Of course."

Sierra flipped the menu over to examine the dessert menu. "I'll have one of each, please."

"Does someone have a sweet tooth?"

"It's *ridiculous*. I wish I could identify which one it is. I'd have it pulled."

He tossed his head back as he laughed.

DAMN, the man was hot, dressed all in black with a little gel to tame his salt-and-pepper hair. He had just the right amount of scruff on his jaw and a smile that lit up his dark eyes. She liked making him laugh. Hopefully, it gave him a moment of lightness in an otherwise difficult time in his life.

"Note to self." He pretended to write something on an imaginary notepad. "Keep her in sweets."

"That's the quickest way to my heart."

His brows lifted in surprise.

"Yikes. That was a big reveal for a first date. Scratch that."

"I will not scratch that. I'm recording all the information I'll need to secure a second date. Whereas my next move might've been to send flowers to say thanks for a great night, I'll skip that in favor of chocolate."

"How do you know it's going to be a great night?"

"It already is."

Game. Set. Match. This guy was next-level, she decided. Not only was he incredibly sexy, but he had good banter, which was super attractive to her. She loved to spar with her friends, and to do that with a guy who interested her was a new experience. Most guys were too easily butthurt by a cutting comment that was intended to be funny.

Not Morgan. He got it, and that was a huge plus in his column. Add that to the lovely manners, the sense of humor, and his obvious interest in her, and a girl could be bowled over by a guy like him.

"Is there significance to those?" she asked of the black bracelets adorned with silver beads he wore on both arms.

Morgan ran his fingers over the beads on his left arm. "After our sister and parents died, Billy and I had these made. Their initials are on the beads. One is mine, and the other was his. I was glad to get it back after they found him."

"That's incredibly sweet."

"It made us feel connected to them. I guess I need to add a bead to them now."

Her heart broke for him. There was almost nothing she wouldn't do to make him smile. *Slow down, woman. He's here temporarily and going through hell. Don't get overcommitted only to end up heartbroken.*

The waitress delivered their drinks and took their dinner order.

After she walked away, Morgan took a sip of his beer. "Did something upset you before she came to the table? You had an odd expression for a second there."

She stared at him, astounded by his insight and how he paid attention—another thing that made him different from other men she'd known.

"Sierra? Are you okay?"

"I was moved by what you told me about the bracelets, and I was thinking about how much fun this has already been and that I need to proceed carefully with you since you're a short-timer around here."

"Ah, I see how that could be a concern."

"Indeed." She took a big drink of her wine after sharing more with him in an hour than she had with other guys she'd dated for months. Something about him made it easy to open up in a way she never had before.

Sierra appreciated that he didn't immediately try to defuse her concerns with platitudes. That, too, made him different. Most guys would say what they thought she wanted to hear to ensure they ended up in her bed at the end of the night—not that many of them did, but a few had snuck past her defenses only to let her down eventually.

"Hey."

She looked up, realizing she'd settled into a full-on brood.

"I don't want you to worry about anything. This place I used to hate is looking better and better to me all the time. Anything can happen."

"You hated it?"

"Intensely. I thought it was the most boring place *in the world* to grow up. There was absolutely nothing to do, or so it seemed to me at the time. I had a literal countdown to graduation on the wall of my bedroom, and two days after that, I headed for the mainland to find a job and a life that didn't take place on a small, remote island."

"What did your parents say?"

"I made them sad with my disdain for our home. I regret that now. Big-time."

"I'm sure they understood. They were kids once, too."

"True, but I was mean about it. I can't even think about that without cringing. If I'd known then what I know now about how fleeting time and life can be, I would've behaved differently."

"You ought to forgive yourself for that. We're all selfish when we're young. How could you possibly know you'd lose them all by the time you were… what…"

"Thirty-nine."

That made him seven years older than her. "That's not fair."

"No, it isn't. What about you? What were you like as a kid?"

"Hell on wheels, as you guessed earlier, and I'm not proud of that. I was sneaking out of the house from the minute I figured out how."

"Did you ever get caught?"

"Not once. Ever."

"Impressive. What'd you get up to on these jaunts?"

"This. That. The other thing."

"In other words, anything and everything you could get away with."

"That's right."

"Where'd you grow up?"

"Providence. My grandparents owned a restaurant on Federal Hill, the Italian neighborhood, and both my parents worked there, so they were gone a lot at night."

"I know Federal Hill. That was my dad's first stop any time we were on the mainland. He loved Mancini's. Do you know that one?"

Sierra laughed. "You could say that. My dad now owns the restaurant his grandparents founded. It's an institution on the Hill."

"It sure is. Wow. I'm impressed. We all looked forward to eating there any chance we got."

"I'm glad you enjoyed it. I miss it when I'm away for too long."

"Do you get back often?"

"Every couple of months. Not enough for my dad, but he comes out to visit whenever he can get away for a day or two. We make do with Face-Time in between visits."

"You're close to him?"

"He's my best friend in the whole world."

"That's so sweet. Do you have siblings?"

"Nope, just me. My mom died about ten years ago, so it's just us two and a wild bunch of aunts, uncles and cousins who keep us from being alone. My cousins are the ones who taught me how to sneak out."

"Another note to self." He held up his pretend notebook again. "Keep kids away from cousins."

Sierra laughed. "That's a good rule. We had all the fun together, but we're lucky we survived adolescence."

"I, for one, am glad you survived. I would've hated to miss out on meeting you."

She fanned her face. "You're good at this."

Again with the raised brows. "At what?"

"This." She gestured between them. "Whatever it is we're doing here."

He reached for her hand and brought it to his lips in a gesture that nearly had her swooning, for crying out loud. Sierra Mancini did not *swoon*. Ever.

"Whatever this is, I'm enjoying the hell out of it."

She cleared the emotion from her throat. "I am, too."

CHAPTER 14

"I want to see baby Dylan," Stephanie said to her husband, Grant, when he came in for dinner at the bar, as he did most nights when she was working at the restaurant. By this point in December, they were usually counting down to their great escape to Southern California for the winter. Normally, they left right after Christmas with their families. This year, they'd be staying home to wait for their baby boy to arrive in January. They hadn't told anyone that he was a boy, nor had they disclosed the name they'd chosen for him: Oren Charles McCarthy.

Grace and Evan's baby was due in February, and they didn't want to miss that arrival either.

Grant said he was cool with spending the winter on Gansett, but Stephanie worried he'd miss being in California. It'd help that Dan and Kara planned to stay this year, too. Grant was always happier when Dan was around.

"I'm texting Dan to see if they're ready for visitors yet," Grant said as he sent the text.

Stephanie sat next to him and thanked her bartender, Max, for the glass of ice water with lemon he put on the bar in front of her. She looked forward to being able to drink wine again someday.

"Are you having dinner, too, Steph?" Max asked.

"Just a house salad for me, please. If I eat a big meal this late, I'll die of heartburn."

"Sounds good. Usual for you, Grant?"

"Please."

He was a sucker for the shrimp scampi.

"Dan said to come tonight if we want to. The baby slept all day, so they're anticipating a long night."

"Is there a chapter on that scenario in the manual?" Stephanie asked.

"There's a manual?"

"No, but there should be. What's the latest from Providence?"

"Mom texted the group chat to say the babies are doing great and that Abby is tired but thrilled to be up and about again."

"I don't know how she could bear to be in bed for all that time. I'd go mad."

"From what Adam says, she nearly did."

"Thank goodness the babies are here, they're doing well, and, hopefully, they'll be home soon. That's when the real fun will begin."

"I can't imagine bringing four babies home at the same time," Grant said with a shudder. "One is going to be more than enough for me."

"For now, though, right? We've got to give this guy a sibling."

"Definitely, but I'm a little scared of the outbreak of multiples going on in my family. Twins and quads in the same year."

"Yeah, no kidding. With our luck, we'll get the triplets."

Grant nearly choked on his beer. "I can't believe you said that out loud!"

Laughing at his horrified expression, Stephanie said, "I take it back, universe. No triplets for us."

"Stop saying that word. Right now."

She couldn't stop laughing at his horrified expression.

After they ate, Stephanie left the restaurant in the hands of her capable staff and went with Grant to visit Dan, Kara and baby Dylan. She was glad she'd put the baby gifts she'd bought ages ago in the car for when they got the chance to see the new arrival.

"Did Dan say how Kara is feeling?"

"He said sore and tired, but thrilled, too."

Stephanie was incredibly stressed about the looming childbirth experience and was hoping Kara would put her mind at ease. She hadn't said much about her anxiety to Grant or anyone else, for that matter, but it hung over her like a dark cloud of worry that was getting worse as her due date drew nearer.

She'd thought about mentioning it to Victoria, but what could the midwife say that would make Steph feel better about it? That women gave birth every day? That she was young and strong and would do great? How did anyone know how it would go ahead of time? They didn't because each situation was unique. The unknowns, the possible complications, the pain… It was almost all she thought about, which she knew was unhealthy.

Grant turned the car into the Torringtons' driveway and cut the engine.

"Can you grab the gift bags in the back seat?" Steph asked him.

"Yep."

Stephanie stood back while Grant gave a soft knock on the door.

Dan came to the door, smiling so big it was a wonder his face didn't break. Steph had never seen him smile quite like that.

"Come in!"

The baby was crying in the arms of her mother, who was rocking her.

"She's got a set of lungs, huh?" Grant asked as he hugged Dan.

"Hell to the yes," Dan said. "She's loud like her mother."

"Right," Kara said. "Like anyone thinks I'm the loud one."

An older woman emerged from the extra bedroom. She had short, white, curly hair and blue eyes.

"Grant, Stephanie, meet our Bertha," Dan said. "Kara's grandmother and my girlfriend."

"Haha." Bertha hugged Grant and then Stephanie. "He wishes. Heard so much about you two."

"Likewise," Steph said. "We couldn't wait to meet you."

"Welcome to our island," Grant said. "What do you think so far?"

"It's almost as beautiful as my corner of Downeast Maine."

Kara had told them how Bertha was still lobster fishing almost every day well into her eighties—and wouldn't have it any other way.

Steph moved closer to Kara and the baby, eager for a look at the new arrival. "She's gorgeous. Just like her mother."

"That's nice of you to say, but she's the spitting image of her father, God help us all," Kara said with a teasing grin for her husband.

"I can't deny it," Dan said.

"That poor kid," Grant replied.

Dan gave Grant a shove that had Grant retaliating with a headlock.

"Business as usual," Kara said to Steph. "Would you like to hold her?"

"Can I?"

"Of course."

Kara transferred the precious bundle to Stephanie, who looked down at baby Dylan in amazement. She was so tiny and pretty.

"How're you feeling?" Steph asked as she gazed at the baby.

"Not too bad, all things considered."

"So it was horrible?"

"I wouldn't say that. It just took longer than I thought it would, but the end result is so incredibly worth it. Look at her."

"She's perfect."

When the baby started to fuss, Bertha came to get her. "I'll change her."

"Thank you, B." Kara smiled at her grandmother. "I'm so happy you're here."

"I'm happy to be here."

"Bertha never leaves Maine for any reason."

"I'm standing here as living proof that isn't true," Bertha said.

Stephanie laughed at their banter.

"It's the first time she's left in ages."

"For a very good cause," Bertha said, gazing lovingly at the baby.

After Bertha took Dylan into Dan and Kara's bedroom, Kara said, "How lucky am I to have my grandmother here with me after having my first baby?"

"So lucky. She's as great as you said."

"She's the greatest of all time. It's such a gift to have her here. Slim and Erin fetched her the minute they heard I was in labor."

"Aw, I love that."

"Can I get you anything, hon?" Dan asked.

"Maybe a lift up. I need to pee. And what a blast that is right now."

Stephanie winced. "It's that bad?"

"It's a temporary inconvenience for a lifetime with my baby girl. It's no big deal."

After Kara had walked away, Stephanie sat for a second with that comment. *A temporary inconvenience for a lifetime with my baby girl.* That was exactly what Stephanie had needed to hear, not that Kara could've known it. While Kara's words didn't completely alleviate the fear she was dealing with, they helped to give it some perspective.

Grant sat next to her and reached for her hand, giving it a squeeze.

Dan plopped down into a chair across from Grant.

"How're you doing, old man?" Steph asked Dan.

"I'm keeping it together but just barely. No one tells you how emotional it all is. I've been a weepy disaster since she arrived."

"Aw, that's so sweet."

"Waited a long time for my girls. You know?"

Grant glanced at Steph and smiled. "Yeah, I get it. But it was so worth the wait to get it just right."

"You said it, pal. Any word on how Abby and the boys are doing? I'm trying to picture this," Dan said, gesturing to the baby equipment that'd taken over their living room, "times four."

"I know. We were talking about that earlier. Linda sent a text that said Abby and all four babies are doing great, and they're hoping to be home within a week or so."

"That's great news," Dan said. "It's such a relief that they're here, and they're okay—and that Abby is, too."

"I know," Grant said. "I hadn't realized how stressed I was about it until we heard the good news."

When Kara and Bertha returned with the baby, Dan held out his arms.

Kara transferred baby Dylan to her daddy, who teared up at the sight of her.

"He's a red-hot mess," Kara said, smiling warmly at her husband.

"Can't help it. Look at her."

"She's perfect," Stephanie said. "Open your gifts, Kara."

Kara oohed and aahed over the embroidered tote bag and the oatmeal-colored sweater with Dylan's name on them. They'd known what her name was but not whether she was a boy or a girl, so she'd gone with neutral colors. She'd also included some staples like onesies and a few toys.

"These are great, Steph," Kara said. "Thank you so much to both of you."

"We're so excited for our babies to grow up to be best friends," Dan said.

"We are, too," Grant said.

"What if they end up getting married someday?" Steph said.

"On this island," Kara said, "anything is possible."

AFTER DINNER, Sierra and Morgan moved to the bar to listen to Julia Lawry's performance. She opened with "No One" by Alicia Keys and then went right into "Someone Like You" by Adele.

Morgan put his arm behind Sierra's chair, trying to decide whether he dared to actually touch her. It'd been a while—years, in fact—since he'd debated such a thing when it came to a woman. Usually, the path forward was obvious to him. But with her, he was uncertain. Not because he thought she wasn't into him. He sensed she was having as good a time tonight as he was. No, it was more about the rare feeling that this could be something special if he handled it right.

Did he want something special right now? Not even kind of, but he couldn't deny it was happening regardless of whether he was ready for such a thing. After a few hours with her, he already knew he'd regret letting her slip away. Not only was she stunning to look at, but she was easy to talk to. That last part had been a problem in the past. He hated having to pull information out of a potential partner.

Sierra gave it up willingly. She told him stories about her life and was refreshingly blunt about her own shortcomings, which apparently included math, anything mechanical and sometimes a lack of tact.

"That one gets me in trouble with my friends," she confessed, "because if I think they're doing something stupid, I don't hold back."

Refreshing, he'd thought.

As they listened to Julia's beautiful performance, he wanted so badly to raise his hand from the back of Sierra's chair to her shoulder, which was bare since she'd removed her sweater during dinner, revealing her stunning sleeve tattoos. Would she welcome him touching her? Almost as if he conjured him, he heard Billy's voice saying, *Why don't you just ask her? You like that she's straightforward, so why don't you be, too?*

He sat riveted, feeling as if Billy was standing right next to him.

Sierra looked over at him. "Are you okay? You just got all tense."

"Did I?"

She nodded. "What happened?"

"I was having an internal argument with myself, and I heard Billy's voice telling me what to do, as if he were standing right here."

"What did he say to do?"

"He said I should ask you if it'd be okay if I did this." He moved his hand from the back of her seat to cup her shoulder, moving his thumb over her soft skin. "Is it?"

She flashed a cute little grin that revealed a dimple he hadn't noticed before. "I was wishing you'd do *something*."

"Why didn't you say so?"

"Why didn't you ask?"

"Because Billy hadn't told me to yet."

"Thank goodness for him moving things along for us. Otherwise, we might've wasted a lot of time."

Morgan grinned at her, and since he had permission to *move things along*, he leaned in to kiss her, hoping she'd kiss him back.

She did—and *whoa*.

What he'd intended to be a quick kiss, a promise of more to come later, turned into a fiery collision of desire that had him pulling back to stare at her. What the actual hell? A kiss had never delivered such a punch. It had him wanting to take her by the hand to get a room at the hotel since it was closer than either of their places.

"Oh, to be a fly on the wall for whatever you're thinking right now," she said with that sexy little grin.

"I'll bet you're thinking the same thing I am."

"I'm not that kind of girl, Morgan. This is our first date."

Morgan wasn't sure if she was serious or if she was screwing with him. He desperately hoped it was the latter, because after that kiss, he wanted to be alone with her as soon as possible. "Oh, um, well... Okay, then."

His entire body vibrated with the kind of energy he'd rarely experienced from a simple kiss—although nothing about that kiss had been simple. This woman had *complication* written all over her gorgeous self, but all he wanted was more, and he wanted it right fucking now.

However, she was in charge. She said what, she said when, she said how much—or she said no.

Her husky, sexy voice cut into his thoughts. "You want to get out of here?"

"More than I've ever wanted anything ever."

As they stood and headed for the door, he pulled a twenty out of his wallet and dropped it in Julia's tip jar.

She thanked him with a smile.

Julia Lawry was a beautiful, talented woman. In another life in which she wasn't with Deacon Taylor, and he wasn't following Sierra in an all-fired rush to get her somewhere they could be alone, he might've been interested in getting to know Julia better. However, now that he knew Sierra Mancini existed, he wasn't looking to get to know anyone but her.

Was it possible for a single kiss to change a life? He wouldn't have thought so until about ten minutes ago.

Now… He wasn't so sure.

Outside, she took hold of his hand and towed him along with her to the parking lot.

When they were standing next to the passenger door, she stepped forward, put her arms around his neck and fused her lips to his in another kiss that was somehow even hotter than the first one. This one included tongue and teeth and her fingers buried in his hair, pulling him closer.

His arms were wrapped around her so tightly, he hoped he wasn't hurting her. His right hand slid down her back to grip her ass and pull her in as close as he could get her, which still wasn't close enough.

The blustery, cold air blowing in from the ocean was no match for the heat they generated. Turning them, he pressed her against the car and pulled her right leg up to improve the angle.

She moaned.

Morgan couldn't recall the last time he'd wanted anyone the way he wanted her. When he had no choice but to come up for air, he rested his forehead on hers as she sucked in greedy deep breaths of cold air right along with him.

He pulled the keys from his back pocket and managed to unlock her door. As desire throbbed through every inch of him, he got her settled and then walked around to the driver's side. "Your place or mine?"

"Mine."

"I don't have—"

"I do."

Okay, then.

The short ride across town gave him enough time to recall the many reasons why he shouldn't be getting involved when his whole life was unsettled.

However, the thought of pulling back, of putting a stop to this while he still could, was so revolting that he pushed that out of his mind to focus on reliving the hottest kisses of his entire life. No matter what happened next, he already knew he'd relive those memories over and over again for the rest of his days.

CHAPTER 15

This, Sierra thought, was the *thing* she'd often witnessed happen with other couples but had never experienced herself. It was the thing that'd made Duke fall headfirst into love with McKenzie and her son, Jax, without a single hesitation. It'd happened to Jace and Cindy, as well as Kevin and Chelsea and countless other friends. If she hadn't seen it unfold, up close and personal, among her circle of friends, she might not have recognized the significance of this moment.

Every cell in her body was attuned to him sitting two feet from her, gripping the steering wheel with both hands as if he didn't trust himself to touch her while he was driving.

He stared intently at the road as a muscle in his cheek pulsed with tension.

Knowing he wanted her so much made her acutely aware of her own power, which was another thing that was new to her. Sure, she felt powerful in her own little domain at the studio, but in the rest of her life? Not so much.

The five-minute ride from the hotel to her home was among the most erotically charged interludes of her life, and they didn't so much as look at each other or exchange a single word.

It was the knowing… What they were capable of together, what would happen the second they were behind a closed door… And the wondering… What might this become? Was this what she'd been looking for all this time?

As they went up the stairs to her place, she felt his urgency moving her forward from behind. Her hands didn't want to cooperate as she tried to put the key into the lock.

He took the key from her and got them inside with the same haste he'd shown on the stairs, nudging her forward and following her in, kicking the door closed as he reached for her.

Nothing like this had ever happened to her. Not even close. She wanted to fully experience every second of it, but it was happening so fast, she almost couldn't keep up with him as clothes were tossed aside and hands were touching her everywhere he could reach as they fell to the floor right inside the door.

Holy. *Shit.*

JULIA HAD BEEN on pins and needles since her noon appointment at the clinic when she'd gotten confirmation of what she already knew. Her set at Stephanie's had seemed endless as she counted down to Deacon coming to pick her up and take her home so she could finally tell him the news.

Her heart did a happy little jolt when she saw him come in, smiling at her the way he always did. No one had ever been so happy to see her. While she was working, he'd been over to visit their new nephew at his brother's house. Julia couldn't wait to hear how that had gone. She looked forward to meeting baby Adrian tomorrow on her day off.

Soon, Stephanie's would close for the winter, and his harbor master duties would be vastly reduced for the off-season. The winter had become her favorite time of year because they had more time to hibernate together. He oversaw police department training in the fall and winter, so he was still busy, but not like he was in the summer.

As she did every night, she ended her set with "Can't Help Falling in Love," the song she thought of as theirs, especially since she'd sung it for him at their secret wedding after the storm in which she'd nearly lost him.

Hearing that song, Pupwell lifted his head off the bed she kept for him under the piano, knowing it was time to go home. She loved that he recognized the song and knew what it meant.

This season with Deacon and Pupwell was the happiest time in a life that'd been full of trauma, starting with her abusive father and continuing through an eating disorder that'd nearly killed her once upon a time, not to mention a few terrible relationships with men who turned out to be far too much like her father. All that felt like a long time ago now that she had her little family to go home to.

And it was about to get even better. She couldn't wait to tell him the news.

"Thank you so much for coming in, everyone," she said to the full house. "I'll be off for a couple of days but back at it on Thursday. I'll see you then."

She never got tired of the applause from an enthusiastic audience. At one time, she'd been afraid to perform in front of people, which was another thing her asshole father had tried to take from her.

He was in prison, where he belonged, and she tried very hard to never think of him or the way he'd treated her, her mother and siblings for years. Each of her siblings had carried deep trauma into adulthood—and each of them had found a way to overcome it, for the most part, anyway.

Everyone was worried about Johnny, though. He hadn't been himself since he'd come back from the mainland after taking care of their youngest brother, Jeff, who'd been seriously injured during the hurricane. And Johnny wasn't talking to any of them about what was wrong.

She emptied the tip jar that overflowed with cash and tucked the bills into her purse to count later.

Deacon met her at the stairs to the stage, taking Pupwell's leash from her and leaning in for a kiss. "Hi, honey."

"Hi there. How was the visit with Adrian?"

"Awesome. He's so cute. Wait until you see him."

"I can't wait."

"Tiffany said to come over any time tomorrow."

"I want to sleep in, and then we can go over there."

"I can't wait to sleep in. I've been thinking about that all day."

He'd been incredibly busy in recent weeks as they hauled and winterized most of the harbor master boats and prepared to hunker down for the long, cold winter.

Deacon put an arm around her as they left the hotel and walked outside into the bitter chill.

The scents of woodsmoke and seaweed filled the air. They were among the scents of "home" to her since she'd lived full time on Gansett, where she and her siblings had spent idyllic summers with their grandparents as kids—in the very hotel where she now worked, doing the thing she loved the most.

Deacon held the door to his police department SUV for her and then helped Pupwell into the back seat, clipping him into his seat belt for the ride home.

The second they pulled out of the parking lot, Deacon reached for her hand, the way he always did.

She wrapped his hand inside both of hers.

After the dreadful scare of him being missing for hours during the storm, she'd never miss a chance to hold on to him with everything she had. The horror of those endless hours, of fearing she'd lost the love of her life, would stay with her forever. Every second with him felt like a miracle after that, and she loved him even more than she had before—if that was possible.

"When we get home, I have a surprise for you."

"Oh yeah? What kind of surprise?"

"The kind you'll like."

"I already knew that because I like everything with you."

"This is an extra good surprise."

"You have my attention, Mrs. Taylor."

Keeping their marriage a secret until the wedding they had planned for next summer had made being married even more special, because it belonged only to them and the few people who knew they'd tied the knot after he'd been found. They'd wanted to be married right away after learning how quickly they could lose everything.

Since she'd be hugely pregnant by the summer, she planned to scale back the wedding to a big party to celebrate with their family and friends.

At home, Julia went directly to the bathroom to retrieve the positive pregnancy test she'd hidden three days ago. She'd wanted it confirmed by Victoria before she told Deacon the happy news.

Deacon and Pupwell were curled up together in a snuggle on the sofa when she joined them.

"Where's this surprise I was promised?"

Julia held up the stick with the two lines.

His eyes went wide. "Yes?"

She smiled and nodded. "Confirmed today by Victoria. We're due in late July."

Deacon let out a loud whoop that scared the dog. "Sorry, buddy, but Mommy just told us we're having a baby. You're going to be a big brother!" He reached for her over the dog and kissed her soundly. "This is the best news ever."

"We did a crap job of family planning, though. The baby will arrive during our busiest time of year."

"Who cares? We'll figure it out."

Pupwell got tired of being squeezed between them and got down from the sofa to settle in his bed on the floor.

Deacon brought her in closer to him, placing a hand on her still-flat abdomen. "I can't believe our baby is in there. He'll be close in age to Adrian."

"Or she will be."

"I think he's a boy."

"How come?"

He shrugged. "Just a feeling I had when I was holding Adrian that I was going to have one just like him before long."

"I'm thinking she's a girl, but either way, the cousins will be best friends."

"Or they'll bicker like Blaine and I did until recently."

"Nah, cousins don't fight like brothers do."

"That's true."

"He'll be close in age to Shane and Katie's baby, too, and the new quads and Mac and Maddie's twins. So many kids."

"They're going to have to add on to the school."

"Seriously."

"The town council is already talking about it."

"Really?"

"Yep."

Julia laughed. "That's funny. The great Gansett Island baby boom."

"Our baby will be lucky to grow up with so many friends."

"That crew will be something as teenagers."

"I can't wait for a front-row seat to that show."

.   .   .

ON THE ADVICE of her husband, Charlie, Sarah had given her son Johnny space to deal with whatever he was going through.

"If he needs you, he'll say so," Charlie had said when John first retreated from them.

But Sarah wasn't so sure of that. Her children had become experts at hiding their true feelings during an upbringing marred by violent outbursts from their unpredictable father. She wasn't at all convinced that Johnny would ever tell her—or anyone else, for that matter—what was making him so desperately unhappy.

She'd talked to Jeff about it that morning, asking him if anything had happened when the brothers had been together in Providence after Jeff was first injured.

"Nothing that would cause him to act like this for months," Jeff had said.

He and his fiancée, Kelsey, were living with her and Charlie while they continued to recuperate from the injuries they'd sustained when the roof at Kelsey's home had collapsed on them during the hurricane.

"I don't know what to do," Sarah had said. "The longer this goes on, the more worried about him I am."

Johnny had all but retreated from anything that wasn't work in recent months, hunkering down in the guesthouse on Charlie and Sarah's property since her parents, Russ and Adele, were in Florida for the winter, and rarely joining in any family get-togethers. She went days without laying eyes on him. His car coming and going was the only proof of life she got.

After having been through a suicide attempt when Jeff was much younger, she'd like to think she was more alert to the kind of trouble that needed to be addressed with her kids. Johnny was a grown man who deserved his privacy, but her maternal radar was attuned to something seriously amiss.

So she made meatloaf, mashed potatoes and corn and invited him to come for dinner after work, hoping to tempt him with his favorite meal.

Sorry, he'd replied. *Can't make it.*

I'm not asking you. I'm telling you to come for dinner. And don't give me any excuses. Dinner is at six thirty. Be here.

She could see that he'd read the message, but he didn't reply.

Charlie came up behind her and massaged her shoulders. His love was such a gift in her new life on Gansett, with six of her seven children living close to them, along with his daughter, Stephanie. "Why's my honey so tense?"

"I told Johnny he's coming for dinner after he said he couldn't, and he hasn't replied."

"If he knows what's good for him, he won't defy his mama."

"What if he does?"

"Then we'll go over there after him. Whatever it takes."

"So you agree that this has gone on long enough."

"I woulda said that a couple weeks ago, but he's not my kid."

"You said to wait him out."

"For a while, maybe, but not forever."

"I'm glad you agree." She turned to face the man who'd changed her life in every possible way by giving her proof that true love really did exist. "I hope you know you can say whatever you want to me about any of them."

"Normally, I would, but this feels… I don't know. It feels a little different for some reason, and I don't know him as well as I know the others. Does that make sense?"

"Yes, it does, but if you've got a thought about any of them, feel free to share it with me. I've been guilty in the past of overlooking things I should've paid more attention to. I don't want to do that anymore."

"You're a wonderful mother, Sarah, and I have no doubt you always have been."

"I should've taken my kids away from him. I'll always regret that I didn't."

"You survived a horrific situation, and every one of those kids loves you and lives near you and is in your house every other minute. They don't blame you, and you shouldn't either."

"It's hard not to when I see each of them dealing with things they brought from their difficult childhoods."

"From where I'm sitting, they're all doing extremely well, except for Johnny. We'll figure out what's up with him and get him the help he needs."

She rested her head on his chest. "What'd I ever do without my Charlie to make me feel better about everything?"

His gruff laugh made her smile as he tightened his arms around her.

"What would I ever do without my sweet Sarah to make every day the best day I ever had?"

"Okay, you win."

"It's not a contest, sweetheart. We've been around long enough to know how lucky we are, and we'll never take this for granted."

"Not ever."

Jeff came into the kitchen on the crutches he still used after his pelvis was shattered during the roof collapse.

Sarah pulled back from Charlie.

"Don't let me interrupt the lovebirds," Jeff said.

"Oh hush. You and Kelsey are the lovebirds around here."

"Not just us, Mama," Jeff said with the quick grin that came right from his father, not that she'd ever tell him that.

"Can I get you something?"

"I'm looking for some water, and I'll get it myself."

"Don't be silly. I've got it."

"Let her dote on you, son," Charlie said. "She loves every minute of having you here—and so do I."

"Thanks for having us. Not sure what I would've done without you guys, Kelsey and the rest of our amazing family these last few months."

"We're thankful to see you standing upright again," Sarah said as she handed him the glass of water.

He leaned on his crutches to take a drink.

"What time is Kelsey due back?"

After getting her cast off and being cleared to drive again—finally—she'd gone to see the McCarthy kids she'd cared for before being injured.

"She said she'd be home for dinner. Is it weird that I miss her like crazy even though we've spent twenty-four hours a day together for months?"

"Not at all, honey," Sarah said. "That's how it should be."

Once upon a time, she might've objected to her son sharing a room with his fiancée before they were married. Now she couldn't care less. Those two kids were obviously madly in love, and Sarah was so thankful to have Jeff home and recovering after a long stint in physical rehabilitation that having them sleep together was fine with her.

"Mom... What're we going to do about Johnny?"

"We were just talking about that," Sarah said with a glance at Charlie.

"I told him he's coming to dinner tonight whether he wants to or not, and we'll try to talk to him."

"Good," Jeff said. "He's been weird since we were together in Providence before you guys got back from Italy, and he won't tell me what's wrong."

"He won't tell anyone," Sarah said. "We're hoping to get to the bottom of it tonight."

"That'd be good," Jeff said, "because something's definitely not right."

CHAPTER 16

*A*s he drove home from his job as the director of security at the Wayfarer, John Lawry was pissed off at the command performance demand his mother had levied on him. He didn't want to deal with a family dinner and intended to blow it off. Yes, he felt guilty because she'd made his favorite meal, and he was well aware of why she'd done that.

He'd been keeping his distance from everyone lately, and of course, they'd noticed because that was how his family rolled. Usually, he didn't mind that, but sometimes a man wanted to be left alone—and this was one of those times. As a fully grown adult, he shouldn't have to explain himself to anyone, especially his mother, sisters and brothers, who'd been texting and calling him relentlessly, asking him what was wrong and what they could do to help.

He knew he ought to be grateful to have people in his life who cared. It was just that right now, he wished they cared a little less than they did. Was it too much to ask to be left alone? Apparently so, because it wasn't like his mother to demand the presence of any of her children, especially since she was now happily married to Charlie and living the kind of life she deserved with a man who worshipped her.

John was glad to have one less thing to worry about. The years she'd spent alone with their father after the last of them left home had been hard on all seven of the Lawry kids. Knowing she was safe and happy was a huge load off their minds. The downside was having more mental and emotional energy to devote to his own life and the many ways he'd screwed it up lately, starting with the relationship he'd had with his ex-boss that'd blown up in his face, and now the thing he'd started with Niall that'd turned messy.

He'd known he was gay from the time he was about seven years old, and his monster of a father had tuned in to it around that same time, which had made his life a living hell as he set out to prove his father wrong about his suspicions. "No son of mine is gonna live like that," he'd say, along with other derogatory words that'd scarred John's soul so deeply that he couldn't function in a healthy relationship without that son of a bitch's voice in his head ruining everything.

He should've known better than to get involved with Niall, who'd been unique from the start in the way he worked his way into John's heart and mind one casual conversation at a time. Nothing had ever been easier than it was with him, which was how it was supposed to be. At least that's what he'd heard.

It'd been so easy that his heart was all in before his head caught up to remind him of how damaged he was by childhood trauma, by years of not being free to live his truth, by always looking over his shoulder, expecting his father to jump out of the bushes and say, "Aha! I always knew you were a fucking deviant."

That was one of the general's favorite words. *Deviant.* "I expect my kids to toe the line," he'd say in his big, booming voice that drowned out every other sound in the house. To Johnny, he'd add, "If you think you're going to live like some kind of deviant freak, you, my friend, are sadly mistaken."

John used to tremble for hours after one of his father's homophobic outbursts. One time, their father had punched Owen in the face for daring to tell him to leave Johnny alone when he'd been calling him a little wimp, which was another of the general's favorite things to say to Johnny. Seeing Owen hurt because of him had broken Johnny more than just about anything else, because Owen was always there for all of them. He'd told Owen to never defend him again. Owen had thought John was mad, but really, he was heartbroken to see Owen, whom he loved more than almost anyone, hurt for trying to help him.

As John pulled into the driveway at the palatial home his mother shared with the amazing Charlie Grandchamp, he realized his face was wet from tears he hadn't realized were there. He shouldn't be surprised by them. Any time he thought about that shit from the past, his emotions overflowed, making him feel almost as helpless as he had then.

A knock on the window startled him. His former-cop sensibilities had deserted him after all this time on a small island where not much of anything happened—thankfully. He wiped his face and put down the window to talk to his stepfather.

"Are you okay?" Charlie asked.

"I guess."

"Your mother is waiting for you."

"I know."

"Whatever it is, son, we'll work it out, but you'll never fix what's wrong by running from it. Trust me on that."

To his intense mortification, John broke down into sobs that came from the deepest part of him.

Charlie opened the door, reached in to release John's seat belt and helped him out of the car and into his waiting arms. "Let it all out. It's not healthy to keep these things bottled up."

He sensed his mother approaching, but Charlie must've signaled her to give them a minute.

John tried to pull back. "I'm sorry."

"Nah, we're not doing that, Johnny. You've got nothing to be sorry about."

"You don't need me crying all over you."

Charlie released him but stayed close as John wiped the tears from his face. "You know what I need? A wife who isn't sick with worry over what's going on with her precious son, because we can all see that it's something, and we want to help."

John shook his head. "It's not that simple."

"Nothing ever is but keeping it all to yourself won't fix it. That much I can promise you. Every problem I ever had got easier to handle as soon as I shared it with someone who cares."

John wanted to say thanks but no thanks, but how could he with this man who'd come into his life later, but who'd been more of a father to him than he'd ever had, standing before him, asking to help? The way a good father would. More than anything, he didn't want to disappoint that good man who'd come to mean so much to all of them.

"Okay," John said as he allowed Charlie to usher him into the house, where his mother hovered anxiously.

"Let's give him a minute," Charlie said to Sarah, who nodded and put a beer on the table in front of the seat at the table that Charlie had guided him to. "That meatloaf sure smells good, honey."

John's stomach growled, and they all laughed.

Sarah gave John a kiss on the top of his head, the way she used to when he was little. "You always were a sucker for my meatloaf."

The sweet gesture soothed the ache John carried with him everywhere he went. While his father had been a monster, his mother was an angel who'd saved them from living in utter despair. Some of his happiest child-hood memories had been when his father was deployed for months, and they'd been alone with their mom. She'd made everything fun, with things such as dinner in the living room in front of the TV, which would've been forbidden on the general's watch.

His mother put a plate full of meatloaf, mashed potatoes and corn in front of him. "Thanks, Mom."

"My pleasure, honey."

Kelsey and Jeff, on crutches, came in to join them for dinner, and Charlie jumped up to help Jeff into a chair that had a pillow on it.

Even though Charlie had been in their lives for a while now, it was still remarkable to watch him continuously step up for the Lawry kids, as if he'd always been a part of them. It occurred to John in that moment that if his mother could start over with a new, happy relationship after what the general had put her through, maybe he could, too.

When Jeff was settled, Charlie returned to his seat at the head of the table. "Thanks for dinner, honey. It's delicious."

"Oh, you're welcome," Sarah said, with a note of surprise in her voice. "I'm glad you like it."

His father had never once thanked her for a meal she'd prepared, because he'd seen that as her duty to him and their family.

Charlie saw it as a gift she gave them all.

Kelsey whispered something to Jeff.

"No, thanks, babe. I've got it."

Right here before him were two examples of true love at work among people who'd suffered through the same trauma he had. Sure, it'd had different edges for each of them, but the end result had been the same. His mom was happily settled into a whole new life with Charlie, Jeff had Kelsey, Julia had Deacon, Owen had Laura, Katie had Shane, Cindy had Jace… Their brother Josh, the only one who didn't live on Gansett, had started dating someone special recently, too. They hadn't let the past determine their futures. Why couldn't he have someone for himself, too?

John put down his fork and wiped his mouth with a napkin. He felt the eyes of the other four on him, looking on with concern and bewilderment that made him feel bad for causing them to worry. They'd all been through hell together and were on the other side of it with the general in prison. While his siblings had done an admirable job of getting on with their lives, he was stuck in this strange limbo that was making him as miserable as he'd ever been.

"Are you okay, honey?" his mother asked in that tense tone that reminded him of a time he'd much rather forget.

"No, Mom, I'm not okay."

Everything stopped as his family members waited for him to say more.

"Before Jeff got hurt, I was sort of seeing Niall."

"Yes, we know," Sarah said. "He seems like such a nice young man."

"He is."

"I love his Irish accent," Kelsey said with a smile.

"I do, too."

"Did something happen to upset you?" Jeff asked.

"Sort of, but it wasn't his fault. It was mine."

"How so?" Charlie asked.

John fixated on a framed picture of the seven Lawry siblings that his mother had hung on the dining room wall. "Well… It's just that we, you know, were together, and all I could hear in the back of my mind was *that* voice, telling me all the reasons it was wrong and disgusting and—"

"What?" Sarah asked, shocked. "He didn't know…"

"Yes, he did, Mom, and he tormented me with what he knew every chance he got, and he still is."

"No!" Sarah's forceful tone took the others by surprise. "You will not let *him* have anything to do with this."

"*Let* him," John said with a laugh. "If only I could turn it off, but I've yet to figure out how."

"I feel you," Jeff said. "I turned to drugs to make it stop, but I'm certainly not suggesting you do that."

John huffed out a laugh. "I've been tempted. Niall… He's such a great guy. He's been nothing but supportive, and I've treated him like shit. I'm sure he's probably moved on by now." That thought was profoundly depressing.

"I don't think he has," Charlie said. "I saw him in town the other day. He asked about you."

John perked right up when he heard that. "He did?"

"Yep. Said he was worried about you. I told him we were, too, and that we were hoping we might get you to talk about it at some point."

"Thus the meatloaf," Sarah said.

The love and support from his family made all the difference, even if he'd been ambushed by them.

"I don't know what to do," John said. "I want to be with Niall, but I can't bear the thoughts that run through my head when we're together. It brings it all back…"

"We'll call Kevin McCarthy in the morning," Charlie said. "We'll get you in with him to talk it out, and in the meantime, you should tell Niall what you've told us. I think it'll make a big difference to him."

"You think so?"

"I know so," Charlie said. "That man cares about you. If you ask me, he looked heartbroken to not be in touch with you."

"I hate that I did that to him."

"It's nothing that can't be fixed," Jeff said. "You just have to be honest with him."

"What if it's too late?"

"Then you learn from this and do the work with Kevin so you're ready the next time you meet someone special," Sarah said. "Either way, you have to heal yourself before you can move forward with any relationship."

"If Niall cares like I think he does," Charlie said, "he'll wait for you to be ready."

John couldn't believe how much better he felt after talking to them. "Thanks, you guys, for, you know… everything. A lot of people don't get this kind of support from their families when they come out. It means the world."

"We love you, Johnny," Sarah said tearfully. "We want you to be happy, and being with Niall obviously made you happy."

"It did, until things got real, and the past intervened."

"Let's get that taken care of so it's not an issue anymore," Charlie said. John nodded.

"Now eat your dinner, son," Charlie added. "It's your favorite."

"Yeah, it is," he said with a smile for the man who'd become a father to him at some point when he wasn't paying attention. "Thanks, Mom."

"Anything for you, my love."

NIALL HAD BEGUN to wonder whether he'd be able to stay long term on the island he'd begun to think of as home. Between his gig four nights a week at the Beachcomber and his day job as a producer at the Island Breeze Recording Studio, he was making a very decent living in the music business he loved.

But it was incredibly difficult to go through his days knowing the man he loved was close by but out of reach. Heartbreak leached into every corner of a person's soul, and it was almost impossible to hide the misery from the people he saw every day.

Such as Evan McCarthy, his boss at the studio, who'd noticed something was off but had only asked if he was okay. Niall suspected he was on borrowed time with Evan, that he could either snap out of the funk that was affecting the music or find another job. Not that Evan had said that, but how long would he put up with a sad sack working with him every day without getting fed up?

Probably not much longer.

At the Beachcomber, Jace asked him every night if he was okay and had surely noticed he was drinking twice as much Guinness as he normally did while working.

What did it matter? What did anything matter when he'd had a brief moment of pure happiness, only to have it yanked away by the person who'd made him so happy? Nothing mattered anymore, and that ought to terrify him.

Even his parents in Ireland had picked up on his disturbed state of mind during their weekly calls. His mam had asked him four times if he was sleeping, eating and getting by okay. He'd reassured her that all was well, but he wasn't fooling her or his da. If he wasn't careful, they'd be showing up on his doorstep to check on him. They'd been there for a week in the summer and couldn't afford to come back until next year, so he hoped they didn't decide to come out of concern for him.

Niall hated feeling this way and having everyone asking what was wrong. He yearned for the happy-go-lucky existence he'd enjoyed for years on Gansett before Johnny Lawry came along and turned his life upside down in a matter of weeks. Having such an incredible connection with him and then having him go silent had been one of the most painful things Niall had ever experienced.

He supposed he was lucky to have lived for almost thirty years without going through true heartbreak. All his grandparents were still living, and his parents were robustly healthy, so he'd never lost anyone who meant everything to him. Until now. And it totally sucked.

He got home from another night at the Beachcomber and poured himself a nightcap of Jameson. The whiskey was a new addition to his repertoire and was the only reason he was able to sleep for even a few hours each night.

His time with Johnny ran through his mind over and over, like the rom-coms he used to watch with his mam in which everything worked out and the couple lived happily ever after. Except his own rom-com had ended disastrously for reasons that were still very much a mystery to him. Maybe if he knew *why*, he could find a way to live with it. In the meantime, he was stuck in this purgatory of wondering what he'd done to drive off the one guy he'd truly connected with after years of first dates and relationships that went nowhere.

This one had been different, and he couldn't help but think that'd been what had run Johnny off. Big feelings brought big complications, and perhaps Johnny just wasn't ready for that. He'd only recently come out to his family, so perhaps he wasn't as far along on his journey as he'd thought. If so, Niall would certainly understand, but Johnny wouldn't tell him what the issue was, so there was no way he could do anything about it or gain closure if they were done for good.

Niall sat in his dark living room, sipping his drink and wishing he could think about something else. Anything else. He missed writing new music and watching movies and reading a book once in a while. If only his mind could make space for something other than heartbreak.

How long would this go on? he wondered as someone new to it. Would it ease up in time, or was this it for the rest of his life? If so, how did he unsubscribe?

His phone chimed with a text, which gave him something else to think about for the ten seconds it would take to read it. When he saw Johnny's name on the screen, he sat up so quickly he nearly spilled his drink.

Niall... I'm sorry. I've been dealing with some stuff that has nothing at all to do with you, and I'm very sorry for going silent on you. It wasn't fair, and I wouldn't blame you if you hate me and never want to hear from me again. If that's the case, feel free to say so, and I'll leave you alone. I have an appointment tomorrow with Dr. McCarthy to talk about some things that have kept me from fully embracing the life I want. With you. I have no right to ask for time to get my shit together and to figure myself out so I can be fully available to you, but I'm asking anyway...

Just that quickly, the dark cloud Niall had been living under lifted, and the sun came out again, bringing him out of the deep funk and filling him with the hope and optimism he'd been without since the last time he saw Johnny at the Wayfarer. He'd left that encounter with more questions than he'd had before, but now he knew... He hadn't done anything wrong. It had nothing to do with him and probably everything to do with the difficult childhood Johnny had endured with a violent, unpredictable father.

Johnny hadn't said much about what'd gone down with the general, as they referred to him, just that it'd been horrific, and they were all relieved the man was in jail, where he belonged.

Niall stared at the phone, trying to think of what he should say in response. Johnny would be able to tell he'd read the message and was waiting for him to reply. He thought for a second about making him suffer, the way he had, but in the end he couldn't do that. His response was two words:

I'll wait.

CHAPTER 17

"Do you feel better about things with Johnny?" Kelsey asked Jeff when they were tucked into bed in their room at his mom's house, where they'd been welcomed with open arms after Jeff "graduated" from rehab. She was curled up to him with her head on his chest and his arm around her.

"I'm glad he finally told us what's been eating at him, although we should've known. Of course that was it. That's what it always is with us. Even from prison, he haunts us."

"I hate that for all of you."

"I do, too, and I hate carrying around hate for anyone, but with him… It's hard not to feel that way."

"You have every right to feel like that about him, and so do your mom and siblings."

"Still… It's a hell of a thing to carry around when all you want is to be free from the past so you can enjoy all the good things happening now."

"I hope Dr. McCarthy can help Johnny find a way forward with Niall. I loved them together. They seemed so happy."

"I know. I hope so, too." He ran his hand up and down her arm, which ached badly the day after getting her cast off. "I never got the chance to ask about your visit with the kids."

"They were so happy to see me, and the babies have gotten so big!"

"Did you decide about when you want to go back to work?"

"I'm going to try for part time next week and see how that goes. They really need the help, especially with Mac's brother and his wife about to bring home quads."

"Four babies. That's a lot."

"Sure is, and they're going to need Big Mac and Linda, who've been helping Maddie while I was laid up."

"What a baby boom."

"I know, especially for the McCarthys. They have six new grandkids with two more coming soon."

"That's a lot of kids."

"Sure is."

"How's the pain?" she asked, knowing it was always more intense at the end of the day.

"A little better than it was."

"I'm sorry it's still so bad."

"It's nothing like it was at first, so that's progress." He gave her a squeeze and kissed the top of her head. "I'm looking forward to picking up where we left off when Ethel messed with us."

"Me, too."

"Are you blushing?"

"I don't do that anymore."

Jeff laughed—hard. "Right."

"It's not nice to laugh at your future wife."

"I'm not laughing *at* her..."

"You're the only one laughing!"

"I can't help it. You're so cute when you lie."

"I do *not* lie."

"You're even cuter when you're indignant."

"Let's talk about something else before I forget you're still injured and give you a smack that you deserve."

His low chuckle pleased her because it meant he wasn't thinking about the pain that'd persisted much longer than either of them had expected it to.

"How great was Charlie with Johnny earlier?" Jeff said.

"He's such a lovely guy."

"Before he came along, the whole lot of us probably would've said we had no need for a new father, thank you very much, but we can't help loving him and the way he steps in as needed without forcing himself on us. He's teaching a master class on how to come into a family of traumatized people and make himself at home there."

"That's a such a nice way to put it. You should tell him that."

"I will if I get the chance."

"I think it would mean a lot to him."

"Probably. He has no idea how easy he's made it look, when joining this family is anything but."

"I don't know… I think your family is incredible, especially with the way they've all stepped up to support us during this crazy time. I can't wait to be a Lawry."

"I can't wait for that either. When's it going to happen?"

"You said you wanted to be able to stand without crutches before we get married."

"That's taking longer than expected."

"Are we in a rush?"

"I'm sick of being laid up when we've got big plans."

"And plenty of time to make them happen."

"I want to get going on all of it."

"It'll happen. In the meantime, you need to stay focused on doing your PT and getting stronger."

"*Sick of it*," he said in a protracted whine.

"Is this what our kids will sound like when they don't get their way?"

"Maybe so."

"You're cute when you're cranky."

"I must be cute as hell lately."

"You're cute as hell all the time, and don't worry about the crankiness. It's a small price to pay to have you on the way to a full recovery, even if it's taking longer than we'd like."

"I'm thankful to still be here. I know it was a very close call, and I'm doubly thankful that you weren't hurt any worse than you were. But I'm not meant for sitting around. It's making me nuts."

"I know, babe. Tomorrow, I'll take you out for a ride, and we'll stop to have lunch somewhere. That'll make you feel better."

"Yes, it will. Thanks for giving me something to look forward to."

"Jeffrey... honey... We have *everything* to look forward to. Don't ever forget that."

"Keep reminding me, okay?"

"Any time you need to hear it." She kissed him good night. "Get some rest so you'll be ready for our big date tomorrow."

"More kissing, less sleeping."

"Is that what kind of husband you're going to be?" she asked with pretend annoyance.

"You know it."

"I can't wait for all of it."

"Me either."

THIS WAS HAPPENING TOO FAST. That was the only thought in Sierra's mind as she took the wildest ride of her life, right on the floor inside her front door with a man who needed no instruction on how to bring her more pleasure than she'd ever experienced with a partner. In ten short minutes, he'd upended her entire existence, using lips, tongue and teeth to make her come harder than she knew she could.

Twice.

The sight of his dark head between her legs was almost enough to get her off all on its own.

Then he raised his head, caught her watching him and grinned with total male satisfaction that would've been a turnoff with anyone else. This man, however, had earned the right to be pleased with himself. "We need protection."

"In the bathroom closet. Second door in the hallway."

"Don't move."

"Couldn't if I tried."

Morgan got up and stalked naked across her living room like a panther on the prowl, a thought that should've made her laugh, but she was still too stunned by recent events to do anything other than try to prepare herself for what would happen next. He returned as quickly as he'd left, rolled the condom onto his impressive erection and came back down on top of her, covering her with his warmth and the rich scent of cologne.

"Should we move to the sofa?" He reached down to cup her ass. "I'd hate to see this perfect skin with rug burns."

"I'm okay where I am." She also doubted the ability of her legs to hold her weight, as every part of her felt like a wet noodle after two explosive orgasms.

"Hold on to me."

The way he took care of business was ridiculously sexy, mostly because he made it so she didn't have to think about anything other than chasing the next high. That, too, was an all-new thing to her. Most of the guys she'd encountered had no idea how to pleasure a woman. This one dove right in and went for it, which was a huge turn-on.

She did as she was told and held on tight to him, her arms around his neck as he pushed into her, slowly and carefully so he wouldn't hurt her. All the while, he watched over her with dark eyes that seemed to see deep inside her. He never blinked or looked away or tried to dodge the intensity of the moment.

He pushed deeper into her, making her moan from the tight squeeze that had her already on the verge of another orgasm. When had *that* ever happened? Never. Ever.

"Good?" he asked, still watching her as if he was afraid to miss anything.

"Mmm, *yes*." She smoothed her hands down his back, massaging as she went because she couldn't help herself.

"God, that feels amazing." His gruffly whispered words, lips close to her ear, set off a wave of goose bumps that made her skin extra sensitive.

She kept her hands moving down, digging into his back muscles and then the glutes that flexed as he pressed as far into her as he could go and then held still. Under him, she squirmed, trying to get him to move, but he didn't take the hint. "Morgan…"

"Hmm?"

"Come on!"

"Are you in a rush?"

"No, but…"

He kissed a path of fire up her neck and rolled her earlobe between his teeth as he continued to throb inside her. "You're so busy taking care of everyone else, when was the last time you let someone take care of you?"

Sierra was moved to tears by the astute observation.

"Relax. I've got you."

She closed her eyes, desperately trying to contain her emotional reaction, but a tear slid down her cheek anyway.

He kissed it away as he began to move, keeping a hand under her to protect her from rug burn. Everything he did and said wrecked whatever defenses she had left, leaving her feeling fully exposed in a way she'd never been before. At any other time, she would've run screaming for her life away from that kind of vulnerability, but he made her feel safe in it, as if she wasn't alone anymore.

Wouldn't that be something?

When he picked up the pace, every thought left her brain except for one—he was it. The one she'd waited for. Now she just had to figure out how to keep him forever.

WHAT. The. Hell.

Those were the only words running through Morgan's scrambled brain as he rested on top of Sierra, every cell in his body attuned to her and the aftershocks of explosive passion the likes of which he'd never before experienced.

This was the kind of thing that could change a guy's life if he let it.

Would he let it?

He had no idea which end was up at the moment, so he couldn't answer that or any other deep questions. Not now, anyway. His most pressing concerns at the moment were to get her off the floor and move them to a bed so they could do that again as soon as possible.

Her hands moving on his back felt heavenly as she zeroed in on all his hot spots, working out each knot before moving on to the next one. "That feels so good."

"You're a tight mess of stress."

"Gee, I wonder why."

"You need regular treatment to deal with your stress."

"Are you offering?"

"We can work something out. A quid pro quo, perhaps. Electrical work for massage treatment."

"Deal."

"You're easy," she said with a laugh.

"I'll do whatever it takes to have more of this." He kissed her neck and then raised his head to kiss her lips. "All of this."

"I'd be down with that."

He kissed between her eyes. "What's with this frown I see forming?"

"What frown?"

"This one." Morgan kissed the spot again. "What're you thinking about?"

"Oh, well, let's see… I just had the best sex of my life with someone who may or may not be punching out of here before too much longer, and you know… I'm trying to keep this casual, but that's turning out to be easier said than done. Other than that…"

Morgan wanted to reassure her, to tell her there was nothing to worry about, but the truth was, he didn't know what the future held for him. Everything was upside down at the moment, but this… He hadn't felt this good in a long time, and all he wanted was to hold on to the person who'd given him respite from the nightmare his life had become lately.

"I'm not going to say what you want to hear for the sake of saying something," he said after a long pause.

"Thank you for that."

He loved the refreshing way she said whatever she was thinking. "Tonight was amazing for me, too. And not just what happened here. All of it. Dinner, the talking, the laughing… I needed it more than you could ever know."

"I'm glad you enjoyed it. I did, too. And for the record, I haven't done *this* on a first date since I was twenty and made a vow to never let that happen again."

"So you broke a vow for me?"

"A solemn vow."

"I'm honored."

"You should be. Thanks for making it worth it."

He grinned. "Glad to be of service." After another soft kiss, he said, "Should I go?"

"Only if you want to."

"I don't, but feel free to kick me out."

Sierra curled her arms and legs around him, trapping him in her soft sweetness. "Just relax and get some rest." She ran her fingers through his hair, making his scalp tingle as he exhaled the horror of the last few months and turned himself over to her care.

For now, anyway.

What tomorrow would bring was anyone's guess.

"I CAN'T BELIEVE it's over." Hours after finishing her last exam and turning in her final assignment, Janey Cantrell still couldn't process that she'd *finally* completed veterinary school. She'd celebrated with her husband, Joe, and their kids, PJ and Vi, at dinner and had cake at home afterward, and now that the kids were asleep, she was in bed with Joe and trying to process this moment. School was really over. Forever.

"I'm so, so proud of you, Dr. Cantrell."

"I'm proud of *us*, because none of this happens without you." She turned on her side to face him. "For the rest of my life, I'll never have the words to thank you for everything you did to make this happen."

"You don't have to thank me, Janey. Seeing you achieve this goal is as thrilling for me as it is for you."

"I honestly thought it was never going to happen until you showed me the way forward." She had tears in her eyes as she looked at the man who'd made all her dreams come true, not just the professional one. To think, for the many years she'd been with David, Joe had been right there waiting for her to realize they were meant to be.

"We also got Seamus out of this adventure," Joe said.

"I remember a time when you weren't sure that was a good thing," Janey said, smiling. "I was afraid you might kill him."

"That seems like a long time ago. Now it's like he's always been there, making my mom happier than she's ever been."

"It's crazy to think how everything happened. If David hadn't gotten in the way of me going to vet school after college—and if he hadn't cheated on me—I might've been somewhere else and missed this with you, and your mom never would've met Seamus."

"I guess things work out the way they're meant to, even if it's not as smooth as we'd like it to be." He turned to face her and put his arm around her. "Did you tell Doc you finished?"

"I texted him, and he sent me the hourly countdown until my arrival and his retirement."

"He's as excited as we are."

"I can't wait to be home to stay."

"Me, too. It's been fun to live here in Ohio for a while, but Gansett is where we belong."

"We'll have four new nephews waiting for us, along with Dylan and Adrian and the ones soon to be born. Lots of excitement to look forward to."

"PJ was saying today that he can't wait to play with his cousins every day."

"I'm glad we're getting them home when they're young enough to grow up together."

"Me, too." He kissed her as he ran his hand down her back to cup her ass. "You know what I've never gotten to do?"

"Whatever it is, you should do it because of everything you did to make my dream come true."

"That works out well, because the thing I've never done is make love to a veterinarian."

She laughed. "Wow, I walked right into that trap, didn't I?"

"You sure did. Now what are you going to do about it?"

"I suppose that since you moved heaven and earth for me, I should do the same for you. And PS, you know I never mind making love with my handsome, supportive, sexy husband."

He placed his hand on her face, caressing her cheek with his thumb. "I've never been prouder of anyone than I am of you, my wife the doctor."

"And I've never been prouder of anyone than I am of my husband, who shouldered far more than his share of the parenting load these last few years while teaching classes and helping to run a business from afar. You made it look easy, when I know it wasn't."

"It was so worth it. Every second was leading us to this day. I can't wait to see you running your own clinic on Gansett and living the dream."

"Just so you know, I've been living the ultimate dream with you for a while now. This is just frosting on the cake."

"I wish you could see how happy you looked today when you came home and started dancing with the kids."

"I loved their posters and the balloons and dinner, the cake. All of it."

"We had fun planning a Mommy's Done With School Party."

She pushed a hand under his T-shirt, encouraging him to remove it.

He pulled it over his head, tossed it aside and then did the same to hers. "Mmm, hello, Doc."

"Um, we call Doc Potter that…"

"So what you're saying is that's a mood killer?"

"Sorta."

"Hello, Dr. Janey. Better?"

"Much." She slid her leg between his. "Joseph…"

"Hmm?"

"I love you so, so much. Thank you for everything."

"No need to thank me for anything when being married to you has made my life perfect." He turned them so he was on top, gazing down at her with his heart in his eyes, the way he always did. "My dream girl."

Smiling, Janey put her hands on his face and brought him close enough to kiss as he pressed into her.

"God, there's nothing better than this," he whispered.

"Nothing at all."

When she woke to total darkness, for a second or two, Monique had no idea where she was or whose warm hand was resting on her bare hip.

Then she remembered. Linc. Dancing. Kissing. Tearing at clothes. Doing it like sex was about to be outlawed any second, and they had to get it all in before it was too late. She closed her eyes tight against the flood of memories that had her questioning everything, the way she always did since the man she'd expected to spend the rest of her life with had let her down so terribly.

Linc wasn't Jaden, and he shouldn't be held up to the same light for comparison. He'd never been anything other than lovely to her, but so had Jaden until he'd crushed her with his lies and deception.

She needed to get out of there and find the sanity that had deserted her in the hours she'd spent in Linc's bed. But where had her clothes ended up?

"What's wrong?" he asked when she pulled away from him.

"I need to go."

"Where?"

"Back to Dara's."

"I thought we were hanging out together."

"We did, and now I have to go."

He sat up and turned on the light.

She was glad she had her back to him since her hair was probably wild and her makeup smeared.

"Monique."

"Yes?"

"Will you look at me?"

She shook her head. "I'm pretty sure I look like the Joker after rolling around in bed with you."

He snorted out a laugh. "I highly doubt that."

"No, really. Can you give me something to put on? I have no idea where my clothes ended up."

He handed her his T-shirt, which was on the bed.

She put it on and got up to use the bathroom attached to his room. When she glanced in the mirror, she nearly let out a shriek. Thank God she hadn't let him look at her. She scrubbed her face, did what she could with her hair—which wasn't much—and used some of his toothpaste on her finger to brush her teeth as best she could.

Yet, even after all that, she still didn't feel ready to face him with every flaw and insecurity on full display.

A soft knock sounded at the door. "Are you okay in there?"

"Not really."

"Can I do anything for you?"

She felt ridiculous. The old Monique would've found this version of herself pathetic. Hiding from a man? In what lifetime would that've ever happened? In this lifetime, the one after Jaden, she had no idea who she was anymore or how to face Linc after the way she'd clawed at his back and shrieked like a wild woman in his bed.

Ugh.

She sat on the closed lid of the toilet and dropped her head into her hands.

"Whatever you're in there thinking, you should knock that off. I had a great time, and I can't wait to do it again. But you'll have to come out of there for that to happen."

"I don't want to come out."

"Then can I come in?"

After a long silence, she said, "Yeah."

He stepped into the room and closed the door. Then he took a seat on the floor next to her and wrapped his arms around his knees.

His nearness made her feel better, which had her remembering one of Lewis's favorite stories about Pooh and Piglet sitting with Eeyore when he was sad and how it had made him feel better to have his friends close.

"I'm sorry for the dramatics."

"Don't be. I don't think either of us was expecting that to be so…"

"Wild?"

He grunted out a laugh. "I was going to say incredible or maybe life-changing or something like that."

She raised her head ever so slightly to find him watching her with gorgeous blue eyes that she'd thought of as kind eyes from the first time she met him. Nothing she'd seen from him since then had changed that first impression.

"I don't trust myself anymore."

"How come?"

"If you'd have told me my husband would do what he did, I would've bet my life there'd be no way… I'd be dead."

"That's on him, not you."

"Maybe so, but it's a reflection of me and the life I thought I was living when he was off having a completely different kind of life."

"Monique… Look at me."

She forced herself to make eye contact.

"You shouldn't take responsibility for what he did. I have no doubt you were an exceptional partner to him, and he let you down epically. But it would be tragic if you let him steal your future happiness along with your past happiness."

She wiped away a tear that escaped down her left cheek. "I never saw it coming. That's the part I've had the hardest time coping with. I pride myself on not missing a thing. How'd I miss that?"

"He made sure of it. My dad was like him. He had two kids with two other women in our town—kids I went to high school with—and I had no idea they were my half siblings until the whole thing blew up when I was in college. If you'd asked me, I would've said he was a great husband and father, the kind of man people looked up to, including me and my brothers and our friends."

"That must've been such a shock."

"It was pretty bad, especially for my mom and my two younger brothers, who were still at home when the shit hit the fan. At least I was away for most of it."

"I'm sure it still messed you up."

"I ended up on academic probation that semester, which is a big deal at the Coast Guard Academy." He ran his hand over her calf, setting off a reaction she felt everywhere. "The thing about guys like them is they get off on the deception. That's part of the attraction, the getting away with it, you know?"

"One of my friends thinks Jaden is a sociopath because he lies as easily as he breathes."

"My dad is for sure, and he's a narcissist, which is an awesome combination."

"Yikes."

"Yeah, it's been a lot, but we're all doing better these days. My brothers are married to great women, and they each have a couple of kids and successful careers."

"What about your mom?"

"She's got a significant other who makes her happy, but she'll never marry him."

"Is he okay with that?"

"I think he'd like to be married, but he gets why she won't risk her independence or her financial security."

"I hope that means she took your dad to the cleaners."

"Big-time."

"Good for her."

"We were all firmly on Team Mom."

"Do you see him?"

"Not much. He lives in Colorado with wife number three and has a couple more kids with her. I've never met her or the kids, but my brothers have. They say she's cool and the kids are cute, but they'll never be family to us or anything like that."

"What about his other kids, the ones from when you were in high school?"

"Amazingly enough, they're some of our closest friends. We went through hell together when the whole world found out about our connection, and we turned to each other to survive it. We didn't blame them, and they never blamed us."

"That's really cool that you're close to them."

"Life is so weird."

She laughed. "Sure as hell is. Thank you for sharing that with me. It helps."

"You're beautiful and funny and sexy and smart, and did I say funny? Don't let him ruin a good thing for you. He's not worth it, and I promise you I will be."

"How can you be so sure?"

"Because I have never, ever, *ever* felt like this about anyone, and all I want after tonight is many more nights just like this one."

He extended his hand to her.

Monique eyed it as she tried to decide if she was ready for him and for this. "There might be more steps backward."

"I'm here for that."

She reached out to him.

He curled his hand around hers and kissed the back of it as he looked up at her. "I might be the safest bet you could ever make, because there's no way in hell I'd ever do to anyone what my father did to us."

"Thank you for understanding."

"I do. I get it. And it's not something you have to worry about with me. If I want out, I'll tell you. And hopefully you'll do the same."

"I would. Absolutely."

"For what it's worth, though, I don't expect to want out. I want in. I want you and this and us and all of it. I've been waiting a long time to find you."

"Will your family approve of, well, you know…"

"What?"

"That I'm Black."

He gave her a look that told her everything she needed to know. "The only thing they want for me is the same thing I want for myself—happiness with the right person. Trust me, that'll never be an issue for any of us."

"It's been an issue for me in the past. I dated a white guy once… It was going well until his mother met me, and suddenly it was over."

"He didn't deserve you either."

"No, he didn't."

"You know what my mom will love about you?"

"What's that?"

"Your sense of humor. She loves irreverence and sarcasm and all the rest of it. You'll fit right in with us."

"It's nice to hear the qualities that've caused me trouble with every boss I've ever had will finally pay off."

He flashed that sexy grin. "Are we good now?"

"Yeah, thank you."

"For what?"

"For making me talk about it. I'm famous for running and hiding when things go sideways."

"You can run, but I'll always come looking for you—for as long as you want me to, that is, not in a weird stalker kind of way."

Monique laughed and then let him help her down and onto his lap. "Thank you for clarifying."

He wrapped his arms around her and held her tightly to his chest. "I don't want you to worry about anything. Let's just be together and have all the fun for as long as we can. Like four or five decades maybe."

"That's an awfully long time," she said as she looked up at him.

He kissed her sweetly. "Won't be long enough for me."

Sierra woke before Morgan, cocooned in his arms with her head on his chest and their legs intertwined, as if they'd been sleeping together for years rather than one night. She who normally preferred her own space in bed had never slept better than she had snuggled up to him after three sizzling rounds of life-altering sex.

After being burned in every previous relationship, a girl would normally be thinking about self-preservation at a moment like this, but oddly, that was the last thing on her mind this morning after. A slight adjustment in position gave her a view of his handsome face, relaxed in sleep with morning whiskers covering his jaw.

Except for the scruff, he looked almost boyish, as if he had not a problem in the world. She wished that were true. When she thought about all he'd lost, she ached for him. She'd never had siblings but had grown up close to her cousins. Losing any one of them was unthinkable, as was the thought of life without her dad. They were her essential people since her mom and grandparents had died. He'd lost all his essential people and was forced to go forward alone.

That idea of him completely alone in the world made her feel fiercely protective of a man she barely knew. Although… after last night, she knew him better than she'd ever known any other guy she'd dated.

This whole thing should've been terrifying, but for some reason, it wasn't, which was unsettling. Her normal MO after a hookup—not that she had a lot of them or anything— would be to get the hell out of there and try not to run into the guy anywhere until he forgot about her.

Sometimes they tried to track her down, but she'd become a master at dodging guys she never wanted to see again, which was most of them.

This one, however…

She wasn't thinking about how to get away from him. Nope, quite the opposite, in fact.

"What're you thinking about so hard first thing in the morning?" he asked in a raspy voice that made her tingle with awareness of him.

From his voice, for fuck's sake.

"Nothing much."

"You gonna start lying to me right out of the gate? Usually, it takes a while for the lying to start."

"Has that been your experience?"

"Every time. Easier to stay single than to put up with the drama."

"God, isn't that the truth?"

"You've had your share of it, too?"

"That's all it is. Nonstop drama and picking fights for the sake of fighting so we can make up and start the whole stupid cycle over again. It's exhausting."

"That sounds very familiar. I dated this woman Cheri a couple of years ago. Things were going really well until she got mad when I couldn't go to her mother's birthday party because I had Patriots tickets with some of the guys from work. That'd been planned for months, before I ever met her."

"What did you do?"

"I went to the game, and I never saw her again. Whatever."

"Don't you just want to say please be so for real right now?"

"Yes. A thousand times yes."

"I dated a local guy, Kyle, for six months a while ago. He works on the ferries and isn't exactly on fire with ambition, but he's a nice enough guy."

"What happened?"

"We ran out of things to talk about in the third week, and after that, it was just… boring. Which made me lonely for something he'd never be able to provide. It just gets so tiresome after a while, to the point that I'd convinced myself I'd be better off alone than playing the game anymore."

He caressed her arm with a light touch that set off goose bumps. "And now?"

Sierra hesitated, wondering how truthful she should be on the morning after the most momentous night of her life.

"Tell me what you're thinking. There's no wrong answer."

"Well, this feels pretty good."

"Only pretty good? I need to up my game."

She choked on a laugh. "If your game was any better, I'd be in the hospital."

He gave a satisfied smirk. "Is that right?"

"Don't get cocky."

"Speaking of cocks…"

"Put it on ice, pal. I've got to get to work. First client in an hour." Thank God for the off-season and a first client at eleven rather than nine, the way it would've been in the summer.

"I never put ice on him. He deserves better than that."

"Can I ask you something I probably have no right to ask this early in our situationship?"

"Is that a word?"

"I believe it is."

"Ask away."

"If you're planning to leave here at some point, will you tell me sooner rather than later? Because…"

"Because what?" he asked, continuing that maddening glide of fingers over skin that had her wishing she had more time.

"I… um, well… After all this… You could probably break my heart pretty easily, and that would totally suck. You know?"

"I do know, and for what it's worth, that's the last thing in the world I'd ever want to do."

"That means a lot, but I think maybe you need to figure out your life before we let this go any further. I don't want to be another complication you have to deal with at an already complicated time."

"You're a ray of light in the darkness, Sierra."

"Oh, well… Like that doesn't make everything worse."

His laughter was the best thing she'd heard in a while, because she knew he hadn't had much to laugh about. "I mean it. Let's try to enjoy this for what it is. We've both been around long enough to know this sort of thing doesn't come along every day."

"No, it doesn't, and that's what makes it scary."

"Don't be scared. I promise I'll talk to you about what I'm thinking and any plans I'm making. For right now, today, I'm focused on getting through another day cleaning up after my brother while looking forward to seeing you later. If you're not busy, that is."

"I'm not busy."

"Then this day is already looking up."

CHAPTER 19

After Morgan left, Sierra floated through her morning routine feeling oddly disconnected from reality. Everything seemed softer, sweeter, full of possibilities and new beginnings. He'd said all the right things when she expressed concern about diving all in with him, only to be devastated if or when he decided to return to his life on the mainland.

She recalled when Duke had faced a similar dilemma the first time he was engaged and his fiancée decided she couldn't handle living full time on the island where Duke had found the first real family he'd ever had. Duke had struggled with the conundrum of trying to make the relationship work when she didn't want to live where he'd made a real home for himself, not to mention the successful business he now owned after working there for years.

Ultimately, he'd ended it with her because he couldn't conceive of living anywhere else, and while he'd suffered over the loss for a time, he'd done the right thing. His friends had agreed that he wouldn't have been happy living on the mainland, even if it meant he got to be with her.

Now that he was madly in love with McKenzie, he could see that he'd truly done the right thing in letting go of the relationship with Lynn. He never would've met McKenzie if he hadn't stayed on Gansett and stepped up for her after Hurricane Ethel flattened the home she'd inherited from her grandmother.

Things worked out the way they were meant to. She believed that and had seen it happen more than once. Like for her friend Jace Carson. At one time, all the odds had been stacked against Jace, and look at him now, playing a role in the lives of his sons and happily in love with Cindy Lawry. His story had inspired her to chase her own dreams, which had included finding a partner to share her life with who lifted her up rather than dragged her down.

Would Morgan turn out to be that partner?

She didn't know yet, but after last night, she'd begun to think he could be.

Her first client of the day was her friend Piper, who came breezing through the door at five minutes before eleven with a coffee for Sierra.

"Bless you," Sierra said as she took the cup and gave Piper a quick hug. "How's everything?"

"Couldn't be better."

"I take it things are going well with Jack?"

"Can you keep a secret?"

"Duh. Of course I can."

Piper laughed. "I know, but it's so weird to say it out loud."

"Say what?"

"That I think I'm in love."

"Again—duh. I've known that for weeks now."

"What do you mean?"

"Piper… Honestly… You can't talk about that man without lighting up like a woman in love."

"Really?"

"Yes, silly."

Piper frowned and seemed to be less than thrilled by a development that should've made her deliriously happy.

"What's wrong?"

"I'm not sure how he feels. We're together every night, and it's so, so good, and he seems totally into me the way I am with him, but…"

"What?"

"I don't know. There's something not quite right, and I'm afraid to ask him because I might not like what he says."

Sierra put an arm around Piper and guided her into the break room at the end of the hallway, while knowing the delay would throw off her schedule. What did that matter when her friend was in distress? They sat at her little table with their coffees.

"I'm sorry to dump this on you, but my friends at the hotel are so excited about Jack that I couldn't bring it up with them…"

"What do you think is going on with him?"

"If I had to guess… It's probably that things got real between us very quickly, and maybe he wasn't quite ready for that after losing his wife."

"I don't think that's it," Sierra said. "I've seen you two together. The man is wild about you. He barely takes his eyes off you and is always touching you and making sure you're okay. I think he feels the same way you do."

"Really?"

"Yes, of course he does."

Piper rubbed her abdomen. "I just have this feeling, right here… Something isn't right."

"You need to ask him."

"I can't." Tears filled her eyes and spilled down her cheeks. "If he says we're over, I don't know if I'd survive it. And yes, I'm aware that sounds ridiculously dramatic, but it's true. When I think about how I almost married the wrong guy…" She shuddered. "Jack has shown me how it's supposed to be, and all I want is more of that. More of him."

"Just say that to him—exactly that."

"It makes me sick to think about what he might say."

"You don't need to worry. I'm sure of it. Maybe he's wrestling with something that has nothing to do with you, and you're picking up on the tension. You might be making yourself sick over nothing."

"You're right. I need to be a big girl and confront it head on."

"You'll feel better after you talk to him, and don't worry about him wanting out. That's not it. I'm sure of it."

"Thank you, Sierra. I really appreciate your advice."

"That's what I'm here for. Relaxation and life advice."

"Haha, right."

"Let's get your treatment started. You'll feel better after that, too."

"I always do."

While Piper got settled in the room, Sierra refilled her water bottle and ate a protein bar. She hated to see her friend so upset when things had been going well for her since she started seeing the handsome state police officer. Several years ago, he'd lost his wife to breast cancer, and Piper was his first serious relationship since that difficult loss. She'd said once before that she knew the odds were stacked against them, as the first relationship after a loss like that often failed. She'd been determined to beat those grim odds.

Sierra knocked on the door.

"Come on in."

Inside the room, she got busy making sure her friend had a nice, relaxing treatment that would enable her to talk to Jack about the things weighing on her.

"Now for breaking news," Piper said as she lay facedown on the table. "How'd it go with Morgan?"

"It went all night."

Piper's head came up off the pillow. "Okay, what? You let me go on and on about Jack when you were sitting on *that*?"

Sierra laughed. "Your thing is more important."

"No way, girl. Spill the tea, and don't leave out any of the dirty details."

She gave her friend an overview of the evening's events without giving too much away.

"Oh, I love this for you!"

Sierra worked on Piper's neck and shoulders. "Don't get too excited. I'm trying to keep myself in check over here. Who knows how long he'll be here before he has to go back to his real life?"

"What's he saying about that?"

"He's not sure of anything yet, and he's being honest about that, thus me trying to proceed with caution, which didn't go so well last night."

"Was it fun?"

"Um, yeah, you could say that."

"So it was good, then?"

"'Spectacular' is a better word."

Piper let out a girlish shriek. "I love this so much!"

"We're not getting excited yet, remember?"

"How's that going for you?"

"Not so great. I really like him. And we have a connection, the kind that doesn't come along very often."

"I know all about that rare connection."

"He's like your Jack in some ways. He's been through *so* much. I'm not sure he's ready for anything like this."

"I get it. It's a gamble to go all in with someone who's grieving a big loss, but it can also be thrilling to bring light and joy back to their lives."

"That's a nice way to put it."

"Every time Jack laughs or smiles, it feels like a victory of sorts. It happens a lot more often than it did when we were first together."

"Which is another reason why you have nothing to worry about where he's concerned."

"We're not talking about me. We're talking about you and Morgan."

"There's no me and Morgan. We had a fun night. Who knows if it'll go anywhere from there?"

"I bet it will."

"I guess we'll see, won't we?"

"Yes, we will, and I can't wait to hear all about it."

THOUGH HE HADN'T SLEPT much during the night, Morgan pushed himself through a workout while Terry watched the gym's reception desk for him. As he lifted free weights with much more energy than he should've had, Morgan relived his night with Sierra for the third time since he'd left her place, wanting to commit every second of it to memory.

From when he'd picked her up until they parted company this morning, their time together had felt almost magical to him, which wasn't a word he used lightly. Not much in his life had been *magical*. He'd had much more tragedy than magic and was almost afraid to trust his own instincts when trying to describe how it'd felt to be with her.

She'd given him something he hadn't known he needed until she provided it—soft sweetness, which he wouldn't have expected from her before last night. While she was always super friendly and warm, there was an untouchable aura about her, too. Like she didn't let just anyone get close, and if you were lucky enough to make the cut, you damned well better be worth it.

Morgan was fairly certain he'd met the moment, but he wouldn't know for certain until he saw her again.

Duke Sullivan came over to say hello while Morgan was resting between sets. "How's it going?"

"Good. You?"

"Every day is a good day on Gansett Island."

"Is that right?"

"Sorry. Shouldn't have said it like that."

"What do you mean?"

"You've had a few not-so-great days here."

"I knew what you meant. No worries. And today's been a great day so far."

"Glad to hear it. So you know how news travels around here. Heard you were out with Sierra last night."

"That's right." Morgan looked up at Duke, who was muscular and covered in colorful tattoos. "Something you want to say, Duke?"

"Just that she means a lot to me and a bunch of other people. Wouldn't want to see her get hurt."

"That's certainly not my goal."

Duke nodded, seeming a bit flustered or something. "I don't mean to step out of line."

"You didn't. You're looking out for your friend. I get it."

"She's more like family than a friend, and she's got this tough outer shell that might make you think she's tough on the inside, too. But she isn't. Not at all."

"I've already figured that out for myself."

"Then I guess we understand each other. No hard feelings?"

"None at all. I get wanting to protect the people you love from being hurt."

"That's all it is."

"Understood."

"If you could maybe not tell her we had this conversation, I'd appreciate it. She might be tempted to kill me."

Morgan laughed. "No worries." He raised his hand for a fist bump.

"Thanks, man."

"Any time."

Morgan wasn't surprised to discover that Sierra had close friends looking out for her, especially since she'd been such a good friend to him since Billy went missing and in the months since they'd found his body.

She sprinkled friendship and compassion like fairy dust, and he was glad to know she had great friends like Duke looking out for her.

After his workout, he showered and went to Billy's office to pick up where he'd left off the day before, determined to clean up the mess so he could figure out a plan for the gym—and himself.

Two hours later, he'd made a dent in the filing and paperwork when his phone lit up with a text from his boss, Devin.

Hey, man, hope you're doing okay. We're all thinking about you. Also wondering if you've decided whether you're coming back to work. We just landed a new contract for an apartment complex in Dorchester, and I need to get my ducks in a row. Would love to have you on the electric, if you're available. Work scheduled to begin in mid-January, so I'll need to know soon. Let me know when you can, and again... hope you're hanging in there.

Well, there it was, Morgan thought. Decision time.

Dev had been super supportive from the minute Morgan found out Billy was missing and had never wavered in telling Morgan to take the time he needed. Three months had gone by in a flurry of activity as he kept his brother's business running while cleaning out Billy's home and working to settle his estate. And yet, he felt no closer to being capable of making any long-term decisions than he had when it had first happened.

If anything, he was more conflicted than ever after spending so much time on the island and becoming part of the community. Yes, he had friends at home, people he enjoyed spending time with, but when he wasn't working, he spent most of his time alone. That got old after a while. Here, he was rarely alone, and while he would've expected to be annoyed by the constant parade of people through his days, he'd begun to find it comforting.

Did he want to go back to being somewhat of a lone wolf?

Or did he want to stay here, where he'd made new friends, not to mention the start of something promising with Sierra?

But then he thought about the fifteen years he'd spent with Devin's family's company, working first for his father and now for him as the business grew bigger all the time. They'd been good to him, paid for him to get his master electrician's license and had steadily increased his salary over the years, putting him well over six figures.

He'd had a comfortable life that had suited him for years.

But now, everything had changed, and it'd happened without him even realizing it as one day became two and one month became three as he learned to live without his brother while figuring out who and what he was now that his entire immediate family was gone.

The thought of going back to that quiet existence didn't appeal to him the way it would have before Billy went missing. When he used to come out to the island to visit Billy a few times a year, he usually couldn't wait to get back to reality. He'd eagerly board the ferry and leave the tiny island behind without much of a thought for the place he'd once called home, except for daily text exchanges and weekly calls with Billy.

"Morgan."

He looked up at Terry, realizing he'd been talking to him.

"Sorry. What's up?"

"Are you okay? You were really spaced out for a minute there."

Morgan blinked his surroundings into focus, wondering how much time had gone by while he contemplated the dueling narrative running through his mind. "Yeah, I'm good. What's up?"

"I was just going to ask if you mind if I take an early lunch."

"No, go on ahead. I'll cover the desk."

"Thanks, man. Can I bring you back a sandwich? It's my turn to buy."

"Sure. Surprise me."

"Will do."

Morgan went to the desk to cover for Terry while he was gone. Terry and the other employees had hung a framed photo of Billy on the wall. He stopped to stare at his brother's handsome, smiling face, wondering what he'd tell Morgan to do if he were still there. Although, if Billy were there, Morgan would get on the ferry and go home because he didn't belong on Gansett anymore.

But that was no longer true, and Devin's text had been a reminder that the island interlude in his childhood hometown would end eventually.

Or would it?

He'd never been more confused.

In the meantime, he responded to Dev. *Hey, man, thanks for your note, and congrats on the big new contract. That's awesome. I'd love nothing more than to tell you I've worked everything out here and can head home, but that's not the case. I need a little more time. I'd understand if you need to move forward without me.*

Morgan tried to think of something else he could say beyond the nonanswer to Dev's question, but what else was there to say? He sent the message.

Like all things, his return to his job was up in the air.

The state of indecision would normally drive him crazy, but after what he'd been through lately, it would take more than that to send him over the edge.

Dr. Kevin McCarthy came into the gym, smiling the way he always did as he said hello to Morgan. "How's it going?"

"Not bad, all things considered."

"You were a million miles away when I came in. Everything okay?"

"Yeah, I mean… Some big decisions to make, but nothing I can't handle."

"If it gets to be too much, you know where to find me."

"Thanks, Doc. That's nice of you to offer."

"My offer covers everything from formal sessions in the office to a beer with a friend. Whatever you need."

"Thank you."

"You got it."

As Kevin headed for the locker room to change, Morgan was reminded once again of the community that'd surrounded him since he'd come home to look for Billy. People he'd known all his life and those he'd never met had propped him up in so many different ways that it would take the rest of his life to process the outpouring.

One thing he knew for certain as the dilemma occupied his mind for the rest of the afternoon was that it wouldn't be as easy to leave this place as it used to be.

CHAPTER 20

*I*n Providence, Abby's doctor and the neonatologist had declared mother and babies cleared to go home the next day.

Adam and Abby had looked at each other in complete terror at the thought of being entrusted with the care of four tiny humans without the assistance of the incredible nurses who'd been such a godsend to them. If there was an upside to leaving the hospital, it would be the end to the "fundus massages." No one had warned her how unpleasant it would be to "encourage" her uterus to return to its normal size after the birth. Add that to the engorged breasts and the litany of other aches and pains, and Abby was thrilled to be done with childbirth forever.

"You'll be coming with us, right?" she asked Ellen, their daytime nurse who'd quickly made herself essential.

Ellen laughed. "You've got this, Mama."

"Do I, though?"

"I have faith in you."

"We do, too, honey," her mother, Carol, said.

"You have to say that. You raised me."

Linda McCarthy laughed. "You're doing great, Abby. You're ready to take this team home."

"I wish I felt as confident as you all do."

"We've got this, babe," Adam said.

"No, we don't."

"You'll have lots of help," Carol reminded her. "Linda and I will take turns spending the night until you find a groove."

"Thank goodness for the grannies," Adam said. "They'll save us from messing up too bad."

Despite all the reassurances, Abby was filled with anxiety at the thought of taking four newborns—and their two-year-old brother—to the remote island they called home. What if something went wrong that they couldn't handle there? What if—

"Abs." Adam massaged her tight shoulders. "It's going to be fine. I promise—and I always keep my promises."

She was reminded of how he'd promised her everything would be okay after she was diagnosed with PCOS and given the devastating news that she might never conceive. Look at them now.

Five sons.

Even with months to prepare, it still boggled her mind that they had *five* sons.

And then Kane woke from a nap with a hearty cry that roused his brothers, beginning the change-feed-burp cycle once again.

Thank goodness Big Mac and her dad, Tom, had stepped up to take care of Liam, who wanted nothing at all to do with the babies.

They were hoping he'd come around in time, when they stopped making such a racket that he couldn't hear the TV or get a second of his parents' attention before one of the babies needed something.

When they got home, they would make a point of spending one-on-one time with Liam each day so he wouldn't resent his brothers. Liam's lack of interest in the babies was a challenge they hadn't expected. Linda had assured her it was normal. She said Mac had had no use for Grant when he was first born, and look at them now, the best of friends.

She burped Kane and walked him around the room until he dozed off again while her mom, Linda and Adam tended to the other three.

Four babies was a lot of babies.

Haha, no shit, Sherlock. What'd you think it was going to be like?

When the babies were back to sleep, Adam flopped onto the sofa next to Abby and put his arm around her.

She rested her head on his chest, closed her eyes and fell off the cliff into sleep.

The next thing she knew, it was time for another round of change-feed-burp.

"Too bad this isn't an Olympic event," Adam said as they went through the motions once again. "We'd be gold medalists in no time."

"Right?"

"Aren't you glad I bought stock in the diaper company?"

"Did you really?"

"Nah, but I should've."

Abby laughed as she burped Beckett while Adam handled Murphy. Her mom had Rory, and Linda had Kane. All bases covered. She'd begun expressing breast milk so each baby would get some every day, as feeding them one by one just wasn't feasible.

"I know it seems hard to believe right now," Linda said after they'd settled the babies once again, "but this will all be routine to you guys in no time."

"I find that very hard to believe," Abby said.

"Linda's right," Carol said. "In a week or two, it'll be like they've always been here, and you'll be able to handle two at a time like old pros."

"I guess we'll see about that," Abby said, full of anxiety over the looming trip home with four infants and a toddler whose entire life had been turned upside down by the arrival of his brothers.

What could go wrong?

AFTER RECEIVING a text from his dad letting the family know that Adam and Abby would be bringing the babies home the next day, Mac McCarthy sprang into action by calling his father-in-law, Ned.

"I need a huge favor," Mac said when Ned picked up the call.

"What's up?"

"Well, it's like this. The babies are coming home tomorrow—"

"Heard that. Excitin' news. Can't wait to meet 'em."

"Me, too, but what I need more than anything is a night out with my wife before we lose the help of half the grandparents for a while."

"Ah, I see whatcha mean. What can I do?"

"Can you and Francine babysit tonight until about midnight or so?"

Ned chortled with laughter. "That's way past our bedtime."

"I know, and I feel bad about asking you, but desperate times call for desperate measures. You can sleep over so you don't have to wait up." And that would give him more time alone with Maddie. He'd take as much as he could get.

"Lemme check with the missus to make sure she ain't got somethin' else planned for tonight. I'll call ya back."

"Thanks, Ned."

"You got it."

What would they do without the grandparents on call at a moment's notice? If there was one huge benefit to living on the island, it was having his parents and Maddie's close by to help out as needed—and they needed the help a lot, especially since their nanny, Kelsey, had been injured in the storm.

That reminded him he was supposed to meet Morgan for a beer after work. He texted his childhood friend. *Hey, can we push our beer to tomorrow night? Let me know! Looking forward to it.*

He wanted to say that something had come up, which was true, sort of. If things worked out as he hoped, he'd be up in more ways than one. Mac laughed when he imagined what his wife would have to say about the juvenile direction his thoughts had taken.

"What's so funny?" Julia Lawry, the manager of his construction company, asked as she came to the door of his office.

"Nothing I can tell you."

"Ah, it's like that, is it?"

"Yep. I'm plotting and scheming to get a night alone with my wife before my four nephews get home and steal half the grandparents from us."

His phone lit up with a text from Morgan. *No problem at all. Let's talk tomorrow.*

Mac gave that message a thumbs-up.

"What're you planning for your big night out?" Julia asked as Pupwell came in and curled up at her feet. He rarely let his beloved Julia out of his sight.

"I'm not sure yet. Before I plan anything, I need to make sure I've got babysitters lined up."

"I can do it if the grandparents can't."

"What? No way. I'd never ask that of you."

"You didn't. I offered. I could use the experience."

He tipped his head as he studied her, noting a rosy glow to her fuller cheeks. "Are you trying to tell me something, by any chance?"

She smiled as she shrugged. "Perhaps."

"Congratulations."

"Thanks, but you have to keep it secret. We haven't even told our parents yet."

"My lips are sealed. I'm happy for you and Deacon."

"We're pretty happy for us, too. But we're clueless when it comes to babies and kids, so if you want some help, we're available."

"While I'd hate to look a gift horse in the mouth…"

"I assume I'm the horse in this analogy of yours?"

"Stay with me… Our kids are a lot. Twin babies. A toddler. Two older kids who fight. This isn't your average babysitting gig. You might want to start out with something a little less—how can I say this?—savage."

Brows raised, she said, "Are you calling your children savages?"

"If the shoe fits…"

Julia laughed. "Wow, something tells me your romantic evening with Maddie might not go as you hope if she hears you describe her children that way."

"I think she said it first, actually."

Julia collapsed into laughter. She laughed so hard, she had tears in her eyes.

"In case you were wondering what's ahead for you…"

"Gee, thanks for scaring the shit out of me."

"Word of advice… Don't have three babies in eighteen months when you already have two."

"I believe there's zero chance that'll happen to me."

"I would've said the same thing myself a few years ago, and look at me now."

"So what's your plan for romancing your wife?"

"I haven't gotten beyond finding a way to escape."

"To go where?"

"Haven't figured that out yet."

"Doesn't your cousin own a hotel?"

"In fact, she does. Great idea."

Julia rolled her eyes. "That was a gimme."

"Don't get cocky. We've got more work to do here." He sent a text to

Laura, asking if he could reserve a room for the evening. *A fireplace would be a bonus*, he added. "Okay, I asked her. What else have you got?"

"What's the dinner plan?"

"You'll be shocked to hear I haven't gotten to that yet."

"Don't you have a sister-in-law with a restaurant in your cousin's hotel?"

"You're good at this."

"You're an idiot."

"Believe it or not, I've been told that before."

She cackled with laughter. "Believe it."

"Oh hey, Laura responded that she's got the perfect room for us, so that's all set."

"Why don't you call the florist and have some flowers sent over?"

"Another great idea. I don't deserve you."

"I tell you that every day. Do you want me to do that?"

"No, I want to do it myself so it doesn't seem like I farmed this out to others, you know?"

"I respect that, even if you're still an idiot."

"Stephanie is in to deliver dinner to the room."

"Doncha just love when a plan comes together?"

"You have no idea how much I love this plan." He stopped short of mentioning he hoped to get lucky for the first time in months, but more than anything, he couldn't wait for some precious time alone with his love to reconnect as a couple. "No one tells you how tough kids can be on a marriage, even though we love them more than anything and wouldn't trade a second with them. It's just a lot sometimes."

"Five kids is a ridiculous number of kids."

"Six, actually. We count Connor, the one we lost, too."

"Of course. Six is a ridiculous number, too."

He grinned. "But they bring a ridiculous amount of joy in addition to the mess, the screaming, the diapers, the never-ending bickering… Maddie likes to remind me that while the days are long, the years are short, and we need to enjoy every stage for what it is. But I'm looking forward to the time when they're all out of diapers and a bit more portable."

"That's fair. The baby years are intense, even when you don't have three in eighteen months."

"I wonder if Adam and Abby know what they're in for with four babies."

"I bet they're finding out."

"Probably. Okay, what else am I forgetting?"

"How can you surprise Maddie and get her to pack for a night away, too?"

"Hmmm, that's a tough one. Could I pack for her?"

Julia gave him a withering look.

"Right. Bad idea."

"How about asking her mother to do it?"

"That's a thought. Remind me I owe you a bonus."

She pretended to do something on her phone. "I'll add that to my to-do list."

"Despite your sarcasm and snark, you're rather handy to have around."

"You already knew that."

His phone rang with a call from Ned that he took on speaker so Julia could hear, too. "What's the good word, my man?"

"Yer all set. Francine and I will take the overnight shift so you kids can have a night off."

"God bless you both."

Ned guffawed. "Happy ta do it. Ya know we love bein' with the kids."

"Thank goodness someone does—besides us, of course."

"Haha, I won't tell yer wife ya said that."

"She knows. Believe me. Do you think you guys could go over a little early, and Francine could pack a bag for Maddie?"

"Yep, we gotcha covered."

"You're the best. Both of you. Please tell her I said thank you."

"Will do. Been a busy week fer the grandparents with baby Adrian arriving."

"How's he doing? I need to get over there to see him."

"He's a sweet little guy. His sisters are smitten with him."

"In case I forget to tell you, old pal, seeing you in grandpa mode is one of my favorite things ever."

"Aw shucks, thanks. Best time o' my life. I'll collect Francine, and we'll get over ta yer place ta get this mission started."

"I'll be there around six. Thanks again."

"Any time."

"He's the absolute sweetest," Julia said. "He reminds me of our Charlie."

"I can see that."

"It takes a special man to step up for someone else's children."

"Does that make me special, too?" His son Thomas was born before he met Maddie, but he was his child in every way that mattered.

"You're special, all right."

"You're a tough crowd."

"You already knew that, too. What else do you need to make tonight perfect?"

"Just my beautiful wife. That's all I ever need."

CHAPTER 21

"I have to go home," Monique said to Linc late in the afternoon after they'd spent the entire day in bed.

"To Boston?"

"No, silly, to Dara's to get my stuff."

"Oh, phew. I thought you were quitting me already."

"Nah, not yet. But a girl has her needs."

"I thought I'd seen to all her needs."

She giggled. She actually *giggled*. "I'm talking about the cosmetic kind."

"Ah, I see. Want to grab dinner while we're out?"

"Wouldn't it be lunch since we never got around to that?"

"If breakfast and lunch is brunch, what's lunch and dinner?"

"Linner."

"That's what we need. Linner." He gave a mighty stretch. "I've never been this lazy in my entire life."

"Me either, and yet, it's the best day I've had in far too long."

"Same." He leaned over to kiss her. "Shall we shower and return to civilization?"

"As long as our return is brief, I'm down for it."

"We'll only stay out for as long as it takes to acquire supplies and sustenance, and then we'll return to our slovenly ways."

"Perfect."

He held out a hand to her.

She wrapped her hand around his.

He kissed the back of hers. "'Perfect' is the word. Every minute of this has been perfect."

Nodding, she let him help her out of bed and followed him into the shower. While they waited for the water to get hot, he put his arms around her and propped his chin on the top of her head. They stood there like that, lost in a moment, until steam from the shower reminded them of what they'd planned to do.

Linc laughed as he gave her a nudge toward the water. "You make me forget my own name, woman."

"Same. Don't get my hair wet. I don't feel like dealing with that right now."

"Got it." Standing behind her, he washed her back and then brought his soapy hands around to caress her breasts.

"Keep that up, and we'll be right back where we started."

"Would that be so terrible?"

"I need my stuff, and we both need food. Focus on the mission, Commander."

"Yes, Captain, my Captain." He rubbed his erection against her back. "Keep me on task."

"*That* is not on the agenda."

His hands slid down her back to cup her ass. "We could be so quick."

Before she knew it, he'd turned and lifted her, pressing her back against the cool tile, perfectly aligning their bodies.

She wrapped her arms around his neck. "That was sneaky."

"Being ready for the sneak attack is a critical part of our training."

Her face hurt from smiling and laughing. She did a lot of both those things with him. "I must've missed that day."

"What do you say, my Captain? Shall we fire the missile one more time to hold us over until after the mission?"

Monique lost it laughing. "Fire the missile…" She howled.

"You like that, huh?" He nudged at her with his metaphorical missile.

That thought made her laugh even harder.

"My missile is feeling a bit wounded by your laughter."

"What can I do to make this right?"

He affected a grave expression. "I think you know, Captain."

"Whatever must be done to advance the cause. I'm on board. Get it? On board? A little Coast Guard reference."

"Very clever." He gave her his full length in one deep thrust that made her moan. Then he held still, making sure she was okay before he continued.

She loved the way he took care of her even in the throes of wild desire. Her gaze met his in utter unity, a moment so charged with potential and emotion and all the things, it rendered her breathless as she tried to process each new realization while he made her come twice in rapid succession before he found his own pleasure.

"You got me all dirty again," he muttered as he raised his head off her shoulder, withdrew from her and put her down carefully, making sure she was steady on her feet.

"*I* got *you* dirty? I think it was the other way around, sailor."

"Oh, I've been demoted after two orgasms? How is that fair?"

She gave his shoulder a playful smack when he would've started the soaping process all over again. "Hands to yourself until we're dressed. We have a mission to execute."

"I like when you boss me, my Captain."

"Don't get any ideas."

"I'm full of ideas. I have so many ideas where you're concerned, I could write a book about them all."

She'd never had such silly fun with a man before, and found she quite enjoyed it. Hell, she'd enjoyed every second she'd spent with him. It was *easy*, and dear God, was there something to be said for that.

"I'd give anything to know what you're thinking right now," he said as he toweled off.

"I'm thinking about how easy this is."

"How do you mean?"

"Our groove feels a bit effortless, which is new to me. I'm much more used to watching everything I say."

"That's no fun."

"Not at all, but I thought that was just how it was, you know?"

He was quiet as they got dressed and left his place to head to the light-house where her sister and brother-in-law lived for now. Dara had texted to say they'd gotten the house they'd put the offer on and would be moving in after their year at the lighthouse was finished. Monique was thrilled for them.

When they were on the way, he asked, "Are your parents still living?"

"My mother is. She lives in Florida with two of her sisters. They're having the time of their lives after being married to difficult, exacting men."

"Were your parents divorced?"

"No, but it might've been better if they had. They stayed together for Dara and me, but they really did us no favors. We grew up watching her tiptoe around his mercurial moods, always trying to please him and falling short every time."

"Why was he like that?"

"I don't know. He had a lovely wife, a beautiful home, daughters who loved him, but nothing was ever good enough for him. While Dara broke the cycle with her wonderful Oliver, I fell right into the same trap as my mother with a difficult, complicated, hard-to-please husband who went and cheated on me. Everyone we knew said they couldn't believe it was him and not me who cheated. They said they wouldn't have blamed me if I'd done it years ago, which was sort of humiliating."

"How so?"

"It made me realize that everyone else saw him for what he really was, while I was still dancing around him, trying to make it work when it was never going to. Like, how did they see it, and I didn't?"

"You were in the thick of it. You couldn't see the forest for the trees, or whatever that saying is."

"I guess, but I like to think I'm a pretty savvy person. He made me realize I'm not so smart."

"Knock it off with that crap. It wasn't your fault. I have no doubt you tried your best to make it work, and he was an asshole for treating you that way. He didn't deserve you."

"That's nice of you to say, but how do you know I wasn't a nasty bitch of a wife?"

He grinned as he gave her a side-eyed look. "Were you?"

"Not until he gave me reason to be."

"Well, there you have it. His loss. My gain."

"Is that right?"

"You know it." He reached over to put his hand on her leg. "I'm sorry you had to go through such a rough thing, but I'm glad you were free of him when we met."

"I am, too. I would've hated to miss out on this because of him."

He took the turn onto the lighthouse property that her sister had called home for nearly a year.

Monique eyed the lighthouse. "In many ways, this place saved them. They weren't doing well when they got here. And now… I'll always be thankful to Gansett and the people here who helped them get back on track."

"It's a special community. I'm not looking forward to getting orders that'll move me away from here."

"When will that happen?"

"In the next year or so, probably."

"Oh. Where will you go?"

"I put in for the West Coast this time, but that was before I met someone who made me want to stay on this side of the country."

"What's her name, and where do I find her?"

"Haha, her name is Monique, and she's right here with me where I want her to stay for a long, long time."

"That'd be nice."

"Yeah?"

"I think so."

"How would you feel about spending a few years out west?"

"Would I be able to come home to visit my new niece as often as possible?"

"That could be arranged."

"Then I'd definitely give it some careful consideration."

He turned to her, his expression as earnest as she'd ever seen it. "I'm dead serious, Monique. I want to make this work."

A knock on the window interrupted the intense moment.

Oliver, wearing a goofy grin, waved at her. "You broke curfew."

"Shut up and go away, Ollie."

"Dara said you're grounded."

"You're going away now."

He laughed as he walked around the car and into the lighthouse, probably to tell Dara that her wayward sister had returned home.

"He's funny," Linc said.

"No, he isn't."

"He is, and it's obvious he loves you."

"I love him, too. He's the brother I never had." She kept her gaze fixed on the lighthouse, waiting for Dara to come bursting out. "I'd better go face the music."

"I'll come with you."

"You don't have to."

"It's fine. They don't scare me."

They went inside and up the spiral staircase to the combined living room and kitchen, where Dara and Oliver sat at their little table, eating dinner and pretending they weren't trying not to act like complete fools.

"Well, look who it is, Ollie."

"Our little girl decided to come home."

Dara gave her hair a judgy look. "Because she needs her bonnet, among other things."

"All right, kids," Monique said. "That's enough."

"But we were just getting started," Oliver said.

"That's what I was afraid of." Monique went to the corner where she'd stashed her things and quickly packed her bag. "I'm running upstairs for a second. Do not interrogate him. You hear me?"

"The details must be really filthy," Oliver said to Dara, who giggled like a fool.

"Shut your trap." Monique ran upstairs to the bathroom to grab her toiletries, while hoping they wouldn't grill Linc while she was gone. She scooped up her things and tossed them into her cosmetic bag, trying to hear what was being said downstairs. As she rushed down the spiral stairs, she nearly tripped in her haste to get back to Linc.

"What're your intentions, young man?" Oliver asked right as she landed on the main floor.

"I'm going to kill you, Oliver, and I'm going to make it hurt."

He lost it laughing.

Dara, that bitch, laughed, too.

"Well, as nice as this visit has been, we're outta here," Monique said.

"Was it something we said?" Dara asked.

She glared at her sister. "Gee, I wonder."

"Seriously, though," Dara said. "It's nice to see you guys. Hope you're having a nice time together, which you must be since you were gone all night."

Monique gave Linc a push toward the stairs. "Bye, ya'll."

"Don't forget to call or write," Dara called after her. "You know how I worry."

"Sheesh," Monique said as they reached the entryway on the first floor. "What a couple of ass pains."

"They're funny."

"No, they're not."

"Are."

"Are not."

"Is this our first fight?"

"If you think they're funny, it's gonna be."

"Good to know," he said, obviously trying not to laugh as he put her bag in the back seat.

"Let's get out of here before they think of something else they need to say."

As Linc drove them through the gate, Monique received a text from Dara.

All kidding aside, we're thrilled to see you happy with a good man who will treat you right. Everyone around here loves him, which means a lot. Go be happy. You've earned it. We love you.

"Well, damn it. Now she's making me cry." Monique read Dara's message to him.

"That's very sweet, and she's right. You have earned it."

"We both have."

"Is this happening too fast for you?"

"Probably, but it's nice to feel good after feeling like shit for so long."

"I hope you never feel like that again."

"I'd be down with that."

"I'll do everything I can to make you happy. I promise."

"Same."

"Then let's go be happy, shall we?"

"Yes, please."

CHAPTER 22

After her last appointment of the day, Sierra went next door to Duke's tattoo studio and found him working with a female client. She did a double take when she realized the woman was McKenzie. "What is happening here, citizens?"

McKenzie had been steadfast in her refusal to let Duke give her a tattoo out of fear that it would hurt.

"My love decided she wants her unicorn after all." Duke beamed with pride. "So while our little Jax is visiting with his new best friend, Lily Harris, we decided to go for it, and here we are."

Sierra stretched around him to see McKenzie.

Her grimace made Sierra laugh. "You've got this. It doesn't hurt that much."

"You're a couple of lying liars."

"Did you give her the numbing stuff?" Sierra asked Duke.

"Yep. Just waiting for it to kick in."

"Let me see the design."

Sierra would know a Duke Sullivan original drawing anywhere, but this one was truly special. She wouldn't have been able to find the words to describe the unicorn drawing that somehow managed to convey unity, love and acceptance. "It's beautiful, Duke. Truly."

"The drawing is what changed my mind," McKenzie said. "I saw what he'd done, and I wanted that gorgeous image to be part of me forever."

"Aw, you gals are gonna make me misty."

"Can I watch for a minute?" Sierra asked. "Or is this one of those intimate, couples-only moments?"

"You can watch if you hold my hand," McKenzie said.

"I'd be happy to do that." Sierra walked around to the far side of Duke's station and pulled up a stool to sit next to McKenzie.

"Can you feel that?" Duke asked her.

"Nope."

"Great, then let's get started."

She immediately went tense.

"Don't do that," Sierra said as she began to massage McKenzie's hand and arm. "Focus on me. We've got this."

"Do you guys charge extra for the tattoo and massage package?"

Duke grunted out a laugh. "This is our first package deal."

"I feel special."

"You are, babe."

"Thank you, Sierra."

"My pleasure. You're doing great." Sierra was happy to be sharing this special moment with Duke and McKenzie, who'd become a good friend in the months since she started keeping Sierra's books—and making her best pal happier than she'd ever seen him.

"Did you hear that Evan and Owen are playing at the Wayfarer tonight?" Duke asked without looking up from the masterpiece he was creating on McKenzie's left arm.

"No, I hadn't heard, but I'd love to go. They're so great together."

"That they are. We're hoping to get there."

Sierra wondered if Morgan would enjoy doing that.

"How was the big date last night?" McKenzie asked.

"Excellent. It ended this morning."

McKenzie let out a girlish squeal.

"Don't move, love, or you'll end up with something other than a unicorn."

"Tell me everything. Leave nothing out."

Sierra laughed. "We had a nice time. Neither of us wanted it to end, so it didn't."

"Does that mean… you know…"

"It means what you think it means, and I'm not feeling the slightest bit guilty for putting out on the first date, if that tells you anything."

"This is the best news I've heard all day! Isn't it, Duke?"

"Uh-huh."

Sierra glanced at him, noting his intense concentration as he inked the love of his life. Only because she knew him so well did she also see the tic in his cheek, which happened whenever he clenched his teeth. He did that when he was stressed. "Something on your mind, Duke?"

"Nothing other than making sure this lovely skin gets the art it deserves."

"You wouldn't lie to me, would you?"

"What is happening right now?" McKenzie asked.

"Duke has something he wants to say about me hanging out with Morgan, but he's pretending otherwise."

"Is he doing that thing with his cheek?" McKenzie asked.

"Yep."

"Then it's definitely something."

"If you ask me, he wants to lecture me about getting involved with a guy who might be a short-timer here. He's worried I might get my heart broken if I'm not careful."

"That sounds like something he'd say."

"Are you two done putting words in my mouth?" Duke asked gruffly.

"We're just getting started," McKenzie said with a grin for Sierra. "When you go grumpy and silent, we gotta do the talking for you."

"Wow, she already speaks Duke, huh?"

"She sure does," Duke said. "She's *fluent*."

"Ew."

"What? She is. And I'm not grumpy. I was in a pretty good mood until the two of you started talking about me like I'm not right here."

"You wanted us to be friends," Sierra said. "Be careful what you wish for."

"No kidding. So what's the deal with Morgan, anyhow?"

"No deal. Just having some fun."

Duke gave Sierra a quick glance. "And that's all it is? Fun and games?"

"For now."

Sierra rarely lied to herself—or to him. This thing with Morgan was already way more than fun and games. It had taken a hard turn toward serious, and she wanted more than anything to ask them how she should handle that.

"Did you know, MK, that when Sierra is lying, she gets a tiny wrinkle right down the center of those perfect eyebrows of hers?"

"Does she?" McKenzie asked.

"She sure does."

Sierra stared at him, astounded. "I'm not lying!"

"Yes, you are, and there's no point in denying it. The question is, why do you feel the need to lie to your best friends about something so important?"

"I don't. I'm not. I'm…"

Duke cut the power on the machine he was using and sat back to get a better look at her. "Talk to me."

"And to me," McKenzie said.

Oh shit. Was she going to cry? Absolutely not! That couldn't happen.

McKenzie reached for her, hugged her tightly and wouldn't let go. "Whatever it is, we're here for you. We want to help."

"It's so stupid."

"Nah, don't do that," Duke said. "I've never once seen you get emotional over a guy, so it's gotta be something big."

"That's just it. I'm afraid it could be something big, and I guess I'm not quite sure what to make of that."

McKenzie released her.

Duke handed her a tissue.

"What can we do?" McKenzie asked.

"I have no idea why I'm even upset. I should be elated. This is what I've been waiting for, so why am I a wreck?" Embarrassed by the emotional outburst, Sierra wiped the tears from her face. "I feel foolish."

"You're not," McKenzie said. "You're scared because you recognize the significance of what's happening with Morgan. If you ask me, you'd be crazy not to be a bit freaked out. I was the same way when things with Duke took a turn for the serious. I mean, here I was, alone and homeless on an island with a baby and a flattened house, and along comes this absolute cinnamon bun of a guy—"

"A *what?*" Duke asked with a scowl.

McKenzie patted his chest. "Trust me. That's a good thing. But I was in no way prepared for what he very quickly became to me and Jax. There's absolutely nothing you can do to adequately prepare yourself for meeting *the one.*"

"She's right," Duke said with a warm smile for his fiancée. "It was the same for me. Incredibly overwhelming in every possible way, but also… so incredibly thrilling. Best thing to ever happen to me, hands down."

McKenzie leaned into him and then winced when her freshly tattooed skin protested. "Me, too. Best thing ever. This tattoo, on the other hand… The jury is still out."

Sierra laughed at the face she made. "You're going to love it in the end. I'm sure of it."

"I am, too, or he never would've gotten near me with his needles."

"Are you going to be okay, Sierra?" Duke asked. "I hate to see you upset."

"Of course I'm going to be okay. It's ridiculous to be so emotional over one great night. Like, what the hell is wrong with me?"

"Nothing is wrong with you," McKenzie said, "and this was much more than one great night, or you wouldn't be feeling so undone by it."

"You got yourself a smart one here, Duke."

"Believe me. I know. She's way out of my league, but for some reason, she loves me, which makes me the luckiest dude in the world."

"I'm not out of your league, and you know it makes me mad when you say that."

"But that leads to makeup sex, which is my favorite of all the sex."

"And with that, I'm out," Sierra said as she got up to leave.

"Don't let us run you off," Duke said.

"You're not. I've got another night with Morgan to get ready for."

"See you at the Wayfarer?" McKenzie asked.

"Yeah, maybe. I'll see what he wants to do."

"I bet I know what he wants to do," Duke said with a dirty laugh.

He and McKenzie laughed at his little joke.

"Grow up, people."

"Nah, we'll pass," Duke said. "Hey… If you need us, you know where we are."

"Always. Thanks for listening."

"We love you," he said.

Damn if he didn't get her all emotional again by saying that. "Love you, too." As she walked past his reception desk, she helped herself to a piece of the candy he kept in a bowl and popped it into her mouth as she left Duke's studio and headed upstairs to shower and change.

Her friends had given her a lot to think about.

Piper was on pins and needles as she waited for Jack to get "home" from work. Her room at the Sand & Surf had begun to feel like their home after spending months of nights wrapped up in each other in her bed. Some nights, they didn't even bother with dinner before they were right back to doing their favorite thing for as many hours as they could before they fell into exhausted sleep and then started the whole cycle again the next day.

She loved every second she spent with him, and during the long days apart, she counted the hours until she could be with him again. Weekends had taken on all-new meaning as they got two full days and three nights to spend alone together.

Everything about him and them felt like magic to her, but…

That *but* loomed large over everything lately, and it came with a sense of impending doom that she couldn't shake no matter how hard she tried.

She hated being a worst-case-scenario thinker, but she couldn't rewire herself at this point. By preparing for the worst, she reasoned, she could be ready for whatever happened. But honestly, how could she ever be ready to lose someone she loved as much as she loved Jack? There was no way to prepare for such a thing. Not that she thought she was in danger of losing him, but for some reason, the idea of broaching the subject of where this was headed terrified her.

It'd been such a big deal for him to have this much with her after losing his precious wife, Ruby, to cancer. What if the status quo was all he was capable of? What if she pushed him for more, and he pushed back? What would she do then? By the time she heard his key in the door, she'd worked herself into a full-blown panic.

The second she saw his handsome, smiling face and windblown hair, she felt better, even if she was still full of self-inflicted unease. Why did she put herself through this shit? Probably because she'd learned not to trust her own judgment in these matters. Although, Jack had given her no reason at all not to fully trust him.

Jack pulled off his heavy coat and tossed it aside as he began quickly removing his state police uniform. Because he could never wait to shed his work clothes, she told him he reminded her of a little boy tearing off his tie on the way out of church. "How was your day?"

"Great, especially the massage."

"Ah, right. You were looking forward to that." Stripped down to boxers, he gave her a look that could only be called sizzling. "Are you all loose and limber now?"

"Yes, I guess I am." That was a lie. Her muscles were tighter than ever due to the question she needed to ask him.

He came to her, rested his hands on her shoulders and gave a light squeeze. "Hey, what's this? Why are you all tense after a massage? What's wrong?"

He'd given her the opening she needed to ask her burning question, but now that the moment was upon her, she couldn't get the words past the huge lump in her throat. What they had now was more than she'd ever had with anyone—even the man she'd planned to marry, until he called off their wedding. It was enough, wasn't it?

"Piper. You're scaring me. Are you okay?"

"Yes," she said, forcing a smile. "I'm good. What do you want for dinner?"

He shook his head. "Nah, let's not do that. I could tell the second I came through the door that something was off. How am I supposed to think about dinner when I can tell you've got something weighing on you?"

Of course he knew. He was intuitive that way. That was one of the things she loved about him. Who was she kidding? She loved everything about him, and that was what had her tied up in knots as she tried to find a way to ask him the one thing she most needed to know.

"What's wrong, sweetheart?" he asked as he sat next to her on the bed and put his arm around her. "Whatever it is, I can't help if I don't know what's troubling you."

Who was this perfect man who'd been sent from heaven to say and do all the right things? Most of the time, anyway... He was coming along with not leaving his clothes on the floor and the seat up on the toilet, but who cared about stuff like that when he got so much right?

"I... I've been thinking about life outside this room where we've spent so much time."

"I need to take you out more often. I was thinking that same thing."

"No, that's not it."

"Don't tell me you want out, Pipes. I'm not sure I could handle that."

She loved how he'd given her a nickname that no one else had ever used for her. "I don't want out. I want in. All the way in."

"What do you mean?"

"That night when I went after you when you were upset... You said you wanted everything with me. I want that with you, too. Every day, I get deeper into this thing with you, and I have this knot of fear." She put her hand on her belly. "Right here."

"What're you afraid of?"

"I don't know exactly, but it's got me wondering what you and I look like outside this bubble we've been living in for months now."

"Hmm, well, let me set your mind at ease. I want to be wherever you are for the rest of my life. I don't care where we are or what we're doing, as long as you're there, I have what I need."

"Jack..."

"I love you, Piper. I love everything about you and us and how you've made me feel hopeful and optimistic again. I hadn't realized how much I missed those things until you brought them back to my life."

"I love you, too. Everything about you."

He grinned. "Except the clothes on the floor and the toilet-seat problem, right?"

"No one is perfect."

"You are."

She shook her head.

"No, you really are. You took on me and my grief and made space for Ruby... Do you have any idea how special that makes you?"

"I... um..."

"It makes you very special. Not everyone could successfully navigate the minefield that comes with dating a widower, and you managed it just right. I'll never have the words to thank you for that. Whatever you're worried about or fearing, don't. You and me are forever, if that's what you want, too."

"It is. You know it is."

"Did something happen to make you feel anxious?"

"Nothing specific. It's just how I'm wired, especially after getting dumped right before my wedding."

"If you stick with me, kid, you'll never get dumped again. I promise you that much."

She rested her head on his shoulder, feeling much better.

"Now, all that said, I have been thinking that we need to go out more and stop hiding out here like a couple of newlyweds."

"I have no complaints about how we've spent our time thus far."

"You're very sexy when you use words such as 'thus.'"

Piper laughed. "Is that all it takes?"

He shook his head. "You're sexy when you breathe, too." Leaning in to kiss her cheek, he added, "And when you blush."

"I don't blush."

"Whatever you say, babe. You know what we need to do?"

"What's that?"

"Get our own place together. What do you think?"

"Ah, well, so we'd like…"

"Live together—and not in a hotel room."

"Laura will miss getting to see Hot Cop in his uniform every day."

He scowled at that name the way he always did when they called him that. "I bet she'll survive."

"I'm not sure she will. I know I wouldn't if I didn't get to see that every day."

"I'm offering you free viewings every day for the rest of your life. Are you in?"

As she gazed into his lovely eyes and saw everything she ever wanted reflected back at her, she nodded. "I'm in."

CHAPTER 23

Mac arrived to the usual chaos at home. Kids running around, babies crying, and in the middle of the madness was the woman who made it all work for him and their kids. Every day, he had the same reaction to seeing her after a long day apart—gratitude, delight, love. So much love.

Sometimes he thought about the day they met and how she could've ridden right by him on her bike, neither of them aware that the love of a lifetime was getting away. Thank goodness he'd taken one wrong step and ended up with everything he ever could've dreamed of.

Before her, he hadn't dreamed big enough because he never could've imagined the life they had together. Before her, he would've said he didn't want the wife and kids and the white picket fence. Before her, he'd been a shell of the man he was today, thanks in large part to her love.

"Mac?"

He'd been staring while she talked to him.

"I'm sorry, what did you say?"

"I asked if everything was all right. You had a strange look on your face."

He picked up their son Mac and gave him a snuggle as he made his way to the sofa, where she was holding court with the twins while Hailey and Thomas ran circles around them.

Little Mac always seemed relieved to see him when he got home, which was endlessly adorable. Of all their kids, he looked the most like his daddy, which his mommy found amusing. Two Macs, mirror images of each other. Just what she needed.

He sat next to Maddie on the sofa with Mac snuggling up to him and gave her a kiss. "Hi, honey, I'm home."

"Can you tell me why my mother was here to do something upstairs that she couldn't tell me about?"

"I could, but then it wouldn't be a surprise anymore."

He loved when her smile was so big it included her eyes. "Tell me."

"Not yet, my sweet. Give me the babies and go get ready for a night out. I'll make dinner for them."

"Gramps said he's bringing Mario's," Thomas announced loudly.

"Well, then, I guess I'm not making dinner." He put Mac down to play and took Emma from Maddie. "Go on."

"They might be getting hungry soon."

"I've got this," Mac said.

"No, you don't," Thomas said with a snort of laughter.

"Hey, whose side are you on?"

Thomas dissolved into giggles. "Mommy's side."

"I see how it is. Go," he said to Maddie. "While you can."

"I'm gone."

Mac gazed down at the sleeping face of his baby daughter as her twin sister snoozed in the baby swing.

"I can help you, Daddy," Hailey said.

"That's very nice of you, sweetie. Thank you."

"No problem."

As she skipped off to bother Thomas, which was her favorite thing, Mac could picture her at fifteen, gorgeous like her mother and swatting boys away with a stick. He couldn't even think about having three teenage girls who were as pretty as their mother without wanting to wail.

He'd almost dozed off himself when Francine and Ned arrived, bearing pizza. The scent made Mac's stomach rumble.

Thomas and Hailey attacked the pizza as if they hadn't been fed in a week.

"Let's see some manners, you guys," Mac called to them. "And a big thank-you to Gramps."

"Thank you, Gramps."

"Yer welcome. Chew it good, will ya?" He lifted little Mac into the high chair and cut up his pizza like the professional grandfather he'd become. "Whatcha lookin' at?"

"Grandfathering looks good on you, old friend," Mac said.

"Best thing ever."

"I'll take her, Mac," Francine said. "Go get ready."

He transferred Emma to his mother-in-law. "Thank you for this."

"We love every minute with them," Francine said.

Sometimes Mac couldn't believe she was the same woman who'd been so bitter and jaded when he first met her. Her relationship with Ned and the arrival of eight grandchildren had changed everything for her.

Leaving the kids in the capable hands of their grandparents, he went upstairs to change, checking his phone as he went.

He read a text from his brother Evan. *Playing at the Wayfarer with O tonight if you guys can escape.*

Got some other plans, but we may stop by.

Would love to see you. Grace is going to text about a welcome-home party for Adam, Abby and the babies at the ferry landing tomorrow.

Sounds good!

Mac couldn't wait to meet his baby nephews, but first, he had a rare night alone with his beautiful wife, and he was going to make sure they both enjoyed every second of it.

WAITING for the phone to ring was the most stressful thing Lizzie James had ever done. On the one hand, she wanted to hear from Kendall that the situation had been resolved and they had nothing to worry about. On the other was the fear of getting bad news that would ruin her life.

So, yeah, waiting for the phone to ring was complete torture. It had taken over every thought, emotion and action, weighing her down with unbearable stress.

In the meantime, she tried her best to stay focused on her precious Violet and keeping the torment hidden from her. All the books said that babies were incredibly perceptive and could tell if their parents were stressed or upset about something.

She didn't want Violet to have any inkling that everything they held dear was in jeopardy from a man they'd never met and might still never know. So she forced herself to remain joyful around her daughter, to play and laugh and sing and do all the things they did every day as if nothing was wrong.

But on the inside, she was shattered.

What would she do if a judge ordered them to give Violet to her biological father?

They would run. Jared had the resources to make it possible for them to disappear into the world, never to be seen or heard from again. They'd have to leave everyone else they loved behind, but they'd do it to keep their family together.

Jared came into the room and smiled at them as if everything was normal when nothing was. He loved Violet as much as she did, but more than anything, he loved seeing her as a mother. He'd told her more than once that it was his favorite thing ever to witness her immense love for their child. Losing her would break his heart just as much as hers.

"I'd ask how you're doing, but…"

"I'm trying to hold it together for her, but it's hard to hide the torment."

"I know, love. But you're doing great. She's happy as always." He reached out a hand to Violet, smiling when she gripped his finger.

"Can we run away, Jared? Just take her and disappear?"

"I think that's harder to do than you might think. People know who I am."

"But we could try?"

"If we run and we get caught, we lose her. If we stay and fight, then we stand a chance to get the outcome we want."

"But we could lose her."

"Yes, we could, and we always knew that was possible until the adoption was final. We talked about this at the beginning, how we were taking a huge chance falling in love with someone who wasn't ours to keep yet."

"What were we supposed to do? Not love her? That'd be like asking me not to breathe."

"I know, honey, but we went into this knowing the risks. We can't forget that now that our worst-case scenario has come to pass."

"How can you be so calm about this?"

"I'm not calm. I haven't had one second of calm since Kendall told us

Violet's biological father had reached out. I'm just trying to deal with the situation we're in as best I can, and running away won't fix anything."

"I can't just sit here and do nothing."

"We're not doing nothing. Kendall and Dan are all over it. We have to trust them to help us get the outcome we want."

"The court will give him custody."

"Maybe not. We know nothing about his background. For all we know, he's got a criminal record or he's a drug addict or any number of things that could prevent him from getting custody. Maybe he has other kids he's not taking care of. Anything is possible."

"I can't stand the not knowing. It's going to break me."

"I won't let it. I've spoken with Kendall, and she assured me we'll have more information today. We just have to keep the faith."

"That's getting harder to do."

Jared's phone rang, startling them.

Lizzie's heart couldn't handle the jolt of fear that accompanied every phone call since they'd first heard about Violet's father.

"It's Kendall. Hey, you're on speaker with both of us."

"I've just got off the phone with the attorney for Violet's biological father. His name is Brooks Ward, and he's in medical school at Yale. He dated Jessie for a few weeks last summer and had no idea she was pregnant until he ran into a mutual friend who told him about the baby."

Lizzie's heart was pounding so hard, she wondered if Jared could hear it. "Wh-what does he want?"

"He wants to meet her."

The floor dropped out from under her.

"Is he going to contest the adoption?" Jared asked.

"The attorney said he's not sure what his intentions are beyond meeting his daughter."

"Does he understand the nightmare this is for us?"

"That's been conveyed to him, and he's sorry about that, but he still wants to meet her."

"When?"

"As soon as possible."

"Let's do it this weekend and get it over with. Lizzie and I can't live in this unbearable purgatory indefinitely."

"I suggested this weekend and asked if he could get to the island. The attorney will get back to me as soon as he hears from him."

"What's your gut saying, Kendall?"

"I think it's good news that he's in medical school and has no time to care for a young child. That said, he probably has parents who could, so I don't know what to think. We have to take this one step at a time, as excruciating as it is."

"It's the most unbearable thing either of us has ever been through."

Jared's tears gutted Lizzie. He was always so strong, and to see him break down was heart-wrenching.

She took his hand and rested her head on his shoulder while Violet played on the floor, oblivious to the drama swirling around her.

"I know," Kendall said, "and I'm working as hard as I can to get you some resolution. But we have to play this out, as hard as it is. He wants to see her, and we have to let him. I'll be back to you as soon as I hear anything more."

"Thanks, K."

"Hang in there. Love you guys."

"Love you, too."

"How are we supposed to breathe until we know if he's going to take her from us?" Lizzie asked.

"We have to keep it together for our daughter," Jared said. "Let's focus only on her, like we always do."

"I'm so scared."

"I know, honey. I am, too."

By the time Morgan knocked on her door shortly after seven o'clock, Sierra was about to spontaneously combust from excitement. She couldn't recall the last time she'd been so amped up for anything as she was to see him after the long day apart. And while a tiny voice inside her head said to slow her roll and chill the hell out, she couldn't seem to make that happen when he came through the door, smiling and obviously as happy to see her as she was to see him.

Then he wrapped his arms around her and kissed her, and her knees went weak under her. Only his tight hold on her kept her standing as he kissed her face right off.

"Mmm," he said when he finally came up for air. "I've been looking forward to that all day."

"Me, too. Was it a particularly long day, or did it just seem like it?"

"It was endless, but it just got a whole lot better." He nuzzled her neck. "What do you feel like doing tonight?"

"I, um, my brain is currently scrambled, and I have no coherent thoughts."

His low rumble of laughter against her neck made her shiver from the sensations that rippled through her.

"Do you want to go out?"

"I heard there's good live music at the Wayfarer tonight."

"That sounds fun. Should we go check it out?"

"I mean, we could, but we could also stay right here."

"I don't want you to think that's all I want."

"What if it's all I want?"

He pulled back to look at her, seeming alarmed. "Is it?"

"No, not at all, which is terrifying, actually."

"How come?"

"Things are unsettled for you right now, but I'm very, very settled, and, well… That's kind of scary."

"How about we go have some dinner, enjoy some music, talk about this stuff and come back here later?"

"That sounds good. I'm starving."

"Me, too."

"Let's get to it, then." He kissed her again. "To hold me over."

"Once more should do it."

He smiled as he brought his lips down on hers for a kiss that quickly turned hot and had her moaning as he ended it minutes later. "If we don't cut that out, we'll never go."

"Fine. Be that way."

"One of us has to be an adult around here."

She gave him a playful push toward the door. "Haha, very funny."

When they were downstairs next to his truck—or Billy's truck that he was using—he put a hand on her arm. "Hey."

"What's up?"

"I don't want you terrified. This… with you… It feels so good that you've got me pondering some life changes after one incredible night."

"Oh." She licked lips that had suddenly gone dry as the desert. "I do?"

"Yeah. You do. You have me rethinking my whole damned life, so please don't be afraid of anything other than how quickly this is happening and how epic we might turn out to be."

Was this really happening, or was she dreaming? "Epic, huh?"

"You never know unless you try, and I intend to go for it. That is… if you're going for it with me." He backed her up against the truck, pressing his aroused body to hers. "I was guilty as fuck for feeling so good today when the last few months have been nothing but one shitty day after another. But today… Today it was like the sun had come back out after a long, dark, cold winter. All thanks to you."

CHAPTER 24

*S*ierra had never been more moved by anything in her entire life than she was by his beautiful words. As she tried not to cry, she rested her head on his chest and breathed him in. Not only was he handsome as all hell, but he smelled delicious, too. The scent was new to her, as was the sense of completion that came with him.

If this was what she'd spent all this time waiting for, he'd been worth the wait.

He broke the spell when he said, "Let's get out of this cold."

"Is it cold? I hadn't noticed."

Smiling, he held the door and kissed her before leaving her to get settled.

She couldn't believe this was happening. It was finally happening, and if the feeling of elation that came with him was anything like Duke had felt for McKenzie, Sierra could honestly say she got it now. She got why he'd gone off the deep end over her and had changed his whole life to accommodate her and her son.

In fact, she owed him an apology for being such a skeptical bitch during the first weeks they were together, when she'd begun to feel like she'd lost him or something.

"Everything okay?" Morgan asked as he drove them the short distance to the Wayfarer. In the summer, they could've walked. In December, it was too damned cold to walk anywhere.

"Yes, of course."

"Did I say too much just now?"

"Not at all. No one has ever said anything like that to me before."

"I find that hard to believe."

"Well, believe it."

"That's a crying shame, but I'm secretly glad I got to you before anyone else snapped you up and out of reach. That would've been the biggest shame of all, if you weren't single when I first saw you."

"You first saw me months ago."

"Believe me. I know."

"So what're you saying?"

"I'm saying that the first time I ever saw you, I almost swallowed my tongue."

She sputtered with laughter. "Is that even possible?"

"I wouldn't have thought so until I laid eyes on you."

His hand on her thigh set her on fire.

Holy. Shit.

And then he gave a little squeeze.

She moaned.

"Don't make that sound unless you want to be naked in the cold."

"Then don't touch me like that."

He squeezed again. "Like that?"

"Morgan…"

"Yes, Sierra?"

"You're making me crazy."

"I owe you months of payback for every time you came prancing into the gym looking like a fucking goddess and making me hard behind the counter."

"I do not *prance*, and you were hard?"

He took her hand and brought it over to feel how hard their conversation had made him. "Like that. Every single time."

Sierra squeezed and stroked until he was the one doing the moaning. "Stop."

She didn't stop.

He grabbed her hand. "I don't feel like walking around with wet britches all night."

"Don't start trouble you can't finish."

"Oh, I'll finish it. As soon as we eat something, it's on."

She shivered.

And not from the cold.

"Why didn't you say something about your… um… interest… sooner?"

"Because I wasn't ready for what this might turn out to be. But I kept asking around about whether you were seeing anyone, and every time someone said not that they knew of, I was incredibly relieved. One time, I said to Terry, who works at the gym, 'What's her story?' and he said, 'Not really sure, but she's hot as fuck, right?' I almost punched his teeth out for talking about you that way."

Sierra cracked the window because she needed a dose of cold air to cool her off before she combusted. Hearing that he'd been pursuing her before she was even aware of it made her whole system buzz with incendiary desire.

"What would you have done if you heard I was seeing someone?"

"I probably would've tried to mess it up."

"You would not!"

"I might've…" He glanced over at her. "Tell me the truth. Am I coming on too strong or freaking you out?"

"Not at all. It's kind of refreshing to hear how you really feel and not have to wade through a bunch of crap to get to the truth of the matter."

"I think I suspected months ago that last night would go the way it did, and I needed to be ready, you know?"

She nodded. "You've had a lot to deal with."

"Worst thing that's ever happened to me, and that's saying something when you consider the previous losses. This one really did me in. But even in the midst of it, I saw you. I wanted to know you. I couldn't wait for you to stop by to check on me. And when you offered me a free massage…"

"What?" she asked breathlessly.

"I can't say it. You'll be horrified."

"Now you have to tell me."

"Let's just say the thought of you massaging me gave me some rather vivid thoughts."

"How vivid are we talking?"

"Positively filthy."

Sierra snorted with laughter as he pulled into one of the last remaining parking spaces at the Wayfarer. Owen and Evan had drawn a crowd.

When he would've gotten out of the truck, Sierra stopped him. "I'm not sure if it matters, but if we walk in there together, we'll be making a bit of a statement to half the town."

"Does that matter to you?"

"Not at all, but you might not be ready to deal with that."

"If I wasn't ready, we wouldn't be here, but I appreciate you thinking of me that way."

"Okay, then."

He stole a kiss. "Let's go."

When she met him in front of the truck, he wrapped an arm around her to hustle them toward the entrance as the wind whipped off the water in South Harbor. The fishing boats that lined the pier during the summer and fall had been put away for the winter, leaving nothing to break the icy blast of wind.

He opened the door and ushered her inside, following her with a muttered curse about how freaking cold it was.

"It gets worse in January," she said over her shoulder, smiling at his grimace.

She stopped at the hostess stand, and he wrapped an arm around her from behind as he whispered in her ear. "Will you keep me warm in January?"

"Will you be here in January?"

Before he could answer, the hostess came to show them to a table by a roaring fireplace that cast some much-needed heat on the big, crowded room.

Sierra felt every eye in the place on her and Morgan as they took their seats and accepted menus from the hostess.

"Is everyone looking at us, or does it just seem like it?" Morgan asked as he kept his gaze fixed on the menu.

"Oh, they're all looking. Nothing fuels the gossip machine around here like a potential new romance."

"I see how it is."

"You don't. Not yet. But you will."

"What does that mean?"

She gave him a sly grin. "You'll find out."

Morgan was completely captivated by her, but then again, like he'd told her, he'd known he would be. That was why he hadn't dared get too close before he'd taken care of some of the more onerous tasks that followed the death of a loved one. It wouldn't have been fair to her to start something when he was an emotional disaster area.

Not that he was "healed" from the tremendous loss, or anything close to it, but the sharp, ragged edges of early grief had subsided somewhat, leaving him with a dull ache that would probably be with him for the rest of his days.

He'd learned to live with that ache after losing his parents and sister, so it wasn't new to him. What was different was that he no longer had Billy to commiserate with. No one else in his life could understand the magnitude the way he did, and now that he was gone, too, Morgan was very much alone with the tragedy of it all.

That'd been the hardest part, losing the one person who understood what he'd been through. Part of him would never forgive Billy for getting himself killed in a storm, leaving him all alone to face the rest of his life.

But he didn't want to think about that shit when he had the glorious Sierra Mancini sitting across from him, looking more beautiful than ever in the glow of the fire, which brought out red highlights in her hair that he hadn't noticed before.

"Why are you staring at me?" she asked from behind her menu.

He ducked his head so he could see around the menu. "How can you see what I'm doing?"

"Don't answer a question with a question."

"If you were me, you'd be staring at you, too."

"You can't see me through the menu."

"I don't want to miss anything when you put the menu down."

The menu landed on the table. "Are you for real with these lines?"

"They're not lines. They're truths. You make me want to stare. Among other things."

"What other things?"

"We should talk about them when we're not in a room full of nosy islanders."

Their waitress came to take their order, which was clam chowder for both of them to start with, as well as wine for her and a beer for him.

Duke and McKenzie came over to say hello.

"We thought that was you," McKenzie said.

"Oh please, don't be ridiculous. You want the scoop."

"That, too," McKenzie said with a laugh.

"How'd the tat come out?" Sierra asked her.

"It's half done. We'll finish it tomorrow. But who cares about that? Tell us everything about you two."

"Well…" Sierra leaned toward them like she was going to say something top secret. "We're both having clam chowder."

Duke cracked up. "That's what you get for being a busybody, MK."

"That wasn't nice, Sierra. You wouldn't want to hold out on your bookkeeper, now would you?"

"We'll talk," Sierra said. "But not now."

"Fair enough." To Morgan, McKenzie said, "I don't know you very well, but everyone says you're a good guy."

"I try to be."

"Be nice to our girl, or else I'll send Duke to talk to you."

"He's already talked to me."

"*What?*" Sierra and McKenzie said, zeroing in on Duke.

Duke's face flushed as he laughed nervously. "It was a friendly conversation between men. Nothing to see here."

"He wanted to make sure I have good intentions toward you," Morgan said to Sierra.

"I'm going to gut you like a fish," Sierra said to Duke.

"I'll help you," McKenzie said.

Duke held up his hands. "I was just looking out for my friend the way she did for me when you came along, MK. That's all it was."

Everyone looked to Morgan to confirm it. Part of him wanted to make Duke squirm some more, but more than that, he wanted Sierra's friends to like him. "I told him he has nothing to worry about."

"Which made me feel better," Duke said.

McKenzie took him by the hand. "Let me get you out of here before she makes good on the gutting she promised you." MK patted the six-pack that'd come from hours at the gym. "I like your gut just the way it is."

"Have a nice evening, and MYOB, Duke," Sierra said.

"What fun would that be?" Duke asked as McKenzie dragged him away.

"You two are cute," Morgan said.

"He's the brother I've never had, but tell me the truth… Was that all he said to you?"

"That was it. Just a guy looking out for his friend."

"He never had a family of his own. We're it, so he can be a bit protective. That's never bothered me before."

"I hope it doesn't now either. I got where he was coming from. He was mostly concerned about me starting something with you and checking out of here."

"Funny, I have the same concern."

Morgan took a sip from the beer the waitress had delivered. "It's weird… If you'd have told me before Billy went missing that I'd ever want to call this place home again, I would've laughed my ass off. But now…"

"What?" she asked, sounding a bit breathless.

"Now everything looks different to me, especially since yesterday."

"It's been one day, Morgan."

"And yet… Everything looks different."

He hoped he wasn't getting ahead of himself with her, but with a decision to be made—and soon—he needed to know he wasn't the only one falling fast and furious into whatever this was that was happening with her.

CHAPTER 25

"Thanks for coming out to see us tonight, everyone," Evan McCarthy said from the stage, where he was seated on a stool next to his best friend, Owen Lawry, his favorite person to perform with. "It's always nice to play for the home crowd on Gansett Island."

That was met with a huge cheer from their friends and family.

"You know, a lot has changed for me since 'My Amazing Grace' became a number one hit—"

He was interrupted by more applause and cheers.

"Aw, thanks, but I was going to say… Some things never change, especially my love for Gansett Island and everyone who lives here. This is for you guys, with all my love."

He and Owen strummed the opening chords for "Home," originally performed by Phillip Phillips on *American Idol*.

As the crowd sang along to the familiar tune, Evan grinned at Owen, who was perfectly in sync with him, as always.

In the audience, he spotted his wife, Grace with Stephanie, Laura, Sydney, Katie and Julia, while Grant, Luke, Shane and Deacon were huddled next to them. At the next table, his cousin Riley and his wife, Nikki, were seated with Riley's brother, Finn, his wife, Chloe, as well as the Gansett Fire Chief Mason Johns, his fiancée, Jordan Stokes, Cooper

James and his fiancée, Gigi Gibson, who were home on Gansett for the holidays.

In January, the season of the Jordan and Gigi reality show that they'd shot on Gansett would begin to air and would make Mason and Cooper stars along with their partners.

As he sang along with Owen, Evan found his love in the crowd, glowing with pregnancy and smiling the way she always did when they got to spend time with their closest friends and family. Deciding to stay home on Gansett for a while had been a good move for both of them, after a year of relentless touring in support of his hit song.

Grace had come out on the road with him and had stood by him through the wild ride of achieving success he'd only dreamed about before the song he'd written for her had become a massive hit. But she hadn't been happy like she was now, surrounded by the best friends she'd ever had in the place that had become her home as much as his.

Soon, they'd welcome their first child, surrounded by all the people they loved best, and would get to raise him or her in a pack of cousins and friends who would grow up together.

Life was good and about to get better.

They finished the song and announced a ten-minute break. "We'll be right back," Evan said, "so don't go anywhere."

After they'd stashed their guitars, Owen extended his fist.

Evan bumped it. "Just like riding a bike to play with you."

"I was scared. We hadn't played together in a while."

"I had no doubt we'd pick right up where we left off, the way we always do."

"Feels like coming home to play with you."

"Same, brother. Let's go see what we've missed while we were up here."

They went to join their wives, who'd ordered cold beers for them in anticipation of their break.

Evan put an arm around Grace. "How lucky are we, O?"

"The luckiest." Owen kissed Laura. "Thanks for taking such good care of me."

"Haha, we both know it's the other way around," Laura said.

"Who's got your kids tonight, Laura?" Evan asked.

"They're having a sleepover with the grandparents," Laura said.

"Thank God for Sarah and Charlie, who have them tonight—and Dad and Betsy. They're always willing to take the hooligans to give their exhausted parents a night off."

"I hope you weren't planning on getting much sleep tonight," Owen said with a dirty grin for his wife.

"Shut your face. There will be sleep or else."

"Uh-oh, bro," Evan said.

"Don't worry," Owen said with a cocky grin. "When push comes to shove, she'll want what I want."

"One more time, in case you missed it the first time," Laura said, "*shut your face.*"

The others howled with laughter.

"You love when my face is open and pressed to your—"

Laura put a hand over his mouth as he rocked with laughter. "I'm going to kill you."

"You'd miss me."

This was the shit Evan lived for with their friends and family. Laura was his first cousin and had grown up spending summers with him, his siblings and her brother, Shane. Those had been the best of times until they all grew up and got to do the rest of life together, too. All the McCarthy cousins had ended up on Gansett Island, which was just another reason to love being home.

Even the "babies," Riley and Finn, had landed there and were loving life with Nikki and Chloe, their dad, Kevin, his second wife, Chelsea, their baby daughter, Summer, and another sibling on the way.

Evan took Grace's hand and brought her with him when he went to say hi to their crew, sitting around one of the big circular tables. "What's up, babies?" They hated when their older cousins called them that, which was what made it fun to trot out the dreaded nickname.

"You're getting on in years, cousin," Riley said. "I could drop you on your ass."

"I'd like to see you try."

Riley stood.

Nikki grabbed his arm. "Sit your ass down."

The others cackled with laughter.

"Just so you know, I could," Riley said to Evan.

"If your mom lets you come out to play."

Nikki released her husband. "Go kick his ass."

Evan took off running as Riley chased after him, the two of them laughing their asses off as they collided in a wrestling match right in the middle of the big dance floor.

"Fools," Grace said. "Will they ever grow up?"

"Probably not," Nikki replied.

A crowd had gathered to watch the cousins' wrestling match.

"And people say I'm the jackass of the family," Mac said.

Where had he come from?

Evan took his attention off Riley for one fateful second and ended up pinned to the floor by his younger cousin.

"Say uncle," Riley said, grunting from the strain of holding Evan in place.

"Eff you."

"*Uncle.*"

"Whatever."

"I've got all night, bro."

"Fine. Uncle. You win. Are you happy?"

"You bet I am." Riley stood and extended a hand to help Evan up.

Evan gave a mighty pull and had Riley pinned to the floor in two seconds flat. "Who's your uncle now, *bro?*"

"Your ten-minute break is up, Evan," Nikki said.

She was the manager of the Wayfarer.

"I'm doing this gig for free."

"Get back to it before people get bored and go home."

"Welp, we can't have that, but let's call this one a draw, cousin."

"I beat you fair and square," Riley said as he dusted himself off.

"Keep telling yourself that," Evan said as he went to say hi to his brother Mac.

"Thanks for distracting me at the worst possible time."

"That baby kicked your ass," Mac said.

"Shut up. How'd you two get out of the house tonight?"

"Grandparents," Maddie said. "My wonderful husband arranged the whole thing, and we're free until tomorrow morning."

"What the hell are you doing here, then?" Evan asked.

"We heard there was going to be music," Mac said, "but we arrived to WWE."

"The music is coming back momentarily."

"Well, get to it," Maddie said. "We have other items on our agenda for this rare night away from our five children."

"Yes, ma'am. I'm on it."

Evan kissed Grace and returned to the stage, amused by the interlude with his family and how they still treated him the same, which was a huge relief in the craziness that came with fame.

As he tuned his guitar for the next set, Evan was thrilled to be home.

"WHY YOU GOTTA WRESTLE your cousin right on my dance floor?" Nikki asked her husband. And yes, it was still weird to think of him as her husband three weeks after they tied the knot over Thanksgiving weekend.

"He started it."

"Did he, though?"

"All in good fun, babe."

"I know."

"He had to defend our honor," Finn said. "That baby shit was old when we were in high school, and it's ancient now."

"They do it because you react every time," Chloe said. "If you just ignored them, it would ruin their fun."

"We'd rather wrestle them," Riley said.

"Hell yes," Finn said. "They can't stand that the babies can take them."

"We're younger, stronger and sexier than they'll ever be," Riley said.

"Did you just refer to yourself as sexy?" Chelsea asked, her eyes twinkling with amusement.

"They weren't raised that way," Kevin said.

"I think they actually were," Chloe said. "We've all seen you with your brothers, Kev. The apple doesn't fall far from the tree."

"She's got you there, Dad," Finn said, laughing.

"I can't deny that the original McCarthy brothers may have set a less-than-stellar example for our offspring," Kevin said.

"In all seriousness, you set the best possible example," said Evelyn Hopper, Nikki and Jordan's grandmother. "I love how close all you McCarthys are to your siblings and cousins."

"It's fun having everyone here and working together," Riley said. He and Finn worked for Mac's construction company, along with Shane.

"How're you feeling, Chloe?" Nikki asked her sister-in-law. Her rheumatoid arthritis had been giving her grief again.

"I'm okay. The cold is always a challenge."

"I need to take you somewhere warm for the winter," Finn said.

"Maybe someday when we're old and retired, we'll do that."

"We need to do it now so you won't suffer like this all winter long."

"I'm fine, honey. Don't worry about me."

"I'll always worry about you. I hate when you're in pain."

Chloe rested her head on his shoulder. "Don't fret. We're supposed to be having fun tonight."

They all wished they could find the magic elixir that would soothe the pain Chloe lived with every day, but she was a trouper and didn't want anyone fussing over her.

Nikki's twin sister, Jordan, yawned for the fifth time in five minutes. Pregnancy was making her so tired she could barely function.

Mason suggested they head home.

"Yes, please. I can't stay awake."

They all got up to hug Mason and Jordan.

"Call me tomorrow," Nikki said to her sister.

"I will."

"You're a regular drag, old lady," their best friend, Gigi, said when she hugged Jordan.

"Wait until you're knocked up, bitch. You'll see what it's like."

"When can we do that?" Cooper asked. "I'm here for knocking up any time."

"Easy, stud. We're in no way ready for that."

"I'm ready when you are."

"You're starting a new business this summer. I've got the publicity tour for the new season of the show that I'm doing solo because someone is too pregnant. Where do you see time for a baby in all that mess?"

"I'll let you have this fight while I go home to sleep," Jordan said. "Love you all."

"Love you, too," everyone at the table said.

"We can go whenever you want," Riley said to Nikki.

"Let's stay for one more set."

"I'm with you, babe. Whatever you want."

As far as Nikki was concerned, marriage to Riley McCarthy was the best thing ever, and it was getting better all the time.

THE CHOWDER HAD WARMED them up, and the McCarthy cousin wrestling match had kept them entertained, and now... All Sierra wanted was to get the hell out of there so she could be alone with Morgan.

People had stopped by their table to say hello, to ask how Morgan was doing and probably to try to figure out what was going on between them, not that they were giving anything away.

Everyone was being nice and friendly and supportive of Morgan, which he appreciated. They asked about his plans for the gym, and he assured them it would stay open one way or the other. What he didn't say was whether he'd be the one to manage it or if he planned to turn that role over to one of the employees.

Sierra would like to know the answer to that question, but she wasn't about to press him for big decisions on their second official date.

But with every minute they spent together, this thing with him became a bigger deal for her. There was no denying the sizzling chemistry between them or the wild attraction that simmered on low boil the whole time they sat across from each other at the Wayfarer, surrounded by the entire island population—or so it seemed.

Evan McCarthy and Owen Lawry returned to the stage and began to strum their guitars in perfect harmony. They were always so fun to watch.

"Not sure if you heard that I have four new nephews," Evan said to cheers from the crowd. "I want to send a big shout-out to my brother Adam and his superstar wife, Abby, and to their four new sons—Murphy, Rory, Kane and Beckett McCarthy. Look out, world, four more McCarthy boys are about to come home to Gansett! I'd like to ask my friend, and Owen's sister, Julia Lawry to join us for this one. Julia, you got a song in you tonight?"

Julia got up to come to the stage. "For you, always!"

When she was in place at the microphone, Evan and Owen played the opening notes to "In My Life."

"This is for my nephews," Evan said. "Welcome home to Gansett Island."

"Wow, they sound amazing together," Morgan said.

"They really do. They're all so incredibly talented. I wish I had something like they do."

"From what your clients say, you've got your own very special talent."

She shrugged. "I'd rather be able to sing like Julia, but I'd be too nervous to stand up there and do it in front of people."

"She seems incredibly comfortable performing in public."

"From what I've heard, that wasn't always the case. The Lawrys had a very difficult upbringing with an abusive, overbearing, critical father who would say things like, 'No daughter of mine is going to perform in public like a common whore.'"

"Jeez. That's harsh."

"That's the least of it. He's in prison now for assaulting his ex-wife, Sarah."

"Sarah, who's married to Charlie now?"

"Yes."

"Good Lord, she's the sweetest person ever."

"She really is, and she's so happy with Charlie. They both traveled a long and difficult road before they found each other here on Gansett."

"This place has magical powers."

"Did you think that when you were a kid?"

"Oh hell no. I hated it here. I wanted off this island in the worst possible way."

"What did you hate about it?"

"I wanted to be able to jump in my truck and go to the mall or the movies or to restaurants I'd only ever heard about on TV but had never been to. I wanted to see the world."

"Couldn't you go to the mainland once in a while?"

"Sure but having to schedule your vehicle on the ferry weeks in advance sort of takes the spontaneity out of things."

"Speaking of vehicles on the ferry, I've got mine scheduled for next Wednesday to go home to Providence for Christmas."

"Oh, okay. You must be looking forward to seeing your family."

"I was."

"What do you mean?"

"Not sure if you've noticed, but it's been a rather monumental twenty-four hours around here. The thought of leaving right when things are getting interesting doesn't seem so appealing anymore."

"Ah, I see," he said with a satisfied grin.

"You want to go with me?" The question was asked before she took two seconds to ponder whether it was far too soon to take him home to meet the family. Of course it was, but the thought of him powering through Christmas alone after losing his last remaining family member was unbearable to her.

"Oh, um, well… You won't want me underfoot when you're going to spend time with your dad and cousins."

"I do want you underfoot, or I wouldn't have invited you."

"What will your dad say if you show up with some random dude for Christmas?"

"A, you're not random. B, I'd prepare him in advance. C, he wants me to be happy, and if I tell him that being with Morgan makes me happy, he'll welcome you with open arms."

"Does being with Morgan make you happy?"

She gave him her best withering look. "Duh."

"That's very profound, Sierra. Thank you for being so articulate."

"Ask a dumb question, get a dumb answer."

Oh, how she loved what laughter did to his handsome face. It took years off, lightened him and seemed to relieve some of the terrible burden he carried. She vowed to make him laugh as often as she could.

"Why are you looking at me like that?"

"I like how laughter looks on you."

"Feels good to laugh. It's been a minute since I had anything to laugh about."

"I hope you don't feel guilty for enjoying yourself. I had a hard time with that after my mom died. I thought, what's wrong with me to be laughing and having fun when she's gone forever?"

"I know that feeling all too well. Went through it after each loss and felt the same way. But what I've learned is that life marches on, and you have no choice but to pick yourself up and get back to it. What else can you do? Being a sad sack for the rest of your life isn't going to bring back the person you lost, and it's only going to waste the gift of time you have left."

"Waste the gift of time. That's well said."

"Time is all we have, and you never know when you're going to run out of it, so you have to make every day count. Billy and I talked a lot about that, especially after we lost our sister so suddenly. Her time here was cut far too short, so we made a vow to live fully in her honor, and we really tried to do that. I've thought a few times… maybe that was why Billy was on his boat in a storm. He thought it would be a story he could tell for the rest of his life."

"How do you feel about that possibility?"

"It makes far more sense than him recklessly risking his life for no good reason. I just hope they were drunk as skunks during the worst of it."

"Yeah, for sure." She shivered, thinking about what they must've gone through.

"Do yourself a favor and don't try to imagine it. It'll give you nightmares."

"Have you had them?"

"Yeah, which is why I try not to think about it."

"Let's go back to talking about you going home with me for Christmas."

"Are you sure about that?"

She reached across the table for his hand.

He met her halfway and curled his hand around hers.

"I'm sure."

CHAPTER 26

He'd wanted to take her out, show her a good time, prove he wasn't only after the one thing all guys were after... But as fun as it was to spar with her across the dinner table while being entertained by quality music, Morgan couldn't wait to have her all to himself.

While she watched Owen and Evan, he watched her. He noticed the glow of her expressive face, the way her eyes lit up with pleasure when the guys played a song she loved and how everyone who walked by their table greeted her by name.

She loved it here, was loved by her friends and had established a successful business through years of hard work. It didn't take long to understand she wouldn't be happy anywhere else.

The message from Devin weighed heavily on him. Dev and his family had been good to Morgan, supporting his career growth by paying for continuing education as well as giving him regular bonuses and pay increases. His current salary far exceeded his wildest expectations when he'd entered the field. The thought of giving up that level of security and comfort in his work was intimidating, especially as he stared down forty and his future retirement.

But now that he knew Sierra existed in this world, could he be happy or content without her close by, without evenings with her to look forward to after a long day of work?

Two fucking days.

That's how long it had taken for him to rethink every aspect of what it meant to be happy or content.

Morgan had seen that happen to other people, but it sure as hell had never happened to him. He'd never met anyone who had him rethinking his entire life plan in the span of forty-eight consequential hours.

"You want to get out of here?" he asked her when he couldn't wait any longer.

"Yeah, let's go."

As they made their way to the exit, everyone wanted a word with Sierra—and a few stopped him to thank him for keeping the gym open.

"I love it there," Grant McCarthy said. "Best gym I've ever belonged to."

"That's all thanks to Billy."

"Absolutely, but you've kept up the vibe, and we all appreciate it, especially in light of what you're dealing with. Just wanted to say thanks."

"Nice to hear how popular the place is."

"I know people who started working out because they heard how fun the gym is," Grant's wife, Stephanie, said.

"I love that," Morgan said. "Leave it to Billy."

"We're doing that beer tomorrow night, right?" Grant asked.

"That's the plan."

Grant shook Morgan's hand. "Looking forward to it."

"Me, too."

"You guys have a nice evening," Stephanie said.

"You do the same," Sierra said with a hug for Stephanie.

Stephanie said something to her that made Sierra laugh.

When they got outside, Morgan asked her what Stephanie said.

"I can't tell you. It was dirty."

"Then I definitely want to know."

"She said, and I quote, 'I hope you're having your wicked way with that hunk of man.'"

Morgan sputtered with laughter. "Well, all righty, then. Let's get to that. Right now."

Holding hands, they ran through the cold to the truck and were on the way to her place in the span of a few minutes. He drove so quickly that the heater didn't even have time to warm up before he was parking outside her building.

Like the night before, he was right behind her as they sprinted up the stairs. Again, the key and lock gave her some grief. He reached around her to help. They were laughing as they almost fell through the door, dropping their coats on the floor. Morgan put his hands on her hips to steer her straight into the bedroom, tugging at her top, easing it over her head and tossing it aside in the smoothest of smooth moves.

Then he wrapped his arms around her from behind and rested his chin on her shoulder. "This feels so good, Sierra. Better than anything ever has."

She covered his hands with hers. "For me, too."

"All I want is more of it. More of you."

"Same." She patted his hand. "Let me turn around."

He held on tighter. "In a minute."

Mac bided his time. He enjoyed watching Maddie cut loose with their friends and family as they listened to their favorite performers. Seeing her talking and laughing with their closest people reminded him of a hundred other similar nights before they had five kids and rarely left the house anymore.

This season in their lives would pass, probably long before they were ready, but he vowed to get her out more often, to make sure she had fun with her girls and that they got more time alone together.

"You're quiet tonight, brother." Grant took the seat next to Mac's, bringing fresh beers for both of them. "Which is unusual enough to be concerning."

"Haha. I'm relaxing and taking it all in. I've missed nights like this with you guys. It's been too long."

"You've been a little busy with baby twins and such."

"Yeah, for sure, but we needed this night away from it all, and thank God for grandparents who step up at a moment's notice."

"Are you ready to share them with the rest of us?"

"Not one bit ready."

Grant laughed. "Ready or not, here come four new McCarthy babies."

"I can't wait to meet them."

"Me, too."

"And I can't wait to meet yours and Evan's. Exciting times around here."

"Good thing no one took your no-more-babies edict seriously, huh?"

"You're all a defiant bunch of SOBs."

"And you're not the boss of us."

"I'll be glad when they've all safely arrived, and we can settle in to watching them grow up together."

"Can you imagine what it's going to be like around here in about fifteen years?"

"I can't. We'll need to double the number of cops on the island to keep the McCarthy grandchildren under control."

"Because we'll be too old to do it by then."

"Speak for yourself, asshole."

"I'm not the one about to turn forty."

"Is that really necessary?"

Grant laughed. "Truth hurts."

"Ah, it's just a number, and I'll remind you that you're right behind me."

"Trust me, I know. I talked to Morgan before they left. He's looking forward to our beer tomorrow."

"Yeah, me, too. I'm going to offer him a job. Did you know he's a master electrician?"

"What? No way."

"Yep, and I talked to Dad about him. The town wants him working on the electrical upgrade that we needed twenty years ago. There's a lot of work for him here if he wants it."

"Do you think he'll want it?"

"Hard telling. I'm not really sure what his situation is on the mainland, but we sure as hell need him here if he's up for it. He was like us growing up, though. Couldn't wait to be rid of this place, so I'm not sure what he'll say about staying."

"He said he's planning to keep the gym open."

"Let's face it. The gym makes bank. He could hire someone to run that place for him if he doesn't want to stay."

"True. Looks like there's something brewing with Sierra. That might be incentive enough to keep him around."

"I guess we'll see."

Maddie came over to them. "Take me to bed or lose me forever, Malcolm."

"Whoa," Grant said with a laugh. "She's pulling out the big guns, Malcolm."

Mac glared at his brother. "*She* can call me that. *You* cannot."

"Whatever you say, Malcolm."

"Are you going to fight with your brother or take me to bed?" Maddie asked.

"We're outta here." Mac held her in front of him to hide his instant reaction to the *take me to bed* order. "Have a good night, everyone."

"Don't do anything we wouldn't do," Evan called after them from the stage.

Mac shot him the bird over his shoulder and kept moving so nothing would impede the goal of following his wife's order. He patted her ass. "That was hot as fuck, babe."

"What was?"

"'Take me to bed or lose me forever.'"

"You gotta love a little *Top Gun* between friends."

He rubbed his erection against her back. "My top gun loves the hell out of you."

Her giggle was the best thing he'd heard all day. Then she hiccupped, and they both cracked up.

"I might be a tad bit tipsy," Maddie announced.

She'd only recently weaned the twins, and since tonight was the first time she'd drunk wine in more than a year, it hadn't taken much to make her silly.

"No worries, love. I've gotcha."

"I know," she said with a sigh. "I'm so happy we got to go out tonight."

"We need to do it more often. I miss nights like this with the gang—and with you."

"Same. Just cuz we have five kids doesn't mean we can't leave the house."

Mac held the door to his truck for her. "That's right." When she was settled, he stole a kiss. He didn't expect her to meet fire with fire, but before he knew it, they were engaged in a full-on make-out session right there in the frigid parking lot. "Hold that thought, babe."

"Hurry up."

Her eagerness lit a fire in him like only she ever had, and that it still burned so brightly between them after years together and six children, including the precious son they'd lost, was the greatest gift in his life.

He drove them quickly to the Sand & Surf and ushered her in ahead of him through the side door that led straight up the stairs to the room he'd checked them into earlier. Francine had dropped off Maddie's bag with Laura, who'd promised to deliver it to their room.

While he carried his bag, he kept his arm around Maddie on the stairs so she wouldn't trip. She was all goofy giggles as he juggled his bag and the key while keeping an arm around her.

"You'd better not be asleep in five minutes, Mrs. McCarthy," he said as they went into the room that featured a king-sized bed, a dresser and a small bathroom, which was all they needed.

She dropped her coat onto the floor. "I'm not at all tired."

"That's a bald-faced lie."

She flopped down on the bed. "The flowers are gorgeous. Thank you for arranging all this."

"Steph is sending up dinner in thirty minutes."

She held out her arms to him.

Mac didn't need to be asked twice. He came down on top of her and let her trap him in her web of soft, fragrant skin and the hot, sexy kisses he'd missed so much during the months they'd been consumed with kids and babies. Not that they hadn't kissed plenty during that time, but they'd kept the lid on things until he'd gotten the all clear following his vasectomy.

They were done having kids and were finally able to get back to enjoying each other without the fear of conception.

"The first time might be quick," he whispered against her sweet lips.

"I'm okay with quick."

He caught the look of apprehension that crossed her expressive face before it was gone as fast as it had come. "What's wrong?"

"What? Nothing."

"Don't lie to your husband, Madeline. I know you too well."

"It's just… What if we slip one past the goalie, and it's triplets this time or something? And don't say that can't happen with twins and quads in this family in the same year."

Mac smiled as he brushed the hair back from her sweet face. Could she be any cuter? "David assures me that all my pucks are gone, so there's no chance the goalie will miss one."

"I still feel like I'm playing with fire."

"I'm hot, but not that hot."

"It's not funny, Mac! We can't have any more kids."

"I'm not laughing."

"You are on the inside, and don't try to deny it."

"Maybe just a little, but only because you're adorable."

"I'm dead serious."

"I know you are, and we've done everything humanly possible to prevent further conception. Now it's time to go back to enjoying ourselves with no fear of consequences."

"Did you just refer to our children as *consequences*?"

Mac laughed at her indignation as he quickly undressed them both. "They are, in fact, the consequence of this." He was careful as he slid into her, watching as her face flushed with color and her eyes rolled back with pleasure. "Oh, how I've missed this, my love. So, so much."

"Me, too."

For the longest time, he stayed still as he held her close and wallowed in her soft sweetness and the scent that he'd know anywhere as the woman he loved with all his heart.

Her hands slid down his back to cup his ass and pull him deeper into her.

Lord have mercy, the move almost took him right over the edge. He began to move, slowly and carefully since it'd been a while, and the last thing he wanted was to hurt her in any way.

"I'm okay, Mac."

And that she sensed what he was thinking was one more reason to love her madly. She knew him better than anyone ever had.

He pushed up on his arms so he could see her face as he made love to her. Her eyes were closed, her lips parted. "Madeline."

"Hmm?"

"Look at me."

She opened those caramel-colored eyes and smiled.

"I don't want you to forget who you're doing this with."

Rolling her eyes, she said, "As if you'd ever let me forget."

"I can't ever let you forget who loves you more than anything."

She raised her hands to his face. "I never could."

"Thank goodness for that."

Mac picked up the pace until they were both crying out from months' worth of built-up desire and years of love that had only gotten deeper through all the ups and downs they'd experienced together.

Afterward, he rested on top of her, enjoying the slide of her fingers sifting through his hair as her other hand caressed his back.

"Things get so busy with kids and work and life in general that I almost forget how great it is to be just us once in a while," she said. "Thank you for the reminder."

"Since we have amazing grandparents always willing to help out, we'll do it more often going forward. I promise."

"We're going to be sharing half of them with the quads."

"That's okay. We'll still find time for just us, even if we have to have date night at home."

"I'm down for that."

He kissed her neck, her cheek and then her lips. "I'm down for anything that gets me more time alone with you."

"Yes, please."

CHAPTER 27

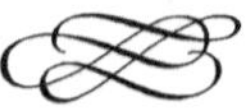

*S*ierra woke to Morgan kissing a trail of fire down her back and taking a bite out of her right cheek. She startled and would've turned to face him, but he held her in place.

"Like this," he said, entering her from behind. "Just like this."

With his hand flat against her belly, he held her in place as he pumped into her, arousing her to the point of madness. Then he moved his hand down to between her legs and coaxed a screaming orgasm from her.

Before him, she wouldn't have thought herself capable of a screaming orgasm, but he'd shown her otherwise.

He kissed the back of her shoulder and continued to stroke between her legs until she was coming again.

Holy. Shit.

"How do you do that?"

"Do what?"

"Make that happen more than once."

"I can't seem to stop touching you, so that might have something to do with it."

"You've turned me into a noodle. I couldn't move if I had to."

"This is a good thing, right?"

"Mmm, the best."

In the past, sex had been transactional. *You get off. I get off. Everyone goes home happy.* This was something else altogether. Something much more intense, profound and exciting. She was quickly becoming addicted to the way he made her feel every time he touched her.

"Do you have clients tomorrow?" he asked after a long silence.

"No, tomorrow's my admin day to order supplies and clean."

"Would that be a good time to examine your wiring, ma'am?"

She laughed. "Sure, if you have time."

"I'll come over after I open the gym."

"Thank you so much. This is almost as exciting as the two orgasms."

"Do I need to improve my technique?"

"Not at all, but this electrical issue has been plaguing me for years. If you can fix it, I'll owe you big."

"Mmm, how will you repay me?"

"I'll think of something."

"I'll work very hard to solve your problem as I look forward to whatever you come up with as my reward."

"I've already got a few ideas that I think you'll like."

"I like all your ideas, especially the one you had in the middle of the night. What a way to wake up."

Sierra's entire body felt overheated at the reminder of what had gone down overnight. *She* had gone down, and he'd whimpered in his sleep until he woke to discover he wasn't dreaming. "You liked that, huh?"

He tightened the arm he had around her and slid his leg between hers. "Oh yeah."

And just like that, she was ready to go again—and so was he.

"We can't keep this up," she said. "We'll be dehydrated."

She loved when he laughed like that—and loved being the one who made it happen.

"What a way to go."

Sierra yawned from the mostly sleepless night and early wakeup. "You need to go open the gym." People started arriving at six a.m., which was in twenty minutes.

"Do you mind if I borrow your shower?"

"Feel free."

He kissed her shoulder again. "Go back to sleep."

"There's a key on the hook by the door with the Patriots keychain that'll get you in when you come back."

"Got it."

The next thing she knew, he was crawling back into bed with her and gathering her into his cold embrace.

Sierra shivered. "You're freezing."

"Coldest day yet out there."

"Let's stay here all day."

"You have stuff to do downstairs, and I'm looking forward to getting my hands on your wiring."

She groaned.

He cupped her backside. "Get this sweet ass out of bed before I have to resort to other tactics."

"What other tactics?"

"I'll never tell. I'm saving them for when I really need them."

"Ah, okay. I'll stay on guard then."

He pinched her ass, making her jolt. "First tactic delivered."

"Knock it off! I'm getting up." She sat on the edge of the bed to stretch.

His arm came around her midsection, and the next thing she knew, she was flat on her back again with him above her.

"What is this tactic called?"

"This one is commonly referred to as 'one more minute in bed won't hurt anything.'"

She turned her face so he couldn't kiss her. "I need to brush my teeth."

"I don't care."

"I do, now get off me and let me up."

"I will, but I want the record to show I didn't want to."

"Duly noted."

He rolled over, putting his impressive erection on full display.

"Does that thing ever get tired?"

"He doesn't like being referred to as a *thing*."

Sierra got up and walked toward the bathroom. Over her shoulder, she said, "That doesn't answer my question."

"He's in a permanent state of readiness when you're around."

"I see how it is."

"Do you?"

Sierra was smiling as she brushed her teeth and hair and washed her face. Then she went to the doorway and struck a pose, her arms over her head. "I do. I see that you have a problem controlling yourself around me."

He got up and crossed the room to hook an arm around her. "You're damned right I do." Then he kissed her thoroughly. "Good morning."

"I thought we already did the good-morning thing."

"I didn't get to kiss you then, so it didn't count."

"You have a lot of rules. Is there a list somewhere?"

"Nah, I make them up as I go."

"This is fun."

"Most fun I've ever had."

"Really?"

"Uh-huh."

"I texted my dad to tell him I'm bringing a friend home for Christmas. He had questions."

"What'd you tell him?"

"I said he'd like you and to not be a dipshit about it."

"You shouldn't talk to your father like that."

"That's the least of what I say to him. We're more like best girlfriends than father and daughter, so it's no-holds-barred."

"I love that." He paused before he said, "Wait, you don't tell him *every-thing*, do you?"

She shrugged and laughed. "That's for me to know and you to find out when you meet him."

"I think I'm busy on Christmas."

"Wimp." She stepped back into the bathroom and closed the door in his face, feeling rather pleased with herself—and with him.

IN PROVIDENCE, panic was setting in as discharge time drew closer. A week after their arrival. Abby simply could not believe they were going to be allowed to leave with four infants to care for on their own. How would they manage without the amazing nurses, many of whom had become like family in the course of the last three months? While there was a different team of nurses working with them now that the babies had arrived, the original group checked in frequently and came to say goodbye on discharge day.

The nurses supervised the bathing of the four babies, each one assigned to a parent or grandmother, and now the boys were dressed in matching navy-blue going-home outfits and buckled into their infant car seats, including the bumpers that Linda had bought to cushion their heads. Abby hadn't even known they'd need them, so how in the world was she going to be allowed to take these precious babies from the safety of the hospital to a remote island?

She felt like she was hyperventilating.

Adam's hands landing on her shoulders startled her. "Why are you tight as a drum, babe?"

"Gee, I wonder."

"Everything is going according to plan. The boys enjoyed their baths, and they're settling in for their first ferry ride."

"Do you hear the wind howling out there? You know what that means, right?"

"I asked my dad to grab some seasickness medication for you."

"You did?"

"You think I don't remember that day on the ferry when you and me became we?"

She melted into his embrace. "You make me feel like I can handle anything, even taking four infants on the ferry to our island."

"You've got this, Mom."

"*We've* got this, Dad."

"You bet we do. Now, how about we go home?"

"You're sure we're ready for this?"

"Hell no, but we'll figure it out one minute at a time."

Abby took a deep breath and released it slowly, searching for the inner calm she'd need to get through the next few hours. The desire to be home, after months away, was the thing that propelled her forward. She couldn't wait to sleep in her own bed, with Adam, and to finally have their five sons together under their own roof.

Five sons.

She wanted to laugh hysterically at the sheer absurdity of it all.

"You ready, hon?" Adam asked, his brows furrowed with concern.

"As ready as I'll ever be, and before I forget to say so, thank you for making all my dreams come true times five, Adam McCarthy."

Smiling, he hugged her tightly. "You're the one who's making dreams come true around here. Thank you for the many sacrifices you made to bring our boys safely into the world. You're a rock star, Abigail McCarthy, and I'm so, so proud of you."

"I'm proud of *us*. I'd never have gotten through it without you and Liam and our family and friends who rallied around us."

"I'm so ready to be home. What do you say we get going?"

Abby took a long look around at the room that'd been home for months and nodded. She still felt apprehensive—who wouldn't, bringing four infants home—but the minute alone with her husband had fortified her for the challenges ahead.

Adam pulled her suitcase as they crossed the hall to the room where the babies had been left in the hands of their grandmothers while Abby packed the last of her belongings.

Big Mac held Liam, who watched the scene with the same apprehension that Abby was feeling. He was probably putting things together to realize the squalling babies were coming home with them, and he wasn't at all happy about it.

"Are we ready, everyone?" Adam asked in a cheerful, upbeat tone that belied the anxiety he was surely feeling, too.

"Let's do this," Linda said as she picked up the carrier that held Beckett, while Abby's dad took Murphy, and Adam carried Kane and Rory.

The nurses and other staff had lined the hallway in a send-off party full of applause and elation for the successful arrival of high-risk quads, and for their parents, who'd become friends over recent months.

Dr. Coleman hugged them both. "I'm just a phone call away if you need anything at all."

"Thank you again for everything. We did it."

"*You* did it, and I couldn't be prouder of what a trouper you were. Go enjoy every minute with your beautiful family."

"That's the plan."

"Call me if you need anything. I mean it."

"I'll miss you."

"I'll miss you, too. I'll be telling the story of my incredible quad mom for years to come."

The next thing Abby knew, they were in the elevator with the babies and Jessica, the nurse accompanying them to the exit. Abby had refused the wheelchair they offered, wanting to walk after having to spend months in bed.

Beckett was a bit fussy, but the others were quiet, taking it all in with big eyes that probably weren't seeing much of anything quite yet. Abby had read about that during the long weeks she'd spent in bed with nothing to do but read everything she could get her hands on about infancy and child development.

But now that the moment was upon her, all the books in the world couldn't have prepared her for the awesome responsibility of taking four babies home to their remote island in the sea.

What had they been thinking, choosing to raise their family in such a place? Before the hysteria could set in once again, Abby reminded herself that she'd been raised on that island, along with her sisters, Adam and his siblings. They were all fine, and these babies would be, too.

Outside, the babies were loaded into Big Mac's truck and Adam's SUV, each with a parent or grandparent assigned to them for the forty-minute ride to the ferry landing.

Adam kissed Abby. "Call if you need to stop."

"You'll be the first to know."

He flashed that irrepressible McCarthy grin. "Let's go home, shall we?"

"Yes, please."

"I'm looking forward to sleeping with you tonight."

"Me, too."

"Let's do this!"

Liam was riding with Abby, Big Mac, Linda, Kane and Rory. No matter how this went, in two hours, they'd be home with their five sons to begin the rest of their lives together.

She was so ready to get this next chapter started.

CHAPTER 28

$\mathcal{A}$dam was worried about rough seas, knowing how much Abby hated being on the ferry when it was rocking and rolling. After pulling away from the hospital, he called Seamus on the Bluetooth to get a weather update.

Seamus picked up on the third ring. "Hey, Big Daddy. How's it going?"

"We're on the way."

"We're ready for you with two spots on the noon boat."

"How bad is it out there?"

"It's sporty but shouldn't be too ugly. I've seen worse."

"That's hardly comforting coming from someone who rode out a *hurricane* on a ferry."

"*That* was truly sporty. This is only kinda."

"How reassuring. My wife hates it when it's rough."

"Most people do, but we'll get you there safely. Don't worry. Looking forward to meeting those wee lads of yours."

"We'll see you in thirty minutes."

"See you then."

"Abby won't be happy out there in this," her dad said.

"I know," Adam said, "especially since she decided not to take the Dramamine because she's pumping."

One of the babies woke up with an outraged squeak a few minutes later, which gave Adam something to think about other than how rough the seas would be. Thankfully, the baby was quickly pacified by his grandmother and settled down before he woke his brother.

As he drove south, with an eye in the mirror to keep Big Mac's truck in sight, Adam was comforted to think that at least their babies hadn't been born on the ferry or in a helicopter, not during a tropical storm with no doctor on the island or any of the other crazy things he'd worried about before Abby was moved to Providence—on a helicopter.

Babies tended to join their family with a bit of drama. In their case, the fact that there were four of them was all the drama they needed.

He called his father, and when he answered, Adam heard babies crying in the background. "I'd ask how it's going over there, but…"

"We're fine," his dad said. "The boys are just making themselves heard."

"I bet Liam is thrilled about that."

"He's had a few choice words for his brothers."

Adam laughed. He hoped Liam would outgrow his disdain for his brothers, but he didn't expect that to happen overnight. After all, the little guy had had him and Abby all to himself for almost two years and now had to share them with four loud, needy brothers.

"How's Abby doing?"

"She's a champ. Nothing to worry about over here."

"Okay, thanks, Dad."

"Welcome, Dad. See you soon."

Adam ended the call, smiling at his father calling him Dad, a title he'd once wondered if he'd ever hold. After all the struggles and heartache, he and Abby had five sons to love and raise and enjoy for the rest of their lives. If they had to withstand some rough seas to get home, so be it.

When they arrived at the ferry landing, Seamus was waiting to show them to a special lane so they could be the last on and the first off the boat when they reached the island. While they waited to board, Adam got out to check on Abby. In the back seat of Big Mac's truck, she was holding Kane and trying to soothe him.

"He's not happy, huh?"

"Not so much."

Linda was comforting Murphy while Big Mac took Liam for a walk to see the fishing boats.

"How are the others?" Abby asked.

"They're good. A few squeaks here and there, but no real outrage so far."

Abby eyed the dark gray sky. "We're almost there."

"One more hour, babe."

Seamus came to tell them they were ready for them.

"Here we go," Adam said, stealing a kiss before he went to back his SUV onto the boat.

Big Mac was right behind him and would be the first vehicle off the ferry when they landed on Gansett.

Adam noticed that the lowest deck was mostly empty, with about a quarter of the vehicles that would've packed it to capacity during the summer months. Only year-rounders were "crazy" enough to be on the ferry this time of year, because they had no choice in the matter.

They unloaded the four baby seats and carried them to the second floor, where they were set on picnic-style tables for the last part of the ride home.

Linda took a photo of the four babies about to embark on the first ferry ride of their lives. "Liam, do you want to be in the picture?"

He shook his head and rested it on Adam's shoulder.

Linda captured that moment and all the others that transpired before the horn sounded to let them know the boat was about to depart. Liam loved that horn and perked up when he heard it.

"Time to go!" he said.

"That's right, buddy," Adam said. "Let's take these babies home."

"Wanna go home."

"Me, too. What are we going to do when we get there?"

"Play!"

"Yay for playing."

"Yay for playing!"

The second they cleared the Point Judith breakwater, the boat began to dip and roll through the high seas.

"Oh my God," Abby said as she clung to the table and one of the baby carriers to keep it from sliding off the table.

It got worse from there.

The babies were moved to the floor so they couldn't fall off the tables, and each had a parent or grandparent holding on tight as they crested one wave after another, only to fall into the deep trench that followed.

Abby was green.

Her mother was a slightly lighter shade.

Liam loved every wild second of it, demanding that Adam put him down to let him "surf" the big waves. He stayed close to the little guy as he laughed with delight at every big wave and the crash of water hitting the windows that came with it.

"Sweet Jesus," Linda said as she held on to a baby with one hand and Big Mac with the other. "This is like the first day I ever came to the island."

"Best day of my life," Big Mac said.

"Once I stopped wanting to puke, that is."

"Abby and I had a similar memorable ride once upon a time. Remember, hon?"

She gave the briefest of nods. "This is worse."

"Forty minutes to go, people," Big Mac said to groans from the rest of the group.

Adam battled his way to the snack bar, where he grabbed some puke bags and brought them back to the group.

Abby grabbed one and held it close to her face.

The babies slept through it all.

"Our boys are made for island life," Adam said to Abby, who barely acknowledged him as she tried not to get sick.

"I see the island," Big Mac said. "Should get better once we're in the lee."

The island would block the worst of the wind, and sure enough, once they cleared the bluffs, the seas were noticeably calmer.

"Anyone want clam chowder?" Adam asked.

"Shut up, Adam!" his wife said.

"What she said," his mother added.

"I'm just asking."

"Good one, son," Big Mac said with a chuckle. He'd never met a rough sea that he didn't thoroughly enjoy.

"Shut up, Mac," Linda said, making the others laugh, including Abby, whose laughter quickly turned to vomit in the bag.

"Damn it," she said as she gagged through a dry heave. "I was holding it in until you fools made me laugh."

That set off more laughter as Adam took the bag from Abby and handed her a new one.

"Not funny Mommy sick," Liam said.

"Not funny at all, buddy," Adam said.

Liam went to his mother and patted her head. "It's okay, Mommy. We almost home. Look."

Abby reached for him and hugged him close. "I can't wait to be home. What's the first thing you want to do?"

"Play trucks."

"Then that's what we'll do."

GRANT AND STEPHANIE, along with Grace and Evan, had been hard at work at Adam and Abby's house for two days, making sure everything was ready for them to bring home the babies.

They'd decided to turn the downstairs guest room and bathroom into a bedroom for Adam and Abby so they could base all operations on the main floor of their two-story home.

"I hope they'll forgive us for this," Stephanie said as she eyed the four bassinets on wheels that the guys had put together, along with the two changing tables that had been moved from the nursery upstairs to the living room.

"They'll be thanking us," Grace said. "It'll be so much easier for them to have everything down here."

Grant checked his watch. "We need to get going to meet the boat."

Grace had summoned the entire family, asking them to be there when the ferry arrived to welcome their new nephews and cousins as well as Adam, Abby and Liam, who'd been away from the island for months.

The four of them took a good look around at the setup they'd labored to put together.

"I think it's perfect," Grace said. "They'll be so thankful."

"That we broke into their house and rearranged everything?" Evan asked.

"Yes, exactly," Grace said. "They didn't know they needed this, but they'll appreciate it."

"I agree," Steph said. "They're all set to maintain first-floor operations for as long as it takes to get the babies into the nursery upstairs, which could take months."

Grace rested her hand on her pregnant belly. "Thank God I'm only having one."

"Same," Steph said. "Four would take me over the edge."

"Abby is the perfect person for this challenge." Grant had dated her for ten years a lifetime ago. "She's had a lot of craziness in her life. What's a little more?"

"Four babies," Evan said with a shudder. "I couldn't do it."

"Of course you could," Grace said. "What choice would you have?"

"You're not trying to tell me something, are you?"

"Relax. Still only one in there."

They rode together in Grant's car to the ferry landing, where they met up with the rest of the family. Laura had brought balloons, and Katie had made a big banner for the kids to hold that said Welcome Home, Liam, Murphy, Rory, Kane and Beckett!

Thomas and Ashleigh took charge of the banner while Hailey and Mac ran in circles around them, full of excitement.

Mallory and Quinn arrived, followed by Riley and Nikki, Finn and Chloe, Kevin, Chelsea and baby Summer, as well as Big Mac's older brother, Frank, and his fiancée, Betsy. Bringing up the rear were Luke and Sydney Harris, with their daughter, Lily.

"Where are Mac and Maddie?" Shane asked.

"Good question," Ned muttered. "Haven't resurfaced from their night away yet." He held baby Emma while Francine had Evie. "Ready to turn these hooligans back over to their parents."

"Stop that, Ned," Francine said. "They were angels. The babies slept all night."

"Don't tell Maddie that," Tiffany said to her mother as she held baby Adrian as Ashleigh and Addie ran around with the other kids. "She'll make you stay there every night."

"My lips are sealed," Francine said with a smirk.

"Here comes the boat!" Thomas said. "I see it!"

Grant took a visual headcount and saw that everyone was there except for Mac and Maddie. He texted his older brother. *Earth to the lovebirds. Are you coming to meet the ferry?*

He hoped the boat got there soon because it was fucking freezing, and he wanted to get Stephanie—and Grace—out of the cold. "Do you want to wait in the car, hon?"

"Hell no," Steph said. "I don't want to miss a second of this."

Her dad, Charlie, arrived with his wife, Sarah. "We didn't want to miss the fun," Charlie said as he hugged Steph like he hadn't seen her in weeks. They never missed a chance to hug each other now that they could any time they wanted after he'd spent fourteen years in prison for a crime he hadn't committed—and she'd spent every minute of that time trying to get him out.

"Hey, hey, hey," Dan Torrington said from behind Grant. "We heard there was a party happening today."

Kara held baby Dylan, who, like Adrian, was bundled to within an inch of her life in a snowsuit. "I told him it was too cold to take her out, but he said it's only for a few minutes, and I so want to see those babies."

"I hear you, Mama," Tiffany said. "I couldn't miss this either. Adrian promised me he'd be fine if we came."

"Funny that Dylan promised me the same thing," Kara said. "How're you feeling?"

"Like I got run over, but so happy he's here. His daddy is over the moon to have a little testosterone to offset all the estrogen in our house."

"That's right," Blaine said as he slipped an arm around his wife from behind.

"Oh, you made it," Tiffany said to him.

"Just in time."

"How about you?" Tiffany asked Kara.

"Same—like I got hit by a bus, but I'm elated to have her here finally."

"I love that our babies will grow up together," Tiffany said.

"*All* our babies," Stephanie said.

"That's right," Kara said. "More coming soon."

"Who else is thankful to be having them one at a time?" Stephanie asked as the others laughed.

"Me, too," Tiffany said.

"Me, three," Grace said.

"Me, four," Katie said with a smile for her husband, Shane.

"Wait, what?" the others said as one.

"Are you holding out on me, little brother?" Laura asked.

"Yep," Shane said. "We're pregnant and almost through the first trimester." He held up crossed fingers. "We're hoping for the best this time." Katie had suffered a miscarriage with her first pregnancy.

The others swarmed around them, offering hugs and congratulations.

"Today is not about us," Katie said. "It's about the quads."

"It's about all of us," Grant said. "The whole damned family."

"Yer derned right about that," Ned said.

When the ferry cleared the South Harbor breakwater, Captain Seamus gave the horn four long blows to herald the arrival of the quadruplets.

Mac and Maddie ran up to the group just as the ferry backed up to the pier.

"Nice of you to join us, bro," Grant said.

"We overslept," Mac replied, using his thumb to point at Maddie. "She kept me up half the night."

Maddie punched his arm. "Shut your mouth, or it'll never happen again."

The other guys lost it laughing.

"He never learns." Ned shook his head as he grinned. "Yer daddy needs ta take ya out ta the woodshed."

"I'm incorrigible," Mac said with a grin for his wife.

Maddie rolled her eyes as she and Mac were mobbed by their children, who'd just noticed their arrival.

"Mommy, Thomas wouldn't go to bed last night," Hailey said.

"That's not true!" Thomas said, sputtering. "I went to bed. Eventually."

"Hailey, don't be a tattletale." Mac picked up his little girl while Maddie hugged Thomas and little Mac. "The other kids won't appreciate that."

"But it's true. You told me not to lie."

"That's right, I did. But it's not a lie to *not* tell us what Thomas didn't do."

Her cute little face twisted into a confused expression as she tried to make sense of that.

"How did our little ladies do overnight?" Maddie asked her parents.

They exchanged a guilty glance that said it all.

"If you tell me they slept through the night, I'm never coming home again."

"No, Mommy!" Mac said. "Come home!"

"I will, honey. Mommy is just kidding."

"We won't tell ya they slept through the night, then," Ned said.

"I don't believe this," Maddie said. "All I had to do was leave for the night?"

"Or we gots the magic touch," Ned said, smiling as he cuddled the sleeping Emma.

Not even the loud horn from the ferry could wake those two girls when they were asleep. Mac had told Grant that it was because they'd been listening to noise since before they were born.

Adrian and Dylan weren't at all happy about the horn, however.

"The new babies are coming home to the chaos they'll grow up in," Grant said as Big Mac drove his truck off the ferry, tooting the horn as he went.

Adam was right behind him, also on the horn.

The older kids were out of their minds with excitement as the two vehicles parked and were swarmed by family members and friends, straining for a look at the new arrivals.

"Oh my gosh," Stephanie said as she hugged Abby. "Look at those little faces."

"They're so cute!" Grace said from the other side of Big Mac's truck. "How'd they do on the boat?"

"Better than I did. Adam made me puke."

"That's not true." Adam handed Liam to Grace, who was one of his favorite people. "She always pukes when it's rough."

"Let's get these boys home," Big Mac said.

"Can we come?" Grant asked his brother.

"We'd be bummed if you didn't, right, Abs?"

"Absolutely. Everyone is welcome as long as you're willing to change diapers. We need all the help we can get."

"Let's roll, citizens," Mac said. "We've got diapers to change!"

Grant laughed as he held hands with his wife and followed his older brother to their vehicles for the ride to Adam and Abby's house.

This might go down as one of his top ten best days on Gansett Island, the day they welcomed home four new McCarthy boys. He just hoped they grew up to be more like him than Mac.

CHAPTER 29

$\mathcal{W}$inter was Alex Martinez's favorite time of year. Other than opening the shop for a few hours each day to sell Christmas trees, they were off until the spring after being straight-out from April through November. He loved nothing more than lolling about in bed with his wife, Jenny, until their son, George, woke up to start their day.

George was a great sleeper, and sometimes he made it as late as nine a.m.

Alex brought coffee to Jenny in bed. "He's still asleep."

"I wonder if his brother will be as good of a sleeper."

"I sure as hell hope so, because I love my mornings in bed with Mommy."

He handed her coffee to her and brought his own with him when he got back in bed. "Cheers to winter," he said, raising his mug to her.

"Cheers to winter, which is something I never thought I'd say as a girl of the summer all my life until Alex Martinez made me love winter."

"Alex Martinez made you love a lot of things," he said with a dirty grin.

"And he's a little full of himself this morning, I see."

"He's always full of himself, which you knew before you shackled yourself to him for life."

"Can he quit talking about himself in the third person?"

"Why would he do that when you like it so much?"

"When did I ever say I liked it?"

"He thought you did."

"Stop!"

Alex laughed and put his mug on the table so he could snuggle up to her. Even after waking her with slow morning lovemaking, he still wanted to be as close to her as he could get, like always. He'd never gotten over his complete obsession with all things Jenny Wilks Martinez, love of his life and mother of his children.

"What're you up to, Martinez?" Jenny asked as he ran his hand over her naked body, cresting the hill of her pregnant belly and heading south. "Don't make me spill my coffee."

"Then you'd better stay very still."

"Alex!"

He was laughing when his phone rang, turning his laugh to a groan. Turning back toward his side of the bed, he took the call from his brother, Paul.

"What?"

"The care home just called. They think Mom has had a stroke. She's being transported to the clinic."

"Oh shit. Okay. I'll meet you there."

"What's wrong?" Jenny asked.

Alex got out of bed and ran for the closet. "They think my mom had a stroke."

"Oh no. I'm so sorry, Alex." She got up, put on a robe and was tying it closed when he emerged from his closet after pulling on jeans and a Henley and jamming his feet into boots.

He let her hug him for a full minute, drawing strength from her the way he did any time things went sideways—and they'd gone sideways with his mom a lot over the years. "Is it terrible to hope that maybe this is it? That her suffering—and ours—might end?"

"It's not terrible. It'd be merciful at this point."

Dementia had been a ruthless bitch. His mother hadn't recognized him or Paul in years, but she still called Paul's stepson, Ethan, and her friend Daisy Lawrence by name any time she saw them.

"Do you want me to come with you? I can get George up real quick."

"Nah, let him sleep. I'll call you as soon as I know anything."

Jenny kissed him. "I love you. I'm sorry this is happening."

"Love you, too. Thanks."

"Drive carefully. Please."

"I will. Don't worry."

"Right."

After withstanding the tragic loss of her fiancé Toby, she'd always worry. And because he didn't want her to suffer, he checked in with her every chance he got.

Alex drove too fast on icy island roads on the way to the clinic, his mind racing with scenarios as he tried to prepare himself for what was waiting for him when he arrived. He pulled into the parking lot just as his brother ran for the main entrance.

He followed Paul inside a minute later.

Dr. Quinn James and his nurse wife, Mallory, who served as the medical directors for the senior care facility, were updating Paul when Alex joined them.

"We believe she's suffered a severe stroke," Quinn said for Alex's benefit. "David is with her, and we'll need to thoroughly evaluate her to get a definitive diagnosis. We'll let you know as soon as we know more."

"Thank you," Paul said for both of them as he ran a hand through his hair, trying to bring order to it. He looked as if he'd run out of the house before bothering to comb it.

Alex hugged him, and then they took seats in the waiting room. They were like the survivors of a disaster, only theirs had taken years to unfold, slowly at first and then so quickly, they'd barely had time to react before more was lost.

People referred to dementia as the long goodbye, and truer words had never been spoken.

"What're you thinking?" Paul asked after a long silence.

"That part of me hopes this is it, because her quality of life is nonexistent."

"Yeah, me, too."

"The other part of me feels disgusted with myself for even thinking such a thing."

"I get it. Believe me. In her right mind, she'd never want to live like this."

"We've said that for years now." He glanced at his brother. "Did you remind them about the advance directive?"

"No, but they're aware. They won't do anything crazy to save her."

Alex sent a text to Jenny to update her on what he knew so far, which wasn't much.

George and I are praying for you and Marion, Jenny replied. *Do you want me to reach out to Daisy?*

Yes, please. Tell her to feel free to come here if she wants to.

I will.

Thanks for thinking of that.

"Jenny is going to text Daisy and tell her to come if she wants to."

"Oh, good thinking."

Do you want us to come? Jenny asked.

Let me hear what they have to say first, and I'll let you know.

OK, we'll get ready just in case.

"Hope is asking if they should come."

"I told Jenny to hold off until we hear more."

"Yeah, good call."

They waited an hour before Mallory came out to talk to them. "David and Quinn are with her and have confirmed she suffered a severe stroke. Without more extensive testing, we can't be a hundred percent certain, but we know you wouldn't want to put her through that."

"No," Alex said, his voice barely more than a whisper. "So is she dying, then?"

"We believe she'll pass in an hour or two unless we provide life support."

Paul was shaking his head before she finished saying the words. "No to life support. She's suffered enough."

"I agree. If there's anyone who should be here with you, now would be a good time to call them."

"Thank you for everything," Alex said. "You and Quinn and the staff at the home have been a godsend to us."

"We love your mom and your family very much. We'll miss her."

Alex's eyes flooded with tears. How could he be so fucking sad over something he'd hoped would happen for years now?

"I just want to add… No mother could ask for more from her sons than what Marion has gotten from you guys. If she knew the full story, she'd be very, very proud."

"Thank you," Paul said as he wiped away tears. "That means a lot to us. We wanted to make her—and our dad—proud."

"You've done that a million times over. If you want to sit with her, you can come back with me."

Alex looked at Paul, who nodded. "We'd like that. Let us just text our wives to tell them to come in with the kids."

After they sent the texts, they followed Mallory to the exam room, where their mother was hooked to monitors as she seemed to sleep peacefully, her chest rising and falling like usual, but he noticed her breaths were spaced out more now. Each of them took hold of one of her hands.

"You can talk to her," Quinn said. "She might still be able to hear you."

"It's Alex, and Paul is with me, Mom. We're here, and we love you. If you're ready to go see Dad, we understand."

"You must be so tired after everything you've been through," Paul added. "It's okay to go now if you're ready."

They shared old family memories and updated her on what was going on with the business she'd founded with her husband, George.

"Martinez Lawn and Garden is in good hands with us, Mom," Paul said. "We hired McKenzie to keep the books the way you used to. She's told us a bunch of times how meticulous your books were. No one can ever take your place, but we think you'd be happy with how things are going."

"We're almost sold out of Christmas trees," Alex said, "and soon we'll close for the long winter's nap. Remember how much you and Dad used to look forward to that? Now we do, too."

"We're going to take the kids to Disney this winter," Paul told her. "We're going together before have the new babies in the spring. You'll have five grandchildren soon, Mom. Can you believe it?"

Hope and Ethan arrived a few minutes later with baby Scarlett, who was handed off to her daddy so they could give kisses to Marion. Paul had met Hope, who was a nurse, when she'd come to the island with her son, Ethan, to help take care of Marion.

Jenny and George arrived fifteen minutes later.

Alex wondered if they were doing the right thing letting him see his grandmother on her deathbed, but the little guy needed closure, too.

"Grandma sick," George said as Alex held his lookalike son.

"Yes, she is, and she's going to go to heaven to be with Grandpa George. That will make her so happy to be with him again."

"But we miss her."

"We sure will."

Normally, George would be trying to break free to run around, but he put his head on Alex's shoulder, as if he knew his daddy needed his love and comfort.

Daisy came rushing in a few minutes later, seeming relieved to have arrived in time. They made room for her to come in and kiss Marion and whisper some final words to the woman who'd become her friend when she'd ended up on Daisy's porch in town after she wandered off.

After she had the chance to see Marion, Daisy hugged her husband, David, while she cried softly, and he did his best to comfort her.

All the people Marion loved best were by her side when she took her last breath at two fifteen that afternoon.

"She's with Dad now," Paul said through his tears.

"They're having one hell of a reunion." Alex couldn't believe how heartbroken he felt to realize they were both gone.

Jenny was right there to provide love and comfort while Mallory and Victoria entertained George and Scarlett in the room next door.

"Grandma was ready to go," Ethan said as he stared at Marion. "She told me she was ready."

"When?" Alex asked.

"Last week. She said it was time."

Alex would never get over the way Marion had taken to Hope's son. Their bond had been immediate and deep. Long after she stopped speaking to anyone else, she still had something to say to Ethan any time she saw him.

"She loved you very much," Paul said.

"I loved her, too. I'll miss her." He glanced at Paul, who was now his dad. "She's the reason we're here, that we're part of this family and get to live on Gansett."

Alex had noticed that his nephew had gotten taller in recent months, and his voice was starting to get deeper. "We'll always be thankful for the joy you brought to her final years."

"I won't forget her," Ethan said, his chin quivering as his parents hugged him.

"We'll take care of calling the funeral home on the mainland," David said. "They'll be in touch with you about arrangements."

"Thank you all for everything," Paul said. "I know I speak for my brother when I say we never would've survived these challenging years without all of you. David, for your never-ending care and compassion as Mom's condition came on. Mallory and Quinn, for making her final years so peaceful and for helping us to keep her close to home."

When Paul became choked up, Alex took over for him. "Daisy, for your unwavering friendship to Mom and to us. Hope, Ethan, Jenny, George and Scarlett, for all the love and support, for helping us to focus on the joy you all bring to our lives, and Jenny, for helping us so much at work. Thank you all. We're incredibly grateful to you guys."

Jenny hugged him, and Alex held on to her, the love of his life, the woman who'd saved him from the utter despair of his mother's rapid decline with her unwavering love and devotion.

"Let's go home." Jenny took his hand to lead the way, and with a backward glance at his mother, he followed his wife from the room.

"Marion Martinez has passed away," Jared told Lizzie when he sat next to her at the kitchen table while Violet napped.

"I'm sorry to hear that. People say such nice things about her. How are the guys doing?"

"Okay, from what I hear. I'm sure there's a bit of relief after the long illness."

"Yes, for sure."

He put his hand over hers and was shocked by how cold she was. "You're freezing."

"Can't seem to get warm."

"Come with me."

"That's okay. I'm fine."

"Come." He helped her up and led her to their room, tucking her into bed and then getting in next to her to wrap himself around her. "I can't bear to see you suffering like this."

"I can't breathe, Jared."

"I know, honey. I can't either. We just have to get through tomorrow, and hopefully that'll be it." Violet's biological father was coming to meet her. That was all they knew about his planned visit, and not knowing his intentions was sucking the life out of them.

"What if it isn't the end of it?"

"We're taking this one step at a time. If we try to speculate on all the scenarios, we'll lose what's left of our minds. Dan and Kendall are confident something can be worked out. Perhaps he'll ask for visitation once or twice a year, which would be no problem to accommodate."

"What if he wants full custody?"

"We'll fight him."

"On what grounds?"

"That she's bonded to us after living with us for all this time, and he'd do irreparable harm to her if he tried to uproot her life at this juncture. We have rights in this, Lizzie. Don't think we don't."

"He has more rights as the biological father who didn't even know about her until recently."

"If a judge is considering Violet's best interests, he or she will see that we have her best interests at heart."

"I can't even allow myself to get to the point that a judge could be involved." She shuddered at the thought of a protracted fight. "I can't bear this. Any of it. I used to think I was a strong person, but I'm not."

"Yes, you are. You're the strongest person I know, and together, we'll fight for our girl. Don't give up, Lizzie. I need you to stay in the ring with me."

"I'm here, but I'm hobbled."

"One more day and we'll know what we're up against. Let's just keep breathing until then, okay?"

"I'm trying."

CHAPTER 30

*A*bby couldn't believe what Grace, Evan, Grant and Stephanie had done for them. Everything was organized and ready for four infants, all on the main floor. Changing tables put together, rolling bassinets set to go and what seemed like a year's worth of supplies stacked on shelves that had once housed books that had been packed away for now.

They'd even thought of Liam, with new toys from Abby's shop to give him something to focus on while everyone else fawned over his new baby brothers.

"You guys," Abby said tearfully. "This is amazing."

"Hope you don't mind that we made some executive decisions for you," Grace said.

"I don't mind at all. This is just what I didn't know I needed." She hugged her sisters-in-law, who were also among her best friends.

"Laura consulted," Grace said, "since we have zero experience with babies, and she's had multiples."

"You did a fabulous job," Laura said from the kitchen, where she was making coffee and setting out some of the food that had been dropped off for the new family.

"This is awesome," Adam said as he eyed the spread on the kitchen table. "We need to have quads more often."

"Don't even say that out loud, Adam McCarthy," Abby said while the others laughed. "It's not funny."

"It's kinda funny," Mac said.

Abby glared at her brother-in-law.

"Sorry, Abby," Maddie said. "I'll get him out of your hair." Maddie hugged her. "Let me know what I can do to help."

"You've got your own hands full, Mama. Hopefully, we'll be having cousin playdates before too long."

"I can't wait for every minute with those boys. Congratulations. You're a stud, woman!"

"At least they weren't born on a helicopter," Mac said when he hugged her.

"There is that," Abby conceded, amused by him as usual.

"Can we talk about my super sperm some more?" Adam asked his brother. "And how I topped you by two whole babies?"

"Can we talk about how that super sperm isn't getting anywhere near me until that thing is snipped?" Abby retorted.

The others howled with laughter.

"I'm sorry, girls," Linda said to her daughters-in-law. "They weren't raised this way."

"Weren't we?" Mac asked.

"No, you were not! Did you ever once hear your father talk about his super sperm?"

"Did he ever once father four babies at once?" Adam asked.

"He's got you there, Mom," Evan said.

"This family is ridiculous," Linda said.

"You're just realizing that now?" Maddie asked.

"No, I've known it for quite some time, but the first time one of my grandsons starts talking about his super sperm will be the day I quit you all," Linda said.

"You can't quit us, Voodoo Mama," Grant said.

"Watch me."

Four babies awaking all at once, demanding to be changed and fed, redirected everyone's attention, thankfully.

Abby had heard more than enough about super sperm to last the rest of her life.

· · ·

WHEN THEY LEFT Adam and Abby's, Mac drove his family home in the big SUV he'd bought when he and Maddie were first together, not realizing he'd one day need every seat in the vehicle for their family.

He helped her get the kids inside and supervised lunch for the older three while Maddie tended to the babies. "I'm heading to work for a few hours and then meeting Morgan for a beer around five. I'll be home by six at the latest, and I'll bring something for dinner."

"That sounds good. Thanks."

Mac bent over the back of the sofa to kiss her. "Thank you. Last night was amazing. Just what we needed."

"Thanks for planning it and executing our escape."

"We'll do it again soon. Love you."

"Love you, too. Have a good day at the office."

"I'd rather be here with you guys."

"We know."

"Daddy stay home!" Mac said as he ran after his dad.

Mac scooped him up and swung him around, making the little guy laugh. "Be a good boy for Mommy today, and we'll wrestle when I get home, okay?"

"Okay."

Mac set him down to toddle off to find Thomas and Hailey.

"Go while you can," Maddie said, smiling.

"I'm out."

As he drove into town, Mac reflected on his many blessings, which began with his wife and children and included his still-active, healthy parents and uncles as well as his siblings, cousins, their spouses and children. The McCarthy family was rapidly expanding, and in a few short years, their kids would be running roughshod over their parents.

Mac couldn't wait for all of it and to get to know his four new nephews as well as Adrian, Dylan and the children Evan and Grant would soon welcome to the family with their wives.

To think, not that long ago, he'd had no plans to relocate to Gansett Island, and here he was now, running two businesses, surrounded by his entire extended family and countless friends. Life was good and getting better all the time.

He stopped at the marina to check on a project his business partner,

Luke Harris, was overseeing—the installation of new washers and dryers for summer guest use.

"How goes it?" he asked Luke when he stepped out of the blustery cold into a slightly warmer space where Luke was working.

"It's going. These things are bulky and awkward to move around, but I've got two more to go."

"Thanks for handling it."

"No problem. Fun to see the new babies this morning. They're cuties."

"Of course they are. They're McCarthy boys."

"Do you ever get tired of the sound of your own voice?"

Mac pretended to think about that for a second. "Nope. Not really."

Luke laughed. "Why'd I even ask? What's up with you today?"

"Since it's already almost two, I'm going to the office for a few hours to do some estimates and other paperwork, and then Grant and I are meeting Morgan Weyland for a beer at the Beachcomber at five. He wants to talk to us about island life as an adult when, like him, we couldn't wait to get the hell out of here. You should come if you want."

"Maybe I will. I'll see what's up at home. So is Morgan thinking about staying?"

"I think he might be."

"That'd be cool. I always liked him. It's been nice having him around again, even if I hate the reason."

"Same. All right, carry on, pal. I'll see you at five, I hope."

"I'll try to get there."

"Sounds good."

Mac zipped his coat against the frigid blast of air coming from the Salt Pond, which was frothy with whitecaps. In the summer, the pond was so packed with boats, you could barely see the other side. Now, there wasn't a single boat to be found. Mac looked forward to this time of year, when the marina was all but shut down and he could focus on the construction business.

He worked hard all fall to get projects to the point where he and his guys could work inside during the coldest part of the winter. They had several renovations going and were finishing the inside of the wedding facility at the alpaca farm this winter.

Back in his truck, he read a text to their family group chat from Grant. *Marion Martinez passed away.*

"Aw, shit," Mac said as he sent a text to Alex and Paul. *So sorry to hear about your mom. She was a great lady who was always so much fun to be around. Let us know if there's anything we can do for you.*

He sent another text to Grant and Morgan, confirming their five o'clock meeting.

Looking forward to it, Morgan replied.

Same, Grant said.

Me, too. Invited Luke Harris to join us.

Great, Morgan said. *See you then.*

MORGAN STASHED his phone in the back pocket of his jeans and opened the electric panel that powered Sierra's studio and her apartment upstairs. As he worked, he had to stifle a yawn, realizing he was getting far too old for a mostly sleepless night. Not that it hadn't been worth every second of lost sleep. It'd been more than worth it.

Sierra was everything he'd spent his adult life looking for without even knowing it. She was fun, funny, smart, witty, sexy as fuck and easy to talk to. If he wasn't careful, he might fall in love with her.

Would that be so terrible?

Not at all, but her whole life was here, and so he needed to figure out if he could handle living on the island full time. He looked forward to hearing what Mac and the others had to say about making the transition to full-time island life.

He quickly determined that Sierra's building needed to be completely rewired because everything about her panel and setup was outdated and out of current code. She was lucky she hadn't had a fire.

When he went to find her, he followed the sound of her voice to the lobby, where she was on the phone with one of her suppliers, placing an order.

She smiled at him. "Nope. That's everything. Thank you." After she ended the call, she made a check on her list. "I'm getting it done today. How's it going back there?"

"I have good news and bad news. Which do you want first?"

"Give me the good."

"Your building hasn't burned down."

"Jeez. If that's the good news, what's the bad?"

"You need a complete rewiring with all-new circuit breakers."

Her throat bobbed when she swallowed hard. "How much will that cost?"

"About five thousand for materials. Labor is free."

She winced. "You have to let me pay you something!"

"Nah, I don't need it, and I love jobs like this. I'm happy to take care of it for you."

She stood to hug him. "Thank you." Pulling back, she looked up at him but kept her arms around his neck. "So it's bad, huh?"

"Really bad. Needs to be done ASAP. I'll order the stuff today."

"I don't have five grand just sitting around, so can I give you a credit card to put it on?"

"Sure. I assume you want me to expedite delivery due to the afore-mentioned fire risk?"

"Yes, please."

"Will do."

She handed him her credit card, and he sat at one of the chairs in her lobby to order what he needed to rewire her building. Twenty minutes later, he said, "I used my company discount and got it all for forty-four hundred. Will be delivered early next week."

"Excellent. Thank you. Can I give you that long-promised massage in exchange for you saving my business and home from a future fire?"

He gave her a sexy side-eyed look. "Would I be required to get naked?"

"Absolutely."

"Would you?"

"Absolutely *not*. I'm a professional." She nudged him backward toward one of the rooms. "Everything off. Put your things on that chair or hang them on the hook." She pointed to the O-shaped pillow at the head of the bed. "We'll start facedown."

"Got it."

"Be back in a few."

"I'll be here."

Sierra went into the break room to add some ice to her water bottle, preparing for the most meaningful massage of her career for the man she was quickly falling in love with. She couldn't deny the feelings were big and overwhelming and getting more so with every minute she spent with him.

When he was around, the air cracked with potential and electricity—no pun intended in light of her current predicament. Ugh, forty-four hundred dollars. That was a big hit, but at least she didn't have to pay labor.

She knocked on the door to his room. "Ready?"

"Yep."

When she walked in to him bare-ass naked on her table, she laughed. "Most people get under the covers."

He raised his head to look at her. "I'm not most people, and it's nothing you haven't already seen."

"That's true." Was it hot in there, or was it him? It was definitely him. She rubbed some lavender oil on her hands and held it beneath the pillow. "Take a couple of deep breaths."

"Smells good."

"That's the idea."

She took her sweet time as she worked on his shoulders, back and arms, for once not paying attention to the clock. Time ceased to exist as she kneaded knots until they released their hold on him.

"Feels so good, babe."

"Glad to hear it."

His hand hooked around her leg and slid up to cup her ass.

"No molesting the masseuse."

"Why not?"

"It's not allowed."

"I want my money back."

"Haha."

He continued to squeeze and shape her ass while she moved down to do the same to his. "If you keep that up, things are going to happen."

"This is a place of business, Mr. Weyland. Your behavior could get you banned for life."

He turned so he was face up, which was when she noticed he was hard. "What a way to go." Somehow, he managed to lift her so she was on the table with him.

She let out a huff of protest. "I'm not finished with your treatment, sir."

"I can't take having your hands all over me and not being able to touch you, too. If you want me to relax, I need your help." He nuzzled her neck and nibbled on her earlobe as he eased her top up and over her head. "Have you ever done it on a massage table?"

"Of course I haven't. I'm a licensed professional, Mr. Weyland."

"I love when you scold me. It's hot as fuck." He arranged her so she straddled him and sat up to release the clasp on her bra. "Tell me to stop if this is messing with your feng shui or whatever."

Amused, she said, "I'm surprised you know what that is."

"I know stuff."

"You're exceptionally good at removing female clothing. You must've had a lot of practice."

He shrugged as he tucked a strand of hair behind her ear. "None of that matters now that you're here. It was all preparing me for you."

"You think so?"

"I know so." With his hands on her face, he kissed her with the kind of wild passion she'd heard about but never fully experienced until he came along to show her what she'd been missing. "Can this table hold us both?"

"We're going to find out."

"What's the over-under?"

"It's good for up to six hundred pounds, so we should be okay."

"Good to know." He moved smoothly to put her under him and tugged at the button to her jeans, peeling them off along with her panties. With his feet on the floor, he buried his face between her legs, sliding his fingers into her and taking her right to the precipice of release before backing off and doing it again.

As she looked up at the ceiling she'd painted herself with stars and moons and planets to give her clients something fun to look at, she couldn't believe this was happening in one of her treatment rooms. How would she ever step foot in that room again and not think of the sight of his dark head between her legs as he brought her to a screaming orgasm?

He slid her to the edge and pushed into her as he leaned over to tug her nipple into his mouth.

Sierra wrapped her legs around his back and buried a hand in his hair as she held on for the wild ride. On her massage table. If she had an ounce of sense left, she might find that ridiculously funny and slightly scandalous. But at the moment, she couldn't find the wherewithal to care about anything other than the divine way he made her feel.

Once again, he made her scream as she came so hard, she saw stars.

And then she froze when she heard something outside the door.

"Sierra! Sierra!"

Oh my God, it's Duke.

"Let me up. Quick." She had time to put an arm across her breasts before Duke burst into the room, looking panicked.

"One of the guys heard you scream. I… uh… Okay, then." His face bright red with embarrassment, he backed out, closing the door.

Behind her, Morgan rocked with silent laughter.

"It's not funny!"

"Yes, it is."

"It's not! Poor Duke." She grabbed a robe she kept behind the door for clients and ran after her friend. "Duke, wait!"

"Sorry to barge in on ya," Duke said without turning back. "Was worried about you."

"I know, and I'm sorry. I didn't mean to scare you."

"Didn't know what to think when the guys heard screaming."

His building and hers shared a common wall, which she'd forgotten while she'd screamed her head off.

"Thank you for checking on me."

"No problem. You'll understand if I can never make eye contact again with either of you."

Smiling, Sierra took his arm and made him turn around. "There," she said when he looked at her. "Was that so hard?"

"It was very, very hard."

She laughed. "I guess now we're even. We've both barged in on each other at inopportune times."

Morgan strolled out of the room, wearing only jeans that were unbuttoned. "Is he still speaking to us?"

"Barely."

"Thank you for checking on Sierra when you thought something was wrong," Morgan said as he put his arm around her. "That makes you a very good friend to both of us."

Duke was so cute when he blushed and totally ruined his bad-boy vibe. "Sounds like things are going well between you two. Glad to never hear it again."

With that, Duke departed, and Sierra buried her face in Morgan's chest. "Mortifying."

"He's going to tell his guys he saved you from a thorough fucking."

Sierra shrieked. "*Stop!* He'd better not tell them that."

"You know he's gonna."

Moaning, she said, "I'll never be able to go over there for free candy again."

He hugged her. "Aw, poor baby. I'll get you all the candy you can eat."

Sierra started to laugh and couldn't stop. She laughed so hard, she would've peed her pants had she been wearing them.

"I'm never going to hear the end of this," she said when she finally caught her breath.

"Neither of us will, so what do you say we go finish what we started, minus the screaming this time?"

"I think we've had enough for now, don't you?"

He surprised her when he lifted her off her feet to carry her back to the room. "I have a feeling I'm never going to get enough of you."

CHAPTER 31

"**I** know it's not what you wanted, sweetheart, but it's what makes sense right now with three little kids to drive around," Blaine said as he showed Tiffany the ugly SUV he wanted to buy to "replace" her precious red Volkswagen Bug that had been squished by a tree during the hurricane. Oh, how she'd loved that car!

He was right, of course. They needed a bigger family vehicle, but not the one he was showing her. "I can't with that. It's ugly."

"It's functional and has an excellent safety rating, which is the most important thing."

"Functional. Such a sexy word."

"Since when are cars sexy?"

"My Bug was!"

"Can we agree that we can't put five of us—including two car seats and a booster—in the Bug?"

"I suppose," she said with a pout. She felt like a spoiled brat but couldn't muster an ounce of enthusiasm for the vehicle he'd shown her.

"Reminder that we were going to need something bigger even if the Bug hadn't gotten squished, so why can't we put the insurance money for the Bug toward this one?"

"I don't like it. What're my options?"

He went to get his iPad and called up the dealer site where he'd found the first one and scrolled through the available choices. Black. Gray. Light gray. Silver. White. Boring.

"Anything?" he asked with the patience of a saint.

She shook her head. "Can we look somewhere else?"

"What is it that you've got in mind that's not the size of the Bug?"

"Something fun and sexy and red."

"Fun, sexy and red. Okay, got it. I'll keep looking."

"Sorry to be difficult."

"It's okay. I'm used to you by now."

She sputtered with outrage that made him laugh.

He kissed her. "You've been trying me since the day we met and every day since. Why should today be any different?"

"Are you going to get sick of me someday?"

"God no, sweetheart. I'd be lost without you. And PS, you know you never need to worry about that with me."

She rested her head on his shoulder. "I know."

He took her hand and laced his fingers with hers. "Do you really? Do you know how hard it is for me to go to work every day when I'd much rather be here with you and our kids? Do you know how much I think about you when I'm not with you, how the scent of strawberries makes me hard, regardless of where I am, and how I'm so happy to have you driving me crazy every day of my life?"

She sniffed as tears spilled down her cheeks.

"Are you crying?"

"Postpartum hormones. Nothing to see here."

"You know how I feel about girl tears."

"I'm very sorry, but you have your own sweetness to blame."

"I don't want you to spend one second worrying that I might do to you what he did, because I could never, ever, ever live without you."

Her now-late ex-husband, Jim, had shattered her by suddenly leaving their marriage for reasons that had taken her years to fully understand. Even now, she sometimes still thought about that time and tried to see warning signs that hadn't been there.

"I'm sorry to still be weird about that even after all this time, when you've given me no reason at all to be insecure."

"It's okay. I get it. When it happens once, why wouldn't it happen again? Any time you feel worried, you let me know, and I'll remind you of how obsessed I am with you."

A tiny squeak came from Adrian's bassinet.

"I'll get him," Blaine said. "Hey, little man, how was your nap?" The rapturous look on his handsome face as he picked up his son made Tiffany fall in love with him all over again. "Did you have some sweet dreams?" Blaine put him on the changing table and unsnapped the sleeper to get to his diaper.

"Don't forget—"

"Oh shit, he nailed me." Blaine grinned as baby pee ran down his face. "You were saying?"

"Don't forget to cover the package."

Blaine used a towel to wipe his face. "Did you just pee on your daddy?" he asked as he nibbled playfully on baby toes. "I don't think he's one bit sorry."

"The things babies get away with before they're old enough to know better is legendary. Ashleigh once loudly loaded her diaper while she was sitting on my mother's lap."

"That must've been funny."

"We laughed about it for months."

Blaine handed the baby to her for feeding and then sat next to her to watch. "I never get tired of seeing you feeding our babies. You're never more beautiful than you are in Mom mode."

"Even when I'm huge?"

"You're not huge. You just gave birth to our son. Be nice to my wife. She's the most precious thing in the world to me."

"He's so handsome, like his daddy."

"He looks like you."

"No way. He's all you. Even your mom says so. She says he looks just like you did as a baby."

"Poor guy."

"Oh hush. His daddy is the sexiest man alive."

Blaine snorted with laughter. "Whatever you say, babe."

The next day, Kendall arrived at Jared and Lizzie's at eight thirty, a half hour before Violet's father was due to arrive with his attorney on the eight o'clock boat from the mainland.

She'd done a deep dive on Brooks Ward online and found him to be an accomplished student, a star lacrosse and soccer player and a well-regarded colleague and friend. In short, there was nothing about him not to like—at least on paper, that was. She was reserving judgment until she met the man in person.

Jared and Lizzie moved like survivors of an apocalypse or something, going through the motions of coffee and breakfast for Violet, who was thankfully unaware of the drama playing out around her. She banged her spoon on her high-chair tray, laughing at the sound it made as her parents watched with none of the usual delight for everything she did, as if they were already preparing themselves to have her ripped from their lives.

That couldn't happen.

She was surprised when Dan Torrington walked in, looking every bit the part of one of the most successful attorneys in the country. Dan knew she could handle this meeting, but he also understood that his presence would be intimidating to opposing counsel.

"Thanks for coming," she said when he sat next to her at Jared's table.

"No problem. How're they doing?"

"Terrible."

"Thanks for being here, Dan," Jared said in a dull, flat tone. He had purple circles under his eyes and looked as tired as Kendall had ever seen him. "How's the baby?"

"She's great."

Lizzie sat on the edge of her seat, as if she was afraid to get too comfortable even in her own home. "And Kara?"

"She's feeling much better and settling into a routine of sorts with the baby. I understand that once you get used to things, they change the game."

"That's right," Lizzie said with a loving glance at Violet. "They keep you guessing." Lizzie abruptly stood and left the room.

Jared went after her.

Kendall's heart broke for both of them as she watched Violet cheerfully eat the dry cereal from her tray, oblivious to the stakes of this day that seemed like every other one to her.

"This is unbearable," Kendall said to Dan.

"Truly."

"How do you think today will go?"

"I honestly don't know. The lawyer has played it cool from the start."

"Yeah, with me, too. He doesn't give anything away."

Jared and Lizzie returned a few minutes later. Her face was red and puffy from crying, and Jared looked so tense, Kendall feared for his health.

They sat in uneasy silence that was broken up only by spurts of laughter from Violet, who was amused by the way the cereal pieces jumped around on the tray when she banged her spoon on it.

The sound of a car arriving outside had them all sitting up straighter.

"I can't do this," Lizzie said tearfully.

"I'll be right here," Jared said. "We've got this, honey. Just stay strong."

Kendall wanted to hug them both, but there wasn't time for that as their guests arrived at the door.

Lizzie took Violet out of the high chair and quickly washed her hands and face.

The lawyer, Mr. Martin, came in with a young dark-haired man who was obviously Brooks, along with an older couple.

Shit. He'd brought his parents.

Kendall glanced at Dan and saw that he didn't like that development any more than she did.

"I'm Kendall James. This is my colleague, Dan Torrington."

Martin shook hands with both of them. "Pleasure to meet you both. I'm a big fan of your work, Mr. Torrington."

"Thank you," Dan said.

"This is my brother, Jared James, and his wife, Elisabeth, and their daughter, Violet."

Brooks and his parents stared at the child, without blinking, or so it seemed, since the minute they crossed the threshold into the house.

"My client, Brooks Ward, and his parents, Denise and Hunter Ward."

Everyone shook hands and said hello as if this were a normal social event, when nothing about this was normal.

"Can I offer you anything to drink?" Jared asked.

. . .

LIZZIE COULDN'T DO THIS. She simply couldn't make polite conversation with people who might want to take away the most important person in their lives. She wanted to leave with Violet. She'd do it if it wasn't for the fact that she was on an island and could go only so far before they'd find her.

The guests declined refreshments, and Jared suggested they move to the family room so Violet could play while the adults talked.

How could he be so calm and rational when her heart was about to explode out of her chest at any second?

"We all know why we're here," Dan said, "so how about we get right to it?"

"That works for us." Martin turned to Jared and Lizzie, who sat together on a love seat. "My client was unaware that he'd fathered a child until recently. Needless to say, the news came as a shock to him, and he was at once very eager to meet his daughter."

"She looks like you did as a baby, Brooks," his mother said tearfully.

"I was thinking the same thing," his father said, his voice gruff.

"Are you going to take her from us?" Lizzie asked, her voice hitching on a sob. "Because if you are, I want you to know we'll fight for her until our last breath. She's lived with us for more than six months. We've sat up with her all night while she was teething and when she had a fever. We've tucked her into bed every night and woken up to her happy squeaks every morning. For one hundred and ninety-two days, she's been the center of our lives. If you try to take her from us, we'll fight you."

As an attorney, Kendall would've advised her sister-in-law to take a more conciliatory approach. But as a mother, she wholeheartedly approved of Lizzie's blunt words.

"We don't want to upset her life," Brooks said haltingly. "But I'm not sure how I'm supposed to go on with my life, knowing I have a child in the world being raised by people who are strangers to me."

"So get to know us," Jared said. "Come to visit any time you want. All of you. There's no reason you can't be part of her life, but as my wife said, if you want to take her from us, we will fight you. We can either spend years raising this child with your reasonable involvement, or we can spend years in court."

Wait. What did he say? She hadn't expected him to say that and didn't want strangers involved in raising Violet.

"We understand that you weren't told of her existence," Jared said, "and we feel for you in that situation. We really do. But we hope you have some empathy for us, as well. We've devoted our lives to this child since her mother left her with us, and we're weeks away from the adoption being final. As you can imagine, this situation has been extremely distressing for us."

Violet crawled over to Lizzie, who picked her up.

"I'm sorry for the pain this has caused you," Brooks said. "That's not our intention. I wanted to meet my daughter. Could I... Would it be possible to hold her?"

Lizzie tightened her arms around Violet. No, it was not all right if he held her.

Sensing her mother's disquiet, Violet burrowed into her embrace.

"Lizzie."

She looked at Jared, who nodded as he reached for Violet.

Lizzie feared if she let her go, she might never get her back.

"It's okay," Jared said softly as he took the baby from her and transferred her to Brooks, who sat on the sofa with his parents on either side of him.

"Hey, baby girl," Brooks said. "You're so pretty and sweet."

"She's beautiful," Denise said.

Lizzie thought she might die right then and there watching them fawn over *her* child.

Jared took her hand and held on tight.

Five minutes passed, or maybe it was five hours, for all she knew or cared. *Give her back. Give her back. Give her back.*

Violet suddenly seemed to realize she was with people she didn't know and began to cry the way she did when she was scared.

Lizzie crossed the room to retrieve her child, who immediately settled when she was back in the arms of the only mother she'd ever known. She took her out of the room and went to the rocking chair in Violet's room, where she'd spent hours soothing her baby girl.

That's where Jared found her twenty minutes later.

"Did they leave?"

"Yeah."

"What did they say?"

"Brooks said he'll consider what I said and get back to us."

"When?"

"He didn't say, but Kendall and Dan assured me they won't let it drag on indefinitely."

"He holds all the cards. If he says they want her, we have to give her up to them. There won't be anything we can do."

"We'll delay in court so long she'll be in high school before they see her again. They're well aware that we have the resources to fight them. I think, in the end, he'll take our offer. He's in medical school. He has no time for a child. Dan said both parents have big jobs in New York, so they don't have time for her either."

"They could retire. If they have big jobs, they have resources, too."

"Not like we do."

Jared rarely referred to his fortune, let alone used it to intimidate someone. That told her more about how upset he was than anything else ever could have. He squatted next to her and stroked Violet's soft blonde curls as she slept in Lizzie's arms. "I don't want you to worry. I'm not going to let anyone take her from us."

She wanted to believe he had the power to get the outcome they wanted, but she wouldn't relax until she heard from Brooks himself that he wasn't going to take her child from her.

CHAPTER 32

"That was brutal," Dan said to Kendall as they walked to their cars.

"Unbearable. What do you think they thought of what Jared offered?"

"They'd be smart to consider it. Their son has no time for a child, and from what I read about them, they don't either. They know Jared meant it when he said they're in for a protracted court battle if they try to take her away from Jared and Lizzie."

"It's not like Jared to throw his money around like that."

"I know. I thought the same thing. I'm going to head home. Let me know when you hear from them."

"I will. Thanks again for being here. Your presence sent a big message."

"I wish we could do more."

"It was what we needed, so thanks for taking time away from your family, especially right now."

"It was no problem at all. I want to get this resolved for them as soon as possible." He glanced at the house. "I can't imagine what they're going through. Even more so after a few days of being a dad myself."

"Me either. It's horrible. I'll keep you posted."

"Thanks—and thank you for covering for me so I can take some time off."

"Happy to do it. Enjoy every moment with your little one. She'll be talking back to you before you know what hit you."

"I'm looking forward to all of it, even the sass, which will be world-class with Kara as her mom." He got into his Porsche and waved to Kendall as he drove off, eager to get home to his girls.

Two hours away from home had felt endless, which had him thinking again of Jared and Lizzie and what they were dealing with. What a gut punch. He drove a little faster than he should have as he navigated the curving island roads that led to home. When he pulled into the driveway, he brought the car to a skidding stop. He jumped out and jogged to the door, pulling off his tie as he went. Bertha had left the day before, after four days with them, to get back to lobstering in Maine, and he already missed her as much as Kara did. They'd declared a draw for their bet on how long she'd stay.

"Tell me everything that's happened since I left," he said when he burst through the door.

"Shhh, she's sleeping. Finally."

"Oh, sorry."

Dan went over to sit next to Kara on the sofa, gazing at the perfect face of his daughter as she slept on her mother's chest, her tiny lips making a sweet kiss shape. "Good Lord, but she's beautiful."

"I can't stop staring at her."

"We make very pretty babies. We should do it again soon."

Kara groaned. "Easy, cowboy. It still hurts to pee."

"You want more, right?"

"Yes, give me a year or two."

"I'm getting old, babe," he said without taking his gaze off the baby, not wanting to miss a single one of the myriad expressions she made while sleeping.

"What did you just say?"

"You heard me."

"I can't believe you actually admitted that."

"Well, the truth hurts, and it's true that I'm getting old. I don't want to be sending kids to college when I'm eighty."

"You're not going to be eighty," she said with a snort of laughter. "I thought you were supposed to be so smart, and you can't do basic math. Forty plus eighteen equals fifty-eight. Does that make you feel better?"

"I thought it equaled eighty."

She rolled her eyes, which she did so often with him, it was a wonder she didn't sprain something. "You're a spring chicken, and we have plenty of time to have more kids. Don't rush me."

"Thank you for my sweet, beautiful Dylan."

"Thank *you* for her."

"I don't know how I'll ever go back to work when there's so much fun to be had right here."

"I feel the same way. I can't imagine leaving her for a single minute."

"We can spend most of our time with her. I'll work from home. You'll find someone to manage the launches."

"Is it that simple?"

"Why can't it be? We've worked our asses off so we can set things up the way they work for us."

"Well, you've worked *your* ass off."

"We have. You've got that business in the Salt Pond running seamlessly. You did that. Now you can settle into motherhood and not worry about anything else, if that's what you want."

"I might want to work a little bit here and there."

"Then that's what you should do."

"My mom is asking when we can bring Dylan home to Maine to meet everyone."

"We'll do that. In a couple of months, when she's more portable. In the meantime, invite them to come here."

"I already did. It's nice to be on better terms with them and to know they'll be part of Dylan's life."

"And how are Keith and Kirby doing?"

Her brothers had been wrongly charged with murder last fall, and thanks to Dan and the team he put together in Maine, the charges had been eventually dropped. The time he and Kara had spent in Maine had helped to smooth things over between Kara and her enormous family.

"Kirby's back to work and doing much better, and Keith decided to take some time off to get out of Maine for a while. He went right to work after high school and hadn't traveled much, so I think it'll be good for him."

"I agree. How about we take a little nap while our little girl snoozes?"

"Yes, please. I'm exhausted."

"Let's go, my love."

"WHAT'S WRONG?" Shane McCarthy asked Katie when he found her curled on her side in bed when she should've been getting ready for her shift at the clinic.

"I'm not sure."

Alarmed, Shane sat on the edge of the bed and took her hand. "Is it the baby?"

"Could be. I feel weird."

"Let's get you to the clinic to be checked."

"I don't want to be one of those pregnant ladies who runs to the doctor any time something feels slightly off.

"Why not? Who cares? No one is keeping track of how often you get checked. Let's go."

He helped her up and tried not to panic when she gasped and grabbed his arm. "What?"

"Dizzy."

"Sit on the bed. I'll get you some clothes."

He helped her change into track pants and a sweatshirt and then walked her to the foyer to hold her winter coat for her, zipping it over the tiny hill that made up her pregnant belly. She'd been so excited to start showing. If she lost this baby, too…

That just couldn't happen.

They made the short drive to the clinic in silence that was so unusual, it further rattled his nerves. The two of them always had something to talk about. That was one of the things he loved best about her—that they never ran out of subjects to discuss. He was never bored with her or unsettled or unhappy, except for the time after their first pregnancy had ended in miscarriage.

Then he'd been heartbroken, but they'd gotten through that together and had been so excited for this second chance.

His heart was in his throat as he drove into the clinic parking lot and parked at the main doors to walk her in.

"Hey, guys," Victoria Stevens said as she came toward the door, wearing her coat. "I'm going to get the good coffee." To Katie, she said, "You want a decaf?"

"She needs to be seen," Shane said. "She woke up feeling weird."

Victoria was immediately in professional mode, ushering Katie through the waiting room and into an exam room in the back. She helped her change into a gown while Shane stood by, feeling helpless. He took a second to text Mac to tell him he might not make it into work.

Hope everything is okay, Mac replied.

Me, too.

He knew his cryptic message would put the whole family on notice that something was up right after they'd shared their news, but he couldn't take the time to care about that when something might be wrong with his precious wife and/or their baby.

Victoria hooked Katie up to a monitor that had the baby's strong heartbeat echoing through the room in a matter of minutes.

"Oh, there it is," Katie said tearfully, holding a hand out to Shane.

"Your baby looks and sounds great," Victoria said as she completed an ultrasound and wiped the gel from Katie's belly. "We'll run a few tests and see if we can figure out what's making you feel off."

"Thanks, Vic."

"You got it."

"That's a relief, huh?" Katie said to Shane when he perched on the edge of her bed.

"Yeah, for sure."

"Take a deep breath, Shane. The baby is okay."

"I won't take a breath until I know you are, too."

They did a blood test and took a urine sample, and half an hour later, Victoria returned to the room, smiling. "You, my dear, have a UTI."

"Translation, please," Shane said.

"Urinary tract infection," the two women said in stereo.

"Easily treated by antibiotics," Victoria added.

"How did I not realize that?" Katie asked.

"As you know, they don't always present with the usual symptoms," Vic said.

"It's safe to breathe, Shane," Katie said. "Easily fixable problem, and the baby is fine."

"Okay, I'm breathing again."

"I know it's so hard not to leap to the worst-case scenario when you've been through a miscarriage," Victoria said, "but everything with the baby looks great. We'll get you a script and send you home to get some rest."

"That's okay. I can work."

"You're not working today—or tomorrow. We can cover for you."

"Are you sure? I hate to leave you shorthanded."

"I'm positive. Let me get that script for you."

Shane held out his arms to Katie, needing a hug from her in the worst possible way. "Vic is right. You need to get some rest until you feel better."

"I can't believe I didn't know it was a UTI."

"Even a super nurse like you can't know everything."

"I can't?"

He smiled for the first time in an hour. "Nope."

Victoria returned to tell them the prescription had been called into Ryan's pharmacy, and she handed Katie some discharge instructions. "Nothing you don't know."

Katie hugged her colleague and friend. "Thanks again, Vic."

"Glad it was something easy."

"Me, too."

Shane kept his arm around Katie as they walked to his truck. Once they were inside, he wasn't surprised to see texts from his father and sister, asking if everything was okay.

He sent a text to update them and another to Mac, letting him know Katie and the baby were okay, but he'd be out of work for the day.

Glad to hear all is well, Mac replied. *Take whatever time you need.*

I'll bring you dinner, Laura said.

"Laura's bringing dinner over," he told Katie.

"She doesn't have to do that. It's a simple UTI."

"Are you going to tell her not to?" he asked.

"Why don't you do that?"

"No, thanks."

They laughed at how his big sister still thought she was the boss of him—and Katie by extension. Because she was the most loving, generous big sister ever, they let her get away with her bossiness.

"It's not like she doesn't have enough to do running a hotel and chasing three kids," Katie said.

"She wants to do it, and we have to let her."

"Okay, then."

Shane dropped her off at home and then ran to the pharmacy to pick up her prescription.

"I put a rush on it," Grace said as she handled the checkout.

"Thank you so much."

"I hope Katie feels much better very soon."

"I do, too."

"Are you okay, Shane?"

"I'm better now that we know it's something treatable and the baby is fine."

"Huge relief."

"You said it."

"Let me know if I can do anything for either of you."

"Thanks, Grace. This island…"

"It's a nice place to be when things go sideways."

"Yeah," he said over the lump in his throat. "For sure."

On the way home, he thought about how many times things had gone "sideways" with his first wife and how he'd kept their struggles to himself. Here, it was impossible to do that, surrounded as they were by both their large families, who were always there with love, support or a hot meal when needed.

In the past, he would've said he didn't want everyone up in his business. Now, he couldn't imagine living without the tremendous support system that made life so much easier and sweeter, no matter what was happening.

And of course, everything was better with Katie by his side. Being with her made him happier than he'd ever been. It was weird to think that if things had worked out with Courtney, he might have kids in school by now. His time with her seemed like a million years ago now that he was happily settled with Katie, yet he still thought of her often and mourned her passing far too young.

He pulled into the driveway of the house they'd bought last year and had made into a home he looked forward to getting back to after every long day at work. Inside, he found Katie sleeping on the sofa. When he touched her face, he was alarmed by how warm she was.

Her eyes fluttered open. "Oh hey, you're back."

"I'm back, and you need to take your medicine. You're burning up."

She sat up and took the pills and glass of water from him. "Thank you."

"No problem. Grace said to tell you she hopes you feel better soon."

"I will," she said as she settled back against the pillow. "In a day or two, I'll be fine, so don't worry."

"What? Me worry?"

"I can tell just by looking at you that you're all wound up."

"I'm fine if you're fine."

She took his hand and held on tight. "I have a good feeling about this baby. He or she is meant to be, while our first one wasn't. This pregnancy feels different. It has from the start, but I didn't say anything because I didn't want to jinx us."

"I'm glad to hear you say this one feels different."

"I can't say for sure that everything will be all right, but if mother's intuition counts for anything, this one is for keeps."

"Mother's intuition counts for a lot." Shane bent to kiss her. "Get some rest while you can. I'll be here if you need anything."

"I'm totally fine if you want to go to work. I know how busy you guys are."

"I'm all yours for the day."

"Then let's go to bed so we can snuggle while I rest."

"That sounds like the perfect winter day off to me."

CHAPTER 33

*L*aura ran down the stairs at the Sand & Surf with a twin toddler in each arm. "Hey, Piper. Have you seen Owen?"

"He was in the kitchen with Holden a few minutes ago. Everything all right?"

"Yes, but I need to hand these guys off to him while I run to the grocery store."

"Ah, okay. When you have a second, I wanted to talk to you about something."

Laura came to a halt in front of the registration desk. "Do not tell me you're leaving me."

"I'm not leaving you, but I am moving out of the hotel."

Suddenly having all the time in the world, Laura leaned against the desk while the kids squirmed in her arms. She put them down, and they ran for their toys in the living room. "Are you moving into a place by yourself?"

"Nope."

"Yes! I love this!"

"I'm moving in with Debbie from the salon."

Laura's face fell. "No way."

"Ha! Got you!"

"That was mean—and speaking of mean, you're going to deny me my viewing of Hot Cop every morning?"

"I am. You're going to have to find a way to live without that."

"And here I thought we were friends."

Piper laughed. "We're the best of friends, but it's time to get a real home."

"Yes, it is, and I couldn't be happier for you and Jack. You know that."

"I do, and I can't thank you enough for all your support of—and interest in—our relationship."

"I love when good things happen for good people, and you two deserve all the happiness in the world. But I'll miss having you living close by."

"We live on an island. I won't be far away."

"You know what I mean."

"I do, and I'll miss the pitter-patter of six little feet upstairs and having you and Owen around, too. But I'll still be here every day."

"Thank goodness for that. When are you moving?"

"We rented a place on the west side as of January first, so we'll move in after we get back from Christmas with my family."

"You're taking Jack home to meet the family?"

"I am."

"Wow, these are big steps."

"It's very exciting—and scary, too."

"How so?"

"I love him so much. So much more than I loved the one I was supposed to marry. Everything about this is different and so special. I just worry about something going wrong."

"It won't. He loves you just as much. Try to relax and enjoy the best thing to ever happen. Soon enough, life and kids take over, and that early magic starts to feel like a long time ago. Don't spend too much time worrying about a future you can't control anyway."

"Good advice, as always. Keep it coming, will you?"

"Any time you need it. I'll be back shortly."

"I'll be here."

Laura went into the living room to find her kids and encountered her husband, who gave her a curious look. "What?"

"'The early magic starts to feel like a long time ago'?"

"Oh. You heard that?"

"I did, and what shall we do about that?"

"I… I was just talking to Piper. I didn't mean anything by it."

Smiling, Owen came to put an arm around her as the kids ran in circles through the room. "I know you didn't, but what that says to me is we need a little Mommy/Daddy time to reconnect and find some of that old magic."

"Owen…" She looked up at the love of her life, the man who'd given up everything to stay with her when she was pregnant with another man's child. He'd picked her up off the floor when she was so sick she couldn't move… "Every minute with you is magic. I'd never want you to think otherwise."

He kissed her softly. "I never would, but you're not wrong about life and kids taking the steam out of a hot romance."

"Our romance is still hot."

He nuzzled her neck and brought her in closer to him. "But it can always be hotter, right?"

"Mmm. Uh-huh." Just that quickly, he'd made her forget about why she'd come downstairs in the first place. Oh. Right. Dinner for Shane and Katie. "I need to go to the store."

"Okay," he said, keeping her pressed against him.

"I'm making dinner for Shane and Katie. She's not feeling well."

"Is the baby okay?"

More kisses to her neck and lips that made her stupid in the head. "I, uh… Uh-huh. She has a UTI."

"Ouch."

"Hey, Owen?"

"Yeah?"

"This, right here… It's all magic."

"Even the screaming kids?"

"All of it."

"For me, too."

"Don't ever think that I don't feel that every day, okay?"

"I never would. Don't worry. So our Piper is moving out, huh?"

"That's what she said."

"Good for her—and Jack."

Laura made a pout face. "But no more Hot Cop in uniform every morning."

Owen gave her a light spank on the rear. "I'm in the room."

"I guess I'll have to focus on my own hot man going forward."

"I have to get me a uniform. Gotta keep my wife's attention on me."

"You have her full attention, as you well know. Hot Cop is a hobby. You're my whole life."

"And you're mine." He kissed her again and let her go to tend to kids who were beginning to melt down. Over his shoulder, he said, "Meet me at bedtime for a little magic, okay?"

"I'll be there."

Hope Martinez found her husband, Paul, sitting on the front porch as snow flurries danced in the frigid air. She handed him the mug of hot chocolate she'd made for him with the little marshmallows he liked on top because they reminded him of his mother.

She zipped her coat and sat in the rocker next to him. "What're you thinking about out here in the cold?"

"My mom loved this porch." They now lived in the house his parents had called home for more than forty years. "It was her favorite spot, even when it was freezing."

"I remember. It's where I first met her."

"That's right. The porch was such a blessing to us during the worst of times. She was always happy out here."

"It's where I'll always picture her when I think of her."

He glanced over at her. "Thank you for your support through it all. I'm not sure I would've survived it without you, Ethan and Scarlett. Alex, Jenny and George, too."

"I was thinking earlier how you two have built beautiful families for yourselves during the worst thing you've ever been through. That sorrow and joy have coexisted in this family for years now, and it's the joy that'll sustain us."

His eyes filled as he nodded. "That's a perfect summary of the last five years. I'll never forget having to make that call to Alex, asking him to come home because I couldn't handle her care and the business on my own anymore. He was so, so angry about having to give up his life in DC, and look at him now."

"Happy as a pig in shit."

Paul grunted with laughter. "He's even corrupted you."

Alex's colorful language was the stuff of legends.

"Not completely," Hope said, "but I have picked up a few new expressions from him."

"As has Ethan."

They laughed together over how much their son adored his irreverent uncle.

"Maybe we need to keep the two of them separated," Paul said.

"Good luck with that."

"Thank you for the hot chocolate. It's as good as my mom's."

"That's high praise indeed. Is there anything I can do for you?"

"Just having you right here with me is all I need. Is Scarlett napping?"

"She is." Hope shivered as she raised the collar of her coat. "She went down about fifteen minutes ago, and Ethan is spending the night with Kyle and Jackson."

"Let's go make a fire and snuggle while we can."

"I thought you'd never ask."

Paul smiled as he helped her up. "Your lips are blue, and we can't have that. I need those lips nice and warm."

Inside, he went straight to the hearth to strike the fire he'd laid the night before.

Hope kept her coat on until the fire was providing some much-needed extra heat. Then she took a call from Ethan. "Hey, how's the sleepover?"

"Would it be okay if I came home?"

"Of course. Is everything all right?"

"I'm just really sad about Grandma Marion, and I'm sure Dad must be, too. I feel like I need to be with you guys."

"We'll be right over to get you, honey."

"Seamus said he'd drive me home. He wanted me to make sure you were there."

"We're here. Tell him thanks for us."

"I will. See you soon."

"What's up?" Paul asked when he sat with her on the sofa and pulled a down blanket over them.

"Seamus is bringing Ethan home. He's sad about Grandma Marion and said, 'Dad must be, too.' He wants to be here with us."

Tears filled his eyes. "What a sweet kid he is to think of me like that."

Hope snuggled into his warm embrace. "He loves you so much."

"Life is so strange. If my mom hadn't had dementia, I'd never have met you or Ethan. I wouldn't have the best wife, son and daughter anyone has ever had, not to mention a new baby on the way."

"I'll always believe your dad was looking out for all of you when he connected Alex with Jenny and me with you during the hardest time in your lives."

"I wouldn't put it past him. Taking care of his family was always his top priority."

"Sounds like someone else I know."

"I learned from the best." After a long pause, he said, "Can I tell you something kind of weird?"

"You can tell me anything."

"I didn't expect to be this sad when she finally passed."

"You're sad for the mom you knew before her disease progressed, and probably a little extra sad now that both your parents are gone. I've heard that can be a difficult transition, even when your parents are very old. You lost both of yours far too soon."

"That's true. Thank you for understanding. Mixed in with the sadness is a lot of relief, for her and for us."

"Which is totally normal, too."

"Is it?"

"Yes, Paul, it's normal to feel relief that a terrible ordeal has ended and that your mom is finally at peace—and reunited with your dad, which is all she ever wanted."

"She missed him so much. Sometimes I wonder if losing him didn't somehow cause the dementia, like her brain was protecting her from his absence or something like that."

"I suppose that's possible."

"Now that I have you, I have a better understanding of what it was like for her to lose my dad. They were madly in love like we are."

"Are we madly?"

"I am."

She squeezed his arm. "So am I, and you know it."

"And I'm thankful for that every day, but especially on days like today."

Ethan arrived with heavy footsteps on the porch a few minutes later.

Hope got up to greet her son and waved to Seamus from the door. "Thanks for bringing him and have a great trip!"

"Will do," he said. "We'll send pictures."

Hope took Ethan's coat and hung it on a hook by the door as he went to hug Paul.

The boy's shoulders shook with sobs, as if he'd held in his grief until he got home to them.

"I'm s-sorry," Ethan said. "I don't mean to make it about me. She was your mom."

Paul held him close. "And you were her very special friend. Of course it's about you, too."

Hope ran her fingers through Ethan's hair. "You brought her so much joy, honey. From the first day we were here, she adored you. Remember?"

Ethan gave a short nod. "I was her first grandchild."

"That's right." Paul's gaze met hers over Ethan's head. "And she loved every minute of being your grandma."

"I won't forget her."

"That's good to know, buddy. Thank you for the many ways you honored her while she was still here and for honoring her again by remembering her."

Hope wiped away tears as her heart filled to overflowing at the sweet moment between the man she loved and the son he'd made his own. Their bond was one of the most beautiful things in her life. The three of them were family in every way that mattered, and she would do everything she could to help them through this difficult time.

MAC WAS the first to arrive at the Beachcomber bar and ordered a beer from Jace, who'd left work at the construction company half an hour ago. "How'd you get here so fast?"

"I've only been here a minute," Jace said, smiling as he drew Mac's beer from the tap.

"Are you taking over with the boys in the morning?" Mac asked of his sons, Jackson and Kyle.

"Cindy and I are staying there tonight since Seamus and Caro are on the early boat in the morning."

"Ah, I see. I sure do wish I could go to see my little sister officially become a DVM."

"It's a hell of an accomplishment."

"She's worked so hard for years—and Joe has, too, managing kids and dogs and his own classes. It'll be great to have them back here full time."

"I'm looking forward to getting to know them better. They've been gone most of the time I've lived here."

Grant landed on the stool next to Mac's. "I'll have whatever he's having," he said to Jace.

"Coming right up."

"How goes it?" Mac asked his brother.

"All is well. You?"

"Same. I don't have four infants at home—only two—so life is good."

Grant laughed. "Thank God I'm only having one. I was there for two hours today, and I swear they changed twenty diapers."

"Easily."

"They sure are cute, though."

"Of course they are. They're McCarthy boys."

Grant cracked up. "I can't believe *Adam* outdid us all."

"And that we have to listen to his super-sperm bullshit forever."

"Excuse me?" Jace said, brow raised as he put Grant's beer on a coaster.

"That's all Adam is talking about since he got Abby pregnant with quads. His freaking super sperm."

Jace laughed. "What would you say if you'd fathered quads?"

Smiling, Grant said, "Wow, he's really gotten to know you, Mac."

"Whatever," Mac said. "My sperm is super, too. I have twins, don't forget."

"As if you'd ever let us," Grant said. "I'm more than happy with one at a time, thank you very much."

Morgan took the stool on Mac's left. "Sorry I'm late. Got tied up with a project and lost track of time."

"No worries," Mac said as he and Grant shook hands with Morgan. "Glad we could do this."

"Me, too."

"What're you working on?" Grant asked.

"Rewiring Sierra's building. It's a mess."

Jace pulled a beer from the tap for Morgan and put it in front of him. "Nice to see you, Morgan."

"You, too. Thanks, Jace."

"Put that on my tab," Mac said.

Morgan lifted his beer. "Cheers, and thank you for meeting me."

"We were looking forward to it, and Luke said he'd catch you another time," Mac said. "His wife is having a tough time with this pregnancy, so he went home to relieve her with their daughter."

"Ah, I see. Hope his wife is okay."

"She's just really tired. And speaking of your electrical talents, we sure could use someone with your skills around here. Our power grid is a disaster waiting for a place to happen. We've already had one major blackout, and any time we lose power, it's for days."

"What's the town doing about that?"

"Our dad and the other town council members are working with the state to secure funding for an upgrade," Mac said, "but they're looking for someone to oversee the project and not getting any takers."

"Huh. That's interesting."

"It'd be a multiyear project with a lot of one-of-a-kind aspects to it," Mac added. "Not to mention the regular need I have for electricians for my company. I bring people over for a week at a time, but it sure would be nice to have someone local."

"Is this an organized campaign, by any chance?" Morgan asked, smiling.

"Nothing of the kind," Mac said. "I'm merely passing on info that I hope you'll find intriguing."

"It's a great company to work for," Jace said. "I can attest to that."

"I am, in fact, intrigued. Talk to me about living here year-round. How do you keep from going batshit crazy?"

"It's all about the company you keep," Grant said. "I usually decamp for Southern California in the winter, but I'm staying local this year because my wife is due with our first baby in January. She wants to be near her midwife and our family when the baby arrives."

"Understandable," Morgan said.

"But even knowing we aren't escaping this year, I'm fine with being here because we have so much fun with family and friends—and especially when it's just us hanging out at home. We're never bored."

"Spare us the gory details, bro," Mac said.

"Shut up. Your details are just as gory."

Morgan laughed. "Nothing like brothers to keep it real."

"We sure are sorry you lost yours," Mac said.

"So am I."

"Any time you need some brotherlike bonding, we've got you covered," Grant said.

"I may take you up on that."

"We wish you would," Mac said. "Back to your question, though. Grant is right, as much as it pains me to say it."

Grant snorted.

"We have a lot of fun with our people all year long, and you'd be welcomed into our crew if you decided to stay. Everyone is welcome. Our gatherings just get bigger and louder all the time, and as long as you don't mind a shit-ton of kids, you'll have a great time."

"I don't mind kids. I still hope to have a couple of my own before all is said and done."

"Life comes at you fast, and all of a sudden, you're staring down forty," Mac said.

"When will you hit the big four-oh?" Morgan asked.

"February. What about you?"

"May."

"I'm the year after," Grant said. "And I can't believe it."

"You're getting a late start with kids," Morgan said, "as I would be as well."

"That's okay," Grant said. "I wasn't ready before now, so the timing is perfect for me."

"Good way to look at it," Morgan said.

"Do you have a candidate in mind to mother these children of yours?" Mac asked.

"You already know I'm seeing Sierra, because you saw us together the other night."

"He wants details," Grant said. "That's why he asked you."

Morgan laughed. "I see how it is."

"Mac is the biggest gossip on the entire island," Grant said. "If there's a scoop to be had, he sniffs it out."

"Whose idea was it to invite Grant?" Mac asked.

"I believe it was yours," Morgan said.

"Big mistake," Mac said. "Anyway, about Sierra…"

The other two laughed.

"I rest my case," Grant said.

"Sierra is amazing, and we're having a great time. But I've been wrestling with the push-pull of making a life here and going back to the one I have on the mainland. I have a kick-ass job, and the boss wants me back. I've been trying to picture myself here full time after spending my entire childhood trying to get the fuck out of here."

"I feel that so hard," Mac said. "That was me, too, as you know."

"I remember how much you hated being trapped here."

"If it helps you at all, I never feel trapped here anymore. I have everything I could ever want right here, and as an adult, I can leave any time I want. But I go months without going anywhere, and I'm completely fine with that. I have my wife, our kids, our extended families, tons of friends, satisfying work that keeps me so busy, I barely have time to breathe. What else is there, you know?"

"For what it's worth, I feel the same way," Grant said. "When we get back here in the spring, we rarely leave until we go to California for the winter. And after a couple of months there, we can't wait to come home and see everyone. Once our child is in school, we'll be here full time, too, and that's fine with us."

"You guys have given me a lot to think about," Morgan said. "I appreciate you taking the time."

"Always a pleasure to catch up with an old friend," Mac said. "Impartially speaking, I sure as hell hope you decide to stay. I can keep you busy for years."

"Helps to know there'd be work in addition to the gym. As much as I love that place, it's not my calling, you know?"

"Yeah," Grant said, "it was Billy's thing, but everyone is thankful you're keeping it open."

"That's the plan."

Mac downed the last of his beer and signaled Jace to cash out. "I hate to drink and run, but my wife is alone with five kids, and the sooner I get home, the better."

"I appreciate you taking the time when you're so busy," Morgan said.

"Happy to do it. You've got my number if you want to talk about the work."

"I'll be in touch."

"I've got to run, too," Grant said. "It was great to see you, Morgan."

"Thanks for the input." Morgan shook hands with both of them. "You really helped to give me some perspective."

"Any time," Mac said.

CHAPTER 34

Shell-shocked. That was the only way to describe the parents who boarded the eight o'clock ferry on the way to their daughter's graduation in Ohio. They'd been up all night with four baby grandsons, helping out wherever they could as they were changed, fed, soothed, rinse and repeat.

Big Mac went straight to the snack bar for two coffees while Linda landed at a picnic table, too tired to keep her head up.

They were leaning against each other, eyes closed, hands wrapped around coffee cups, when Seamus and Carolina joined them.

"Well, isn't this a lively group?" Seamus said as they slid onto the bench across the table from them.

"Up all night," Linda said as she yawned. "Four babies is a lot."

"How're the parents doing?" Seamus asked.

"Probably better than the grandparents, since they're thirty years younger than us," Big Mac said.

Seamus chuckled at their sorry state.

"How's the leg, Caro?" Linda asked.

Carolina had fallen in the shower and broken her leg months ago. "Better all the time, but I brought the cane because it acts up when I overdo it."

"Good call." Linda returned her head to Big Mac's shoulder. "Wake me up when we get to Ohio."

They slept the entire way to Point Judith and on the way to the airport while Seamus drove Big Mac's truck. They nodded off in the waiting area before they boarded the plane and then slept all the way to Columbus, waking up feeling slightly more rested but still dragging as they were greeted by Joe, Janey, PJ and Vi in a flurry of hugs and kisses and frantic excitement.

"I thought they were going to spontaneously combust waiting for you guys to get here," Janey said of her kids as she hugged her parents.

"I thought *you* were going to," Joe said to his wife.

Janey laughed. "I almost did. This is what I was picturing every minute of the last few months—the second you guys would arrive for graduation, and we'd never have to be apart again."

"I'm here for that," Big Mac said, yawning.

Janey took a closer look at her parents. "You guys look rough. Was the flight bad?"

"They're hungover from wrangling quadruplets all night," Seamus said.

"Ah, I see," Janey said. "We'll put you down for a nap."

"No naps!" PJ said to laughter from the adults.

Janey and Joe led the way to where they'd parked both their cars. "Caro, you're walking so much better than you were the last time we saw you."

"I'm getting there. Slowly but surely."

"Will you be ready to swim at the beach next summer, Gran?" PJ asked her.

She slung an arm around her grandson. "You bet I will."

"In case I forget to tell you later," Janey said, "this is the greatest week of my life. Not only do I get my degree—finally—but we get to come home to where we belong—finally."

"Before I forget to tell you, sweetheart," Big Mac said, "I've never been prouder in my life than I am of my new DVM."

"Thank you, Daddy. Thank you all for making this possible."

"What Dad said," Linda added. "We couldn't be happier to see this dream come true for you. Better late than never."

"Cheers to Dr. Jane McCarthy Cantrell, DVM," Big Mac said.

. . .

"SURELY THEY'LL SLEEP at some point, right?" Adam asked Abby after the longest night of their lives. The only one who'd gotten any sleep was Liam, who was now up and running around, full of energy and wanting to know what they were doing that day.

"Dada, we go to the park?"

"Maybe later, pal. Dada is cooked."

Liam's dark brows furrowed in confusion.

"The babies were awake all night, and so were we."

"No babies," Liam said with a scowl. "Park."

"How about some breakfast?" Abby took his hand and led him into the kitchen as Ned and Francine arrived with coffee and doughnuts.

"I'd ask how it's goin'," Ned said, "but one look at ya tells the story."

"Bless you," Adam said as he took a coffee from Ned.

"What can we do to help?" Francine asked.

"You know anything about babies?"

"As a matter of fact, I have twin training," Francine said. "Take a break. Grandma Francine is on the job."

"Thank you both," Adam said, choked up all at once. "You don't have to…"

Ned squeezed his shoulder. "Yer kids are our kids. Just how it is. Plus, yer down a coupla grandparents for the next little while."

"This is true."

"We gotcha covered."

"You're the best. Thank you."

"Our pleasha."

Francine had Beckett in her arms and was walking him around the room with grandmotherly expertise.

Ned soon followed with Kane on one shoulder and Rory on the other.

With things temporarily under control, Adam took one of the coffees to Abby. "Ned and Francine to the rescue."

"That's so lovely of them."

"We're blessed with an abundance of grandparents who'll get us through this."

"Thank God for them." Abby sat with Liam while he ate his cereal. "This guy is all out of sorts."

"Maybe a trip to the p-a-r-k with Dada might fix what ails him," Adam said, though it was the last thing on earth he felt like doing.

"You might be right. I read that keeping his routine as close to the way it was before the babies arrived will help him make the transition, and trips to the park with Dada are his favorite thing."

"Park!" Liam banged his spoon on the high-chair tray. "Park now!"

"Jeez, who's the boss around here, anyway?" Adam said, amused by his son.

"It appears we've been relegated to hired-help status for the next eighteen years."

Adam kissed his wife. "I wouldn't have it any other way."

EVERY TIME the phone rang for days after Brooks's visit, Lizzie's heart stopped as she wondered if this would be the call that would ruin her life forever. By the third day, she was fighting to hold on to what was left of her sanity when Jared's phone rang.

"It's him," Jared said. "Brooks."

Lizzie couldn't think or breathe or do anything other than sit perfectly still while her daughter slept in the other room, unaware that her whole life could change as the result of one phone call.

He put the call on speaker. "This is Jared James."

"It's Brooks."

"Hi, Brooks. We're glad you called."

Were they glad? Really? That would depend on what he had to say.

"I'm sorry it took a few days to reach out. I can't imagine how hard this is for you guys, and I'm also sorry for putting you through this. It's just that… Well… I needed to see her. My daughter."

Lizzie's heart fell into her stomach as it became clear she wasn't going to get the outcome she'd hoped and prayed for.

"It was a shock to find out she existed, and I hope you understand that I needed to see her."

"We do," Jared said as his warm hand on hers made her realize how cold she was. "We get it."

"Look, I'm not out to upset her life—or yours. It's obvious that you love her very much. It's just that… Well, I'd like for her to know me. And my parents. Do you think that might be possible?"

"Yes," Lizzie said without hesitation. "We'd be fine with that."

"Really? You would?"

"All we want is to be able to raise her as our daughter." Lizzie's gaze was locked on Jared's as she hoped he agreed. "If that means we share her with you on occasion, we can live with that."

Jared nodded and squeezed her hand.

"I… I didn't think… Despite what you said the other day…" A soft sob echoed through the phone. "I thought you'd say no."

"We're not saying no," Jared said. "Does this mean you won't contest the adoption?"

After a long pause, Brooks said, "I won't contest it."

Oxygen flooded Lizzie's system as her chest expanded for the first time since Kendall had told them Violet's father had reached out. Tears poured from her eyes and Jared's.

"Thank you," he said for both of them. "Thank you so much."

"Thank you for letting me be part of her life. I promise not to get in the way."

"You're welcome in her life—and in ours. We'll stay in touch, okay?"

"That sounds good. Tell her… Tell her I love her, will you?"

"We will," Jared said.

They said their goodbyes, and Jared ended the call.

Then Lizzie was in his arms, sobbing her heart out as he did the same. And then they were laughing even as the tears still flowed.

"She's ours," Lizzie said. "She's really going to be ours."

"She's always been ours. We're just making it official."

"We need to text Kendall and Dan."

"I will." He held her as tightly as he ever had. "In a minute."

THE DAYS FLEW by in a flurry of preholiday madness for Sierra, as many of her regular customers treated themselves to some relaxation amid the chaos of preparations, family gatherings, parties, shopping and wrapping. At six o'clock on the twenty-third, she closed the studio door for the next ten days, excited for a much-needed break and visit to Providence to see her dad and extended family.

If only a sense of dread wasn't hanging over the festive season as she tried to keep herself from completely losing her heart to a man who might or might not be leaving the place she called home before too much longer.

They'd spent every night together for weeks. She'd never felt closer or more connected to a man than she did to Morgan, and despite her best efforts to contain her feelings for him, she'd fallen deeply in love for the first time in her life. What should've been the happiest time ever was overshadowed by unanswered questions that kept her awake long after Morgan had drifted off to sleep at night.

She was running on fumes and letting her emotions rule her, but how could she help it? Her phone buzzed with a text from her dad.

Got time to talk?

They'd been playing text-tag for days, and even though she was eager to see Morgan, she took a few minutes to call her best pal.

"Is this my long-lost daughter who has no time for her old man these days?"

"Um, hello? I'm not the one who's been hosting parties every day for weeks."

"I'm getting out of the holiday party business next year."

"You've said that every December for twenty years."

"This time, I mean it."

"I'll believe it when I see it."

"When am I going to see *you*?"

"I'm on the noon boat tomorrow, so around one or so." *Tell him. Tell him you're not coming alone. Why are you being so weird about this?* "So, um, Dad, you didn't have much to say about me bringing a friend home with me. I hope it's okay."

"Because you never said what kinda friend you were bringing."

"The boyfriend kind."

"Well… This is an interesting development. My little girl using the 'boyfriend' word."

"I know, right?"

"What's his story?"

"Remember how I told you that two local men were killed in the storm?"

"Yeah, and I read about them. Sad stuff."

"Definitely. One of them was his brother, the last remaining member of his immediate family."

"Not that lawyer who got himself in trouble?"

"No, the other one. He owned the gym out here, and Morgan, his brother, has been here since September, dealing with Billy's business and estate. We've gotten to know each other, and I don't want him to spend Christmas alone."

"Course not. Bring him. The more the merrier."

"He'll stay in my room with me—and you're not going to make a thing of it. You hear me?"

"I hear ya."

"What? No arguments? No reminders of how I was raised or what my mother would have to say about me living in sin?"

Her dad chuckled. "Clearly, I don't need to tell you any of that. All I'll say is I've waited a long time to see you find someone who makes you happy. If your Morgan does that, then all is well."

"Thank you, Daddy."

"I can't wait to see you, Boo."

"Same. I'll text when we're on the way to Providence."

"I'll make the manicotti for you."

"Guess what? Morgan loves Mancini's."

"Find out what his favorite is, and I'll make it, too."

"Love you."

"Love you, too, baby girl. Can't wait to see you."

"Same here."

Sierra was relieved to have him on board and excited to meet Morgan as she took the stairs to home, planning to shower and change before he arrived for dinner. After he'd completely rewired her building, she planned to take him out for a nice dinner to thank him for all the time he'd spent on the project. But when she threw open her door, she stopped short at the sight of candles, a bottle of wine and a sexy man waiting for her.

CHAPTER 35

"What's this?" Sierra asked.

"I made us some dinner."

"I was supposed to take you out."

"We'll do that another time." He held a chair for her at the small table she'd bought at a yard sale. "Have a seat."

Filled with curiosity, she took the seat he held for her and shivered when he kissed her neck.

"How was your day, dear?"

"Long and tedious."

"How come?"

"I couldn't wait to see you."

"I seem to have that very same problem. No matter what I'm doing, I'm wondering where you are and how long I have to wait to see you again." He sat across from her. "Do you know how slowly the time goes by when you're dying to see someone?"

"As a matter of fact, I do know. It's something I've only just realized in the last few weeks. Work has never been more of a chore than it's been lately."

"For me, too, except the time I spent working at your place when I could steal kisses in between installing new circuits."

"Sexiest electrician I ever met."

He tipped his head adorably. "How many electricians have you known?"

"Never mind. Take the compliment."

Smiling, he filled their wineglasses with the rosé they both liked. "Cheers to you, Sierra Mancini. Thank you for the best weeks of my life."

As she touched her glass to his, she feared he might be planning to tell her their time together was ending.

"Why did you frown like that?"

"Can I ask you something?"

"Anything you want."

"Are you leaving?"

"Only to go to Providence with you tomorrow. If I'm still invited, that is."

"You are invited—and I just talked to my dad. He's excited to meet you and wants to know your favorite dish from Mancini's so he can have it ready for you."

"That's easy. Lasagna."

"Got it, but what about after Providence? What happens in the New Year?"

"What do you want to happen?"

Suddenly, Sierra couldn't take it anymore. She couldn't bear to sit across from him as his gorgeous face was lit by candlelight, dreaming about a future that might not happen. She stood and went into her room to curl up on her bed, feeling madly vulnerable and undone by feelings so big, she didn't know how to manage them. She'd never had to before.

He crawled onto the bed and curled up to her. "What's wrong?"

She took a few minutes to try to settle her emotions before she said words that could never be unsaid. "I'm scared."

"Of what, honey?"

"This. You. All of it."

He pushed himself up on his arm. "Turn over so I can see your gorgeous face."

"Don't want to."

"Please?"

Reluctantly, she turned onto her back and gazed up at the ceiling because looking at him was akin to staring at the sun. He blotted out everything that wasn't him.

"Sierra."

"Yes?"

"You're not looking at me."

"I know."

"Tell me what you're afraid of."

"I'm losing myself to this thing with you, and I have no idea where you'll even be a few weeks from now."

"I'm sorry to have upset you this way."

"I'm not upset. I'm trying to keep my wits about me so if you decide to go back to your old life, I'll still be able to enjoy mine here."

"After these last few weeks, I don't think I could enjoy any life that doesn't include you."

At that, she finally looked directly at him. "Really?"

He caressed her face with a light slide of his fingers over her cheek. "Really. It seems, at some point, I'm not exactly sure when… No, wait, that's not true. I know exactly when. It was when you looked at me at Billy's funeral and made me feel stronger just because you were in the room. That's definitely when it happened."

"When what happened?"

"I fell in love with you."

"You… You fell… Oh."

Smiling, he said, "That was articulate."

"No one has ever fallen in love with me before. I'm not quite sure how to process that."

"I'm so very honored and thankful to be the first man to fall in love with you. I'd also like to be the last one."

She was so overwhelmed by emotion that she barely noticed when tears slid from the corners of her eyes.

But he noticed, and he kissed them away. "Am I out on this love limb all by myself?"

She shook her head. "Not at all. Why do you think I was freaking out?"

"I'm sorry it took me so long to tell you these things, but I was working to figure out my shit before I talked to you."

"Your boss wants you back to work."

"I resigned from that job yesterday."

She sat up. "What? You did? Why didn't you tell me?"

"Because I was waiting for my new job to become official, and it did today. I'll be working for the town of Gansett Island to upgrade the island's power grid—in addition to providing electrical services to Mac McCarthy's construction company. I wanted to have everything resolved before I told you."

"I thought you didn't want to live here full time."

"I didn't until I met someone who has a business and a life here that she loves. She wouldn't be happy anywhere else, and I wouldn't be happy without her. In the end, the decision was much easier than I expected it to be. As I thought about leaving here—and leaving you—everything in me objected."

"Can you be happy here full time when all you wanted was out of here as a kid?"

"Will you be here with me?"

"For as long as you'll have me."

"Then I should be set to spend the rest of my life right here with you."

"Is this really happening?"

"Only if it's what you want."

She held out her arms to him, and he made himself at home in her embrace. "I was all set to tell you that you couldn't come to Christmas after all."

"Ouch."

"I know my dad will love you, and I didn't want to get his hopes up if you weren't planning to stick around."

"And now?"

"I can't wait for my two favorite guys to meet each other."

"I can't wait to meet him, too. How would you feel if I asked for his permission to propose to you?"

Her heart simply couldn't contain the emotional overload. "He'll tell you it's up to me, but he'll appreciate the gesture."

"Good to know. Is there anything you want to tell me?"

At first, she didn't know what he meant, and then she got it. Only one of them had said the actual words. "I love you, Morgan."

The way he looked at her... She'd waited all her life for someone to look at her like that and was thankful now that she'd waited for him.

He put his hand on her face as he gazed into her eyes. "Right when I'd lost the last of my family, there you were to give me a whole new one. If you put your faith in me, Sierra, you'll never be sorry."

"I already know that—and likewise. We'll make a whole new family of our own, even if it's just the two of us."

"That's all I'll ever need, but maybe we can add a few little Morgans and Sierras to the mix at some point?"

"I'd consider that."

Everything was different when he kissed her this time, sealing their deal in a passionate embrace that was so much more now that she knew for certain he loved her, and they were going to spend their lives together.

He made her truly happy, and she would spend the rest of her life doing the same for him.

EPILOGUE

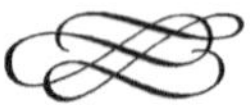

On New Year's Eve, right at midnight, Morgan proposed to Sierra, who said an enthusiastic yes as he slid his mother's engagement ring onto her finger and promised to love her forever.

The following week, Erin Jackson gave birth to a son named Tobias Fitzgerald Jackson III, named for his father and his late uncle. His dad, Slim, was looking forward to taking him on his first flight and starting his pilot training.

In mid-January, Stephanie McCarthy gave birth to her and Grant's son, Oren Charles McCarthy. His grandfather, Charlie, was positively smitten at first glance, as were Big Mac and Linda.

In late January, Jordan Stokes gave birth to a son whom she and Mason Johns named Wyatt. Two months after Wyatt's birth, his parents were married on a windy day in March, a week before the finale of the wildly successful season of *Jordan and Gigi: Live From Gansett Island*, which had made Mason, and Gigi's partner, Cooper, into instant stars.

On Valentine's Day, Grace McCarthy gave birth to a son who she and her husband, Evan, named Maddox. His dad planned to start teaching him to play the guitar as soon as he could sit up.

In mid-February, Monique relocated to Gansett Island to live with Linc in his Coast Guard apartment as they pondered a wide variety of options for his next duty station. In the end, he put in a request to stay on

Gansett Island. Monique had decided to open a dance studio at Tiffany's, and they wanted to stay close to her niece, Hazel, who was born to Oliver and Dara Watkins in early March.

Later in March, Daisy Lawrence gave birth to Helen Marion, and her husband, David, immediately fell madly in love with his little girl—and her perfect name.

In April, Jenny Martinez and her husband, Alex, welcomed a second son. They named him Henry Hugh, because the name means "ruler of the estate." Alex noted that someday Henry, George, Ethan, Scarlett and the new baby coming soon to Hope and Paul would rule the Martinez estate, so the name seemed fitting. Hugh was in honor of Jenny's father.

In May, Sydney Harris and her husband, Luke, welcomed a son they named Elias. Their daughter, Lily, declared her baby brother the cutest boy in the world.

Over Memorial Day Weekend, Cooper James opened his bachelor-and-bachelorette booze cruise business with every weekend of the summer and fall sold out. His girlfriend, Gigi, was his first mate on most voyages.

In early June, Paul and Hope Martinez welcomed a second daughter, named Charlotte Marion Martinez.

On the summer solstice in June, Chelsea and Kevin McCarthy welcomed a second baby girl, named Faith.

That July, Julia Lawry and Deacon Taylor were "officially" married in a ceremony at the bluffs, followed by a reception at the new alpaca farm venue that opened for business that summer. Their daughter, Ella, was born a month later.

In August, Piper Bennett married Jack Downing on the porch at the Sand & Surf Hotel. Laura Lawry was her matron of honor. Per their request, Jack wore his uniform.

On Labor Day weekend, Jeff Lawry married Kelsey Gordon, also at the Sand & Surf, standing on two feet with no crutches in sight.

Later in September, Katie McCarthy gave birth to a son, who she and her husband, Shane, named Benjamin Francis, honoring Shane's father with his middle name.

The following fall, John Lawry married Niall Fitzgerald in a ceremony at the Beachcomber, followed by a party that lasted until dawn.

Early the next year, construction began on a new wing of the Gansett Island School.

~

Soooo, this might feel like a goodbye to Gansett Island, but it's not! This is the end of part one. My hope is to move the storyline forward into the future to start a new series featuring the kids—and there are a LOT of them! I haven't got a handle on that plan yet, and I'm hoping to take next year to get my Remington Family Law Series launched before I start this new direction for Gansett. More to come on that!

I do have Gansett Island news for 2026, however! April of 2026 marks FIFTEEN YEARS since MAID FOR LOVE's debut, and we're celebrating with special edition hardcovers. Sign up here *https://marieforce.com/gansetthardcovers/* to be notified when they're available for preorder.

For now, I hope you enjoyed the arrival of the quadruplets as well as the other new babies, Sierra's romance with Morgan, Monique's romance with Linc and updates to so many other stories. I was sad to see Marion pass away, but it was time, and it gave me a chance to bring together all the people who'd loved her for one last goodbye.

Join the Delivery After Dark reader group at *www.facebook.-com/groups/deliveryafterdark/* and the Gansett Island Reader Group at *www.facebook.com/groups/McCarthySeries*. If you're not on my mailing list, please go to marieforce.com/subscribe to sign up.

As always, a huge thank you to the amazing team that supports me behind the scenes, including my husband, Dan, and my tremendous HTJB crew: Julie Cupp, Lisa Cafferty, Jean Mello, Nikki Haley and Ashley Lopez, as well as my daughter and sidekick, Emily Force.

Thank you to Dr. Sarah Hewitt, family nurse practitioner, for checking the medical details and for helping me to "give birth" to six babies in this book! I want to add that I took significant liberties to somewhat "simplify" the arrival of quadruplets at thirty weeks. Sarah pointed out that they'd probably spend a few weeks in the NICU and the visiting would be severely limited. I wanted their people around, so I'm taking a "this is fiction" mulligan with how their arrival unfolded.

To my editors, Linda Ingmanson and Joyce Lamb, thank you for always being ready to help me whip a new book into shape, and to my primary beta readers, Anne Woodall, Kara Conrad and Tracey Suppo, thank you for your many contributions. Gwen Neff reads for continuity, which is a huge help as this series hits book 28. I'm thankful for all the help that Gwen and the other Gansett Island betas provide. They include: Jennifer, Andi, Doreen, Judy, Amy and Jaime.

Thank you so much for your incredible support of Gansett Island—and me! Turn the page to see the updated Who's Who on Gansett Island AFTER the *Delivery After Dark* baby boom!

Much love,

Marie

WHO'S WHO ON GANSETT ISLAND
AFTER DELIVERY AFTER DARK

The McCarthy Family

- **Malcom John "Big Mac" McCarthy Sr.,** brother to Frank and Kevin, co-owner of McCarthy's Gansett Island Marina and McCarthy's Gansett Island Inn, married to:
  - **Linda McCarthy,** co-owner of McCarthy's Gansett Island Marina and McCarthy's Gansett Island Inn

BIG MAC and Linda are parents to:

- **Mallory Vaughn James,** daughter of Big Mac McCarthy and Diana Vaughn (deceased), nursing director at Marion Martinez Home for the Aged married to:
  - **Dr. Quinn James,** brother of Jared, Cooper and Kendall James, trauma surgeon, medical director at Marion Martinez Home for the Aged
- **Malcolm John "Mac" McCarthy Jr.,** son of Big Mac and Linda McCarthy, co-owner of McCarthy's Gansett Island Marina and owner of McCarthy Construction, father to Thomas, Hailey, Malcolm John "Mac" McCarthy III, Connor (Deceased), Emma Linda, and Evelyn Francine, married to:
  - **Maddie Chester McCarthy,** daughter of Francine Chester Saunders and Bobby Chester, sister to Tiffany Taylor, former housekeeper at McCarthy's Gansett Island Inn, mother to Thomas, Hailey, Malcolm John "Mac" McCarthy III, Connor (Deceased), Emma Linda, and Evelyn Francine
    - **Thomas McCarthy,** son of Maddie Chester McCarthy and Tom Wilkinson, adopted by Mac McCarthy
    - **Hailey McCarthy,** daughter of Mac and Maddie
    - **Connor McCarthy** (deceased), son of Mac and Maddie
    - **Malcolm John "Mac" McCarthy III,** son of Mac and Maddie
    - **Emma Linda McCarthy** (twin), daughter of Mac and Maddie

- **Evelyn Francine McCarthy** (twin), daughter of Mac and Maddie
- **Grant McCarthy,** Academy Award winning screenwriter, father of Oren Charles McCarthy, married to
  - **Stephanie Logan McCarthy,** daughter of Charlie Grandchamp, owner of Stephanie's Bistro, mother of Oren Charles McCarthy
    - **Oren Charles McCarthy,** son of Grant and Stephanie
- **Adam McCarthy,** computer programmer, father to Liam Callahan McCarthy, married to:
  - **Abby Callahan McCarthy**, daughter of Tom and Carol Callahan, owner of Abby's Attic, mother to Liam Callahan McCarthy
    - **Liam Callahan McCarthy,** son of Adam and Abby
    - **Murphy Callahan McCarthy,** quadruplet son of Adam and Abby, identical twin to Rory
    - **Rory Callahan McCarthy,** quadruplet son of Adam and Abby, identical twin to Murphy
    - **Kane Callahan McCarthy,** quadruplet son of Adam and Abby, identical twin to Beckett
    - **Beckett Callahan McCarthy,** quadruplet son of Adam and Abby, identical twin to Kane

- **Evan McCarthy,** singer, performer, owner of Island Breeze Records, father of Maddox McCarthy, married to
  - **Grace Ryan McCarthy,** owner of Ryan's Pharmacy, mother of Maddox McCarthy
    - **Maddox McCarthy,** son of Grace and Evan, born on Valentine's Day
- **Dr. Janey McCarthy Cantrell,** DMV, owner of the Gansett Island Veterinary Clinic, mother of Peter Joseph "P.J." and Vivienne Cantrell, married to:
  - **Joe Cantrell,** son of Carolina Cantrell O'Grady and the late Pete Cantrell, co-owner of the Gansett Island Ferry Company
    - **Peter Joseph "P.J." Cantrell,** son of Joe and Janey
    - **Vivienne Cantrell,** daughter of Joe and Janey

Big Mac and Linda's Grandchildren:

- **Thomas McCarthy,** son of Maddie Chester McCarthy and Tom Wilkinson, adopted by Mac McCarthy
- **Hailey McCarthy,** daughter of Mac and Maddie
- **Connor McCarthy** (deceased)
- **Malcolm John "Mac" McCarthy III,** son of Mac and Maddie
- **Emma Linda McCarthy,** daughter of Mac and Maddie
- **Evelyn Francine McCarthy,** daughter of Mac and Maddie
- **Peter Joseph "PJ" Cantrell,** son of Janey and Joe
- **Vivienne Cantrell,** daughter of Janey and Joe
- **Liam Callahan McCarthy,** son of Adam and Abby
- **Murphy Callahan McCarthy,** quadruplet son of Adam and Abby, identical twin to Rory
- **Rory Callahan McCarthy,** quadruplet son of Adam and Abby, identical twin to Murphy
- **Kane Callahan McCarthy,** quadruplet son of Adam and Abby, identical twin to Beckett
- **Beckett Callahan McCarthy,** quadruplet son of Adam and Abby, identical twin to Kane
- **Oren Charles McCarthy,** son of Grant and Stephanie
- **Maddox McCarthy,** son of Grace and Evan, born on Valentine's Day

RI Superior Court Judge Frank McCarthy, (retired) eldest brother of Big Mac and Kevin, widower of the late Joanne McCarthy, engaged to:

- **Betsy Jacobson,** mother of Steve (deceased)

Frank McCarthy is the father of:

- **Laura McCarthy Lawry,** daughter of Frank and Joanne McCarthy, sister of Shane McCarthy, mother of Holden Newsome, Joanna Sarah Lawry and Jonathan Russell Lawry, co-owner of the Sand & Surf Hotel, married to:
    - **Owen Lawry,** son of Mark and Sarah Lawry, brother to,

Julia, Katie, Cindy, John, Josh and Jeff Lawry, co-owner of the Sand & Surf Hotel

- **Holden Newsome,** son of Laura McCarthy Lawry and Justin Newsome, stepson of Owen Lawry
- **Jonathan Russell Lawry,** son of Laura McCarthy Lawry and Owen Lawry, twin to Joanna
- **Joanna Sarah Lawry,** daughter of Laura McCarthy Lawry and Owen Lawry, twin to Jonathan

- **Shane McCarthy,** ex-husband to Courtney (deceased), father of Benjamin Francis McCarthy, married to:
  - **Katie Lawry McCarthy,** nurse practitioner, daughter of Mark and Sarah Lawry, sister to Owen, Julia (twin), Cindy, John, Josh and Jeff Lawry, mother of Benjamin Francis McCarthy
    - **Benjamin Francis McCarthy,** son of Shane and Katie

Frank McCarthy's Grandchildren:

- **Holden Newsome,** son of Laura McCarthy Lawry and Justin Newsome, stepson of Owen McCarthy
- **Jonathan Russell Lawry,** son of Laura and Owen, twin to Joanna
- **Joanna Sarah Lawry,** daughter of Laura and Owen, twin to Jonathan
- **Benjamin Francis McCarthy,** son of Shane and Katie

- **Dr. Kevin McCarthy,** youngest brother to Big Mac and Frank McCarthy, psychiatrist, divorced from Deb McCarthy, married to:
  - **Chelsea Rose McCarthy,** former bartender at the Beachcomber, mother to Summer Rose and Faith McCarthy

Kevin is the father of:

- **Riley McCarthy,** son of Kevin and Deb McCarthy, employed by McCarthy Construction, married to:

- o **Nikki Stokes McCarthy,** manager of McCarthy's Wayfarer, identical twin sister of **Jordan Stokes,**
- **Finn McCarthy,** son of Kevin and Deb McCarthy, employed by McCarthy Construction, married to:
  - o **Chloe Dennis McCarthy,** owner of Curl Up and Dye Salon
- **Summer Rose McCarthy,** daughter of Kevin and Chelsea
- **Faith McCarthy,** daughter of Kevin and Chelsea

The Lawry Family

- **General Mark Lawry,** imprisoned former husband of Sarah Lawry Grandchamp, father of Owen, Julia, Katie, Cindy, Josh, John and Jeff Lawry
- **Sarah Lawry Grandchamp,** daughter of Russ and Adele, ex-wife of General Mark Lawry, mother to Owen, Julia, Katie, Cindy, Josh, John and Jeff Lawry, married to:
  - o **Charlie Grandchamp,** father of Stephanie Logan McCarthy

Sarah is the mother of:

- **Owen Lawry,** co-owner of the Sand & Surf Hotel, brother to Julia, Katie, Cindy, John, Josh and Jeff, stepfather to Holden Newsome, father to Jonathan Russell Lawry and Joanna Sarah Lawry, married to:
  - o **Laura McCarthy Lawry,** co-owner of the Sand & Surf Hotel, sister of Shane, mother of Holden Newsome, Jonathan Russell Lawry and Joanna Sarah Lawry
    - **Holden Newsome,** son of Laura McCarthy Lawry and Justin Newsome, stepson of Owen Lawry
    - **Jonathan Russell Lawry,** (twin) son of Laura McCarthy Lawry and Owen Lawry
    - **Joanna Sarah Lawry,** (twin) daughter of Laura McCarthy Lawry and Owen Lawry
- **Julia Lawry Taylor,** officer manager, McCarthy Construction, performer at Stephanie's Bistro, sister of Owen, Katie (twin), Cindy, John, Josh and Jeff, mother of Ella Taylor, married to:

- ○ **Deacon Taylor,** Gansett Island Harbor Master and police officer, brother of Police Chief Blaine Taylor, father of Ella Taylor
    - ▪ **Ella Taylor,** daughter of Deacon and Julia Taylor
- **Katie Lawry McCarthy**, nurse practitioner, sister to Owen, Julia (twin), Cindy, John, Josh and Jeff, mother of Benjamin Francis McCarthy, married to:
    - ○ **Shane McCarthy,** employed by McCarthy Construction, brother of Laura, father of Benjamin Francis McCarthy
        - ▪ **Benjamin Francis McCarthy,** son of Shane and Katie
- **Cindy Lawry**, hair stylist at Curl Up and Dye, sister to Owen, Julia, Katie, John, Josh and Jeff, engaged to:
    - ○ **Jace Carson,** biological father of Kyle and Jackson Chandler, ex-husband of Lisa Chandler (deceased), bartender at Beachcomber and plumber at McCarthy Construction
- **John Lawry**, former police officer, director of security at the McCarthy's Wayfarer, brother of Owen, Julia, Katie, Cindy, Josh and Jeff, married to:
    - ○ **Niall Fitzgerald,** from Ireland, musician at Island Breeze Records, and performer at the Beachcomber
- **Josh Lawry**, engineer, brother of Owen, Julia, Katie, Cindy, John and Jeff, not present on Gansett Island
- **Jeff Lawry**, computer science degree, employed by McCarthy's Construction, brother of Owen, Julia, Katie, Cindy, John and Josh, married to:
    - ○ **Kelsey Gordon Lawry,** nanny for Mac and Maddie McCarthy

The Martinez Family

- **George** (deceased) **and Marion Martinez,** co-founders of Martinez Lawn & Garden, parents of Alex and Paul Martinez
- **Alex Martinez,** son of George and Marion Martinez, brother of Paul, father of George Alexander Martinez II and Henry Hugh Martinez, co-owner of Martinez Lawn & Garden, married to:

- ○ **Jenny Wilks Martinez,** former lighthouse keeper, was engaged to the late Toby Barton, mother of George Alexander Martinez II and Henry Hugh Martinez
    - **George Alexander Martinez, II,** son of Alex and Jenny
    - **Henry Hugh Martinez,** son of Alex and Jenny
- **Paul Martinez,** son of George and Marion Martinez, brother of Alex, adoptive father to Ethan Russell Martinez, father of Scarlett Marion Martinez and Charlotte Marion Martinez, co-owner of Martinez Lawn & Garden, member of Gansett Town Council, married to:
    - ○ **Hope Russell Martinez,** nurse, mother of Ethan Russell, Scarlett Marion Martinez and Charlotte Marion Martinez
        - **Ethan Russell Martinez,** son of Hope Russell Martinez, adopted son of Paul Martinez
        - **Scarlett Marion Martinez,** daughter of Paul and Hope Martinez
        - **Charlotte Marion Martinez,** daughter of Paul and Hope Martinez

The James Family

- **Jared James,** billionaire, co-owner of The Chesterfield and Marion Martinez Home for the Aged, adoptive father of Violet James, married to:
    - ○ **Elisabeth "Lizzie" James,** co-owner of The Chesterfield and Marion Martinez Home for the Aged, adoptive mother of Violet James
        - **Violet James,** adoptive daughter of Jared and Lizzie James, biological parents are Jessie Morgan and Brooks Ward. Brooks's parents are Denise and Hunter Ward.
- **Jessie Morgan,** seasonal worker at the Beachcomber, abandoned infant daughter now in the care of Lizzie and Jared James
- **Dr. Quinn James,** trauma surgeon, medical director at Marion Martinez Home for the Aged, brother of Jared, Cooper, Kendall James, married to:

- ○ **Mallory Vaughn James,** daughter of Big Mac McCarthy and Diana Vaughn, sister to Mac, Grant, Adam, Evan and Janey McCarthy, nursing director at Marion Martinez Home for the Aged, EMT for Town of Gansett Island
- **Kathleen "Kendall" James,** attorney, divorced from Phil Tobin, mother of:
    - **Elias Tobin,** 12, son of Kendall James and Phil Tobin
    - **Henry Tobin,** 10, son of Kendall James and Phil Tobin
- **Cooper James,** owner of party boat, youngest brother of Jared James and Quinn James, living with:
    - ○ **Gabrielle "Gigi" Gibson,** lawyer, reality TV star, friend to Jordan Stokes and Nikki Stokes McCarthy

Other Gansett Island Residents...

- **Luke Harris,** co-owner of McCarthys Gansett Island Marina, father of Lillian Alice "Lily" and Elias Harris, married to:
    - ○ **Sydney Donovan Harris,** interior designer, mother of Lily and Elias, widow of Seth, mother of the late Max and Malena
        - **Lillian Alice "Lily" Harris,** daughter of Luke and Sydney
        - **Elias Harris,** son of Luke and Sydney
- **Ned Saunders,** best friend to Big Mac McCarthy, Gansett Island cab driver and real estate owner, stepfather to Maddie McCarthy and Tiffany Taylor, married to:
    - ○ **Francine Chester Saunders,** ex-wife of Bobby Chester, mother of Maddie McCarthy and Tiffany Taylor
- **Tiffany Taylor,** daughter of Francine Chester Saunders and Bobby Chester, sister to Maddie McCarthy, mother to Ashleigh Sturgil, Adeline "Addie" Taylor and Adrian Robert Taylor, owner of Naughty & Nice, married to:
    - ○ **Police Chief Blaine Taylor,** brother of Deacon Taylor, stepfather to Ashleigh Sturgil, father to Adeline "Addie" Taylor and Adrian Robert Taylor
        - **Ashleigh Sturgil,** daughter of Tiffany Taylor and Jim Sturgil, stepdaughter of Blaine Taylor

- **Adeline "Addie" Taylor,** daughter of Tiffany and Blaine Taylor
    - **Adrian Robert Taylor,** son of Tiffany and Blaine Taylor
- **Jim Sturgil,** ex-husband of Tiffany Taylor, father to Ashleigh Sturgil, deceased in *Hurricane After Dark*
- **Jack Downing,** RI State trooper assigned to Gansett Island, widower of Ruby, married to:
    - **Piper Bennett Downing,** employee at the Sand & Surf Hotel
- **Seamus O'Grady,** from Ireland, manager of the Gansett Island Ferry Company, guardian to Kyle and Jackson Chandler, cousin to Shannon O'Grady, married to:
    - **Carolina Cantrell O'Grady,** mother of Joe Cantrell, grandmother to P.J. and Vivienne Cantrell, guardian to Kyle and Jackson Chandler
- **Lisa Chandler,** (deceased) ex-wife of Jace Carson, neighbor to Seamus and Carolina O'Grady, mother to:
    - **Kyle Chandler,** son of Lisa Chandler and Jace Carson, guardian child of Seamus and Carolina O'Grady
    - **Jackson Chandler,** son of Lisa Chandler and Jace Carson, guardian child of Seamus and Carolina O'Grady
- **Dan Torrington,** celebrity defense attorney and friend to Grant McCarthy, father of Dylan Adele Torrington, married to:
    - **Kara Ballard Torrington,** daughter of Chuck and Judith Ballard, granddaughter of Bertha Lively, owner/operator Ballard's Launch Service, mother of Dylan Adele Torrington
        - **Dylan Adele Torrington,** daughter of Dan and Kara
- **Chuck and Judith Ballard,** Kara's parents
- **Bertha Lively,** Kara's grandmother
- **Dr. David Lawrence,** Gansett Island doctor, former fiancé of Janey McCarthy Cantrell, father of Helen Marion Lawrence, married to:
    - **Daisy Babson Lawrence,** friend of Maddie McCarthy's, housekeeping manager at McCarthy's Gansett Island Inn, mother of Helen Marion Lawrence
        - **Helen Marion Lawrence,** daughter of David and Daisy
- **Truck Henry,** Daisy Babson McCarthy's abusive ex-boyfriend

- **Tobias "Slim" Fitzgerald Jackson Jr.,** Gansett Island pilot, father of Tobias "Toby" Fitzgerald Jackson, III, married to:
  - **Erin Barton Jackson,** twin to the late Toby Barton, who was engaged to Jenny Wilks Martinez, mother of of Tobias "Toby" Fitzgerald Jackson, III
    - **Tobias "Toby" Fitzgerald Jackson, III,** son of Slim and Erin
- **Mason Johns,** Gansett Island Fire Chief, father of Wyatt Johns, married to:
  - **Jordan Stokes Johns,** Activities Director at Marion Martinez Home for the Aged and reality TV star, identical twin sister of Nikki Stokes McCarthy, mother of Wyatt Johns
    - **Wyatt Johns,** son of Mason and Jordan Stokes Johns
- **Victoria Stevens O'Grady,** Gansett Island midwife, married to:
  - **Shannon O'Grady,** from Ireland, deck hand on the Gansett Island ferries, cousin to Seamus O'Grady
- **Rosemary Enders,** (deceased) grandmother of McKenzie Martin, close friend/neighbor of Duke Sullivan
- **Duke Sullivan,** owner of tattoo studio, engaged to:
  - **McKenzie Martin,** bookkeeper, mother of Jax
    - **Jax Martin,** infant son of McKenzie Martin and Eric
- **Eric,** ex-boyfriend of McKenzie, father of Jax
- **Carol and Tom Callahan,** parents of Abby McCarthy
- **Fiona,** took over Ryan's Pharmacy when Grace was on tour with Evan
- **Ace,** works with Duke at the tattoo studio
- **Billy Weyland,** owner of the gym, deceased in *Hurricane After Dark*
- **Morgan Weyland,** brother of Billy, electrician for McCarthy Construction and the Town of Gansett Island, engaged to:
  - **Sierra Mancini,** owner of Refresh and Renew Massage Studio
- **Rebecca,** owner of the South Harbor Diner
- **Doc Potter,** island veterinarian
- **Rev. Joshua Banks,** pastor of nondenominational church

- **Clare Reynolds,** teacher at Gansett Island School, briefly dated Billy Weyland
- **Evelyn Hopper,** owner of Eastward Look, grandmother to Jordan Stokes Johns and Nikki Stokes McCarthy
- **Oliver and Dara Watkins,** lighthouse keepers, parents of Lewis (deceased), parents of Hazel Watkins
  - **Hazel Watkins,** daughter of Oliver and Dara
- **Monique,** sister of Dara Watkins, ex-wife of Jaden, living with:
  - **Linc Mercier,** US Coast Guard Commander, stationed at Gansett Island
- **Terry,** works at the gym
- **Candice,** works at Abby's Attic
- **Dr. Cal Maitland,** former island doctor and ex-fiancé of Abby Callahan
- **Bobby Chester,** estranged father of Maddie McCarthy and Tiffany Taylor, ex-husband of Francine Saunders
- **Matilda,** Gigi and Jordan's show producer
- **Libby,** Owner of the Beachcomber, part-time EMT

The Children of Gansett Island

- **Elias Tobin,** 12, son of Kendall James and Phil Tobin
- **Ethan Russell Martinez,** 9, Son of Hope Russell, adopted son of Paul Martinez
- **Henry Tobin,** 10, son of Kendall James and Phil Tobin
- **Kyle Chandler,** 9, son of Lisa Chandler (deceased) and Jace Carson, guardian child of Seamus and Carolina O'Grady
- **Jackson Chandler,** 7, son of Lisa Chandler (deceased) and Jace Carson; guardian child of Seamus and Carolina O'Grady
- **Thomas McCarthy,** 7, son of Maddie McCarthy, adopted son of Mac McCarthy
- **Ashleigh Sturgil,** 7, daughter of Tiffany Taylor and Jim Sturgil, stepdaughter to Blaine Taylor
- **Hailey McCarthy,** 5, daughter of Maddie and Mac McCarthy
- **Peter Joseph "P.J." Cantrell,** 5, son of Joe and Janey Cantrell
- **Holden Newsome,** 3, son of Laura McCarthy Lawry and ex-husband, Justin Newsome, stepson to Owen Lawry

- **Adeline "Addie" Francine Taylor,** 1, daughter of Blaine and Tiffany Taylor
- **Joanna Sarah Lawry,** 3, daughter of Owen and Laura Lawry, twin to Jonathan
- **Jonathan Russell Lowry**, 3, son of Owen and Laura Lawry, twin to Joanna
- **George Alexander Martinez II**, 3, son of Alex and Jenny Martinez
- **Lillian Alice "Lily" Harris,** 3, daughter of Luke and Sydney Harris
- **Vivienne Cantrell,** 3, daughter of Joe and Janey Cantrell
- **Malcolm John "Mac" McCarthy III,** 3, son of Maddie and Mac McCarthy
- **Liam Callahan McCarthy,** 2, son of Adam and Abby McCarthy
- **Summer Rose McCarthy,** 2, daughter of Kevin and Chelsea McCarthy
- **Scarlett Marion Martinez,** 1, daughter of Paul and Hope Martinez
- **Jax Martin,** 1
- **Violet Catherine James,** 5 months, adopted daughter of Jared and Lizzie James, biological parents are Jessie Morgan and Brooks Ward. Brooks's parents are Denise and Hunter Ward.
- **Emma Linda McCarthy,** 9 months, daughter of Maddie and Mac McCarthy, twin sister of Evelyn Francine McCarthy
- **Evelyn Francine McCarthy,** 9 months, daughter of Maddie and Mac McCarthy, twin sister of Emma Linda McCarthy
- **Connor McCarthy,** deceased son of Maddie and Mac McCarthy

Infants in Delivery After Dark:

- **Murphy Callahan McCarthy,** son of Adam and Abby, identical twin to Rory
- **Rory Callahan McCarthy,** son of Adam and Abby, identical twin to Murphy

- **Kane Callahan McCarthy,** son of Adam and Abby, identical twin to Beckett
- **Beckett Callahan McCarthy,** son of Adam and Abby, identical twin to Kane
- **Adrian Robert Taylor,** son of Tiffany and Blaine
- **Dylan Adele Torrington,** daughter of Dan and Kara

Born AFTER Delivery After Dark:

- **Tobias "Toby" Fitzgerald Jackson, III,** son of Slim and Erin
- **Wyatt Johns,** son of Mason and Jordan Stokes Johns
- **Oren Charles McCarthy,** son of Grant and Stephanie
- **Maddox McCarthy,** son of Evan and Grace, born on Valentine's Day
- **Hazel Watkins,** daughter of Oliver and Dara
- **Helen Marion Lawrence,** daughter of David and Daisy
- **Henry Hugh Martinez,** son of Alex and Jenny
- **Elias Harris,** son of Luke and Sydney
- **Faith McCarthy,** daughter of Kevin and Chelsea
- **Ella Taylor,** daughter of Deacon and Julia Taylor
- **Benjamin Francis McCarthy,** son of Shane and Katie
- **Charlotte Marion Martinez,** daughter of Paul and Hope

ALSO BY MARIE FORCE

Contemporary Romances Available from Marie Force

*The Gansett Island Series**

Book 1: Maid for Love (*Mac & Maddie*)

Book 2: Fool for Love (*Joe & Janey*)

Book 3: Ready for Love (*Luke & Sydney*)

Book 4: Falling for Love (*Grant & Stephanie*)

Book 5: Hoping for Love (*Evan & Grace*)

Book 6: Season for Love (*Owen & Laura*)

Book 7: Longing for Love (*Blaine & Tiffany*)

Book 8: Waiting for Love (*Adam & Abby*)

Book 9: Time for Love (*David & Daisy*)

Book 10: Meant for Love (*Jenny & Alex*)

Book 10.5: Chance for Love, *A Gansett Island Novella* (*Jared & Lizzie*)

Book 11: Gansett After Dark (*Owen & Laura*)

Book 12: Kisses After Dark (*Shane & Katie*)

Book 13: Love After Dark (*Paul & Hope*)

Book 14: Celebration After Dark (*Big Mac & Linda*)

Book 15: Desire After Dark (*Slim & Erin*)

Book 16: Light After Dark (*Mallory & Quinn*)

Book 17: Victoria & Shannon (Episode 1)

Book 18: Kevin & Chelsea (Episode 2)

A Gansett Island Christmas Novella (*Appears in Mine After Dark*)

Book 19: Mine After Dark (*Riley & Nikki*)

Book 20: Yours After Dark (*Finn & Chloe*)

Book 21: Trouble After Dark (*Deacon & Julia*)

Book 22: Rescue After Dark (*Mason & Jordan*)

Book 23: Blackout After Dark (*Full Cast*)

Book 24: Temptation After Dark *(Gigi & Cooper)*

Book 25: Resilience After Dark *(Jace & Cindy)*

Book 26: Hurricane After Dark *(Full Cast)*

Book 27: Renewal After Dark *(Duke & McKenzie)*

Book 28: Delivery After Dark *(Full Cast)*

Downeast

Dan & Kara: A Downeast Prequel

Homecoming: A Downeast Novel

The Wild Widows Series—a Fatal Series Spin-Off

Book 1: Someone Like You *(Roni & Derek)*

Book 2: Someone to Hold *(Iris & Gage)*

Book 3: Someone to Love *(Wynter & Adrian)*

Book 4: Someone to Watch Over Me *(Lexi & Tom)*

Book 5: Someone to Remember *(All Cast)*

Book 6: Someone to Save *(2026)*

Remington Family Law Series

Book 1: Acrimonious

Book 2: Contentious (Sept. 2026)

The Quantum Series

Book 1: Virtuous *(Flynn & Natalie)*

Book 2: Valorous *(Flynn & Natalie)*

Book 3: Victorious *(Flynn & Natalie)*

Book 4: Rapturous *(Addie & Hayden)*

Book 5: Ravenous *(Jasper & Ellie)*

Book 6: Delirious *(Kristian & Aileen)*

Book 7: Outrageous *(Emmett & Leah)*

Book 8: Famous *(Marlowe & Sebastian)*

Book 9: Illustrious *(Max & Stella)*

Book 10: Momentous *(Olivia's story, coming 2026)*

*The Green Mountain Series**

Book 1: All You Need Is Love (*Will & Cameron*)

Book 2: I Want to Hold Your Hand (*Nolan & Hannah*)

Book 3: I Saw Her Standing There (*Colton & Lucy*)

Book 4: And I Love Her (*Hunter & Megan*)

Novella: You'll Be Mine (*Will & Cam's Wedding*)

Book 5: It's Only Love (*Gavin & Ella*)

Book 6: Ain't She Sweet (*Tyler & Charlotte*)

*The Butler, Vermont Series**

(Continuation of Green Mountain)

Book 1: Every Little Thing (*Grayson & Emma*)

Book 2: Can't Buy Me Love (*Mary & Patrick*)

Book 3: Here Comes the Sun (*Wade & Mia*)

Book 4: Till There Was You (*Lucas & Dani*)

Book 5: All My Loving (*Landon & Amanda*)

Book 6: Let It Be (*Lincoln & Molly*)

Book 7: Come Together (*Noah & Brianna*)

Book 8: Here, There & Everywhere (*Izzy & Cabot*)

Book 9: The Long and Winding Road (*Max & Lexi*)

*The Miami Nights Series**

Book 1: How Much I Feel (*Carmen & Jason*)

Book 2: How Much I Care (*Maria & Austin*)

Book 3: How Much I Love (*Dee's story*)

Nochebuena, A Miami Nights Novella

Book 4: How Much I Want (*Nico & Sofia*)

Book 5: How Much I Need (*Milo & Gianna*)

*The Treading Water Series**

Book 1: Treading Water (*Jack & Andy*)

Book 2: Marking Time (*Clare & Aidan*)

Book 3: Starting Over (*Brandon & Daphne*)

Book 4: Coming Home (*Reid & Kate*)

Book 5: Finding Forever (*Maggie & Brayden*)

Single Titles

In the Air Tonight

Five Years Gone

One Year Home

Sex Machine

Sex God

Georgia on My Mind

True North

The Fall

The Wreck

Love at First Flight

Everyone Loves a Hero

Line of Scrimmage

Romantic Suspense Novels Available from Marie Force

The Fatal Series*

One Night With You, *A Fatal Series Prequel Novella*

Book 1: Fatal Affair

Book 2: Fatal Justice

Book 3: Fatal Consequences

Book 3.5: Fatal Destiny, *the Wedding Novella*

Book 4: Fatal Flaw

Book 5: Fatal Deception

Book 6: Fatal Mistake

Book 7: Fatal Jeopardy

Book 8: Fatal Scandal

Book 9: Fatal Frenzy

Book 10: Fatal Identity

Book 11: Fatal Threat

Book 12: Fatal Chaos

Book 13: Fatal Invasion

Book 14: Fatal Reckoning

Book 15: Fatal Accusation

Book 16: Fatal Fraud

Sam and Nick's story continues…

Book 1: State of Affairs

Book 2: State of Grace

Book 3: State of the Union

Book 4: State of Shock

Book 5: State of Denial

Book 6: State of Bliss

Book 7: State of Suspense

Book 8: State of Alert

Book 9: State of Retribution

Book 10: State of Preservation

Book 11: State of Unrest

Book 12: State of Mind

Historical Romance Available from Marie Force

The Gilded Series*

Book 1: Duchess by Deception

Book 2: Deceived by Desire

* Completed Series

ABOUT THE AUTHOR

Marie Force is the *New York Times* best-selling author of more than 110 contemporary romance, romantic suspense and erotic romance novels. Her series include Remington Family Law, Fatal, First Family, Gansett Island, Butler Vermont, Quantum, Treading Water, Miami Nights and Wild Widows. She has also written 12 single titles.

Her books have sold more than 15 million copies worldwide, have been translated into more than a dozen languages and have appeared on the *New York Times* bestseller list more than 30 times. She is also a *USA Today* and #1 *Wall Street Journal* bestseller, as well as a Spiegel bestseller in Germany.

Her goals in life are simple—to spend as much time as possible with her adult children, to keep writing books for as long as she possibly can and to never be on a flight that makes the news.

Join Marie's mailing list on her website at *marieforce.com* for news about new books and upcoming appearances in your area. Follow her on Facebook, at *www.Facebook.com/MarieForceAuthor* and Instagram *@marieforceauthor*. Contact Marie at *marie@marieforce.com*.